She leaned back against the door, and Joss stood in front of her, filling her vision with the wide shoulders of his exquisitely cut suit.

"Everything okay?" he asked, his voice low and sensual.

Eva nodded, when what she really wanted to do was shout. To tell him that no—she wasn't okay. This was far, far from okay. This was confusing and terrifying and oh so much more complicated than she had ever wanted her life to be.

But she couldn't let go of his hand. Couldn't be the one to break that connection between them.

She'd felt it growing as they'd played their parts over dinner. A touch of the hands here. A brush of fingers over an arm there.

The intimacy had grown between them in some strange simulacrum of the relationship they had invented. But she had expected them to walk away from it. Expected to leave it at the table. She hadn't expected it to stalk them into the lift and back up to their suite.

Intimacy was safe in public, where neither of them could act on it. But with her back against this door and Joss in front of her—looking serious, smelling delicious—it was a more dangerous prospect. And Joss knew it, too.

CONVENIENTLY ENGAGED TO THE BOSS

BY
ELLIE DARKINS

First Published in Great Britain 2017
By Mills & Boon, an imprint of HarperCollins*Publishers*
1 London Bridge Street, London, SE1 9GF

© 2017 Ellie Darkins

ISBN: 978-0-263-92330-8

23-0917

Printed and bound in Spain
by CPI, Barcelona

Ellie Darkins spent her formative years devouring romance novels, and after completing her English degree decided to make a living from her love of books. As a writer and editor, she finds her work now entails dreaming up romantic proposals, hot dates with alpha males and trips to the past with dashing heroes. When she's not working she can usually be found running around after her toddler, volunteering at her local library, or escaping all the above with a good book and a vanilla latte.

For Mike

CHAPTER ONE

'Could you help me with this zip, or are you just going to watch?'

Instinctively Joss shut the door behind him, wondering if anyone else had seen, and glanced through the window of the office to make sure his father wasn't nearby.

'Sorry, Eva. I was looking for my dad. What are you doing in his office? And why does it involve being undressed?'

Eva shrugged—he watched her shoulder blades move under pale, exposed skin where the dress's zip was gaping at the back.

'Edward's already gone to the boardroom. Shouldn't you be there too? Never mind. Could you help? I should have been there five minutes ago, but I spilt a cup of coffee over myself and now I've got the zip stuck.'

'Okay, okay—sure,' Joss said, with a glance back at the closed door. 'My dad wanted to see me in here before the meeting, but I couldn't get away from my last call.'

He reached Eva and gently batted her hands away

from the zip, pulling the slider to the top as quickly and impersonally as he could manage.

Eva turned her head to look over her shoulder, and as his eyes met hers he felt the tug of attraction that was ever-present around his father's executive assistant.

'Um… Joss, I meant *un*zip.'

Oh, no, that was *not* what he'd signed up for. No way was he that stupid. He'd been keeping his eyes, hands and mind off this woman for years. He knew the limits of his self-control, and just this proximity to her was pushing it—never mind anything else.

'I'm not sure that's…'

'Joss, would you just do it? Shut your eyes, if you want, but get me out of this thing! It's not like I'm naked under here, in case you're worried about your delicate sensibilities.'

He took a deep breath and unzipped, but the teeth snagged halfway down her back.

'It's stuck.'

'Still? Brilliant. I was hoping it was just the angle I was pulling it. Can you unstick it?'

He wasn't sure he wanted to—not when unsticking it meant exposing more creamy skin and finding out exactly what she'd meant when she said that she wasn't naked under there.

Joss fiddled with the zip, passing the teeth slowly through the slider and unpicking the threads that had got caught. Finally it gave way and slid smoothly down Eva's back, revealing a silk slip in a soft pink colour, edged with delicate cream lace. Worse than naked, perhaps, to be so close to seeing the body that he'd dreamed of, only to find it tantalisingly out of reach.

'At last! Thank goodness for that,' Eva said, stepping quickly out of the dress and reaching for another, which Joss had just noticed draped over his father's chair. As the fabric was sliding over her head he turned for the door, but Eva stopped him. 'Wait—can you zip up this time? I don't want to be any later than I already am.'

Joss let out a sigh, but crossed the office again and reached for the slider of the zip, his fingertips very close to the rose silk at the base of her spine. He lingered for a moment as he swept her hair away with his other hand, revealing the wispy baby hairs at the nape of her neck and the invitingly soft skin behind her ear.

But before he could cover her safely, the door behind him opened.

'Eva, are you in—?'

Damn his father and his terrible timing.

'I'm sorry, Edward. I'll be right there,' Eva said, reaching for the zip herself and pulling it further down in the process of twisting round.

'No, no—I can see I'm interrupting,' Edward said. 'I trust you're both on your way.'

Joss couldn't bring himself to look, but he could almost *hear* the huge grin on his father's face, verging on a full-on laugh.

'We're waiting for you.'

His father left the room before Joss could explain that nothing had been going on between him and Eva. He shot a look at her, and saw she looked as taken aback as he did as she struggled with her dress. He pulled the zip up for her—no lingering this time—and strode for the door.

'What are we going—?' Eva started.

'I'll handle it,' Joss said.

He walked into the boardroom, still fighting images of Eva's lingerie-clad body and the look of intrigue and delight on his father's face when he'd so clearly misinterpreted what had been going on in his office.

He was more used to seeing disappointment from his father, especially when it involved him and women. Since Joss's first marriage had failed, his father had tried to hide his disappointment that he'd not been able to settle down with anyone else. He knew that when he'd first told his parents he was getting a divorce, they'd blamed the break-up on him.

And then, when he'd walked into the office as a single man, emerging from the dark clouds of clinical depression and divorce, he had realised the strength of his attraction to his father's executive assistant.

He'd told himself that he would not be going near her—under any circumstances. His father doted on her, and would not take kindly to her feelings being hurt. And after what Joss had done to his marriage—the destruction he'd been powerless to prevent—he knew that he couldn't expect to make any woman happy.

At least his father respected him professionally. He'd been working for the family's chain of luxury department stores since he was in primary school, and had earned his position as Vice President of UK Stores. But professional respect and personal pride were two very different things, and Joss knew that an abundance of one would never compensate for the lack of the other.

All eyes turned to him as he entered the full board-room, with Eva right behind him. They found a couple of spare chairs in the corner. Sunlight flooded in through the old lead-paned windows, brightening the panelled room, which could feel oppressive on a gloomier day.

Joss tried to catch his father's eye, but he was either deliberately avoiding his gaze or so entranced by the view out of the window that he couldn't bring himself to look away. The well-heeled streets of Kensington were bustling below, and Joss could tell just from the hum of the traffic that the pavement outside the store was filled with shoppers and tourists, stopping to take in the magnificent window displays for which the store was renowned.

Eventually, though, the old man cleared his throat and looked around the room, glancing at each of the board members in turn.

'I'd like to thank you all for being here,' Edward began, with a smile that Joss couldn't interpret. 'Especially at such short notice and on a Friday afternoon, when I'm sure you'd all rather be at a long working lunch. I'm afraid that, as some of you may have guessed, an emergency board meeting is rarely called to share good news, and today is no different. So, it is with regret that I have to announce that due to ill health I will be resigning from the company in all capacities with immediate effect.'

Joss felt fear and dread swell in an all too familiar

fashion in the base of his stomach as the deeper meaning of his father's words sank in. His father *must* be ill—seriously ill—to even consider leaving the business.

But Edward carried on speaking, leaving him no time to dwell.

'You all know that over the years we have taken steps to ensure a smooth transition when the time came for me to hand over the reins, and so—if you are all still in agreement—I will be leaving you in the capable hands of my son, Joss, who will become Managing Director and Chairman of the Board in my place. Eva, of course, will be assisting Joss in his new role, as I suspect she knows more about my job than I do. I know you will continue to support them, just as you have supported me. Now, I imagine there will be questions, so I'll answer them as best I can. Who's first?'

The room sank into silence as Edward finished speaking. Joss looked closely at his father. Ill-health? His father hadn't taken a day off sick in his life, and yet now he was resigning completely? Yes, they'd talked about succession plans. Any sensible businessman had contingencies for all eventualities, and Edward would not have wanted to leave the company in chaos if anything had happened to him. But had there actually been more to it than that? Had his father known that he would soon be stepping down?

The dread in Joss's stomach twisted into stark fear as the implications of the announcement sank in and he realised what this must mean. His father wouldn't resign because of a dodgy hip or 'a touch of angina', as he'd once described a health scare. He'd always sworn he'd be carried out of a Dawson's department store in his coffin. For him to resign must mean he had had some terrible news.

Panic and grief gripped his throat as he noticed for the first time the slight grey tinge to his father's skin, and the lines around his eyes that suggested a habitual wince of fatigue. Why hadn't he noticed before? Why hadn't he been looking? His father wasn't exactly a spring chicken, and he was still working sixteen-hour days long past the age when most people would expect to retire.

He should have made his father take things easier—should have taken more off his plate.

He met his father's eye and saw sympathy and understanding in his father's gaze. He wanted to rush to embrace him, but something froze him to his chair, chilling his blood.

And then warmth crept from the tips of his fingers as a hand slid into his and he heard Eva's voice.

'Edward, are you in pain? What can we do to help?'

Joss's eyes swam and he clenched his jaw, determined not to allow a single tear to fall, to keep control over his emotions. Besides, swiping a falling tear before anyone saw would mean taking his hand from Eva's, and at that moment he couldn't see how he was meant to do that.

'Perhaps we should speak in my office?' Edward said to Joss, his voice gentle. 'And you lot—' he addressed the remaining members of the board 'you have a good gossip while I'm gone and think of what you need to ask me. Head back to the pub and finish your lunch, if you want to. But get your questions to me sharpish, because I'm planning on being on a sun lounger by the end of next week.'

Edward rose and Joss noticed, as he hadn't before, that his father leaned heavily on the table for support.

Joss snapped out of his trance and back into business mode as they walked down the corridor and back to Edward's office, firing questions all the way.

'Dad? What's happening? Are you okay? Was this what you wanted to talk to me about?'

Edward collapsed into the chair behind his desk and rested back against the padded seat. 'Yes. I'm sorry, son. Of course I wanted to tell you first, but you didn't arrive for our meeting—'

'Dad, if I'd known—'

'I know.' He softened the words with a smile. 'I know. But it was difficult for Eva to get everyone here at such short notice. I couldn't delay it any longer.'

'Couldn't delay? What's wrong with you, Dad?'

'Sit down, son.' His father indicated the chair opposite. 'And you, Eva. You both need to hear this. It's cancer, I'm afraid, and there's nothing they can do about it. I ignored it for a bit too long, it seems. So I thought it was about time I took that holiday I've been promising myself for the last thirty years and let you get on with running the business while I'm still around to answer your questions—there's no deadline for you two, of course.'

Joss stared at his father, unable to take in his words. His hand found Eva's again and he gripped it hard, taking strength from the solid presence of her, the warmth that always radiated from her.

'How long, Dad?'

'Oh, you know doctors. Never give you a straight answer. A few months, it seems. Long enough to have a little fun before I go. I love this business—you know that I do—but news like this makes you rethink, and I don't want these four walls to be the last thing I see before I go.'

'I'm so sorry, Edward.'

Joss could hear the tears in Eva's voice, and he squeezed her hand. He knew how fond she was of his father, and that her grief must mirror his own. 'Are you sure you're comfortable? Is there anything we can do?'

'Quite comfortable for now, my dear. Thank you for your concern. Now it's my turn to ask the questions.' He glanced at their clasped hands. 'Is there anything you two would like to tell me?'

Eva sat in shock, silenced by Edward's words. She couldn't believe that the old man was dying. Sure, he'd looked a little creaky around the joints lately, but he'd never complained of so much as a runny nose. It just didn't make sense that he could be terminally ill.

Joss had taken hold of her hand and she could feel the contact burning her skin. She hadn't thought about it when she'd slid her fingers between his back in the boardroom. Hadn't thought about all the times she'd imagined the slide of his skin against hers over the years. All she'd been able to feel was the grief and fear radiating from him, and she had acted on instinct, trying to ease it in any way she could.

And now Edward was calling them on it. Under normal circumstances she'd have cleared up the understanding with Edward the minute it had happened. But this was Joss's father, and they had both just been hit with shocking news. It was Joss's place, not hers, to explain.

'I'm sorry you saw that, Dad—' he started.

'Oh, don't be sorry—I'm delighted. I *do* remember what it was like to be young, believe it or not. I'm just pleased that you two have finally found each other. I can't deny that I've been waiting for this for some time. I take it that if you're bringing your personal life with you to work then it's serious?'

Eva felt her mouth fall open and waited for Joss to correct his father, to sum up what had happened with the dress and the coffee and the zip. But expressions chased across Joss's face faster than she could read them.

She was just about to jump in and explain for herself what had happened when Joss finally spoke.

'Yes, it's serious,' Joss said. 'In fact, we're engaged.'

She was about to call him on being completely ridiculous when she clocked the look on Edward's face. A smile had brought a glow to his face, and he was beaming at them both. Just a moment she was so shocked she couldn't speak. And then real life kicked in, and she remembered the news that Edward had just delivered, that Joss had just received. She found that she couldn't contradict him.

Still, she gently withdrew her hand. She had to maintain some semblance of control if she was going to keep her head.

She'd been trying to pretend to herself for years that she didn't have an enormous crush on this man. That he didn't enter her mind when she was out on a date with any other guy. And now he had to go and pretend to be in love with her. And the only result of calling him on it would be to hurt the man she'd come to care for almost as a parent. She couldn't do it to him. She'd have to talk to Joss in private. He could break it to his father gently.

Funny how being angry with him made him that little bit less fanciable—she'd been looking for something to knock the shine off him for years.

It wasn't as if she *wanted* to be attracted to him— she told herself that often enough. She couldn't think of anyone less suitable for falling in love with than the son of her boss, who spent half his time on the road visiting the UK stores, and the other half in his office, buried in spreadsheets and dodging calls from disappointed would-be dates.

Secretaries talked—hardly breaking news.

As soon as she'd recognised where her feelings were going—the irritating pitter-patter of her heart, the annoying dampness of her palms, not to mention the completely inappropriate but delicious dreams that had her waking flushed and impressed by the breadth of her own imagination—she'd acted.

She'd put space between them at the office, avoided him in the break room and at the pub. She'd thrown herself into dating in a way that was the opposite of

Joss's clinical style: enthusiastically, prolifically, discriminately. She'd found handsome, eligible bachelors who weren't intimidated by her salary or her seven fluent languages—or the handful of conversational ones. She'd dated in Russian, Greek and German, and once—haltingly, but memorably—in Mandarin. She'd gone dancing, cocktail-making, picnicking. Tried blue blood and blue collar.

And not a single one of the men she'd kissed so demurely on the cheek at the end of the night had helped her even start forgetting about Joss. He was beginning to appear annoyingly unforgettable, and now he was pulling her into a deceit that she knew, unhesitatingly, was a BAD IDEA. All caps.

'Well, like I said, I can't say that I'm surprised. I've suspected for a while that you two have a soft spot for each other,' Edward said at last, still smiling.

Eva groaned inwardly. Oh, no, how much of her stupid crush had he seen? How much was he going to figure out? How much was *Joss* going to figure out for himself?

'And it makes me a very happy man to see you settled and in love before I go.'

The three of them sank into silence as the meaning of his words hit home and the reality of his illness intruded once again on the completely insane situation Joss had just created.

'But now I've got work to do—so get out of here, the pair of you.'

Eva kissed Edward on the cheek and mumbled something indiscernible, then let Joss follow her from the room, past the open-plan desks and into Joss's office.

'What the *hell* was that?' she demanded as soon as they were alone, staring at Joss as he sank into his chair and rested his face in his hands.

'Not now, Eva.'

'Not *now*? You just told your father we're engaged— I think I'm entitled to an explanation.'

'He's just told me he's dying. I can't talk about this now.'

She dropped into a chair opposite him, feeling sick to her stomach. Joss was right—he'd just had terrible news. Much as she had every right to give him hell, perhaps now wasn't the time.

'You didn't know anything about it?' she asked gently.

'He didn't say *anything*. Just that he needed to speak to me before the meeting. But I was tied up on a call and I... I missed the meeting. He wanted to tell me.'

'You couldn't have known he was going to tell you that.' She crossed to stand beside him and rested a hand on his shoulder. 'It wouldn't have changed anything. The news would have been the same.'

'It would have felt different if he'd been able to talk to me before having to tell everyone else.'

'You're right. I'm sorry.'

He leaned his head against her arm and she let her hand brush against his hair.

'And I'm sorry for what I told him about us.'

Eva moved her hand away, aware of a sudden change

of the chemistry in the room. She hitched herself onto the corner of the desk, letting her stilettoed feet dangle.

'What was that about? The truth would have been a much simpler explanation. It's going to be a hundred times harder to explain things now. Engaged or not, who knows what he thinks we were up to in his office?'

'I was thinking on my feet. I didn't want him to think that you were involved in something sordid, and my brain went to "engaged" rather than "wardrobe malfunction". You saw his face when I told him that we were getting married. I knew that it would make him happy.'

'Marrying me?'

'Being happy…settled. It's all he wants for me. And since my divorce… You don't want to hear all that. Just trust me on this one. I know my father. I knew it would make him happy.'

'So what's it going to do to him when you tell him there's no engagement?'

And suddenly, from the defiant clench of his jaw and the killer look in his eyes, Eva knew that he wasn't planning on telling his father the truth at all.

'Don't be ridiculous,' she said, keeping her voice low and commanding. 'We have to tell him the truth. I'll tell him about the coffee and the dress. I'll sort this out.'

Joss shrugged, never breaking eye contact, never backing down from the challenge she'd made so clear in her voice.

'We'll explain about the dress. But I see no reason to drop the pretence of our engagement.'

She stood slowly from the desk and took a step towards him, letting him know that she found neither his position in the company nor the six inches in height he had over her intimidating in the slightest. Least of all when he was seated and she could tower over him.

'No reason, Joss? You just panicked and told a bare-faced lie that has implications for us both. I have no intention of lying to your father, so unless you want him to hear from me that you just fabricated a fiancée, I think you would do better to just tell him now.'

'Or we could make him believe that it's true.'

She took half a step back to stare at Joss. 'Have you completely lost your mind? Why would we want to do that?'

'Maybe I have lost my mind. It wouldn't be the first time. I don't know… What I *do* know is that my father has just told me that he's dying, and I—we—can do something to make him happy in the time he has left.'

'By lying to him? Do you think he'd really want that?'

'You saw his face. You tell me if you think the lie hurt him.'

She shrugged, unable to contradict him. 'I know he seemed happy, Joss. But it can't be right. I mean, how long would we have to keep this up?'

She sat down again, losing a little of her anger as she realised what she was asking.

'I'm sorry. I didn't mean…'

'I know. I know you didn't mean anything by it. But, yeah, we would have to keep it up until he dies. Which, apparently, won't be all that long. Don't worry—I don't expect you to actually say *I do*.'

She sat and thought on it for a moment. Remembered the look on Edward's face when Joss had told his lie. She couldn't deny that he'd looked happy. As happy as she'd seen him for a long time.

She loved Edward. He had been the one constant in her life for so long now, and she wasn't sure how she was going to manage without him. A sob threatened, and her hand lifted slowly to her throat as she forced it down. She slumped into the back of the chair, suddenly deflated. Surely if it made Edward happy she could do this. She *should* do this.

'I need some time to think about it,' she said eventually, not wanting Joss to know the direction her thoughts had been heading.

Goodness knew she'd been trying to keep the details of her mind secret from him for long enough. If they were to go through with this completely ridiculous idea, how was she meant to keep that up? To hide the fact that her mouth wanted to part every time she saw him? That she had to stop her tongue moistening her lips and her body swaying towards him?

'Take some time, then. No work's going to get done this afternoon anyway, by the looks of it.'

Eva shook her head. 'Your father will need me.'

'I'm going to my father's office now, and we're going to have a long talk. I'll make sure there's not a problem. If you want, I can say you went home with a headache.'

'While he's still at work with a terminal illness? Thanks but no thanks. Lock yourself in with your father if you want, but I'll be at my desk if either of you need me.'

Joss leaned back in his chair, raising his hands to admit defeat. 'We need to talk, though. And we can't do that in the office. Dinner tonight?'

Dinner tonight.

How many times had she imagined Joss issuing an invitation like that? Though she'd always known that she wouldn't accept. It wasn't even the time that he spent travelling around the country that made her think he was a million miles from boyfriend material. No, it was the fact that even when he was here he wasn't quite…*here*. There was an isolation about him. A distance. Even when he was close enough to touch.

She'd done long-distance before, with people in her life that she'd loved, and she'd hated every second of it. The last thing she needed was a man—a fiancé—who was distant even when he was in the room.

But she couldn't ignore him while he was going around telling people that they had got engaged. She had to convince him to tell his father the truth. And then figure out how they were meant to work together.

'Yes,' she agreed eventually. 'I guess we do need to talk about this. My place? I don't feel like going out after news like this. I don't suppose you do either.'

'No. That sounds good. Eight?'

She nodded, and scribbled down her address.

Walking back to her desk, she grabbed the coffee-stained dress and put it in the garment bag that she'd flung over her chair as she'd raced for the boardroom.

The blinds in Edward's office were drawn—a sure sign that he didn't want to be disturbed—so she sat at her computer, knowing that her work—the one constant she had in her life—was going to change irrevocably, and there was nothing she could do about it.

CHAPTER TWO

Eva CHECKED ON the food and resisted glancing at her reflection in the window. She didn't want Joss to think that she'd made an effort, so she'd not touched her hair or her make-up since she'd got home, and had just thrown on jeans and a comfy jumper. She always wore her skinnies and a cashmere sweater for a Friday night in—that was perfectly plausible.

She didn't even want to think about how the conversation over dinner was going to go, but she had to. Had to be prepared—set out in her own mind, at least, what was and wasn't going to be on the cards.

Joss was crazy, thinking that they could get away with a fake engagement. They'd be under scrutiny every minute they were together at the office. She knew how little fuel the gossip furnace needed to keep it alight. But every time she convinced herself of how terrible an idea it was, she remembered the happiness on Edward's face and the eagerness to please his father on Joss's.

She had to admit to being intrigued.

Joss was a powerful man. A director—now the MD—of a vast luxury group of department stores, with a presence on every continent, property in every major European shopping capital. He was notorious for the coldness of his personal life—the wife and the marriage that he'd neglected, and the transactional nature of the dates he took to industry functions. The women he dated were always clients and colleagues, there to further a business deal or a conversation, and they always went home alone.

She'd always seen something else in him. Something more. Something in the way that he joked with his father in a way he didn't with anyone else. Being so close to Edward, she'd seen their father-son relationship up close. Seen that Joss might not be the cold-hearted divorcee that everyone had him pegged as.

And now he'd invented an engagement just to please his dying father, and her curiosity was piqued again.

The two men didn't have much time left together—and they both seemed happier with this alternative reality than with real life. Who was she to judge? Who was she to tell them they were wrong? If she hadn't been personally involved she'd be telling them to do whatever they had to do in order to enjoy the time they had left together. But to say that she was 'involved' was putting things mildly—and this was *way* personal. She'd be as responsible as Joss if the truth came out and Edward's heart was broken in his last few weeks or months.

And maybe all of this was academic. Because it assumed that they stood a chance of getting away with this charade. Making everyone believe that they were in love. Well, it wouldn't be too hard to convince on her side, she supposed, given the attraction that she'd been hiding for years.

Through the break-up of his marriage—that time of dark black circles under his eyes and an almost permanent blank expression on his face—she was the only one who had seen him lean back against his father's office door after he'd left a meeting, composing his features and erasing all emotion before he went and faced the rest of the office. And in the time since, he'd been working non-stop—not competing with his colleagues but seemingly competing with himself.

It was hard to pinpoint when she had realised she had a heck of a crush growing. Perhaps after the dip in her stomach when she'd won a hard-earned smile, or when they'd argued in the boardroom and he'd held up his hands in concession to her point, never mind that he was a director and she an assistant.

Or when he'd walked in on her today, half-dressed in his father's office, and her whole skin had hummed in awareness of him. She'd had to hide the blush that had crept over her cheeks when his fingertips had clasped the zip and pulled it down—something she'd fantasised about more times than she wanted to admit, even to herself.

But nothing that she had done so far had worked in trying to get herself to forget him.

Perhaps it was time to do something different. She had proved that ignoring this thing wasn't going to make it go away. Maybe getting closer to him was the key. It was easy to maintain a crush, a fantasy, from afar. When you didn't have to deal with wet towels on your bed or dirty dishes left on the table. Maybe what she needed was some old-fashioned exposure therapy.

Because what did she really know about Joss, beyond what she saw when he was occasionally in the office? If there was one sure way to test a romance it was for a couple to move in together.

Was she completely losing her mind thinking that this was even a feasible idea—never mind a good one?

The doorbell rang, shocking her out of her internal debate. Good, she was getting sick of the sound of her own thoughts. At least with Joss here she would have a sparring partner.

She jogged down the stairs to the street-level door, trying to ignore the familiar flip of her heart at the sight of him. Not that he was looking his best—he had clearly come straight from the office. His shirt was creased, his collar unfastened and his tie loosened.

And then she remembered again how his day had been a thousand times worse than hers and had to resist the urge to pull him close and comfort him.

'Hey—you found it okay?'

'Yeah.' He waved his phone vaguely at her. 'Just a little help from this. I've not been here since I was a kid.'

'Of course—your dad used to stay here back then. I'd forgotten you must have been here too.'

She stepped back so that he could get through the door. From her little cobbled mews she could barely hear the traffic from the main road nearby, muffled by the square of white stucco pillared houses around the private, locked garden. She showed Joss upstairs to her apartment—a legacy of the time when the building would have had stables downstairs and living quarters for servants of the wealthy above, all tucked away behind the grand mansions on the square.

Eva loved the understated elegance of her home, with clipped bay trees at the door, original cobbles paving the passage and soft heritage colours on the doors and windows.

'It's beautiful,' Joss said as he reached the top of the stairs and crossed to the living room, where great tall windows flooded light in one side of the room. 'Have you been living here long?'

'Since I started at Dawson's.'

Joss looked intrigued. 'I thought my dad had got rid of this place.'

'He had—sort of,' Eva said, reaching for a bottle of wine and raising a glass in question at Joss.

He nodded and reached to take it from her when it was full.

'He realised it was mostly sitting empty while it was a company flat, so he decided to rent it out. When I started working for the company I was stuck for somewhere to stay. Your dad didn't have a tenant at the time, and needed someone to house-sit, so he offered me this place.'

Joss raised his eyebrows. 'Lucky you.'

'Yeah, I don't like to move a lot, and he offered me a long-term lease. I like it here.'

'So I'm going to have a hard time convincing you to move in with me?'

Eva snorted, and winced at the sting of wine in her nose.

'That part's non-negotiable,' she confirmed. 'This is my home and I'm not leaving it.'

'So you're coming round to the rest of it? Good.'

She should have given him an outright no—told him there and then that there was absolutely no way she was going along with his ridiculous scheme. But somehow, with him here in her home, in her space, she wasn't sure she wanted to. All of a sudden she wasn't sure about anything.

That was what happened when the only stable part of your life upped and threatened to leave. It had sunk in on her short walk home from the office that she could be about to lose her job—the first point of stability she'd ever had in her life. The safe place that she'd built for herself in the twelve years that she'd been with the company.

She would have thought she'd have been used to it by now. She'd had her whole childhood to practise, after all. Every time her mother or her father had shipped out, or they'd all packed up and moved to another army base, she'd told herself it was the last time she'd care. The last time she'd cry.

She'd not managed to stick to her word until the final time. The time her mother hadn't come home at all.

Her father had packed her off to boarding school then, not long after she'd begged him to leave the army, to stop moving her around and give her some stability. She'd taken herself straight off to university after school, and from there straight into business, landing in Edward's team and working her way up to be his executive assistant.

Her parents had never managed to give her the stability she'd craved, so she'd found her own—with Dawson's. It was a family business, its history stretching into the last century and the one before that. The company had been around long before Edward, and she had no doubt that it would continue without him.

But how was it ever going to feel the same after he was gone? And what else was going to change?

The succession plans that had been approved by the board had appointed her as Joss's new EA—she was tied to the job role, not to the holder—but once his father was gone Joss had no reason to stick with that decision. She could be out through the door as soon as Edward was dead.

An engagement to the heir apparent—even a fake one—was another tie to the company. To the family. Another bond to the life that she'd built for herself. An obstacle between her and everything falling away. Was that completely crazy? Maybe. But that didn't mean she didn't feel it.

'Here.' She passed Joss a bowl of potatoes and a salad. 'Can you stick these on the table? The chicken will be just another minute.'

He took the bowls from her and glanced at the pan on the hob.

'That looks amazing. You shouldn't have gone to so much trouble, though. We could have ordered something.'

She shrugged. 'It was no trouble. I'd have been cooking for myself anyway.'

'You cook like this every night?'

She narrowed her eyes as she tried to work out his angle. 'Are you asking if that's part of the deal?'

'I'm making conversation. At least, I'm trying to.'

'I'm sorry.' She shook her head as she grabbed a couple of plates and started serving up. 'Everything just feels so…weird. I can't get my head around it.'

'It doesn't need to be weird.'

'Joss, this afternoon you asked me to pretend to be your fiancée. Now you're asking me to move in with you. How can it be anything *but* weird?'

'Because it's not real, Eva.'

She brandished a set of tongs at him. 'That makes it worse! How can faking something like that not feel weird to you? Lying to your father won't feel weird?'

He held his hands up and shrugged, though his expression belied his casual attitude. 'Do you tell your parents everything that's going on with you?'

'There's just my dad. We're not close. But I've never invented a fiancé.'

Before now, she added in her head. Because this conversation seemed to be gathering momentum, and she wasn't sure she was going to put a stop to it. She hadn't come out and told Edward that it wasn't true yet, so at the very least she was complicit in the lie getting this far.

It was only when Joss had mentioned it that she'd even thought about the fact that she might have to tell her dad. How was it that she'd put more emotional energy into worrying that she was lying to Edward than into the fact that she would also have to lie to her own father? She'd not even considered that going through with this would affect him too.

Maybe it didn't have to. Maybe she could keep the whole thing from him—it wasn't as if they spoke often. Or at all, really.

'You're quiet,' Joss commented as they sat down to eat at the dining table tucked into the corner of the living room.

'Thinking,' she replied, helping herself to salad and potatoes.

'Enlighten me,' Joss instructed, equally economical with his words.

Eva sighed, but he was here to talk and they weren't going to get anywhere if neither of them opened up. And, if what she'd seen of Joss over the years was anything to go by, she would be waiting a long time for an emotional outpouring from his end.

'I'm not sure that this is a good idea.' A good start, she thought. Get her cards on the table. 'We're lying to your father. It's likely we'll be found out. It's a distraction when we should be concentrating on what he needs.'

Joss raised an eyebrow.

'What?' Eva asked.

'We're doing it *for* my father. You saw how happy it's making him.'

Joss had said that they needed to talk, but it was only now she realised that he thought he was here to sort out details—not to convince her. He was assuming that she would just go along with it. He'd taken her decision not to tell Edward the truth from the start as approval, and he was here to iron out the fine print.

'You really think I'm going to go along with this?'

Joss looked up and held her gaze for a beat longer than was comfortable.

'I think you already are.'

A shiver ran through her at the tone of his voice. So commanding. So sure of himself. So arrogant. She'd had no idea before this moment that that did something for her, but the heat between her legs and the tightness in her belly told her it definitely did.

'If you were going to back out,' he continued, 'you would have done it back at the office. Or just told my father the truth on the spot. Why are we bothering to dance around this when we both know you've made up your mind?'

She fixed him with a stare and muttered an Arabic curse under her breath, trying not to show him how right she knew he was. Because she *could* have called a halt to this hours ago. The fact that she hadn't told them both all they needed to know.

'I'm doing it to make your father happy,' she clarified, still holding that gaze, making sure Joss could see that she wasn't backing down or giving in to him. She was making her own decisions for her own very good reasons.

'I know.' He nodded, taking a sip of his wine, breaking their eye contact and cutting into his chicken.

'I mean it,' he said, after he'd polished off half the plate. 'I could get used to this.'

'Good,' she said, standing up and picking up her

plate, suddenly losing her appetite. 'You can get used to doing the washing up as well.'

Joss finished his food and followed her through to the little kitchen. 'You think you're going to scare me away with threats of stacking the dishwasher?'

She gestured around the bijou kitchen. 'You see a dishwasher in here?'

He glanced around. 'Fine. So we'll get someone in. I'll pay,' he added when she started to shake her head.

'It's not about the money.'

'What? It's about me being willing to get my hands wet? Fine. But I'm not a martyr, Eva. If you're hoping to scare me then I might as well tell you now that it's not going to work.'

'You don't want to move in here. There's no space.'

He leaned back against the kitchen counter, a hand either side of his hips. His man-spreading made his intentions clear. It would have been more subtle if he'd marked the doorframe with his scent.

'I decide for myself what I do and don't want, Eva. This is where you live, so it's where I'll live too. You've stated your ground rules; now I'm stating mine.'

She folded her arms and leant back against the kitchen counter. 'There's not even any space in the wardrobe.'

'You can't expect us to live apart.'

'We're going to see each other all the time at work. Isn't moving in together a bit much?'

He took a step towards her, and Eva had to admit that his height *was* a little intimidating in the tiny kitchen.

'And how many people are going to believe our story if we're not living together?'

'We could tell people we're waiting until after the wedding.'

He shook his head and, much as she hated it, Eva knew he was right.

'They'd ask us which century we're living in. Perhaps if this was a real relationship we'd say to hell with what they think. But we need to make them believe us. I don't want to give them any reason not to. I'll start moving some stuff in on Monday.'

He moved to leave, and somehow, although it was what her rational brain wanted, it seemed her body wasn't expecting it. Disappointment washed through her. It wasn't as if she wasn't used to living alone. She loved having her own space. But they'd been through a lot today, and she wasn't particularly keen on being left alone with her thoughts.

'Do you want a coffee before you go?' she asked, flicking on the kettle behind her.

'Sure,' Joss said, watching her carefully. 'Something wrong?'

'No,' she replied, rubbing her forehead and realising she wasn't being very convincing. 'Just a lot to take in. Weird day.'

'Tell me about it,' Joss said, leaning back on the counter.

Eva looked up and realised that it wasn't a figure of speech.

'No, no—it's fine,' she said.

'I can listen. Even help.'

'I can't, Joss. He's your dad. You don't want to… It should be me asking if you're okay.'

'I don't get an exclusive on it, Eva. I know you care for him too.'

'I just can't believe I didn't know…you know.'

She made two coffees and carried them back through to the living room. Plonking them on the coffee table, she just had time to wish she had space for a bigger sofa before Joss appeared behind her.

'Do you sit and spy on your neighbours?' Joss asked, pointing out the way the sofa was angled towards the big picture window out onto the mews.

'More like bask in the sun. I get enough gossip at work.'

He looked surprised.

'What? Don't tell me you hadn't noticed.'

He shook his head. 'What do people gossip about?'

'Oh, you know—the usual. Who's sleeping with who. Who's angling for a promotion. Who's getting fired.'

'So why don't I hear any of this?'

Eva rolled her eyes. With all his expensive business education, did he seriously not understand how an office worked? She was clearly going to have to spell this out to him.

'Of course you don't hear the gossip,' she said. 'One, you're practically the boss. No one gossips in front of the boss. Two, you're hardly ever in the office. And three, you're not exactly Mr Friendly over the coffee machine when you *are* there.'

'People don't think I'm friendly?'

'*I* don't think you're friendly. I can't speak for anyone else.'

He folded his arms and fixed her with a stern look. She was tempted to laugh.

'What's so unfriendly about me?'

Should she go for it? Unload all his faults? All the reasons she'd been telling herself for years why he was a million miles from boyfriend material.

Why not? Perhaps it would be the final straw in this idiotic deception.

'Fine—if you want to hear it. You're not exactly an open book, are you, Joss? You don't talk to people unless it's directly about the business.'

'I don't do small talk. There's a difference.'

'Right: the difference between being friendly and not friendly. It's not a criticism. Just an observation.'

'You think I should be friendlier?'

She sighed and shook her head. Seriously, this man's emotional intelligence didn't even register on the scale. 'I didn't say that. I don't think you need to change. But just don't be surprised if people don't open up around you.'

'Well, *you* don't seem to be having a problem with that.'

She shrugged and gave a resigned laugh. 'Proposing to a girl will have that effect. If you didn't want to know, you shouldn't have asked.'

'Might as well know what people think of me. So—office gossip. Is there going to be a lot of it. About us?'

'Are you kidding?' She laughed properly, genuinely

amused for the first time all day. 'I'm going to be grilled like a fish about this on Monday morning.'

'You could just not go in,' Joss offered. 'Take a few days off. Benefits of dating the boss.'

The smile dropped from her face as the insult hit. As if she could just not show up for work, with no notice, and it wouldn't make a difference to anyone.

'I think we need to get a couple of things straight, Joss. One—I work very hard with your father. My job is important, and I can't just swan off because you say so. Unless you fancy handling his correspondence in Arabic, Italian and French on Monday morning, I'll be at my desk as usual. Two—we are not now, nor will we ever be "dating". If I'd wanted to date you, I'd have asked you out for dinner. I'm going along with your little charade because I care about your father. Don't confuse the two.'

'Would you?' He leaned into the arm of the sofa with a smile that was verging dangerously on smug.

'Would I what?'

'Have asked me out for dinner?'

She sighed. Bloody man. 'The key part of that sentence, Joss, was *if*. I've never asked you because I don't want to date you.'

'You know, you sound like you've given that quite a lot of thought. Should I be flattered?'

'Honestly. Only a man with your ego could find a way to take that as a compliment. Listen to me carefully, Joss. I don't want to date you. I don't want to be engaged to you. I'm going along with it for now. But when the time comes we'll both extract ourselves from this situation with as much dignity as we can muster and forget it ever happened.'

CHAPTER THREE

EVA SPENT THE weekend in a daze. The further she got from having seen Joss the more ridiculous the whole thing seemed. So when she pitched up at her desk at eight o'clock on Monday morning she was almost surprised to see him there waiting for her.

'You're in early,' she commented, unwinding her scarf from around her neck and draping it over the coat-stand. 'Trying to impress somebody?'

'I told you—my father wants to start handing things over today. I thought we'd need an early start.'

'Well, we've both beaten the boss in.' She glanced through the blinds to Edward's darkened office beyond. 'Did you see him at the weekend? How is he?'

'*He* is marvellous, Eva, dear,' Edward said, bowling up behind her. 'Thank you for asking. And I was out of the city this weekend, so I've not seen anyone since I left the office on Friday. How about you two? I hope you did something nice with your weekend and didn't spend it worrying about me.'

'Dinner on Friday night,' Joss supplied truthfully.

'And Borough Market on Saturday,' Eva added.

No need to mention that she'd gone alone. She disliked the taste of the half-lie in her mouth, but the smile on Edward's face softened the blow.

'And arriving together on Monday morning. Were you this indiscreet before or am I really getting old?'

'Actually,' Joss said, 'we thought that now everyone will be finding out our news there's no reason we can't arrive together. In fact, I'll be moving my things over to Eva's place tonight.'

'Well, that's marvellous. Wish it had all worked like that when your mother and I were that age. Now, I'm glad I've found you two alone—I've been thinking, and there's something I want to say to you. I don't know what your plans are, but I don't want you to rush them for me. I know my news has been upsetting, but I don't want you hurrying anything up for my sake. Please?'

It was perfect, in a way, Eva realised. They wouldn't have to find an excuse not to marry before he died.

'But enough about that. I need the two of you in Milan as soon as you can get there. The store manager's feeling jumpy, and we have a couple of major suppliers over there as well who would probably appreciate a visit. I need you to smooth things over. Let people see that you're more than ready for the big job.'

Joss's eyebrows drew together, and she knew he wasn't happy at the implication that his employees didn't trust him.

'Dad, I met Matteo at the conference earlier in the year and it was all fine. The managers all know me. Surely you want me here? I'm not sure now's the time for me to be travelling.'

'Now's the perfect time, son. We need to steady things. You're going to have to visit all the flagship stores. The big suppliers too. They're worried—it's been a long time since this company faced big changes. This is part of your job now.'

'But what if something happens here?'

Eva winced. She knew exactly what Joss meant.

'What if I pop my clogs, you're asking? It's not going to happen overnight, son. We have some time. And I'd like to see the old girl looking straight before I go. I promise if anything changes you'll be the first to know. If it helps you make your mind up, I'm not planning on hanging around London waiting to die. Some places I want to see before I go. But you two need to be on a plane before lunchtime, and I've got an inbox the size of Milan Cathedral to work through with Eva before you go.

Joss walked away, leaving Eva and his father huddled around his computer monitor. Eva was making notes on a pad and occasionally reaching across to touch the screen. It was clear to him how fond she was of his father, and how distressed at the news of his illness.

And now he'd told them that he didn't want a hasty wedding. Yes, it got them out of having to take this charade too far, but Joss saw something else in it.

How much did his father know about his last marriage? About how he had felt rushed, unable to stop the oncoming commitment even after he'd realised it was a bad idea. More than he had let on at the time, it seemed.

He'd been rash and stupid announcing their nonexistent engagement to Edward, and he supposed that he should be grateful that Eva had agreed to go along with it.

She'd told him that it was because she cared for the old man, and Joss didn't doubt that. But that didn't mean he believed she'd given him the whole story. There were things that she was hiding. Layers of secrets, he suspected, from the frequently veiled expressions that crossed her face. Well, he was going to find out what they were—they had hours of travelling ahead of them, and she couldn't dodge his questions the whole way to Italy.

Or maybe he'd sleep instead of quizzing her, because that definitely hadn't been happening enough since his father had dropped his bombshell. He'd have liked to say it was grief over his father's illness that was causing his insomnia, but he knew that it was something else.

It was sleek chestnut hair and hazel eyes. The memory of a rose-pink slip under a serious navy dress. It was the thought of his holdall of clothes stashed in his office, destined for her flat just as soon as they got back from their trip. The thought of living in such close quarters with a woman he'd determinedly avoided since he'd noticed his attraction to her.

Back in his office, he dug out his toothbrush and a change of clothes from the holdall. If they weren't on a plane until lunchtime, he knew that they'd need to stay over. With his dad sending him off in such a hurry, he guessed it wasn't going to be a short meeting at the other end.

A noise caught his attention and he looked up to see

Eva, stalled at the entrance of his office. He felt that familiar pull, the heat in his body he knew was inevitable
when he was near her. Again he silently cursed whatever impulse it was that had made him lie to his father.

He felt a twist of pain in his belly. He knew how dangerous secrets could be—keeping his feelings bottled
up had turned toxic before, and lying to his father felt
unnatural now.

Intellectually, he understood the reasons he'd done it.
Because he'd let his father down so many times over the
years. He'd married his university girlfriend, a friend of
the family, because she was 'the right sort of girl' from
'the right sort of family', and everyone had expected it
to happen. He'd done what he'd thought was the right
thing—stood up in front of their friends and their family and made the commitment that was expected from
him, no matter how wrong it had felt inside.

As his depression had grown and his marriage had
darkened, he'd ignored the problems. Blinkered himself
against his wife's pain and buried himself in his work
rather than go back on his word and end a marriage that
was never going to make either of them happy. Until
she'd upped and left, and he'd seen the disappointment
in his parents' eyes that he had failed. Failed his wife.
Failed both their families.

It had only been after the breakdown of his marriage
that he'd realised he needed help. He'd gone weeks with
barely a couple of hours' sleep a night. Seen his weight
drop and his appetite disappear. It had only been when
he'd looked up his symptoms on the internet that he'd
realised they were classic signs of depression.

As soon as he'd read that, everything had fallen into place—that was the dark tunnel that he'd found himself in as his personal life had hurtled towards marriage while he'd buried his head in the sand, concentrating on the business.

So he'd gone to his doctor, worked hard at therapy. Eaten and exercised well. Taken the meds he'd been prescribed. And he'd recovered from his illness with a clarity and a focus that he'd not felt in years.

He shouldn't have been in that relationship to start with. He should have called it off as soon as he'd had doubts—before his illness had blinkered his vision and left him feeling that he didn't have a way out.

His parents had hinted over the years since his divorce that he should start seeing someone else, get back out there. But he knew he didn't want to be a bad husband, a bad partner, again. He couldn't risk doing that to someone else.

But he also knew that his father wanted to see him settled and happy—that was what had made it so easy for those words to slip out of his lips in the heat of the moment. And it was what made him burn with guilt now, knowing that he was misleading him. He suspected his father felt partially responsible for Joss feeling he had to go along with family expectations. If this lie made Joss feel uncomfortable, it would be worth it if it meant that his father could let his guilt rest before he died.

The recent spate of sleepless nights was a worry, though. It was years since he'd felt this drag of fatigue, and it reminded him of a time in his life he had absolutely no wish to revisit. This time it carried with it an extra shade of dread. He didn't want to be ill again. Didn't want his world to shrink and pale as he fought with his own brain chemistry to feel even the smallest amount of hope.

And right there was another good reason not to listen to the pull of his body when Eva was near. No. They had to keep real life, real feelings, and their charade separate. Regardless of how attracted they were to each other.

He considered his own thoughts. Was he right? Was she attracted to him as he was to her?

'Hey, come in,' he said, remembering that she was still standing, watching him from the doorway.

She shut the door behind her and Joss shifted in his chair at the sudden charge in the room that their isolation created.

'How's Dad getting on?' Talking about his father seemed like the safest option.

'He's great. Same as always. If he hadn't told us, I still wouldn't know there was anything wrong. Says he's looking forward to some more time out of the city. You?'

'I'm good. Could do without this trip, if I'm being honest.'

'Yeah.' She glanced at her watch. 'That's what I wanted to talk to you about. Your dad's asked me to book us a room. Said he thought the meetings might go on a bit. I need to go home and pack a bag, so I'll just meet you at the airport.'

'It's easier if I come with,' Joss said, leaning back

in his chair. 'You're only around the corner. We'll get a cab from there. It means I can drop my stuff off too.'

'You brought it to the office?' Eva looked horrified.

'What? Are you still worried about the gossip?'

'It's easy for you to joke about it. You've not been grilled about our grand romance every time you've so much as looked at the coffee machine.'

'I'm sorry you're getting the brunt of it. Do you want me to say something?'

She sighed and shook her head. 'What? A formal announcement about our fake relationship? A little weird, Joss.'

'Fine. Well, we'll be out of here in an hour. Think the news has reached the Milan store already?'

'Oh, I can guarantee it'll travel faster than we do.'

As the plane lifted from the runway Joss itched to reach into his bag for his laptop, hoping to relax in the familiarity of a working journey. He'd travelled between stores more times than he could count, and he knew he could get plenty of work done before their meeting. Plus staring at the screen of his computer was safer than glancing across at the woman sitting beside him.

He remembered the first time he'd seen her. Well, the first time that he'd really noticed her. For so long during his marriage and his illness, he'd not been able to see any beauty in the world, never mind in a woman. And then one morning, newly divorced and with a fresh hold on his psychological wellbeing, he'd walked into his father's office and heard Eva speaking in quick-fire Italian—to the Milan store, perhaps. Or one of the luxury fashion suppliers. She'd burst into laughter, and as she'd thrown her head back in amusement she'd caught his eye.

Something had caught inside him, too. A spark of intense attraction he couldn't remember feeling since… Forget that. He'd *never* felt anything like that before— the intense pull not only to a beautiful woman, but to one he knew could joke and laugh in half a dozen languages when he was struggling to do it in one.

There had been a time in his past when an attraction like that would have felt like a red rag to a bull. But he knew better now. He knew where a relationship with him would leave a woman, and he had no desire to inflict that on Eva.

The 'Fasten Seatbelt' light was switched off, and Joss kept his eyes down as they both pulled out their laptops. Eva started muttering under her breath as she read through a document, the sound almost lost in the rustle of her hair as she tucked it behind her ear.

Please, not Italian, he pleaded silently. He wasn't sure what it was, but the sound of that language on her lips was his weak spot. He breathed a sigh of relief when he caught an Arabic phrase—something to do with the Dubai store, perhaps. It wasn't Italian but, *God*, she made it sound sexy.

He remembered the last time he'd heard her speak Arabic—at the conference of all their international store managers—the way the sounds had rolled around her tongue, and the confidence and speed with which she'd spoken. It was too much, eventually, and he glanced up from his spreadsheet, promising himself just a quick look at her expression.

But when he looked at her, her eyes were already focussed on him, and once he realised that he couldn't look away.

'What?' she asked him, breaking off from reading, and he knew he'd been staring too long.

He raised his eyebrows and shook his head. 'Nothing. Just wondered if you knew you were talking to yourself.'

He returned his gaze to the columns of numbers that had been dancing in front of his eyes since he'd loaded up the file.

He kept his eyes decisively on his screen until he heard his name pass Eva's lips and couldn't help glancing up to see her expression—he wished he hadn't when he saw the exasperation there. She rubbed her forehead and he glanced at her screen, but couldn't make out any of the Arabic she was reading. From her frustration, it was pretty clear that there was a problem, and he suspected he knew what it was.

'Trouble in Dubai?' he asked.

'They're worried,' Eva replied. 'Your father was due to have a phone conference with the manager of the store tomorrow. Edward's cancelled and asked me not to reschedule yet and the manager is worried about business continuity. I'm going to have to call your dad. See if he'll rearrange.'

'I'll take the meeting,' Joss said. 'What?' he added when Eva grimaced slightly.

'I'm not sure that'll work. In fact, I already tried that. They say they want to speak to Edward.'

'Well, if Dad's taking time off it's not like he doesn't have a good reason.'

'I know that. We'll talk to him about it when we're back in the office. But this is two stores just this morning who are going into crisis mode. I think we have to assume that others will react in the same way.'

Joss stared her down, not appreciating her doubting his ability to do his new job. 'I'm perfectly capable of running this business. I've been preparing for it for long enough.'

'I know that, Joss.' Eva relaxed back into the seat as she spoke. 'Your father does too—and every Dawson's employee, really. But knowing it and feeling it aren't necessarily the same thing. As a rule, people don't like change, and—like it or not—you at the head of the company *is* change.'

He shrugged off her concerns. 'So I'll go to Dubai too. To every single store worldwide if I have to.'

'It might help,' Eva said. 'In Dubai at least.'

Joss nodded, trying to mentally rearrange the next couple of weeks to accommodate another overseas trip. Dubai was too far to hop on a plane for just the day.

'You should come,' he said, thinking how valuable having his father's right-hand woman by his side would be in showing the store that nothing was going to change with him in charge. Yes, that was the only reason he was inviting her along. 'As a show of continuity. They might not know me well, but they know you. It will be reassuring.'

'I don't know, Joss.'

Eva didn't look convinced by his reasoning.

She leant forward, her elbows resting on the table in front of her. 'I never went with your dad. I can make the time to be out of the office for this one meeting, but I can't be constantly on the road or in the air.'

He watched her closely for a minute. The way she shifted in her seat and wouldn't meet his eyes. She might be worried about the business, but that wasn't really why she was refusing to go.

'That's not why you don't want to go. What is it— afraid of flying?'

She snorted a laugh. 'Did I miss you dragging me on here kicking and screaming? As if! And I'm an army brat, remember.'

'You *were* an army brat,' he corrected her. 'You look all grown up to me.'

He could have cringed at his cheesy line, but when her gaze finally locked on to his he didn't care—it was the truth. He didn't want to talk about her childhood. He wanted to talk about them on an all-night flight to Dubai and then getting hot and sweaty together in the desert.

He shook his head, hoping to scatter those danger-ous thoughts. Eva was strictly off-limits, and he'd do well to remember that. Even if she agreed to this trip, as she'd agreed to the engagement, it would be strictly business. There would be no hot and sweaty—in the desert or anywhere else.

'So it's not the flight,' he said. He was intrigued. Who would turn down an impromptu trip to Dubai, with a visit to the city's most luxurious shopping mall guaranteed? 'What is it, then? Fear of catching some tropical disease?'

'It's nothing remotely exciting, Joss.' Eva flicked her fingers at an invisible piece of fluff. 'I prefer not to travel much. I love living in London and I like to stay there.'

Joss laughed with incredulity. 'But you speak six languages. Don't you ever want to use them?'

'Seven, actually. And, hello? How long have we been working together? I use them every day.'

'But is that really the same? Just saying the words, I mean. Or reading emails? Don't you want to go and experience the different cultures? Hear the dialects and the slang on the streets?'

Eva shrugged. 'I've done different cultures, thanks. I've done trying to learn what slang the cool kids are using. I'm happy where I am.'

'So why learn the languages at all?' He knew that talking about something so personal was probably a bad idea. But he couldn't help being intrigued by her. Couldn't help wanting to know more. 'There are plenty of jobs you could do without them.'

'It was a case of necessity at first, I guess,' Eva said. 'When we moved to Germany I wanted to do more than speak to the other kids on the base and at the army school. If I was going to be dragged to another country, I was determined to learn how to express myself there. The same when we went to Cyprus. And, to be honest, it came naturally. I loved learning to speak other languages. Maybe my brain likes the patterns of different grammar. Or hearing sounds that we don't even have in English. Words that can't be translated, because speaking another language makes you think in another language.'

'Okay, so German and Greek I get. But what about Arabic? Did you live in the Middle East?'

There was something more to this, he realised. Something about her parents. Something they'd never talked about before.

She shook her head. 'No, we were based here while Mum and Dad did their tours in Iraq. I'm not sure why I decided to learn. I quite liked the challenge of another new alphabet. A completely different written form of language.'

'And maybe it made you feel closer to your parents?' Joss asked gently. 'To speak the language they would be hearing around them every day?'

Eva remained silent, her eyebrows pulling together in a frown. Had she never considered that? he wondered.

'So, anyway, these meetings this afternoon,' Eva said, shaking off any suggestion of a personal conversation. 'What do you need from me? I've already requested an update from the supply management team on any issues they've had in the last few months, and pulled together the minutes from relevant meetings. As for the manager of the store, Matteo Lazzari, I've put all the correspondence between him and Edward in a folder and given you access. Is there anything else you need me to prepare?'

Joss looked at her closely, noting the swift change of subject but not pushing back. If she didn't want to talk about her personal life, then that was up to her. If this had been a real relationship then maybe he'd have encouraged her to open up, but this was just for show. She wanted to draw a line and that was fine by him.

He drew his eyes back to the spreadsheet in front of him, determined that the rest of the flight would be spent working, rather than trying and failing to guess what was going on in Eva's head.

When the announcement came to pack away all electronic devices and return their tables to an upright position, Joss congratulated himself on his self-control. Just as he'd promised himself, he'd got his work done with barely a thought for Eva.

He glanced sideways, to see if she was still working too, and realised the reason he had been so free from interruptions was because at some point, with her fingers still resting gently on her laptop keys, she had fallen asleep. Perhaps he wasn't the only one to have struggled with insomnia last night.

The cabin crew were making their way down the centre aisle, checking that their instructions for landing had been complied with, so he gently shifted Eva's hands from the computer onto her lap, then closed the laptop and folded up the table. She stirred a little in her sleep, shifting to get comfortable, and then eventually rested her head on his shoulder, letting out a deep sigh and settling back into sleep.

Joss watched her for a moment, unsure whether he should move her. But he thought it was unlikely he could do that again without waking her. So he left her where she was: with the gentle weight of her head against his arm and the smell of her hair temptingly close. The armrest between them was up, and as she fell deeper and deeper into sleep her body pressed closer, relaxing into him as he grew more and more tense.

He couldn't allow himself to enjoy this.

He mustn't allow himself to think about how he had seen that body covered only by the fine silk of a slip. How he'd wanted to run his hands inside her dress to clasp her waist, to pull her back against him as he slid her zip all the way down.

He couldn't allow himself to think about all the places his mind had taken him after he'd left her flat that night. Alone at home, he'd imagined pushing her dress off her shoulders, it gliding down to the floor and landing at his feet…

Another announcement from the cabin crew broke into his thoughts and was loud enough to wake Eva, who sat up with a start.

'Did I—?' Eva began, smoothing down her hair with a shaking hand before she stopped herself. 'Sorry—must have fallen asleep,' she said, briskly this time, looking around her in confusion. 'Did you put my laptop away?'

'They put the lights on for landing,' Joss offered by way of explanation.

'You should have woken me.'

He shrugged. 'Looked like you needed the sleep. I know the feeling. We'll be landing any minute,' he added, keen to move the conversation away from the question of them sleeping even in the same vicinity as one another.

An hour later their car passed the extravagant frontage of the Milan store on its way to their hotel, and he looked up at it in wonder. It didn't matter how many times he saw it, it never lost its magic. He thought of his great-grandfather, who had built up this business in a different century, a different world. And not for the first time he thought how lucky he was to be part of this family, to have such an inheritance, such a legacy to care for. His determination to continue that success, to prove himself, rallied.

And, much as he might protest to Eva that he had spent his life preparing for the top job, and much as that might be true, the job was his far sooner than any of them had imagined. He had thought he had a few more years to work on his relationships with the managers of the overseas stores. To build the connections that would be so important when his father was no longer around.

He was certain he had the experience and the expertise to continue the family success—now he had to prove himself to the rest of the business.

CHAPTER FOUR

EVA STEPPED UP to the desk at the hotel and pulled out the paperwork with the details of their reservation. The receptionist took their reservation number and tapped the screen of the computer for a seemingly endless time, until eventually she looked up with a smile and called over a bellboy.

'Thanks so much,' Eva said, excited to be speaking Italian face to face, despite everything she had said to Joss on the plane. 'Could you send some lunch up to the room?' she asked as the bellboy took their bags.

Their meeting was in an hour, but with the prospect of Italian cuisine when they arrived she hadn't been able to face the thought of airline food.

'Something quick and simple, please.'

She hovered behind the bellboy as he jiggled the key card and opened the door into their room. As she followed him in, she realised that there must have been some sort of mistake, in spite of how long the receptionist had taken to check them in.

Her eye was first caught by the extravagant bouquet of flowers on the beautifully polished table in the centre of the suite's foyer. A bottle of champagne and a note sat beside it, with her and Joss's names picked out in a stylish copperplate hand. Through the open doors leading from the foyer she could see at least one bedroom, a marble-lined bathroom, and a terrace overlooking the city. It was luxury far beyond anything she'd ever experienced. Was this what she had to look forward to as part of the Dawson family?

Not that she was part of the family yet. *Or ever would be*, she reminded herself. This engagement was all for show, no matter how real this suite was making it feel.

She picked up the envelope and turned it over, feeling the heavy weight of the paper in her hand. She read the note inside, fighting against the tear that was threatening at the corner of her eye.

Dearest Joss and Eva,
Consider the suite a little engagement present
from me. Enjoy Milan and don't hurry back.
Love,
Dad

Those last two words made her feel something she had been looking for for as long as she could remember. Included. Accepted. Part of a family. Something her own family had never managed.

Some parts of her childhood had been so privileged she knew she shouldn't complain. She'd always had a roof over her head and food on the table. While her mother and father had taken turns to be away on tour, among families and homes torn apart by conflict, whoever had been left behind had tried their best to fill the space that was left.

But that didn't change the facts. Both her parents had been happy to leave her for months at a time. Hugging her goodbye and promising to be home soon, all the while aware that they had no way of knowing if they could keep their promises. And then—inevitably, it had seemed—her mother had kissed her goodbye, told her she would be home soon, and instead they'd had a visit from a sombre-looking man in uniform. Eva had been left with the knowledge that her mother had never loved her enough to want to spare her the pain that her death would bring, even though she'd tried to convince herself that she didn't care enough to hurt.

She'd thought that would be it for her father. That he would be repulsed by the thought of leaving her again. Of taking the chance of making her an orphan.

She'd been wrong.

Joss came up behind her and took the note gently from her hand.

'The old romantic,' he said, with the beginnings of a laugh. He stepped around her to examine the champagne, but when he caught sight of her face he replaced the bottle in the ice bucket and reached to touch her cheek. 'What is it?' he asked, alarm evident in his expression.

'It's nothing,' Eva said, painting on a fake smile. 'You're right—it is romantic. Shame it'll be wasted on us.'

A knock at the door signalled lunch arriving.

'You show them in, I'll be back in just a minute.'

In the bathroom, she patted cold water on her cheekbones and took a few deep breaths, trying not to think about romance, or the suite, or Joss. It was probably a good job that they were going to be in meetings all the time they were out here. It didn't matter what Edward said—she would be hurrying home. The less time they spent closeted in a luxury hotel suite the better. Or safer, at least. There were a lot of reasons why she might enjoy being locked away with Joss, but it was absolutely not a good idea to think about them. Definitely safer not to.

She left the bathroom and grabbed a couple of pieces of ciabatta from the tray the waiter had left on the table. Eating while she worked, she sifted through the files that she had brought with her, stocking her bag and ensuring that her tablet had enough charge to last the rest of the day. She had access to all the information that Joss might need for their meetings. This was his first test as Managing Director of the company, and it was a matter of professional pride for her that nothing went wrong for him.

She glanced at her watch as she pulled on a jacket. 'Are you ready?' she called to Joss, who had disappeared into one of the bedrooms.

'Be right out,' he called back.

She checked her phone as she waited by the door and was relieved to see a text from their driver, letting them know that he was waiting for them outside.

Joss emerged wearing a fresh shirt and she deliberately averted her eyes, not wanting to give herself any excuse to appreciate the way that man wore simple white cotton. It was a thought that she'd blocked out a lot over the years—when she'd caught sight of Joss in a meeting or walking through the office and tried to work out exactly what it was that made this man so attractive to her.

It wasn't as if he was even *nice*. Sure, he was courteous. He was professional. She couldn't think of a time when he had been outright rude. But definitely not nice. He wouldn't go out of his way to make someone feel comfortable. Wouldn't remember her birthday and drop something small and wrapped on her desk in the morning without a word.

He was nothing like his father, whom she adored. So how was it that for years she hadn't been able to get him out of her head? Why was he the man she measured every date against and found them lacking?

She reached behind her and grabbed the door handle, opening the door into the corridor and stepping out of the suite when Joss was a few feet away. A buffer zone: that was what was needed. Safe space between them that couldn't be breached.

But would people think that was odd? she wondered. She had no doubt that news of their engagement would have reached the Italian store before they did. Her standoffishness might cause more gossip—make people start to question whether the relationship was real. Make them ask what she hoped to get out of it.

She shook her head. It was far more likely that people would see that they were two professionals at work, acting professionally. No one would expect them to be all over each other. Respectful distance worked *for* their story, rather than against it.

'So, when was the last time you met with Matteo in person?' she asked Joss, determined to keep their conversation on a work footing after their earlier diversion into her personal life.

'In the spring,' Joss said. 'But it was at the conference for all the international store managers. You know what that thing is like—between meetings and presentations there's hardly time for a business conversation, never mind anything more personal.'

'Well, we should have lots of time today. You two have all afternoon pencilled in, and there's nothing in your diary for tonight either, so you can always take it to dinner if you feel you need to. Just remember you're trying to make a personal connection. He knows that you're capable. You've been with the company for ever. Just show him that you're someone he's going to enjoy working with.'

Joss caught up with her in the hallway. 'What? You want me to flirt with him? Seduce him?'

Here she was, trying to be professional, and he had to mention flirting and seduction pretty much the minute he opened his mouth. Was he determined to make this impossible for her?

'You know, I think he's been happily married for the last twenty years or so. I'm not sure flirting will get you anywhere.'

Joss tutted. 'You know what I mean. You think I should charm him. That's what he wants?'

'I don't think he wants to be charmed, Joss. I think he wants to get to know you. You could be friendly. That would be a start.'

Friendly. There was that word again. Was that what she wanted from him? For him to be friendly to her? Hardly. That would make things impossible. At least when he was terse and short and—well, *un*friendly— she could remind herself of all the reasons why she shouldn't indulge this crush of hers. If he were to actually start conversing, or—God forbid—laughing like a normal human being, then she was going to be in big trouble.

'I thought we'd already established that I can't do friendly.'

'No, we established that you *don't* do friendly. Only you know whether that's out of choice or not. Do you try to be unfriendly?'

'I just try and get the job done, Eva. It doesn't normally require chatting over a cup of tea.'

'Well, your new job does, Joss. People need to see you, to get to know you. Your dad's illness has been a big shock to everyone. They're going to miss him enormously. It's a big gap to fill.'

Joss stopped in the hallway and fixed her with a stare.

'I'm well aware of that, thank you, Eva.'

She let out a breath and reached out a hand to his arm. 'I'm sorry, Joss. I know you are. And I'm not trying to criticise. Just trying to fill you in on what your father's relationship with his store managers is like. I'm not saying that you need to do business in the same way—I'm just giving you the information that you need to manage this transition. We're all trying to manage this situation as best we can. Myself included.'

He turned back to the lift and pressed the button to take them to the lobby. 'Well, thank you for the information. I'll take it under advisement.'

So that was how today was going to be. Icy cool. Well, that was fine by her, but she wasn't sure what Matteo would make of it.

They walked into the grand entrance of the Milan store to see Matteo waiting to greet them. 'Eva, *bella*. It is always such a pleasure.' He greeted her with a kiss on each cheek and warm enquiries about her health. 'And Mr Dawson, of course.'

He held out a hand to Joss and received a brusque handshake in return.

'Please, call me Joss.'

Unfortunately Joss's tone didn't match the friendliness of his sentiment, but Eva resisted the urge to roll her eyes in front of Matteo.

'And I hear from a little voice back in the office that congratulations are in order! You are to be married?' He kissed Eva again on both cheeks and shook Joss's hand again. 'An office romance. How lovely.'

He picked up Eva's left hand and let out a murmur of dismay.

'Oh, but no ring?'

'Oh, no,' Eva said, trying to think on her feet. 'Everything happened rather quickly, and with Edward's news…'

She let the sentence sit in the air and hoped that her allusion to terminal illness would do away with the need for further explanations.

'Oh, but you have some time now,' Matteo exclaimed with pleasure. 'And you are in the most beautiful store in the world! If you will forgive the slight to your English stores, Mr Dawson. I absolutely insist you come and choose something before our meeting.'

Eva looked at Joss, expecting him to shut down any discussion of shopping and insist they all get to work. But he wore an inscrutable expression that was heading towards a smile, and somehow she knew that meant trouble.

'If you're sure you don't mind waiting a little longer for our meeting, Signor Lazzari. Eva and I would love to do that.'

As they walked through the lobby towards the fine jewellery department, Eva grabbed Joss's hand and hung back a little, allowing the distance between them and Matteo to stretch beyond his hearing a whisper.

'What are you doing?' she asked out of the side of her mouth, glancing round to make sure that no one else could be listening in.

'Being friendly,' Joss replied with that same almost-smile.

'If you're doing this to make a point to me, it's fine. I get it—you're Mr Friendly. Time to drop it.'

Joss shook his head. 'Matteo wants to spoil us in his store. Show it off at its best. I thought it was politic to go along with him. Anyway, we will need a ring. If we wait too long people will start to talk.'

'You know,' she said, a touch of sharpness in her voice, 'some people think of that before they pop the question.'

'Yes, well, I'm not "some people", am I? I have the feeling that you never would have agreed to this if I was.'

She stopped, a hand on his arm turning him towards her. 'And what's that meant to mean?'

'Oh, nothing, darling,' Joss replied as he realised they had reached the gleaming glass counters of the jewellery department and Matteo was looking at them expectantly. 'So—where do you want to start?' he asked.

Matteo pulled out a few rings from the nearest cabinet—diamond solitaires all of them, ranging from the shockingly big to the tastelessly huge.

'Something classic, perhaps?' Matteo said, handing her a platinum diamond ring that must be a good three carats.

Eva held it between her fingertips and then looked up to Joss. He must have sensed her discomfort, because he took the ring from her and placed it back in the tray.

'Something a little more unusual for Eva, I think,' he said, reaching for an equally huge stone, this time flanked with pretty yellow pear-shaped diamonds. 'What about this,' he asked, meeting her eyes as he slipped the ring onto her finger.

She stood staring at it for a moment, reality and make-believe clashing. She knew this wasn't real. She knew it was all for show. But with this rock on her finger the lines were less clear than ever before.

She couldn't deny that she'd fantasised about this moment. All she wanted in her life was constancy... stability. Perhaps, one day she'd meet a man who she wouldn't want to let go. He'd slide a ring onto the third finger of her left hand and she would know without doubt that it was staying there for life.

It wasn't meant to feel like…*this*. It was never meant to be temporary. All she could see when she looked at this ring was the day when she would have to take it off. When Edward was gone, and she and Joss gave up their pretence, she'd have to return it to its snug velvet box and hand it back to him.

Her eyes filled with tears, but she fought them back, knowing that she couldn't lose it in front of Joss, never mind in front of Matteo.

'Ah, look at you. This is a special moment,' Matteo said with a smile. 'And I see I am not quite needed here. If I say I will see you again in an hour, will that be enough time for you?'

He handed Joss the keys to the jewellery cabinets and clapped him on the shoulder. 'I leave you two young lovers alone. Choose something special, yes?'

They both watched in silence as Matteo crossed the jewellery hall, waiting until they were alone and could speak safely.

'You don't like it?' Joss asked eventually, picking up her hand again and examining the ring.

'It's spectacular,' Eva replied with honesty.

'Then why the tears?' he said, gently this time, brushing a finger across her cheekbones.

'I'm not crying.'

'You're not letting them fall. I can see that. But you're upset. Why?'

'It's nothing, Joss. It's just that this is all a bit unnecessary. It feels strange. Wrong.'

'Why?'

There was no impatience in his voice, nor in his expression, as she took her time choosing the right words.

'Because it's all a lie. And a ring like this—it deserves something better. It's meant to be a symbol of love and commitment. We both know that we're not promising either of those things.'

He looked down at the ring for a moment, and then gently pulled it over her knuckle. 'Nothing that looks like an engagement ring, then. That narrows our options. What about this?' he asked.

'That's an eternity ring, Joss. Same problem.'

'You know, I don't think the ring is going to mind.'

She shook her head, not sure if she could make him understand without revealing too much of herself. '*I* mind. I might want one of these things for real one day. When I buy my engagement ring—or an eternity ring for that matter—I don't want to be keeping the receipt for when I have to return it.'

'So that's the problem.' Joss nodded, looking as if he had cracked a particularly difficult problem in the budget spreadsheet. 'You don't want something you like because you won't want to give it back? You can keep the ring, Eva. With everything you're doing for my father, for the business, it's the least I can do.'

Eva let out a breath in frustration. 'It's not about the money, Joss. It's the symbol. It's what the ring's meant to mean. I can't accept an engagement ring when there is no engagement.'

He looked thoughtful, and remained silent for a few long minutes, before reaching for her hand and pulling her gently to another case. 'What about if the ring symbolises something else, then? What if it's a gesture—a friendly gesture—of thanks. Thanks for caring for my father enough to go through with this. Thanks for looking after him and the business for so long. It's a gift—from a friend. The meaning doesn't change, whatever happens between us. And I absolutely won't accept it back from you when this ends.'

She looked at the case of jewellery he had brought her to, and thought about what he had said.

A gift like that she could accept, she thought. A ring was part of making this engagement look realistic, but these didn't look like engagement rings. They looked more like garlands of flowers, or boughs of blossoms. Tiny diamonds, sparkling and weaving their way across bands of yellow gold.

Joss unlocked the case and brought out one of the rings, with pink and blue sapphires scattered amongst bigger diamonds. He slipped it on to her third finger and they both stared at it in silence for a moment, taking in the effect.

'What do you think?' Joss asked.

'Better,' Eva said. 'It feels…friendly.'

Joss breathed a laugh. 'You old romantic. You're right. It's better. But it's not perfect. It's too heavy for those slender fingers. Too busy.'

He slipped it off again, and swapped it for a more delicate one—just diamonds this time, set in a meandering line like a trailing spray of flowers. This time when Joss slipped it on her finger she had no doubts.

'It's the one,' she said, gazing down at her finger.

'Perfect,' Joss agreed.

And before she realised what he was doing he had lifted her hand to his mouth and the warm heat of his lips was pressing against her knuckles.

She stood and stared at him, not quite sure where to begin with her line of questioning on this one.

'Joss… I don't think…'

His lips left her hand and he looked up, meeting her eyes with his intense gaze. She forgot what she had been going to say. Something about how this wasn't a good idea, probably. Except with her hand still encased in his, with the ring warming on her finger, it suddenly felt like the best idea they'd had for a while.

Joss's other hand landed lightly on her waist and for a moment neither of them breathed. Then, as one, they took in a sharp breath, and nudged closer towards one another.

Joss's hand snaked around her back, taking hers with it, twisting her until her back was against the jewellery cabinet. And it would have been so, so easy to relax into him, to loosen her body and let his arms take her weight. Take her anywhere he wanted to go.

Another half-step closer and his body met hers, pressing lightly against her from knee to chest, setting off fireworks everywhere in between.

This was all for show, she reminded herself. Joss was playing a part. For him, all this was just a way of making his father happy. Nothing about this was real for Joss—not in the way that the feelings she could feel growing for him were real.

At that moment she heard Matteo's voice from somewhere behind Joss and pushed gently against his chest, putting some much needed distance between them.

'Ah, I see you two have chosen something. Come—let me see.'

Eva held her left hand out to Matteo, hoping that she would be able to control the slight shake she could feel deep inside.

'It is beautiful,' Matteo said. 'A wonderful choice. But then I would expect nothing else. So, perhaps now we are ready to get to work?'

'Of course,' Joss said, his voice brusque, nothing like the soft tones she had heard when they were discussing her engagement ring.

She hoped that Matteo would put it down to an excess of emotion over their engagement rather than unfriendliness, otherwise the whole 'choosing the ring' exercise would have been wasted.

'And I have just spoken to Signora Lazzari—Giulietta—and she insists that you join us for dinner tonight,' Matteo said.

'Oh, I'm not sure if we—' Eva started.

'We'd love to,' Joss said, interrupting Eva's plan for a polite refusal.

But Joss was probably right. He was here to show the manager that he was the sort of man they could work with. It made sense for them to have dinner together. Eva herself had suggested that they might spend some time together this evening. But eating together as a foursome—that was inviting a world of trouble.

When they were working, it would be simple to explain away the lack of intimacy between them. They *should* keep a professional distance when they were in the office or one of the stores. But at dinner, perhaps at Matteo's home, that would be personal. They would be expected to look like a couple—and they'd have to make it convincing.

But now that Joss had agreed she didn't have much choice. She could hardly *un*accept a generous invitation from the man they were here to charm.

'But I insist that you allow us to take you out,' Joss said, allaying one of her concerns.

At least if they were safely out in public then they would be expected not to indulge in too many displays of affection.

CHAPTER FIVE

EVA PULLED ON the black dress that she always packed in case of emergencies. There was no situation she'd discovered yet that a simple black shift couldn't handle. She caught sight of the diamonds on her left hand and decided to leave off the statement necklace she'd also packed—it would be a shame to overshadow the pretty, understated ring that she and Joss had chosen together.

They'd agreed on dinner in the hotel restaurant downstairs. Its reputation was unparalleled in the city, and Matteo and his wife had happily accepted Joss's suggestion.

She checked her reflection quickly in the mirror and rubbed away a smudge of eyeliner. She'd kept her make-up simple, professional: a subtle reminder to herself that she hadn't knocked off for the day. She still had a part to play.

She heard the shower being shut off in the other bath-room and wondered whether Joss had thought to pack something to wear out to dinner. If it had been Edward taking the meeting she would have provided him with an itinerary of their trip—including likely social possibilities as well as all the meetings that were confirmed in the calendar. She hadn't found that familiarity with Joss yet. That closeness. A way of anticipating his needs even before he did.

She shivered slightly at the thought of developing such a thing with Joss. Even without their fake engagement, the changes at work would have been enough to turn their relationship completely on its head. To break down those careful barriers she'd built to keep herself distant from him at work. To keep her mind from wandering in his direction.

With everything else that had happened, she hadn't stopped to consider the alternative reality that might have existed if Edward had never walked in on them in the office and got the wrong idea. It wasn't as if her life would have carried on unchanged. She and Joss would still be in Milan, for a start. In separate rooms, though, instead of this suite. And Joss would still be moving in to Edward's office, sitting every day in her direct eyeline, on the other end of an intercom, occupying a huge part of her work life.

Joss's presence in her life would have grown anyway. So maybe by agreeing to this engagement she'd actually gained more control than she would otherwise have had. More freedom to discuss the nature of their relationship. To make clear to him that, however it might seem, a romantic attachment was absolutely *not* on the cards between them and never would be.

She shook her head. Most people didn't feel the need to have that sort of conversation with their boss. With most people it was just assumed that there would be nothing extracurricular going on. Just the fact that she was thinking it proved that these changes were always going to have caused trouble.

'Are you ready?' Joss called from the other side of the bedroom door.

What a question. She was ready to jump in a car, get on the first plane home, and pretend that none of this was happening. But was she ready to go out and fake a relationship with the man she'd been burying her feelings for since his divorce? She wasn't sure she wanted to admit the answer to that one.

Instead she opened the door, shut out her feelings and faked a smile.

'Ready,' she said, doing a last-minute check on the contents of her bag as they headed to the front door of the suite.

'You look nice,' Joss said as they headed out into the corridor.

He'd barely looked at her, she noticed. But she couldn't fault his manners.

'You too,' she replied, trying just as hard not to actually to look at him.

Spending so much time together was meant to be curing her of her crush—but so far all the evidence was that it was having the opposite effect. It really was in no way fair. Perhaps it was the vast suite that Edward had arranged for them. With their separate bedrooms the size of palaces they might as well be living in separate apartments, as they had been back in London.

But this was only temporary, she reminded herself. Tomorrow they would be flying back to London, where there was a holdall of his clothes waiting for them in her spare room. And an empty drawer and a few inches of wardrobe space she'd managed to clear out for him.

They rode the lift down to the lobby in silence, and Eva deliberately avoided meeting Joss's eye in the mirrors that surrounded them. Then she remembered what they were doing here, the lie they were meant to be living, and risked a glance at him. She found him already watching her, and gave him a small smile.

'Ready for this?' he asked.

'No. You?'

'No.'

At that she felt the smile spread from her lips and across her cheeks, and saw it was reflected in Joss's eyes. She even risked a small laugh.

'Well, as long as we're in agreement, I suppose.'

She grabbed his hand as the lift doors slid open, and they were greeted by the sight of Matteo and his wife waiting for them in the lobby. Good job they'd got their faces sorted out before the lift stopped, Eva thought.

She greeted Matteo and Giulietta with kisses to both cheeks, but Joss kept her hand locked in his. She held on, in case he needed the support. Anyway, with her body anchored to his like this it made it easier to remember what she was doing—the part she was supposed to be playing. She wasn't just his assistant, greasing the wheels of conversation, providing snippets of information when they were needed. She was half of a couple.

Even as they were chatting over an aperitif she could still feel the warmth of Joss's hand against her skin, and she wondered if that would ever go. This hyper-awareness of his body whenever it was in contact with hers. In twenty years, would she still be getting fireworks if their fingers brushed when she handed him a letter to sign, or a contract to approve?

Twenty years.

Working with Edward, she'd never had any trouble envisaging her future. She'd felt secure. She'd known— or thought she had known—that she would always have a place with Dawson's. But now… Now she couldn't be sure.

One of the reasons she'd agreed to this charade in the first place was because she'd thought it would bind her more closely to the company, and then Joss wouldn't be able to show her the door as soon as his dad was gone. But was that naïve? Did this fake relationship make it more likely, rather than less, that Joss would want to see the back of her once this was over? Surely it would be more realistic that they *wouldn't* want to work together any more if they 'broke up'.

And if people found out that the whole thing was a sham, of course Joss would want her out of the way.

The thoughts crashing through her brain made her realise how naïve they had been, thinking that they could just start this thing with no idea when or how it was going to end. And how had she thought that Joss would want to keep her around after it was over?

A shiver ran through her, and she felt rather than saw Joss turn towards her.

'Cold?' he asked, dropping her hand and placing an arm around her shoulder.

'Just from this,' Eva said, faking a laugh and gesturing to the Prosecco in her hand, condensation beading on the glass.

As they took their seats at the table Eva was still incredibly aware of her body language, and that of Joss, sitting beside her. Were they playing it too cool? This was a dinner with colleagues, and they were out in public, so no one would expect them to be all over each other. But since she'd shaken off Joss's arm, with protestations that she wasn't cold, she was more aware than ever of his presence beside her, of having him so close but not touching.

Should she do something? she wondered, as she stared at the menu in front of her, unable to take in a single word. She glanced at his hand, resting on the table, and wondered if she should reach for it. She could just slide her fingers between his, the way she remembered doing instinctively the day Edward had announced his illness. It would look like the most natural thing in the world to Matteo and his wife. Or maybe she could rest a hand on his thigh, feel under her fingertips those firm muscles which just a couple of hours ago had pressed her against a jewellery cabinet.

She resisted the urge to sigh and tried to concentrate on her menu instead, picking it up from the table and attempting to focus.

'Oh, what a pretty ring,' Giulietta said from across the table. 'Matteo told me you chose it together today.'

Eva smiled at Giulietta and glanced down at her hand. She remembered what Joss had said about it symbolising friendship, her place in the family, and looked up at him with a smile.

'Ah, but you two are so in love,' Giulietta said with a laugh, and Eva felt her cheeks colour. 'It is good that you can be happy after such sad news. I was so sorry to hear that Edward is not well.'

This time she didn't think about it. She reached for Joss's hand and squeezed it tightly in her own, knowing how raw his pain must be, if it was anything like her own.

'Thank you,' Joss said, carefully steady.

Eva glanced up at him and could see from the set line of his jaw how much of a struggle he was finding that composure.

'I know my father values your efforts here highly.'

'And I know that he is so sorry that he's not able to be here himself,' Eva added, hoping that she'd be able to make up for Joss's lack of warmth.

Edward and Matteo had been friends for years, and she knew that the Lazzaris would be feeling the sadness of his loss too. Joss had his own grief to deal with—but she had to make sure that this meeting achieved everything they needed it to. Matteo *had* to see that he would be happy working with Joss.

'I know that he would love to be at this dinner with us.'

'Ah, we understand,' Giulietta said with a kind smile. 'We are just happy to have *your* company this evening. And to be able to send our warmest wishes with you when you return.'

'Of course we will take them,' Eva said, and glanced up at Joss.

They were here to try and show Matteo a more

human, personal side of Joss, but so far he was too distracted. He seemed more buttoned up than ever, and she still had no idea how to get him to open up.

'If you'll excuse me?' Giulietta said, pushing her chair back. 'I'll be back in a few moments.'

Three at the table felt a whole lot more uncomfortable than four, Eva realised after a few seconds' awkward silence.

She attempted to start up a conversation a couple of times, but nothing was thawing between them. Matteo's phone rang, and he excused himself from the table with apologies, saying that it was his deputy at the store.

'What?' Joss asked, as she turned towards him with a concerned look.

She took a bracing breath, knowing that this conversation had to be quick, discreet and effective. 'We're here to show Matteo a warmer side to you, yes? Well, we're not doing a good job so far.'

He sat up a little straighter in his chair. 'We were talking about my terminally ill father. Would you like me to be cracking jokes?'

She shook her head—a small, efficient movement. 'Of course not. And I understand how difficult it will be. But we've come all this way. If we're not going to make it count, then why did we bother? Do you want to go back to the office having failed to achieve our objective?'

She knew that the business-speak would win him over—she'd worked with him for long enough to understand that the company director in him wouldn't be able to resist the threat of a missed objective or deadline.

Giulietta returned to the table and Eva greeted her with a smile, and an offer to top up her glass. Signora Lazzari took hold of her hand and looked again at her ring.

'Forgive me,' she said. 'I can't help looking. They're pretty stones—and such an unusual design. You really have an eye.'

It was the perfect opening she needed—cue Joss's human side.

'Actually, it was Joss's choice. He understood exactly what I would want.' She turned to him with what she hoped would look to their guests like an adoring smile.

'After a couple of false starts,' Joss added with a laugh.

Eva could hear that it was slightly forced, but from the look on Giulietta's face she hadn't noticed.

'Let's just say that Eva had to point out the virtues of "less is more".'

Joss leaned over and pressed a kiss to her temple, and for that second when his lips were on her skin everything else stopped. The noise of the restaurant... the conversation around the table. Her breathing and her heartbeat. Everything was *him*. His lips, his touch, his heat.

And then it was gone, and the world crashed in again—noisy and brash.

'Well, you must be an attentive pupil,' Giulietta said. 'It's truly beautiful. And have you set a date?' she asked as Matteo returned to the table, tucking his phone into the inside pocket of his jacket.

'It is to be soon?' Matteo asked as he took his seat. 'Your father must be so excited to see you married.'

'We don't want to wait longer than we have to,' Joss said, taking Eva's hand. 'But we're not ready to set a date yet. My father has asked us not to decide anything until we've had time to come to terms with his news and all the changes it will bring. He wants us to concentrate on business at the moment. We feel that's the least we can do for him, to ensure the continuation of his legacy.'

'Ah, well, a long engagement is very romantic,' Giulietta said with a sigh. 'Sometimes I wish we could go back and do it all again.' She looked wistfully at her husband. 'Be newlyweds again.'

'I can drink to that,' Joss said with a smile that looked a little more relaxed. He lifted his glass. 'To engagements.'

'And being a newlywed,' Giulietta added.

Matteo lifted his glass as they all toasted.

'And to Edward Dawson,' Matteo said before they all went to replace their drinks on the table. 'He can never be replaced, but I am looking forward very much to getting to know his son better.'

Eva breathed a sigh of relief, and for the first time since they had arrived in Milan thought that maybe this might turn out not to be the disaster she had feared.

The rest of the dinner passed quickly, with conversation flowing in tandem with the wine. They eventually kissed Matteo and Giulietta goodbye in the lobby, late in the evening, and walked towards the lift, still hand in hand, just in case the Lazzaris should look back and see them.

Except Eva didn't drop Joss's hand once they were in the lift. She felt warm and comfortable, relaxed in Joss's company in a way she hadn't been since the day Edward had shared the news of his illness and Joss had come up with his absurd plan.

Until the lift doors slid shut and they were completely alone.

Not so relaxed any more.

In fact every muscle in her body tensed as she glanced around her, seeing them reflected in the mirrors on every side of them. Still their hands were linked together. She looked up at Joss, to find that he was already staring down at her, his expression inscrutable.

She opened her mouth to speak, but the ding of the lift stopping and the doors opening halted her.

Hand in hand, they turned towards their suite, and Joss dipped his free hand in his pocket for the key card, smoothly opening the door so that they barely had to break stride.

Eva realised she was holding her breath. She wasn't sure when she'd started to do it, but as the door closed behind them, and they were truly private for the first time all evening, she let it out—long and slow. All she could think about was Joss's lips. Warm on her hand that afternoon as he sealed their friendship ring with a kiss. And then tender on her temple over dinner.

She stopped at the door, not trusting herself to go any further into the suite. After all, her hand was still locked in Joss's, and neither of them was showing any sign of letting go.

She leant back against the door and Joss stood in

front of her, filling her vision with the wide shoulders of his exquisitely cut suit.

'Everything okay?' he asked, his voice low and sensual.

Eva nodded, when what she really wanted to do was shout. To tell him that no, she wasn't okay. That things were far, far from okay. This was confusing and terrifying and oh, so much more complicated than she had ever wanted her life to be.

But she couldn't let go of his hand. Couldn't be the one to break that connection between them.

She'd felt it growing as they'd played their parts over dinner. A touch of the hand here. A brush of fingers over an arm there. A quick kiss to the temple and too many shared smiles.

The intimacy had grown and grown between them, in some strange simulacrum of the relationship they had invented. But she had expected them to walk away from it. Expected to leave it at the table as they had their dirty glasses and used tableware. She hadn't expected it to stalk them into the lift and back up to their suite.

Intimacy was safe in public, where neither of them could act on it. But with her back against this door and Joss in front of her—looking serious, smelling delicious—it was a more dangerous prospect. And Joss knew it too. That much was clear from his expression. And she wouldn't be the first person in her family to walk headfirst and knowingly into danger. Maybe she had more in common with her parents than she'd realised.

A shiver went through her as the moment to push

him away, to break their contact, came and went, and she knew that she had made a decision. She closed her eyes and pushed herself onto her tiptoes, then gently, as gently as he'd kissed her, she pressed her lips to his.

For a moment she thought she'd miscalculated, misjudged, and that this *hadn't* been where the evening had been heading since the moment she'd walked out of her bedroom and set eyes on Joss. But then his lips came alive beneath hers, tasting, touching, caressing. She let out a long sigh—her body's relief after so many years of imagining this moment.

But her body wasn't the one in charge here—her brain was, and it wasn't exactly cheering her on. She could feel his restraint, too. It was there in his jaw, when she touched it gently with her fingers. It was there when he lifted his hand and it came to rest on the door beside her head instead of on her cheek or in her hair. It was there in the way he held his body ever so slightly away from hers, instead of pressing her hard into the wood.

And it was there in the way she had her hand on his chest, making sure he couldn't get too close.

She broke the kiss and rested her head back against the door, a chagrined look on her face.

'Bad idea,' she said at last as their breathing returned to normal. 'Too complicated.'

'I wish it wasn't,' Joss replied, and she could tell that he meant it.

Except they'd known each other for years before it had got so complicated, and they had known then, too, that this wasn't a good idea. At least it was a kind lie.

'Goodnight,' Eva said at last, after a few long mo-

ments during which one or the other of them might
have decided that the complications didn't matter that
much after all. But this wasn't a fairy tale, and the re-
alities of their lives weren't going to melt away because
of one kiss.

She pushed herself away from the door, determinedly avoiding eye contact, and brushed her hand
gently against his arm as she slipped past him and into
her bedroom.

CHAPTER SIX

'*BAD IDEA,*' EVA had said. Joss couldn't argue with that. It would undoubtedly have been a very bad idea. But a bad idea had never looked so good in his life.

They could have just gone for it. One kiss—how much damage could that have caused? But instead they'd both held back, and the whole moment had turned into a glimpse of what it might have been. Stirring his imagination without satisfying anything.

The next morning that kiss was on his mind all through his meetings with the Milan-based suppliers, even as he was reassuring them that there was no reason to think that there would be any drop in demand for their luxury goods throughout the Dawson's network of stores. And there would be absolutely no problems with the transition from Edward's leadership to his.

And on the plane, with Eva so close and so untouchable, the impression of her lips on his remained distractingly present.

It wasn't until they walked into their office at three o'clock in the afternoon and saw his father packing the contents of his desk into cardboard boxes that he was able to push that kiss from the forefront of his mind.

'What are you doing?' Joss barked at his father as he reached his office, though the answer was startlingly obvious.

'Sorry, son,' Edward said. 'I thought I'd be finished before you were back from the airport. You're the boss now—it's only right that you have the office that goes with it.'

Joss folded his arms, looking around the messy office, unable to believe his father was really going to be gone. 'Dad, I don't need your office. I don't *want* your office.'

'Well, I don't have much use for it now, and it would be silly for it to sit here empty.' Edward held up his hands and shrugged. 'And, really, I'd quite like to see you sitting here. If it makes you feel any better, it means Eva won't have to move desks. You'll want her close, believe me. She knows this job as well as I do. Better.'

He'd want her close. Well, there was the problem, wasn't it? It seemed that neither of them knew exactly how close they wanted to be.

She'd kissed him yesterday, all the while keeping him at a safe distance, never really giving in to what she wanted, even when they were alone. And he'd held back too. Warring with himself, telling himself that he had to stop this. He'd not been able to drag his lips from hers. All he'd been able to do was keep some emotional distance and try as hard as he could not to be dragged by those sensations into doing something they would both regret.

He whipped his head around as he heard the familiar click of her heels behind him.

'Edward—no. You can't be packing up already.'

'Ah, my dear, you as well. It is good to see you and my son so in tune with one another but, really, you must both see that I'm not needed here any more. Joss is more than capable of running this company and, to be perfectly honest, I've got places I would rather be. You know how much this business means to me—both of you do. But a prognosis like mine helps you to see what's really important. I've given this business fifty good years. Now, if I only have a few months left, I'm going to spend them doing some of the things I've been putting off for too long.'

He taped up the box with what seemed to Joss to be an unnecessarily dramatic flourish.

'Now…' He glanced at his watch. 'I've got an appointment, so I guess the rest of this will have to wait until tomorrow.' He laid a hand on Joss's shoulder as he passed him. 'I know this is hard, son. I'm here if you need to talk.'

He left the office and Joss couldn't breathe. It was as if he'd taken all the oxygen with him. He sat stiffly against the edge of the desk, among the abandoned staplers and office supplies that Edward had left lying there.

'Do you?' Eva asked.

Joss stared at her, unable to work out what she meant.

'Do you need to talk? Because I'm here too.'

He absolutely, definitely did not want to talk. What he wanted was to go and lock himself in his own office and get on with his job as if none of this was happening. There was a budget spreadsheet in his inbox that he could happily lose himself in for hours.

But he'd been down that route before, and it hadn't led anywhere good. Anywhere healthy. He had no intention of going there again. Talking to Eva… He wasn't sure that was a good idea. But when he thought about it he wasn't sure there was any other good option. She was the only one who knew the secret they were keeping after all. But what about *his* secrets? What about all the things in his past that he'd carefully hidden from everyone around him.

'Maybe I *should* talk, Eva. But I'm not sure that talking to you is the best idea. After last night…'

'What about last night?'

Really? Was she just going to pretend that it had never happened? Maybe they both should. After all, forgetting about that kiss was just about the most sensible—albeit impossible—option at this point.

'That kiss. It was…nice.'

He had a feeling it might have been incredible—if they hadn't both been holding back. He didn't know what her reasons were, but he was going to have to share his if that was what it took to keep them both from the mistake of making this fake relationship real. She had to see what a bad idea it would be, getting involved in a relationship now, with his father's illness and the knowledge that they would lose him soon.

'But I think we were right to stop it when we did. Taking it any further… It just wouldn't be a good idea.'

'Oh!' Eva's left hand flew to her chest. 'You mean

this isn't for *real*?' She subtly waved her engagement ring at him, but the rolling eyes gave her away. 'I *do* know that, Joss. Really, you need to get over yourself.'

'I know I wasn't the only one holding back, Eva. And I don't need you to tell me your reasons. But I want you to hear mine. It's not like I didn't want—'

He stopped himself before he said something stupid.

He started again. 'I want you to understand why. You know that I've been married before?'

Eva nodded.

'Well, it didn't end well. For either of us. The thing is, before I got married I was ill. But I didn't realise.'

She looked curious at that, but didn't interrupt.

'It was clinical depression. I hid it from everyone. From my family. From my then girlfriend, now ex-wife. I didn't get the help I needed, and then the wedding gathered pace around me, and I found myself in the position of being a really terrible husband.'

Her eyes softened with sympathy. 'But you were ill, Joss. It wasn't your fault. Maybe you need to be kinder to yourself.'

He stood stiffly, determined that she would understand him. 'I know that depression is an illness, but that didn't make our marriage any easier for my wife. Or our divorce, for that matter. I realised after it was all over how wrong it had been to feel the way I had for a long time and I finally got help. Got better. But none of that changes what I put her through. Or the fact that I know that it could come back. I'll never be completely free from it. And I'm determined not to do to anyone else what I did to my ex.'

Eva took a step closer to him and he took half a step back. 'You don't know that you will get ill again,' she said.

'And I don't know that I won't. What I *do* know right now is that my dad is dying, and that seems as good a recipe for depression as any other I can think of.'

'And don't I get a say in this?'

He looked at her closely. Had he missed something? This had started as a way of getting things off his chest, just to make things clear to her. A way to avoid the bottling up of his thoughts that he knew could lead somewhere toxic. She had been holding back too last night, and he'd assumed that meant that she was as wary of this chemistry between them as he was. But was he wrong? Did she want more?

Her answer unsettled him—he'd never really thought that she'd want a say in it.

'Don't look at me like that,' she said. He hadn't realised he was looking at her like *anything*. 'I'm not saying that we were wrong to stop things.'

He walked away from the desk and she shifted herself up to perch on the edge of it. He couldn't tear his eyes away from her ankles, slender and vulnerable-looking atop her smart spike heels.

'Look,' she continued. 'I think we can both say that there is an attraction between us. After what happened last night it would be stupid to attempt to deny it. But I'm as scared of this thing as you are. No offence— and this has nothing to do with what you've just told me—but a relationship with you would scare the hell out of me. I want commitment and stability, and even before I knew what you just told me it was abundantly clear that those things are not of interest to you. I fancy you—okay. But that doesn't mean that wanting you is a good idea. We got carried away last night. It was the first time that we really had to act this thing out, and it was trickier than I expected to slip in and out of character. We'll get better at it. We have to.'

She fancied him? It shouldn't really be news to him—not after that kiss last night. But somehow, despite everything else she was saying, that was all he could hear. And not because it was a nice boost to his ego. But because it made him question so many things from the last few years. All those times he'd avoided her, knowing that she was too much temptation, had she felt the same?

'But just because I don't think this would be a good idea, Joss…' she slipped off the desk and came towards him, laying a gentle hand on his arm, '… I don't think having an illness in your past is a good enough reason to shut yourself off from the idea of having a relationship in the future. There's probably some woman out there who thinks you'll make the perfect boyfriend— and she should probably be allowed a say in what happens. Why don't you give it a chance?'

He thought for a long moment. Some mystery woman who might come and convince him that he had been wrong about the decisions he had made in his life? He just couldn't see that happening. If he couldn't find it in himself to bend his rules for Eva, he just couldn't imagine any other woman who would make him want to.

'Well, we don't need to worry about that, do we?'

he said briskly, wanting out of this conversation before he started questioning his own better judgement. 'For now, I'm an engaged man. And one relationship—even a fake one—is enough.'

'Fine.' Eva said, crossing her arms. But then her expression and her body language softened. 'But I meant what I said. If you want to talk, Joss, or if you think your depression might be coming back…you can come to me. I mean, a fake fiancée can still be a pretty good listener.'

Joss smiled. If things had been different—if he hadn't had this illness lingering in his past—he was pretty sure she'd made a damn good *real* fiancée.

'I appreciate that. So, what about you? No luck finding a stable, committed guy to do this for real?'

'Plenty of candidates,' Eva said, with a shrug that wasn't as nonchalant as he thought she was hoping for. 'None that quite match up to my criteria.'

'Lucky for me, I guess.'

'Damned lucky for you.'

CHAPTER SEVEN

Eva sat at her desk, watching the clock on her screen ticking ever closer to seven o'clock. It was already dark outside and the office had emptied a couple of hours ago—everyone except her and Joss were long gone.

She wondered whether Joss was working late for the same reason she was—putting off the moment when they would have to go back to her little apartment and start living together for real. Her stomach gave a growl, and she wished she had picked up something more substantial for lunch.

Well, one of them was going to have to be the first to make a move, and she was too hungry to wait and see if Joss would cave. She shut down her computer and straightened up her files for the morning.

Joss appeared in the doorway to his office, leaning against the frame.

'Heading home?' he asked.

'Yeah, I'm all done for the day. And starving,' she added truthfully. 'I'll see you back there.'

She opened the door to her flat and headed straight for the kitchen. She hadn't shared her living space since she had left university and started working at Dawson's, and she realised that she had no idea how adult flatmates really worked. Or any form of cohabiting other than student living, really. She'd not seen her parents living together often enough to have formed an idea of it at an early age. How *did* a relationship work with both parties present at least most of the time?

She hated feeling so uncertain in her own home. For as long as she had been working at Dawson's she'd felt settled, secure. She'd known how things worked in the office; she'd had her own place to come home to. No one had started changing things up just when she'd got settled. And now her security at the office had gone, and even her home wasn't the safe haven it was meant to be with Joss moving in.

She chucked the leftover sauce she'd found in the freezer into the microwave and tested the pasta. Still way too *al dente*. A glance out of the window showed no one coming up the mews, and she felt relieved. Perhaps she'd be able to eat and zone out in front of a box set for an hour before Joss came home. At which point she could invent some excuse and escape to her bedroom for the rest of the evening.

Really, Eva, she chastised herself. *Hiding? Not exactly your style.*

But then the glow of a mobile phone outside the window caught her eye and she knew that her plans for a solo dinner had just been thwarted.

When she heard the knock at the door she remembered that Joss didn't have a key—something they'd have to fix. As she walked down the stairs it really hit her. He was going to be here. Every day. Even if not in person, his stuff would be here. He was going to be a permanent presence in her life for the next few months at least.

She tried to think of the last time she'd had a relationship, even a friendship like that, and came up blank. The last man she'd lived with was her father. And that hadn't exactly been plain sailing.

She opened the door and stood aside to let Joss pass her on the stairs, but instead he stopped in the doorway and gave her a considering look.

'What's wrong?'

'Nothing,' she replied automatically, trying to shake off the mood that thinking about her parents always caused. 'Just thinking that we need to get you a key cut. Come up—I've put some pasta on.'

'I thought you told me not to get used to being cooked for?'

'You shouldn't. You're cooking next time.'

'Fine. It's a date. I told you—you're not going to scare me off with threats of domesticity.'

A date. She hadn't meant it to sound like that, but intentionally or not she'd just arranged one. Did Joss see it like that too? Or was it just a figure of speech?

She shook her head as she went back up to the kitchen and gave the sauce a stir. Of course he didn't see it like that. He couldn't have been clearer with her that he didn't want to date her. Good, because she'd already told him—more than once, and in no uncertain terms—that she didn't want to date him either.

And where did that leave her? she wondered, thinking back over the last few years of her love-life—or lack of one. If she didn't want to date the only man she had been remotely interested in in years, then was she resigning herself to a lifetime of being alone?

Maybe there wasn't anything wrong with that. Lots of people never married. Stayed single. Perhaps that was the life she was cut out for. When this engagement was over Joss would move out, she would move a couple of cats in, and settle for the next few decades.

But if she really thought that why had she bothered dating at all? Why download the apps and accept the blind dates and chat to the hopeful-looking men in bars if she wasn't looking for something more?

Window shopping—that was what she had been doing. After their visit to the Italian store's jewellery department yesterday, she recognised it for what it was. Looking at all the pretty things on offer, knowing they weren't right for her, and that she would never be interested in actually buying them. So why wasn't she interested in dating Joss either? If the only reason she hadn't wanted those other guys was because they weren't *him*, surely she should want him if he were offered on a plate.

But it wasn't just about him, she realised. Maybe it had never been about him. If she refused to accept anyone who wasn't Joss, but didn't want the real thing either, then that left her where? On the shelf? Off the market? It left her alone, as she had been for all of her life. Where she was comfortable.

Was that what this was?

'Hey, is it terrible to open a bottle of wine on a Tuesday night?' Joss asked, grabbing one from the rack beneath the kitchen counter.

'After we spent most of Monday night on the Prosecco? I don't think anyone will judge us too harshly.'

She was glad of the distraction as she opened the bottle and found glasses.

'So, what have you got planned for the rest of the week?' she asked, trying to keep their conversation on a safe work footing as they went through to the living room and settled with bowls of pasta on their knees and their wine on the coffee table.

'Ah, I actually need to talk to you about that.'

'Sounds ominous.'

She'd expected him to brush the comment off, but he nodded. *Not good.*

'It's Dad. He's invited us to spend the weekend with him. He wanted an engagement party, inviting the great and the good. I managed to talk him out of it, but he still wants us to spend some quality time together.'

'Just the three of us?'

It was a lovely idea, in theory. She couldn't think of a better way for Joss and his father to spend the time they had left. And she loved Edward—of course she wanted to spend time with him. But this charade of a relationship with Joss made everything more complicated. By spending time together, were they going to expose their secret and do more harm than good?

After what had happened in Milan she knew that spending more time in close quarters with Joss and an audience wasn't a sensible idea. Acting out their relationship with the Lazzaris had led to acting out her desires, and they had both agreed that that had been a bad idea. The last thing they needed was a whole weekend of blurring the boundaries.

But they had to put Edward first. And if it was a weekend of quality time that he wanted, then that was what he deserved.

'Yeah, just the three of us,' Joss replied. 'Unless you want half the county and your business contacts list invited too?'

She shuddered. She wasn't sure what was worse—the scrutiny of the single person who knew them both better than just about anyone, or of everyone either of them had ever met.

'The whole weekend?' she checked, thinking that maybe, if they went for just a few hours over lunch, they might be able to keep up the pretence without doing too much harm to her self-control. Being together a whole weekend, there was no way that they'd be able to get away with separate bedrooms—not when Edward thought they were living together.

'That's what he said. And, given the circumstances, I want to go. It's not like we have time to waste.'

'And he wants me there too? Are you sure?'

Joss nodded. 'Of course he does. He thinks you're my fiancée. He just assumed that you would be coming. And you have to admit it would look strange if you didn't.'

Of course it would.

'Okay. And it's just one night, isn't it? Two at most?'

Joss nodded. 'We'll drive down after work on Friday. Be back on Sunday.'

She drew her brows together in confusion. Edward's house was no more than a fifteen-minute walk from her mews, on one of the smart garden squares that filled this part of London.

'Drive there? Wait—where are we going?'

'The house in Berkshire. I thought you realised that's what I meant?'

She sat back in the sofa cushions, temporarily lost for words at the thought of being isolated down a country lane with Joss. Somehow the seclusion of a country house seemed more intimate than being in London all together. If they were in the city she could make excuses to give Joss and Edward time alone together—pop out and fetch them all coffee, suggest a trip to the gallery she knew was opening on Saturday. In the countryside she didn't even know if there would be a pub nearby to escape to if it all went wrong.

She shook her head, but knew that she couldn't refuse. 'Of course I'll come—it'd be my pleasure.'

Oh, she shouldn't have used that word. Because now all she could think of was all the different types of pleasure that Joss could show her in an isolated country house. Hot breath on cold cheeks after a walk to a secluded spot in the woods… Cold hands on warm skin in front of a roaring fire…

'And the rest of the week?' she asked, knowing that she needed to distract Joss from what she was sure was a tell-tale blush on her cheeks.

'Dubai,' he said, giving her a curious look. 'You were right. I need to show my face. Let them know everything's going smoothly. Make sure everyone's happy with how things are going to work from now on.'

She nodded. 'Sounds like a good idea.'

'I need you to let me know if there are any problems here,' he went on. 'Make sure the place is running okay with Dad not coming in to the office any more.'

'I'm your eyes and ears on the ground. I get it. Do you want me to book your tickets?'

'It's done,' Joss said.

Eva felt piqued that he had bypassed her.

'What?' he asked, when he saw the look on her face.

'I know all this fiancée stuff is pretend, but you *do* know that the job isn't? I'm your assistant. I should know about your travel plans.'

'You're angry that I got someone else to book my plane ticket?'

'I'm angry that you're not letting me do my job. The other thing doesn't trump that, you know. I know it's hard, with everything else that's going on, but we have to find a way to work together as well. Otherwise how will that look? Like you've taken over and I'm instantly getting an easy ride.'

'Well, at least one of us is…' Joss said.

Eva didn't want to begin to unpick all the potential meanings of that sentence. Way too dangerous.

'Fine,' he said. 'While I'm away you can take over everything that's needed. When I'm back you can brief me on anything you think I need to know about from my father's desk that he hasn't already covered. Does that meet with your approval?'

'Fine. Good.'

She knew she still sounded short with him as she took another sip of wine, but she prided herself on her professional skills. If Joss was going to work around her at every opportunity she couldn't see herself *wanting* to stay in her job for much longer—a thought that terrified her. If she didn't want to be at Dawson's any more she didn't know who she was, never mind what she wanted from life.

No, she was being silly. Her job at Dawson's went way beyond her relationship with Joss, and mattered way more. She wouldn't even consider leaving just because she and Joss hadn't worked out the finer details of their professional relationship yet.

'So, when do you leave for Dubai?' she asked, wondering when she would get back the safety and security of living alone.

'I thought I'd go Tuesday, then be back in time to drive us down on Friday. Does that work with my diary?'

'You'll have to tell me. Until we get to work tomorrow I'm officially off the clock,' she said, taking a glug of her wine to prove her point.

CHAPTER EIGHT

EVA GLANCED AT the time, hating herself for doing it even as her eyes were drawn once again to the hands on the old wooden grandfather clock in the far corner of Joss's new office.

Three forty-seven. Exactly four minutes after she had last looked.

And at least twenty minutes after she had expected to see Joss back in the office.

He had been on a half-nine flight, which the live arrivals board told her had arrived at Heathrow at thirteen thirty-three. If he'd jumped into the car that she had booked for him he should definitely be here by now.

It was professional concern, she told herself. He had a meeting at four o'clock. She'd told him he would be cutting it fine if they were to leave to pick up his father this evening and get to the house, but he'd insisted that he would be there in time.

Her eagerness to see him was nothing to do with the way she had lain in bed awake, remembering the hard press of his body and the gentle touch of his lips in that hotel suite in Milan. Thinking about the night they had spent together in her flat, knowing that he was just down the hall. Knowing she could bump into him on the way to the bathroom and get a glimpse of those firm, toned abs and muscular thighs.

She shook off the thought. No, it was absolutely nothing to do with that at all.

A noise behind her made her jump, and she turned to see Joss striding through the office, familiar holdall in hand, glancing at his watch.

'I know, I know—you told me it would be close.'

'And you told me you'd make it. I never doubted you,' she lied.

He came up to her desk and kissed her on the cheek, and it was only as the blush rose that she remembered he was only doing what would be expected from a man who'd just spent a few nights away from his fiancée. He was performing for their audience, who—a brief glance out of the corner of her eye told her—were appreciative of his efforts.

'I told him you'd meet him in his office,' she said after a pregnant pause, suddenly struck with stage fright, unsure of her lines.

'Great. I'll drop this bag and head over there now. We'll still be out of here by six. Promise.'

She smiled and waited for him to walk away, but his gaze hadn't broken from hers and the ghost of a smile passed over his lips.

'Did you miss me?' he asked.

She resisted the urge to draw in a shocked breath, keeping her breathing deliberately slow and even. Was he playing with her? Was this part of their act or was he really asking her—the *real* her, not the fake fiancée?

'Not even a tiny bit,' she said, with a proper smile of her own.

Any eager ears in the office could put that down to normal relationship banter, she decided. And it was worth it to see the expression on Joss's face. She liked taking him by surprise.

He reached out a hand to her cheek, just ghosting the tips of his fingers along the line of her jaw. 'Well, I guess that means I need to make more of an impression,' he said, his voice low. Too low to be for the benefit of their audience. 'Give you something to miss next time I'm gone.'

He brought his right hand up in a mirror of his left, bracketing her with his fingers. She should pull away. Turn her face to her computer monitor in an effort at professionalism. But then she might never know. She would be left wondering whether this was for play or for real. And suddenly, dangerous or not, she had to know.

For the fleeting half-second he held her gaze, she wondered if she would be able to tell. And then she remembered that kiss in Milan. The way that they'd read everything the other person was feeling through the touch of their skin. And she knew that his body wouldn't lie to her, whatever he might say out loud.

With the first fleeting, barely there caress of his lips, she knew that it was real. It held all the promise of their kiss in Milan. Set off all the same fireworks. She lifted her hand to his face, felt the same tension in his jaw— the strength of his desire battling with the strength of his self-control. She could feel herself teetering on the edge, just as she had in Italy, knowing that letting a crack in her resolve show for even a second would mean they were both lost.

Which was why—even as it pained her—she pulled away. Again. Put just a millimetre of space between them, waited for him to move further back. He didn't. Instead he leaned his forehead against hers, and she could sense rather than see his smile.

'Now I'm late,' he said, after what felt like an age but couldn't have been more than a second.

Eva bit her lip with a smile, unwilling to let the moment go just yet. 'Told you so,' she said, stifling a laugh.

Joss sneaked one last peck onto her cheek before he strolled out of the office with an irritating degree of calm and confidence.

When the door shut behind him Eva knew she couldn't avoid looking around her any longer. She glanced over the partition of her cubicle and saw that—as she might have guessed—all eyes had been on her and Joss. She waited for the inevitable jokey comments, but instead the women—and half the men—were looking at her wide-eyed.

Eventually her assistant blew out a slow breath in awe, and muttered something that sounded incredibly like, 'Lucky woman.'

If only she knew.

On the dot of six o'clock, Joss closed his laptop and reached for the jacket he'd chucked over the back of his chair. He'd promised Eva that he'd be done in good time for them to leave for his father's country house for the weekend, and he had no intention of breaking that promise. Especially after what had happened earlier.

What *had* happened?

He wasn't sure what had come over him. But as soon as he had walked into the office and seen her it had been as if something that had been missing for three days was suddenly back and in overload. As if he hadn't even known he needed something, and then was drunk on it.

It had been meant as a polite, friendly hello. The sort of public kiss that anyone would offer their fiancée when they'd been away for a few days. To do anything else would have looked suspicious. But as soon as their eyes had locked it had been so much more.

That night in Milan had come flooding back—everywhere that kiss might have led if they had decided to let it. And then it had been too late to back out, and he'd had no choice but to give in to what his body had been begging him to do. Let his fingers trace the soft skin on her jaw, let his lips brush against hers, setting off a chain reaction that was going to lead them somewhere dangerous.

Thank goodness they were in the office, with an inbuilt safety net of public scrutiny and didn't have to rely on their self-control. Or *his* self-control at least. Who knew? Perhaps hers was still rock-solid, and she'd only returned his kiss for show.

No, he knew her better than that, he realised. He had felt the passion in her, and the iron self-control that was holding her just as fast as it was him. She wanted him, but she wasn't going to let it get the better of her.

And now they were going to be spending a whole weekend together, holed up in an isolated country house. Most people would consider having their dying father there as having something of a chaperone effect—but, as he'd once said to her, they weren't 'most people'.

He had to stop overthinking this. It would only make them awkward. The only thing to do this weekend—if they wanted to keep the lie alive and his father happy— was to jump right in. Forget it was a lie. Live as if they were really an engaged couple, head over heels in love. And lust.

But where could that lead when sustained over a weekend? In Italy it had led to an aborted kiss, when they had both still had just enough self-awareness to keep it from going further. And—importantly—they'd had separate bedrooms to retreat to. When they found themselves alone behind a closed door with a four-poster in the corner how were they going to resist?

Well, they'd just have to find a way. Because the alternative was giving in to this attraction. Getting involved in something real. And he knew that if he let that happen Eva would get hurt—and he wasn't having that.

He opened the door to see that she was still sitting at her desk, concentrating on the screen of her computer, the pen in her hand tapping absent-mindedly at her lip. He couldn't look away, reminded of the feel of those lips less than a couple of hours ago. But she was obviously more aware of him than he realised, because she held up the pen in the universal sign for, *Give me a minute*.

She tapped a few more keys, and then looked up with

a beaming smile. 'Sorry—just had to get that done. Are we ready?'

He nodded, temporarily lost for words. He didn't know how she had that effect on him. But then, why would he? For years he'd been avoiding this. Avoiding finding out the effect that she might have on him. Well, there was going to be no getting away from it this weekend.

He wondered if she was as nervous as he was about them being in such close proximity. His father's house was far bigger than her flat, but there were fewer places to hide. Not when they couldn't drop their act as soon as they were inside the front door and start treating each other like indifferent colleagues again.

Eva wrapped a long scarf around her neck as she stood up, half an eye still on her computer before she finally shrugged her shoulders and shut it down.

'Problems?' Joss asked.

'No...nothing. I'd just hoped to be able to sort something out before we left. It's not a big deal.'

He held out her coat and she slipped her arms in while he resisted the urge to run his hands instead of the sleeves up her arms. To let them rest on her shoulders before brushing her hair aside and pressing a kiss at the nape of her neck.

Eva turned on the spot and was suddenly far, far closer than was comfortable. She barely had to look up to meet his gaze, and he resisted the sensible part of his brain that was urging him to take a step backwards.

'Ready, then?' she asked, glancing past him towards the door.

'As I'll ever be.'

Thankfully the drive out to the house was short and familiar—because, Joss thought, he really couldn't attest to his competency on the road with a car so filled with atmosphere.

His father had seemed chipper when they had picked him up, as Edward had slung his small bag into the boot of the car, but he had been asleep on the backseat within minutes.

'Everything okay?' Eva asked, after they had been driving in silence for another ten.

'Yeah, fine.'

He knew that he was killing any chance of conversation dead with his monosyllables, but for the moment he didn't care. The confined space of his car, with two people keeping secrets from each other, was more pressure than he could take.

It wasn't until he drew on to the driveway of his father's country house, between the old stone gateposts, that he finally felt himself start to relax. It wasn't so much that the pressure of having a fake fiancée was lessened. But out of the city, with space around them, it felt easier to breathe.

He parked close to the front door, and was relieved to see it open before they had stepped out of the car, and Thomas, their groundskeeper, pushing a wheelchair through.

Joss stepped out of the car and stared at the chair for a moment. He hadn't even realised that his father *owned* a wheelchair, never mind needed one. But Edward had slept the whole way here from London, and Joss suspected that he hadn't been entirely honest about how well he was feeling.

He waved at Thomas as he walked up to the steps at the front of the house. 'Thanks for this,' Joss said, gesturing at the chair. 'But he fell asleep while we were driving. We should probably just leave him a few minutes.'

'Probably for the best,' Thomas agreed with a nod. 'And this must be Eva.'

Joss looked behind him to see Eva stepping from the car, glancing briefly through the back window to check on his father. He felt a tug of tenderness at this obvious display of affection for the old man. He had no idea what the next few months had in store for them. How dark things were going to get while his father's body fought and then succumbed to this disease. But, however complicated things might be, he was glad that Eva was going to be by his side.

It was selfish, he knew, to look for her support. Especially when he knew that he wouldn't be able to return it. He was going to need all his strength to look after his father, to look after himself. And that was why he couldn't let this thing with Eva become real. Because she would get hurt.

He had to keep reminding himself of that. It didn't matter how good she looked, how incredible she smelled, how natural it felt to have her skin against his, her hand in his. Her life meshing with his. It didn't matter that it felt right, because it wasn't.

Except... That was not what Eva had said when he'd explained things to her. It wasn't what she believed. He had told her, plainly, the reasons he shouldn't be in a relationship, but they hadn't seemed to be good enough for her. He supposed he was lucky that she had her own reasons for wanting to stay single. Because she hadn't recoiled when he had told her of his depression. Hadn't blamed him when he'd told her about how his last marriage had ended. She had simply told him what he knew intellectually to be true: that he had been ill, and that what had happened had been out of his control.

Well, that might have been true then. But it wasn't now. He wasn't going to let this relationship get out of control. Because when that happened innocent bystanders like Eva got caught in the crossfire.

Eva walked towards him and threw a questioning glance towards Thomas. He loved the way she didn't even break her stride as she held out her hand to shake his. There was something in her posture, her confidence, her self-awareness, in the straightness of her back and shoulders, that he found completely captivating.

'Eva, this is Thomas. He looks after the house and the grounds. And perhaps he looks after my father, too, recently?' Joss said, glancing again at the wheelchair. 'Does he use this a lot, Thomas?'

'Ah…only now and then,' Thomas replied. 'More the last time he was here. He hasn't told you?'

'My father's been keeping secrets.'

'Well, he's not the only one, is he? It's lovely to meet you, Eva,' Thomas said. 'I hear that there are wedding bells in the offing. Congratulations to both of you.'

'Thanks,' Joss said, with a quick side-glance at Eva.

She was still smiling at Thomas, not showing any sign of discomfort at their lie. Once again he was blown away by her self-possession.

The sound of the car door opening behind them caused him to turn sharply on the spot, to see his father stepping out of the car.

'Sorry about that, folks. You know what it's like in the back of a car. Like being rocked to sleep in a cradle.'

Joss took the wheelchair from Thomas's hands and pushed it over to the car, but his father waved it away. 'No need for that, son. But if you don't mind I think I'll go and finish this nap inside. You show Eva around. Enjoy the last of the sunshine—it's been a beautiful day.'

Well, his father was right about that. The sun was low in the sky, casting long shadows over the garden through the leaves, which were just starting to turn shades of red and gold.

'Don't worry about the bags,' Thomas said. 'I'll get those. Your father's right. Go for a walk down to the village. The path's beautiful this time of year, and there's just enough light left.'

Joss turned to Eva with a questioning look, and she smiled. 'Good job I threw some boots in my bag. Sounds like a lovely idea.'

She pulled on her boots as she perched on the bumper of his car, and Joss watched his father walk slowly up the steps to the front door. It had only been a couple of days since he had last seen him, but his father seemed years older. And more sick.

When he reached Thomas he leaned on him for a few

moments before taking the last step up into the house. They would have to talk later. Have one of the difficult conversations they had all known must be coming about what his father wanted for the end of his life and how they could all keep him comfortable.

But for now the sun was just touching the tops of the trees, and he knew that the pub in the village would have good beer on tap. They could keep the real world at bay for an hour longer while his father rested.

He grabbed boots and a coat from the car and looked over at Eva, who was winding a scarf around her neck. Was she going to regret this in the weeks to come? Entangling herself with a man, a family, that was about to reach crisis point?

'Let's go,' he said, heading towards the path at the side of the house that would take them through the gardens and then down towards the village.

He walked quickly around the corner of the house, glancing up at the familiar red brick of the old building. This had never been his permanent home, but it had always been a happy place to escape at weekends and in school holidays. He knew every inch of the brickwork, every hollow and tree in the grounds. And soon it would be his, he realised. Along with the house in London and the dozens of Dawson's stores around the world. A whole portfolio of responsibilities was about to fall onto his shoulders.

'Is it far to the village?' Eva asked, catching up and walking alongside him.

'Not far—about fifteen minutes if we go down the

lane. If we want to stay for a pint we'd better walk the road way back. It'll be dark by then.'

'Sounds good to me,' Eva said, and they fell into silence as they walked.

Joss buried his hands deep into his pockets.

'Your father looked tired,' Eva said eventually. 'I'm glad he went for a lie-down. I was worried.'

Joss stopped for a second. 'Me too,' he said eventually. 'I should have expected it,' he added, walking on.

'Doesn't mean it wasn't a shock. Or that it won't be hard to watch.'

'I'm aware of that.'

As soon as the words were out of his mouth he regretted them. Or his tone, at least. He shouldn't be taking this out on Eva—it wasn't her fault. For a second he had a flashback to his marriage. Fights over nothing, and always with his dark mood at the start of them.

'I'm sorry, Eva. I didn't mean to snap.'

'It's okay. It's understandable,' she said, brushing a hand against his arm.

He shrugged it off. This was exactly what he was trying to avoid. Anyone being in the firing line if his depression came back. He was going to do everything in his power to stop that happening, but if he couldn't do that—if he couldn't beat it again—he was at least going to make sure that he wasn't taking anyone else down with him.

'It shouldn't be. You shouldn't let me get away with it.'

'You're under a lot of stress. I can't imagine—'

'Eva, don't make excuses for me. I don't need them. This shouldn't affect you.'

'If I didn't want it to affect me, Joss, I wouldn't have gone along with this whole charade in the first place.'

Joss turned to her, shaking his head and stopping his stride. 'That's different. Of course Dad being ill is going to affect you. But that doesn't mean that my moods should as well.'

Eva brushed her hand against his sleeve again, and this time he lost the battle to shrug it off.

'We're living together. I'm pretty sure that in a couple the other person's crappy moods are part of the deal. Trust me—give it a couple of weeks and I'll give you a run for your money.'

'We're not just talking about an occasional bad mood with me, though. This is something different.'

'Are you talking about your depression?' Eva asked. 'If you're telling me you think it's returning, Joss, then we can talk about that. We can think about getting you the help you need to get you through a bad patch. But snapping at people is something that we all do. It doesn't have to be a symptom of something bigger.'

'It's no excuse.'

'You're right.' She nodded. 'It's not. So apologise, think about what I've said, and we'll move on.'

'I'm sorry,' he said after a few long minutes of walking in silence. 'I don't want you to be brought down by this.'

'You know, maybe you could trust me to *tell* you when enough is enough. My happiness isn't your responsibility, Joss. I can look after myself. I always do.'

She was right—her happiness wasn't his responsibility. But he'd like it to be, he realised. He'd like his first task in the morning to be to put a smile on her face. He could think of a dozen ways right now that he'd like to try. And then he could spend his whole day keeping it there.

But another person's happiness was too big a responsibility on top of his own. Especially for someone like him, who had so spectacularly failed at the task in the past.

He also suspected there was more in what she said than first met the eye. She had always looked after her own happiness… Well, of course. Everyone had responsibility for their own happiness. But the way she'd said it—there was independence and then there was isolation. He suspected he knew which side of the coin she was on.

'So you always look after yourself?' Joss asked, brushing past some overgrown gorse, the thorns catching on his coat.

'No one else volunteered for the job,' Eva replied, with a flippant smile that didn't reach her eyes.

It was obvious that she didn't believe what she was saying. Which meant she was hiding something. After exposing so much of his own past, his own vulnerabilities, he suddenly realised how little he knew about her. And he hated how unequal that felt. Hated that she might be able to hold that over him. If he was exposed, then she should be too.

That was what was behind him needing to know more, he told himself. It wasn't that he had any other reason to want to know why she hadn't met someone and settled down already.

'Somehow I find that hard to believe,' he said. 'I have a suspicion that plenty of guys were interested and none quite measured up.'

'What makes you think that?'

'Oh, you know. You hear things.'

She gave him a sideways look that told him exactly how unbelievable she thought that was.

'Um… I think we've already established that you *don't* hear things. Try again.'

He shrugged. 'Fine—I'm guessing. Are you going to tell me I'm wrong?'

He watched her carefully, watched her eyes narrow and her forehead wrinkle as she thought hard. So he had hit on something, then.

'Why are you so keen to pair me off, Joss? You're not going to be one of those unbearable people who can't see a single woman in her thirties without assuming there's something wrong with her?'

He'd give her full points for deflection, but zero for accuracy. Well, if he'd hit a fault line it seemed to make sense to keep pushing.

'I don't know. *Is* there something wrong with you?'

Eva threw her hands up and picked up her pace, calling over her shoulder. 'So you *are* going to be one of those people? Great.'

He jogged a few paces to catch her up. 'I just wonder why you think you have to do everything by yourself.'

She slowed down again. 'I never said that I did,' she replied.

'No, but I've watched you. In the office. With me. You like to be in control.'

'So? Who doesn't?'

He gave her a meaningful look. 'But a relationship doesn't work like that, does it? Sometimes you have to give the other person a chance.'

She shook off his comment with a carefully neutral expression. 'Good job we're not *in* a relationship then, isn't it? We're just pretending—which means I don't need to change anything about who I am for you.'

'Right, because *that's* a healthy way to approach things.'

'So now I'm unhealthy? Is that what's wrong with me, or is there something else?'

He tried to reach for her wrist, slow her down, but she dodged away from him.

'I'm starting to think you're impossible—does that count?' he asked.

'Oh, sure—why not add impossible to the list as well? At least you don't have to wonder why I'm single any more. It should be self-evident by now.'

Oh, it was becoming that way. The way she deflected his questions. The way her arms had folded over her body, putting physical as well as emotional barriers between them. The way she was making every effort to appear as unavailable and unattractive to him as possible...

She wanted to be single—fair enough. Relationships weren't for everyone. He knew that. But he recognised something in the way she oh-so-casually brushed off the idea of being involved with someone. He recognised it because it was so familiar. It was the same brush-off he'd given his father for years when he asked if he'd considered dating again, giving married life a second chance. The same expression he'd doled out to concerned friends who asked if he wasn't lonely with his string of meaningless dates.

Something had happened to make Eva feel this way about relationships, and he wanted to know what it was.

'So have you always felt like this?' he asked, as the sun slipped behind the thick hedgerows, leaving them in a twilight that cast murky shadows across her face.

'Yeah, I suppose… Just never thought I'd be the settling-down type.'

'But you do date?' he clarified.

'Of course I date. I'm not a hermit.'

But why bother dating if you didn't want a relationship? He knew that one tended to lead to the other, which was why he had stayed clear of both.

'Why do you date?' he asked.

'I don't know—for fun? To meet new people? Do new stuff?'

'Why meet new people who you're not planning on seeing again?'

He could see from the tight expression on her face that he was annoying her. Well, good—if it meant that they got to the bottom of this issue and she stopped evading his probing.

'I see some of them again,' she said, a note of defiance—or was it simply irritation?—in her voice.

'What—two, three times, I'm guessing.'

'What is this, Joss? Are you stalking me now, or just planning to?' she asked as they reached the end of the lane.

He could see the lights from the pub across the road. They crossed to it in silence, and it wasn't until they were installed at the bar, each with a pint of real ale, that he picked up his line of questioning.

'I'm not stalking you,' he said, just in case she hadn't been kidding. 'I'm just guessing. But I'm pretty sure I'm right, or you wouldn't have reacted that way.'

She took a sip of her beer, and he could see the machinations behind her eyes as she tried to work out what his angle was. Why he was so interested.

'I just don't get why you want to know, Joss. Why it's any of your business, in fact.'

He managed a wry smile. 'You're right. It's not. I mean, if we were *friends* then it would be normal for us to talk about this sort of stuff—the guys you're dating, what you want for your future. But we're not friends.'

'We're not?'

'Of course we're not. How can we be when you're so intent on keeping me at arm's length?'

'Um… I thought we were keeping *each other* at arm's length? I thought we had decided that was the best thing to do? We both know that getting involved romantically is a complication this situation really doesn't need.'

'I'm not talking about romance, Eva. I'm talking about friendship. We've barely spoken since Milan. And I don't know about you but it feels weird to me. We're living together. We're working together. We're spending the bloody weekend together with my dad. If we can't even be friendly to each other it's going to be unbearable. And we don't know how long we're going to be keeping this up. Months in the same house but living as strangers—it just wouldn't feel right.'

'Now you're accusing me of not being friendly? You *do* remember we had this exact conversation the other day, except it wasn't me who was being standoffish.'

'You were talking about being friendly.' He laid a hand over hers, where it was fidgeting with a beer mat. He wanted her to focus on their conversation. He needed her to open up to him, and he didn't want to think too hard about why. 'I'm talking about being friends, Eva. Do you even know that there's a difference?'

'I have friends.' She shrugged his hand away with an annoyed flick of her fingers.

'Do you? Really? People you tell your darkest secrets to? Who know you as well as you do yourself?'

She looked up from the beer mat and met his eye— there was fire in her expression now, and he knew he was close to cracking her. Close to the truth.

'That's a pretty narrow definition of friendship.'

'I don't know… I think most people agree it involves opening yourself up. Being vulnerable.'

'Oh, and you're the expert on that, I suppose? Because you're so open to letting new people into your life. That's why you had to convince your assistant to pretend to be your fiancée rather than find yourself a real one.'

He choked on his beer and then looked at her for a few seconds without speaking. She was right. They had a lot in common—which meant he could tell her the truths he was pretty sure she needed to hear. It wasn't as if *she* was holding back. And she wasn't going to get out of talking about herself by turning the conversation to him. They'd already talked about his vulnerabilities—at length. He had no desire to go over that again.

'That's different. Other people got hurt. I'm protecting them, not myself.'

'You're *so* noble. The fact that you don't have to take a risk on anyone else—that's just a side benefit, I suppose?'

He reached for her hand again, hoping that the contact would bring her closer. Let her see that he was on her side.

'Don't turn this around. We were talking about *you*.'

'We were talking about vulnerability…about letting people get close. I think turning this around is pretty valid.'

'Fine, and we can talk about me later, if that's what you want. But right now we're talking about you. Why is it you don't want to let me in?'

CHAPTER NINE

'THIS ISN'T ABOUT YOU, Joss. It never has been.'

Her hand flew to her mouth as she took in a deep suck of air. She hadn't meant to say that.

Ever since he'd started digging, digging, digging—trying to get her to talk about why she didn't want to get involved—she'd told herself she shouldn't let him in. Letting people in never led anywhere good, and with Joss Dawson it would be downright dangerous.

It had been easier to dodge and deflect his questions when they'd been walking, with shadows to hide her face and the ability to walk off when he hit too close to the bone. But here in the cosy, intimate atmosphere of the pub, with the fire roaring behind them and Joss perching so close to her on a bar stool that she could see the golden flicker reflected in his eyes, she knew there was nowhere to escape.

The only way to shut this conversation down was to give him what he wanted—show him that a relationship wasn't an option for her, the same way it wasn't for him. Perhaps then he'd let the topic lie.

'Look, I know what it's like to have someone you

love leave you and hurt you, okay?' she said after a long pause. 'Is that what you want to hear? Because it's pretty much a description of my entire childhood. Both my parents in the army, taking it in turns to ship out while the other one was stuck at home with me. Me making friends and then being told we were leaving again. Until one day my mother didn't come home from her tour, and my dad—rather than be stuck with a grieving teenager—packed me off to boarding school so he could lose himself in his work. So for the love of God, Joss, don't talk to me about opening up. Some of us have perfectly good reasons for being happily closed books, thanks.'

She watched him as she waited for a response. Fine lines appeared at the corners of his eyes and a muscle in his jaw flickered. He was waiting, weighing, judging. Was he going to push further, or had she revealed just enough to make him back off?

'I'm sorry,' he said. 'I didn't know.'

Bingo. Well, her plan had worked, at least. But with the new information in the air between them, and old wounds exposed for the first time in years, she felt uncharacteristically vulnerable. Small and unprotected.

'It's fine. I just want to drop it now. We should change the subject.'

'Right.'

They sat in silence for a few minutes, while she tried to think of somewhere safe to take the conversation. Work? They had enough of that at…well, at work. His dad? That wasn't exactly going to lighten the mood. And there was no point waiting for Joss to pick up a small-talk baton. They'd already established he was all but incapable of that.

She glanced around them for inspiration and her eyes fell on a framed picture of the manor house, where they had left his father resting. Until she saw the picture, faded behind the bar, she hadn't really thought about the house as being part of the village, of Joss belonging to a community.

'So, has your family always owned the house?' she asked.

Joss's face relaxed immediately with relief at her opening small-talk gambit. Much as he had been pushing, it seemed he was as happy to see the personal topics dropped as she was. Perhaps because it meant that she wasn't turning the conversation back onto him, as she'd threatened.

'No, Dad bought it when I was small,' he said. 'After he and Mum divorced. He wanted somewhere in the country to bring us—get us out of the London fumes occasionally.'

Eva nodded slowly, raising her eyebrows. 'Well, when he wants to escape, he does it in style. How old were you when your parents split up?'

'Young enough not to remember it. It was all amicable. They're still good friends. No deep scars to probe there.'

'I'm glad to hear it.' She smiled, relieved the atmosphere really was lightening between them. 'So you used to come here at weekends?'

'And school holidays. You should see it in the summer—it's beautiful.'

'You're lucky.'

'I am.'

She could tell from the way he said it that he knew how incredibly privileged his life had been. But there was a tinge of sadness there, too. Because next time the house saw summer perhaps it would belong to Joss. And that could only mean one thing. She wondered whether Joss was making that same connection.

She finished her beer and glanced at her watch. 'Do you think your dad will have woken up?'

'Probably. We should head back anyway. I'm not sure whether Dad has asked Maria, Thomas's wife, to arrange dinner. But if he has you won't want to miss it.'

'Another woman who likes to cook for you—should I be jealous?'

Eva could feel a blush rise on her cheeks and turned her face to the fire so she could at least blame her colour on the heat from the flames. Thankfully Joss didn't capitalise on the potential of that sentence to get her confessing more secrets she didn't want to share.

'I'll drink up and you can find out for yourself.'

As they crunched up the gravel driveway towards the front door of the house Eva realised that there was one factor of spending the weekend with Edward they hadn't talked about yet—sleeping arrangements. Thomas had told them not to worry about their bags, which presumably meant that by the time they reached the house they would have been delivered to one of the dozens of bedrooms a house like this must contain—and, despite the copious number, they would have been delivered to the same one.

She could only hope that it contained an enormous bed, large enough for them to share without meeting in the middle at some point in the night. Or that there'd be an elegant chaise longue in the corner of the room that Joss could retire to in a show of gentlemanly manners.

If all else failed there were the flannel pyjamas— long legs and sleeves of course—that she'd packed just in case she found herself needing to protect her modesty.

They walked up the front steps and were met by Thomas at the door.

'How's my father?' Joss asked as soon as the door opened, and Eva couldn't help a small smile at his devotion to his father even in the sad circumstances.

'Still resting,' Thomas answered, with a concerned look. 'I've put you and Eva in your usual room, Joss, and Maria says dinner will be ready at eight. If you look in on your father, could you ask him if he'd like a tray instead and let me know? I think the journey must have taken it out of him.'

'Of course,' Joss said, his voice heavy with worry, and he gestured for Eva to go ahead of him up the stairs.

'Do you think he's okay?' Eva dropped her voice as they climbed, fearful of disturbing Edward, though with the treads carpeted in a lush, thick velvet, she supposed their voices wouldn't carry far.

'I'm shocked,' Joss replied. 'I didn't think that just driving to the country would tire him out so much. Either things are moving quicker than he expected, or he's not been telling the truth about what's going on.'

Eva had suspected as much herself. 'Are you going to ask him?'

'I already have. And I've offered to go to the hospital with him. He brushed me off with barely a word. He said he didn't want me dragged down by it.'

'Sounds like he wants to protect you.'

'Parents, huh?' A grimace crossed his face. 'Sorry, I didn't mean...'

'It's fine. You don't have to apologise for having a great dad. I just feel lucky that I got to know him too. You know, he's something of a father figure to me.'

'It will make him happy to know you think that.'

She shrugged, a little embarrassed. 'Well, let's not go telling him. We wouldn't want him to think we're getting all mushy.'

They reached the top of the staircase and Joss gestured her down the corridor in front of him. His steps slowed as they passed door after door, and eventually Eva had to laugh.

'My goodness—how many rooms *are* there in this house?'

'Last count? Fourteen bedrooms. And half as many bathrooms. Not sure about downstairs. I've never counted...'

'So, fourteen bedrooms and we end up—'

'Here,' Joss said, as they finally stopped and he opened the door.

Well, she'd been right about the chaise longue, at least. It was positioned under the elaborately draped Georgian paned windows, upholstered in a deep navy, with a pattern that caught the light from the chandelier overhead. A fire was set in the grate opposite the bed—a four-poster, naturally. It had a canopy up by the ceiling, and heavy curtains tied back in each corner. Crisp white pillows were piled up at the head of the bed, and instead of the sheets, blankets and eiderdown she'd been expecting there was a fluffy duvet, also covered in simple white cotton.

She turned to Joss and had to suppress a giggle.

'I know. It's a lot. But imagine a normal-sized bed in a room like this. You'd never find it.'

'No,' she said, shaking her head, her eyes wide. 'It's perfect. It's just…'

'Ridiculous? At least I drew the line at frilly sheets.'

'Yeah.' She let out a laugh. 'Yeah, a bit ridiculous.'

She crossed to the bed and had to do a little hop in order to hitch herself up onto the mattress. Joss came and sat beside her as she kicked her heels against the frame, and she turned to look at him, smiling.

'Here I was thinking it was going to be awkward, us sharing a bedroom, and I'm bursting out laughing as soon as we get in here.'

'Not what I'm usually aiming for when I show a woman to my bedroom,' Joss said. 'But I'll take it under the circumstances. You thought it would be awkward?'

'Well, of course. You didn't?'

'I hadn't really thought about it.'

'You're lucky to have me, d'you know that? To do your thinking for you. You really do need someone who knows how to do your job.'

'I never said I wasn't lucky.'

'Good. Let's keep it that way.'

She glanced around the room. Her comments on the decor and the house and the furniture had broken the ice when they'd entered the room but now, as they sat on the bed together she could feel tension mounting between them as they both looked around.

She presumed he was thinking the same thing she was—where were they going to sleep?

'I'll take the chaise longue,' Joss said eventually. 'I'll sneak some stuff from the linen closet.'

'And risk Thomas and Maria finding out that we're not what we say we are?'

'I'll blame it on you. Tell them you feel the cold,' he said, with a laugh that eased the tension again.

Eva pushed him gently on the arm. 'Throw me under a bus, why don't you? You know, the bed's the size of a continent,' she said. 'I trust you not to try anything if you want to share.'

'Wow. You have such a high opinion of me you feel you have to spell that out?'

'It was a generous offer and it comes with an expiry date. Just a warning.'

'Fine. Well I accept your offer.'

'Good.'

'Good.'

And all of a sudden awkwardness was back with a vengeance. She glanced across at Joss, then looked away as soon as she realised he had done the same. Being around this man was worse than being a teenager. At least then you could be pretty sure your crush was as messed up and confused as you were. But neither she nor Joss were hormonal kids. The decisions they made now would have real consequences over the coming days, weeks and months. There was no kissing now and then pretending it had never happened.

Except it was too late for that, Eva realised. Kissing without consequences was what they had tried in Milan, and if the tension between them right now was anything to go by there was no doubt that pretending it had never happened wasn't an option.

'I should check on my father,' Joss said at last, breaking the atmosphere between them.

It was a temporary reprieve; she knew that tension would be waiting for them when they climbed the stairs at the end of the night and found themselves locked in here until morning.

Joss disappeared for a few minutes, and then stuck his head round the door. 'Dad's going to join us downstairs, but I'm going to give him a hand getting ready. Do you need anything?'

She shrugged, and glanced pointedly around the room. 'Well, I didn't pack my tiara. Will I be needing one of those?'

'Oh, don't worry about it. Chuck on any old jewels. Kidding!' he added, when her expression must have shown her surprise. 'I'll see you downstairs.'

Eva descended the stairs, wondering how on earth she was meant to find the dining room without a map or a compass. When Joss had been trying to find her mews house he'd had the benefit of satellites and technology, but she suspected there wasn't an app for navigating your fake fiancé's country home.

She stuck her head around a couple of doors, reveal-

ing grand reception rooms with clusters of uncomfort-
able-looking furniture. In the end she followed her nose
down grand corridors to the back of the house, until the
sound of Radio 4 came into hearing and the smell of
roasting chicken grew stronger.

She checked another couple of doors until eventually she stumbled into a room with an enormous range
cooker and an elegant woman—seemingly in her fif-
ties, and certainly in charge—stirring something de-
licious-smelling.

The door hinges squeaked and the woman turned
around, her face lighting up with a smile. 'You must
be Eva,' she said. 'I'm Maria. I try and keep this house
in order and keep those men fed.'

Eva returned her smile, feeling instantly welcome.
'And you do a beautiful job of both, by the looks of
things. Roast chicken?' she asked, knowing that food
was always a safe conversation-starter.

'With lemon and garlic sauce,' Maria replied. 'Now,
don't tell me that the three of them have abandoned you
to find your own way here?' she said with a tut.

'Oh, Joss is—'

'Never mind what they think is more important.
You're our guest. If I'd known they'd left you to wan-
der the halls I'd have come and looked after you myself.
Now, take a seat and tell me what you'd like to drink.
Tea? Or something more appropriate to the hour? A
little aperitif?'

'Well, I suppose a gin and tonic would go down well,'
Eva said, after thinking about it for barely half a sec-

ond. 'But only if you join me. The dangers of drinking alone and all that.'

'Oh, well, I think I probably should—seeing as I appear to be in charge of you. Right, then, let me find us a lime. I know there were some in the delivery yesterday.'

Maria disappeared for a couple of minutes and returned with two glasses filled almost to the brim with ice, lime and clear sparkling liquid.

'I'm sorry—I should have asked if you want this in the drawing room,' Maria said, her brow suddenly creasing. 'Edward asked me to set the table in the dining room for dinner, but he normally has a drink in here with us first. You can go through, though, if you prefer.'

'No, not at all,' Eva said, raising her glass in a salute to Maria and taking a long sip. 'A drink in here sounds perfect to me. It's ridiculously warm, for one thing.'

'Decision made, then,' Maria said, opening the door of the Aga and peering inside. She pulled out a perfectly golden chicken and placed it on the warming plate on top of the range before sliding a meat thermometer into the flesh.

'Can't be too careful,' she said, glancing over at Eva. 'With Edward's health being what it is. I've tried to get the rest of the house warm for him, but a heater in his bedroom and the Aga in here seem to be the only things that work.'

Eva didn't have a chance to reply before the door of the kitchen opened and Joss, Edward and Thomas all appeared.

'Ah, about time. You gentlemen abandoned poor Eva,' Maria scolded them. 'We both had to take some medicinal gin for the shock,' she added, with a wink to Eva.

'Excellent idea,' Edward said. 'Think I'll have one of those myself. Anyone else?'

He made to walk away from where he was leaning on Joss's arm, but stumbled with his first step. Joss helped him over to a chair instead.

'You sit down, Dad,' Joss said, sharing a concerned glance with Eva over the top of Edward's head. 'I'll get the drinks.'

By the time they were all seated formally in the dining room Edward was looking tired again, ready for another lie-down. Eva and Joss shared another concerned glance, but this time Edward caught the look between them.

'Enough, you two. If you've got something to say, then just say it. I'm having a tiring day. Not sure why, but I suppose it's to be expected under the circumstances.'

'We're just worried, Dad. You seem more tired than you were last week.'

'I *am* more tired,' Edward said. 'But my doctor's not worried. I called him, you know. I'm not just pretending this isn't happening. He said it's completely normal. I just need to rest more. Which means we should get this conversation done with so we can all eat and get to bed.'

'What conversation?' Joss asked.

Eva felt a shiver of foreboding. She could guess what conversation.

Edward reached for a folder of papers that Eva realised he must have stashed on a chair earlier.

'We need to talk about my will,' he said.

'Dad—' Joss tried to interrupt.

But Edward wasn't having any of it.

'No, son. We need to have this conversation at some point and I'd like to do it now, while I'm still well and no one can accuse me of having gone doolally or anything like that. Not that it matters much *what* you say, actually, because it's all finished already. I just thought you might like to know what's in there.'

Joss pushed his chair away from the table and Eva could see him glancing at the door, wondering if he could bail out on this conversation. He'd better not dare leave it to her—she'd make him pay if he did.

'Dad, it doesn't matter to me what's in there.'

'Well, it matters to me. So you can sit there and listen, if you're quite finished talking.'

Eva shifted uncomfortably in her chair. It was hard enough being caught in a family argument. When it was about a will, and it wasn't even your family, she was all for bolting for the door herself.

'Maybe I should leave you two...?'

'Not at all, dear,' Edward said when Eva tried to excuse herself. 'You're part of this family now, and I'd like you to stay. I know Joss will tell you everything anyway, so this way we save him the trouble. Right, I'm not going to go over every detail, because you know all the business stuff already. But the personal stuff we've not talked about before. It's not complicated, though. I'm leaving your mother a large amount of cash, so neither of us have to worry about her being comfortable for the rest of her life. But most of the rest of it goes to you, of course, Joss. Including the London house and this draughty old place. But the mews house is yours, Eva. It's been your home for many years, and I would hate to think of you having to leave it. I hope that you'll accept?'

'Edward,' Eva protested straight away. It was too much. Too generous. 'I couldn't possibly—'

But Edward shook his head defiantly. 'I don't want to hear anything like that. A simple thank-you would be fine.'

She couldn't accept. Of course she couldn't under these circumstances.

If Edward knew the truth about their fake relationship he wouldn't be doing this. It wasn't fair to let him make decisions like this based on a lie.

'Edward, you don't understand. About me and Joss—'

'No, no.' Edward said decisively. 'I'm quite sure that your relationship is none of my business. Really, Eva dear. This is a gift for you. Quite apart from what you and Joss mean to one another.'

She shared a long look with Joss, and tried to communicate what she was thinking without speaking.

Was he angry with her? She would tell Edward the whole ugly truth if she had to. This had gone too far. It wasn't fair on the sick old man. She'd gone along with his misunderstanding when he'd assumed that she and Joss were a couple because it had seemed a small thing to do to make him so happy. But this—this was different. This was legal—a binding contract and the transfer of property—making their little white lie suddenly seem a whole lot more serious.

'The mews house *should* be yours,' Joss said at last.

She wanted to kick him under the table for continuing to lie to his father. They should just tell him the truth. Come clean. She turned and glared at him.

'I mean it,' he carried on. 'I'd give it to you anyway, if it came to me. I'm serious,' he continued, when she widened her eyes at him, trying to get him to stop talking. 'Don't fight this, Eva.'

His voice was softer now, gentler, and she found she couldn't argue with him when he was being reasonable.

And when she thought of her mews house as being really her own… It meant that she would have a little piece of the city that was always there—a safety net whenever she needed it. She fought back tears as she rose from her chair.

'Thank you, Edward,' she said, walking around the table to give him a kiss on the cheek. 'It means the world to me. It really does.'

'Well, let's hear no more about it,' Edward said, his cheeks flushed a little pink.

Maria appeared at the door with such promptness it seemed inevitable that she had been waiting outside, listening for an appropriate break in the conversation.

'This looks delicious, Maria. Thank you,' Eva said as the platters of food were set down in the centre of the table.

With the difficult topic of the will set aside, they all relaxed into friendly conversation, though she could see that Edward's eyes were fighting to stay open halfway through their main course. She glanced at Joss, and saw that he had noticed it too. As their eyes met she felt a flash of connection between them, and knew that in that moment she could read him completely. She wondered if she was as open to him as he was to her. What he could see if she was.

A warmth started in her chest and sank to her belly as she realised how close they had grown over the past week. How she had really started to know him, with their communication becoming subtler, more personal, more intuitive.

She didn't want to think too much about what that meant. About the risk that she was taking in letting him in. Because that *was* what she was doing. Whether she had intended him to or not, he was getting under her skin, into her thoughts, into her life. And now, when she looked at him, she saw something familiar—something that had been part of her life for so long she would recognise it anywhere. She saw the void that he would leave when he left. She saw her life without him. The spaces she would have to try to fill when he wasn't part of her world any more. The voids that would haunt her at night and occupy her thoughts during the day.

She'd seen those voids around both her parents when she was growing up, and had wondered how her life would look if they were gone—really gone—and she was left behind. And then her mother had been killed on duty and she'd found out. She'd lived longer with the space that her mother had left behind than she had with her mother there. It was like a shadow in the corner of the room, reminding her of what she'd lost. What she'd never had much of a claim on in the first place.

And she could see that void around Joss now. See the hole that would be left in her life when this was over.

She'd never meant to let it get this far. It was meant to be a lie. Their engagement *was* a lie. But these feelings that she was having for him—they were very, very real.

She didn't know what to do with them. Her instincts were telling her to run. To get away from him now, while she still had a chance of plugging that space, of rebuilding her life without him in it. But her heart wanted her to stay. She knew that from the way it ached when she thought about leaving. About what they were going to do when they had to get back to real life. When she thought about a life without him in it—or, worse, a life where they were polite to one another in the office and then tried to forget each other existed the moment they left.

Joss frowned slightly, and she realised she had shown too much in her expression. Even if he couldn't understand the minutiae of the struggle she was feeling at that moment, he knew something was wrong. And she had a suspicion that he was going to expect her to explain herself later.

A clatter disturbed her thoughts, finally forcing her gaze away from Joss's, and she realised that Edward had dropped his knife. He'd barely touched his meal, but now he lay down his fork too, and took a sip of wine.

'I think I'm going to retire and leave you young people to enjoy the rest of the meal,' Edward said. 'I'm sure that Maria will have a delicious dessert in store, so please don't let it go to waste.'

She called goodnight to Edward as Joss took his elbow and helped him out of the room and presumably up the stairs to bed. Left alone, Eva wondered whether she should make her escape. But what would Joss think if he came downstairs and found her not at the table? And even if she decided she wanted to, she had nowhere to go.

She could escape to the bedroom, but Joss would be there as well soon enough. She might remember how to get back to the pub in the village, but what would Edward, Thomas and Maria think of her taking off in the dark? They'd know that there was something wrong between her and Joss, and that was the last thing she wanted for Edward just now.

Joss appeared at the door a few minutes later, and made her glad that she had stayed. His eyes looked heavy, as if he was fighting off emotion, and she knew he needed company. That if he were alone his thoughts and fears would torture him.

'Is he okay?'

'Tired,' Joss replied. 'He says he's not in any pain, but I'm not sure I believe him. I'll check on him later, and if he's not sleeping soundly I'll call the doctor. I'm sorry, Eva. I should never have brought you here. You shouldn't have to go through this. It's not fair on you.'

'I'm glad I'm here,' she said automatically.

But as the words passed her lips she realised that she meant them. Even if it *did* mean facing the sadness of watching Edward fade by the day. Despite her earlier thoughts of escape, she knew that this was important. That if she left these men to fend for themselves at this crucial time she would be hurting both of them, and she didn't want that.

It was dawning on her just how far she had let both of them in already. She had told herself after her mother had died and her dad had sent her away that she wouldn't do that again. She would never let anyone leave a hole in her life that she didn't know how to fill. But somehow the two Dawson men had found a way in.

Her affection for Edward was nothing new, but since he had given her the news of his illness, since her closeness with Joss, it had changed. He was no longer the kindly old boss she'd always thought him. He'd become more than that. He'd become like family.

And Joss? She didn't know *what* to think about Joss and how she felt about him. She had never meant to feel *anything* about him. She'd had a crush, yes. But that was all it had been. An appreciation for a handsome face and an enigmatic attitude. So how, in a matter of a couple of weeks, had he come to be so much more than that to her? How was he suddenly so much a part of her life, a part of *her*, that all she could see was the dark outline of the shape he would leave in her life when he inevitably left her?

What she wanted to know was what she was meant to do about it. She knew it was too late to turn back without getting hurt. Hurting was inevitable now. But she needed a plan to get through it when the time came to end their engagement.

'How can you be glad?' Joss asked eventually, rubbing both his hands on his face and then reaching for his drink. 'I'd rather be anywhere than here.'

'I don't think that's true. I think you're glad to be spending time with your father. And I'm here for the same reason you are, I suppose. Because it's important to be with your dad right now. And because it's hard to do that alone.'

'You're right,' he said, looking up and meeting her eyes with a look that might burn her if she wasn't more careful. 'But it's not just that. It's not that I want *someone* here. I want *you* here.'

'Because your father thinks—'

'For reasons that have absolutely nothing to do with my father. Believe me, Eva. What I'm talking about has nothing to do with him.'

He wasn't kidding. She could read volumes in his expression, and filial duty was nowhere to be seen.

She dropped her eyes, breaking their connection. If she hadn't, there was only one place that the conversation would go, and she suspected neither of them was ready to go there. Yet. *Ever.*

The door opened and Maria appeared with a trolley to clear their plates. They sat in silence as she worked, only occasionally glancing across to one another. When they eventually had *tarte Tatin* and *crème anglaise* sitting in front of them, on elegant white and platinum plates, Eva let out a long breath, determined to start a conversation with something completely noncontroversial.

But as she grappled around for a subject she found she was coming up with nothing. Everything felt so loaded with Joss. Their work, their home, their families… They all led to conversations more deep and meaningful than either of them wanted right now. And she hoped to goodness they were beyond the point where they would have to talk about the weather for lack of anything else to say to each other.

She pushed a piece of tart onto her spoon, and let out a sigh of anxious relief when Joss eventually spoke.

'I hear it's going to be a nice day tomorrow.'

So that was where they were. She didn't know whether that made her want to weep or laugh, but at least the ice was broken.

'We should take your dad out,' she said.

'He'd like that, I think. He's always liked to walk in the gardens.'

They fell into silence again, and Eva concentrated on finishing her dessert, counting down the pieces until this awkward dinner would be over. And then, with a mouthful left on her plate, she asked herself what on earth she was doing. The longer she could make this last, the better. At least with six feet of solid mahogany table between her and Joss she was safe from making any huge, irrevocable mistakes. Once dinner was over her safety net would be gone.

She lingered over the last mouthful, and responded enthusiastically and gratefully when Maria asked if they would like coffee. But as she drained the dregs of the drink she knew she couldn't delay any longer.

'Do you want to go straight up?' Joss asked.

And, although she had been expecting it Eva still felt wrong-footed. If she said yes, would that make it seem as if she was desperate to get to their room, into bed with him? If she said no, what would he read into that?

But she could feel her eyelids growing heavy, despite the coffee. It had been an emotionally draining evening, and although it wasn't late she wanted a bed—whatever the dangers of sharing it.

'I think I will,' she replied, stifling a yawn that just thinking about sleep had produced.

'Can you find your own way up?' Joss said. 'I think I'll use Dad's study and just finish up a few things.'

Eva let out a breath, trying not to show how her body had instantly relaxed, relieved at his words.

'I'll be fine. I guess I'll see you in the morning, then,' she said, standing up from her chair.

They both stalled by the table for a moment, and for a second she was unsure what they were waiting for. A formally polite kiss on the cheek? A handshake?

In the end, she darted past Joss, the lure of an empty bed too much to resist.

CHAPTER TEN

JOSS LISTENED TO her climb the stairs, her footsteps elegantly measured despite the way she had darted past him out of the dining room.

He sighed at the thought of having to crack open his laptop and put in another couple of hours' work. Since this thing had started with Eva his schedule had been punishing, with him trying to keep himself busy and out of her way as much as possible. Keeping himself from temptation. And now, knowing he would be returning to a shared bed, not just a shared house, the temptation was stronger than ever.

He wondered whether she had felt it too. That connection when their eyes had met across the dinner table… He shook his head. Of course she had felt it. Something like that couldn't be one-sided. It was the very fact that they were both feeling the same way that gave the moment its energy. Its power. He had to be more careful.

He turned on the computer and pulled up the latest reports from his store managers, scrolling through them without really reading. Despite his earlier concerns over how he was going to shoulder his father's business with so little notice, he needn't have worried. The transition plans they had put in place had worked just as they were supposed to. And, although there was still some anxiety in parts of the business, mostly things were going well.

He forced himself back to the start of the reports and made himself read them properly this time.

When he was done, he glanced at the clock and saw that an hour and a half had passed. Eva had looked pretty tired when she had left the dining room, so surely it would be safe by now for him to go up to bed? Everything would be simpler if she was asleep, he told himself. He could just climb into bed and pretend he was alone. Goodness knew, the mattress was big enough for the both of them.

He climbed the stairs slowly, and remembered the sound of Eva's feet on the treads. Had she been feeling as uneasy as him? Wanting to put off the inevitable?

How on earth was he meant to get any sleep in the same bed with her? Maybe he should stick to his chivalrous guns and sleep on the chaise longue as he'd suggested. If anyone caught him, it could be easy enough to explain away. An argument. Snoring. A dispute over the duvet. A sudden conversion to a conservative religious order. Or just a reminder that their sleeping arrangements weren't anyone's business but their own.

Who was he kidding? Sleep was in short supply these days, and if it was going to be difficult in bed with a woman he was attracted to, it wasn't going to be any easier a few feet away, freezing cold, wishing he were closer to her.

He turned the handle of the door to his room slowly, trying to remember where the hinges squeaked and where the loose floorboards were. If he could get into bed without waking her, maybe he could do an okay job of pretending that she wasn't there at all.

Fat chance of that.

He crept through the door, opening it as little as possible, and saw that Eva had left a bedside lamp on for him. He smiled involuntarily at the small gesture of consideration; it was probably more than he deserved.

Her dark hair was spread on the pillow, shiny with just a hint of red, like a conker, in the warm light from the lampshade. He silently gave thanks that the duvet was plump enough to hide any suggestion of what her body might look like beneath the covering.

And then cursed when his brain reminded him that he'd already seen enough to give him plenty of sleepless nights. That day in his father's office. Pale skin and delicate lace. Pink silk just skimming over the curve of her back.

He shook his head and turned his back to her as he slid open a drawer, careful to ensure that the wood didn't stick and make any unnecessary noise. He pulled out a T-shirt and started unbuttoning his shirt, trying not to think about the fact that he was undressing with Eva barely a couple of metres away from him.

If she were to wake up, open her eyes, what would—?

No. He stopped himself. There was no way he could let himself finish that thought. It wasn't fair on Eva, who had offered to share the bed on the understanding that he would be a gentleman.

It wasn't fair on himself either. He needed sleep, and it would never come if he was thinking about Eva watching him undress…maybe moving to kneel at the edge of the mattress as she watched, and then reaching out to help…

He struck a hand against his forehead. He really had to get this under control, he thought, taking a couple of deep breaths. Usually control was not something he struggled with. Since his diagnosis with depression he had taken back control over his life, bringing order to all those areas he had let his illness take over. Structured goals and routine had woken him from the fog that had clouded him for too long. Focussing on achievable objectives, sticking to his plan—even when he didn't feel like it—that was what had got him better. It would be foolish to slip now, to give the power back to his untrustworthy emotions rather than the techniques that he knew worked for him.

He flicked the lamp off, gently pulled back the duvet and slipped between the sheets, gasping at their icy touch on his feet and legs. For a moment he was jealous of the thick cotton pyjamas he had helped his father into earlier, though he hadn't owned anything like that in his life. Even the T-shirt was an out-of-character nod to decency for Eva's sake.

He glanced at the fire in the grate; it was burning low and doing as little as the central heating was to warm the room.

He shifted on the mattress, stretching his legs and wondering how far he could spread out without disturbing Eva. He needed to know where she was so that he could be sure he wouldn't touch her by accident. He reached out a leg experimentally, and breathed a sigh of relief when it encountered only more shiveringly cold sheet.

He turned on to his side, stretching out his arm as he did so, and his hand encountered warm softness. He froze, but the sharp intake of breath from beside him told him all he needed to know. Well, he'd worked out how much space he had—not enough. Eva must have rolled over at the exact moment he had turned, and landed on his hand. The weight of her was soft and heavy, and as he gently flexed his fingers he had to stifle a laugh. Turned out she had better protection against the cold and their attraction than he did.

'Flannel pyjamas?' he whispered.

He felt a shudder of laughter against his hand in return.

'Are you kidding?' she muttered, her voice heavy and slow with sleep. 'Of *course*, flannel pyjamas. It's freezing in here.'

Her voice was not much more than a breath, and the intimacy of whispering in bed with her made him ache.

She shifted and he acted on instinct, wanting to keep her near. As she turned over to face him he drew her closer, so when she eventually looked up they were practically nose to nose. He ran his free hand down her arm, feeling the cotton soft and warm beneath his fingers. The sensation made him achingly hard.

Who knew? he thought. *Flannel.*

Eva sucked in a breath and he realised she was feeling exactly what he was. That she was as keyed up as him, and had the same reservations.

'Still cold?' he asked, testing the waters.

'I've got goosebumps.'

It didn't necessarily answer his question, but it made him throb with the need to pull her even closer. His hand was still trapped beneath the curve of her waist, and finally it was too much to bear. He slipped it under her, until his arm encased her completely and his fingers could brush against the indentation of her waist.

'Better?' he asked.

She took so long to reply he was scared she'd changed her mind. That he was losing her.

'Hot.'

When she eventually spoke he closed his eyes with a groan. She had to know what she was doing, saying that. It was an invitation—or an acceptance. He wasn't sure who was leading this little dance. And he didn't care, because now his other arm was curving around her waist, drawing her against him until she could be in no doubt about how hot *he* was feeling right this second.

He nudged his nose against hers, asking a question he was already pretty sure of the answer to.

He wasn't wrong. Her hand came up to cup his face and she pressed her lips softly to his. Barely a whisper of a kiss at first. He held still, his arms squeezing her to him. It killed him, but he waited. Waited to see if she'd change her mind, as she had in Milan. If she was still holding back. Doing the sensible thing.

But the noise that came from deep in her throat told

him this was nothing like Milan. Her lips found his again—harder this time, demanding a response.

So he responded the only way he could, by possessing her mouth with his, exploring the textures and contours of her lips. Brushing soft kisses, tasting, touching with his tongue.

His hands bunched the soft fabric of her pyjama top at the base of her spine, pulling it tight across her breasts and revealing a couple of inches of bare skin above her waistband. She gasped softly as he did so, and then louder when his hands slipped beneath the cotton, desperate to know the feel of her skin.

'Okay?' he asked breathlessly, drawing away from her for a moment. It felt like ripping away a part of his own body.

'Freezing!' she said, with a gasp and a laugh.

She reached behind her back for one of his hands and drew it between them, rubbing his fingers and his palm between her own, blowing hot breath onto cold skin. He shivered and it had nothing to do with the temperature of the room. She kissed his palm and her lips branded him.

He barely had time to recover himself before she slipped his hand beneath the covers, cupping it around her breast.

'Better?' he asked, barely controlling the shake in his voice.

'Warm,' she replied, pressing another kiss to his lips, snaking her arms around him. 'Good. *Really* good.'

And then her hands were on his back, exploring, pulling at his T-shirt, and he didn't care whether they were fire or ice—he just knew that he wanted them. Everywhere.

He sat up so he could pull his shirt over his head and Eva rolled beneath him. When he looked down he could just make out her features in the warm glow from the fire. Her eyes were closed, her face relaxed, her body open and languid beneath him. He pinned her with his elbows either side, dipping his head to tease at her neck and her collarbone with his mouth and tongue as he unbuttoned her pyjamas, one tiny awkward button at a time.

With each inch of skin that was revealed he dipped his head lower, determined to learn every inch of her. And as the last button came open he kissed her navel, revelling in her gasp of appreciation.

He hooked his fingers into the waistband of her pyjama trousers, barely able to let himself believe that this was really happening. But her fingers were in his hair, encouraging, demanding. And as he skimmed the fabric down her thighs he kissed her lips again, hard. Knowing that every second of this night would be burned into his memory for ever.

CHAPTER ELEVEN

Eva woke with a delicious fatigue in her muscles, her head so heavy she could barely lift it to turn her other cheek to the pillow. She fought against the fluffy cotton duvet, which had formed a cocoon around her face, and stretched out a toe. The sheets on the other side of the bed were cold.

'Joss?' she called into the still room, lifting her head and propping herself onto her elbows. She strained her ears, listening for water running in the bathroom or footsteps on the landing. Nothing.

She reached for her pyjamas, where they had fallen by the side of the bed, and shrugged her arms into the soft flannel, which had long since turned cold, abandoned on the floor. Pulling on socks, she crossed the enormous bedroom into the en suite bathroom, where there were signs of a hasty exit from Joss. His toothbrush had been flung on the side of the cabinet, his T-shirt was still in a heap on the floor.

But there was no note. No explanation of his absence. No apology.

Nothing to explain the huge empty hole he had left in their bedroom or the ache in her chest as reality sunk in.

He had left her, just as she had always feared he would.

What on earth had she been thinking, going to bed with him?

She hadn't been thinking at all. Or at least not with her head. She'd woken up to find Joss behind her in the bed and herself practically rolling into his arms. He'd laughed about her flannel pyjamas, and then she'd gasped and sighed as they'd had precisely the opposite effect to the one she had intended.

In Milan she had held back, certain that giving in to her lust for Joss would lead to disaster. But things had been different last night. She had already accepted that he had a place in her life. That, however he left it, he was going to leave a space behind that was going to be hard to fill. But the way he made her feel when they were together—it would be worth it. She had never thought she would find a man worth that risk.

And now he had walked away from her without even a word.

Had he at least regretted it when he'd shut the door with her sleeping soundly on the other side?

She felt tears prick at her eyes and turned away from the mirror, not wanting to see them fall. A thick dressing robe hung on the back of the door and she pulled it on, aware how even her heavy-duty pyjamas weren't managing to keep out the chill.

She left the bathroom and glanced at the fireplace. She had no idea how to get any heat back into those dying embers, so she pulled the fabric of the robe tighter around her, holding her breath to avoid Joss's lingering scent trapped in the collar. Dropping on to the chaise longue, she glanced out of the window.

No sign of Joss's car—just neat parallel lines in the gravel leading away from where he had parked it yesterday. A shadow. A reminder that he had been there.

Eva shook her head, trying to shake off the gloom that had settled over her since she had woken in an empty bed. Was she overreacting? She hadn't even checked her phone. Her thoughts had flown straight to her parents—the way they had left her, as they always had. Her fears that anyone else she loved would do the same. She was going to feel pretty bloody stupid if there were half a dozen messages from Joss, explaining what was going on.

She crossed to the bedside table and picked up her phone, checking the screen. Nothing.

Well, she had never sat around waiting for a guy to call before, and she didn't much fancy starting now. She dialled Joss's number and felt her heart-rate jump when it started ringing. Once, twice—and then the voice-mail kicked in.

She frowned. It hadn't rung long enough for it to have redirected automatically. But the fact it had rung at all meant it was turned on. Which meant that he had to have rejected her call. He had seen her name flash up on the screen, known that she had woken without him, and then rejected her call rather than explain himself.

Nausea rose in her belly as she realised that he had really meant to abandon her. To leave her with no explanation at all. She fought the sickness down, forcing herself up from the chaise longue and formulating a plan for what to do next. She found her suitcase in the bottom of the wardrobe and started throwing things into it. If Joss didn't want her here—and he couldn't have made that much clearer—then fine. She would go.

She had tried and tried with her parents, had carried on loving them when they'd left her time and time again. And she had ended up with her heart broken. She had learnt her lesson—there was no point sticking around to let Joss do it to her again. She would get away and make a head start on building those walls she would need in place next time she had to face him in the office.

Eva jerked upright at the sound of footsteps on the landing, but it took only a split second for her to realise they were too light to belong to Joss. The gentle knock at the door confirmed her suspicions.

'Come in,' she called out, and knew before the head poked around the door that it must be Maria on the other side.

'I thought you might like some coffee,' Maria said, shoving the door open with a tray and setting it down on the table beside the chaise longue. 'And Joss asked me to fill you in on what happened last night.'

Mortification spread through Eva's veins. What on earth had Joss said to her? Had he told her what had happened? That they had slept together for the first time?

Then the reality of her situation started to sink in. No, Maria wasn't here to talk about what had happened between them in bed; she was here to make Joss's excuses for him.

Eva had fallen asleep last night, satisfied and safe in his arms. And at some point, when she had been reliving their passion in her dreams, he had sneaked away and arranged for Maria to do his dirty work.

'He didn't want to wake you or worry you,' Maria said.

From the hesitation in her voice, Eva guessed she wasn't any happier about the position Joss had put her in than Eva was.

Maria didn't know the half of it, she thought. Leaving unannounced was ungentlemanly at the best of times. In the middle of the night, following the first time they'd made love, when Joss knew exactly how big a risk she was taking on him... She didn't want to say it was unforgivable, but that was certainly how it felt right now.

'Edward was taken ill,' Maria said. 'We called the out-of-hours doctor and he called an ambulance. He's going to be in hospital for a few days.'

Eva nodded slowly, taking this news in. Perhaps she should have guessed that something like this had happened. She tried to get her head around the news and work out where this left her and Joss. So he had had a good reason for leaving. But none, she could see, for doing it without saying goodbye. Without a quick kiss and an explanation.

Had it not occurred to him that she would want to support him? That she would want to be there for him and Edward—especially when things were tough?

And it didn't explain why he'd rejected her call. Why

he'd not found the time in the last however many hours to drop her a quick message, letting her know what had happened. It seemed he had found time to keep Maria informed, after all.

Her heart ached for Edward, and for Joss watching his father fade. But it ached for herself as well. For the trust she had finally managed to put in Joss, only to see it trampled. To find herself abandoned, with her worst fears coming true.

She went to the tray to pour some coffee, wanting something to focus on.

'I'll leave you to your breakfast,' Maria said, her voice kind, and Eva guessed she had picked up on her distress even if she didn't know the cause.

As Eva sat and drank her coffee she wondered whether she was overreacting. Joss was at the hospital. Perhaps it had just been an inconvenient moment for her to call.

She watched the screen of her phone, wondering if he would call back, and then remembered that she was far too old to be playing those sorts of games.

CHAPTER TWELVE

Joss REACHED INTO his pocket for his phone, and guessed before he looked at the screen that it was Eva calling. He was tempted to fire it off to voicemail again, as he had the last time, but knew that there were only so many times he could do something so cowardly.

As he had sat by his father's bedside last night he had gone over and over his decision to leave without waking her. He had taken his phone out of his pocket and replaced it again, wondering what he could say that would lessen the blow of her waking up alone in the morning, knowing he had left without a word.

It couldn't be undone now. He could apologise, explain that it had been an emergency, he hadn't wanted to worry her.

But he didn't want to lie.

The truth was he hadn't been thinking at all. He had been acting completely on instinct—looking after his father, looking after himself. And that was what worried him the most. Because in a time of crisis his self-ish instincts had led to Eva getting hurt.

He'd not taken the time last night to think about how

his actions might affect her. It was what he had been afraid of all along—his selfishness. His instinct to look after his own needs was evidently incompatible with a relationship. They had only tried it for one night, and already Eva was paying the price. He had to put a stop to this before he did any more damage.

'Eva?' he said, hitting the green button on the screen.

'Hey,' she said, her voice neutral, flat. 'How's your dad?'

'Better, thanks.'

So Maria must have let her know what had happened. At least she had opened with a topic that he knew how to talk about. He could give her the facts, repeat what the doctors had said.

'They've made his breathing more comfortable. He'll be discharged in a couple of days. Maybe even tomorrow.'

'That's good news.'

He waited as the silence between them grew awkward.

'Can I come by and visit?' she asked.

The question was inevitable, but his answer had to be more than that. It had to protect her, to show her that they had got too close last night and needed to find some safe space between them again.

'That's not a good idea,' Joss said. 'He's still very tired. He's been asleep most of the time.'

'Okay,' Eva said, and they fell into silence again.

He thought back to being in bed with her, how they had moved and sighed and breathed as one body, and wondered how it was that intimacy like that could be lost. Easily, he realised, when one of you had walked away with no care for the damage they were causing. This wasn't something that had happened *to* them. It was something *he* had done.

'I'm sorry I had to leave in a hurry.' There—the apology was out. 'If you want to go back to London…' Joss continued, not sure whether or not he wanted her to take the hint, to be gone when he was eventually able to leave the hospital.

'I'll book a taxi to the station,' Eva said, and this time she couldn't hide the slight shake in her voice, that little tell of emotion.

He was doing it again. Being responsible for another person's emotions was too much. The people he loved were always going to be disappointed. Always going to get hurt. Even when he was trying to protect Eva, everything he did just meant she got hurt. It was better to end it now, like this, he told himself. The sooner he did it the better. He'd proved last night—to himself as much as to her—that he wasn't relationship material. If he didn't do this now, he was only going to end up hurting her more in the long run.

On Monday morning Joss pulled his car up to the front of his father's London house and rested his elbows on the steering wheel. Was it two days ago that he had done the same journey in reverse with Eva, or three? With the bright fluorescent lights and the constant noise of a busy hospital, it was hard to tell how much time had passed. Perhaps it was only two nights that he had spent sleeping uncomfortably in a straight-backed chair, aching to be home, to be back with Eva.

Except he'd known she wouldn't be waiting for him at the country house—not when he had all but told her to leave. And he couldn't go back to the mews. It wouldn't be fair to pick up as normal when he knew that they both needed to back off—for Eva's sake.

He'd not called her again. It was spineless, he knew, avoiding her hurt and recriminations like this, but what more was there to say? He didn't need her to tell him how badly he had acted. But now his father had been discharged, and they were back in London, he knew he couldn't put it off for ever.

He would have to see her at work. Tell her that they had to stop this. See if he could persuade her to keep up the pretence to his father, but forget that incredible night had ever happened. He wasn't sure how she was meant to do that—not when his own efforts had been so dismal. But they had to try.

He settled his father in bed and headed down to the kitchen to make them both a drink. When he returned, he eased open the door to his father's bedroom slowly, not wanting to wake him if he'd fallen asleep. But Edward was sitting up in bed.

'I thought you were going straight to the office?' Edward said, his eyebrows high with surprise.

'There's no hurry. I want to make sure you have everything you need first.'

Nothing to do with wanting to delay the inevitable confrontation, he told himself.

'From the way you crept in here, you thought I was sleeping—not likely to need much, in that case.'

So his father could see through him. Could see he wasn't telling him everything even if he didn't know the details of the evasion.

'It doesn't matter,' Joss said, refusing to engage with his father's probing. 'The office can manage without me for one morning.'

'And what does Eva think about this?' Edward asked.

Joss tried not to let his emotions show on his face, tried to keep his voice light. His dad was like a dog with a bone when he got an idea in his head. He wasn't going to be able to shrug his way out of this, he suspected.

'She didn't drive back with us.' Edward continued his line of questioning. 'I take it she left while I was in hospital?'

'One of us needed to be in the office,' Joss said. 'But she sends her love. I'm sure she'll visit soon.'

'Of course.' Joss could tell from the tone of his father's voice that he knew he had hit a fruitful line of questioning. 'Everything okay there?' he asked with fatherly concern. 'With you and Eva, I mean.'

'Of course it is,' Joss said, not wanting to worry his dad with the problems in his fake relationship.

He wished he could sound more convincing, but the truth was that things between him and Eva had never been worse. And their lie was meant to be making their father happy, not making him worry about them.

'I know all this must be putting a strain on things,' Edward said, reaching across to the chair beside his bed and patting the seat.

Joss sat down stiffly, recognising an order when he saw one.

'It's bound to. It's normal to have problems. Do you want to talk about them?'

'We're not having problems, Dad.'

He felt a wrench in his gut at lying to his father. Except he didn't even know at the moment what was a lie and what was true. He and Eva had started as something pretend, but this pain he was feeling—this was real. More real than anything he had felt through his actual marriage.

'And if you were you wouldn't talk to your old man about them anyway, isn't that right? I've been here before, Joss. Watching you struggle, keeping things to yourself. I don't want to do that again. I wished there was more I could do to help last time. I don't want to die wishing the same thing all over again.'

Joss dropped his head into his hands. 'I never knew you felt that way. I know I let you down with the divorce...'

Edward reached out and took his hand. 'Whatever gave you that idea? It broke my heart to see you struggling and not be able to do anything to help. But you have *never* let me down, son. You recovered, and now you have the opportunity to be happy. Please don't waste it.'

He couldn't lie to his father any more—even for his own good. He couldn't go on letting him think he was something that he wasn't. There had been too much unsaid between them over the years. Too many truths hidden.

'This is different, Dad. I'm sorry. Me and Eva—'

'You haven't told me everything about your relationship. I know that. I'm not simple, Joss. I don't need the details, because it's clear that you two care about each other very much. I think that was clear to me before it was to you. You love her, don't you?'

Joss didn't know what to say. He had tried so hard to convince himself he didn't—that it would be better for Eva if he didn't. But he couldn't lie to his father—not after what he had just told him.

'Yes. I do.'

'Then I want you to go to her and tell her that. And no matter what is happening with me, or what is happening with the business, I want you to remember to tell her that often. Okay? Nothing is more important.'

Joss wished it were that simple. That loving her would be enough.

CHAPTER THIRTEEN

EVA'S BACK AND cheeks ached with keeping her spine constantly straight and her expression neutral as she ghost-walked her way through Monday morning in the office, determined not to let memories of Joss break her perfect composure.

She'd been there since before the sun was up, and the streets were still quiet. If anyone had asked she would have chalked her early start up to commitment and professionalism, rather than the fact that she'd woken at five and been unable to bear the silence of her empty house any longer.

It was just the change back from the big, staffed country house to her little mews that had her spooked, she told herself. Nothing to do with the fact that the house didn't feel quite so much like a home now without Joss in it. Without knowing whether he had any intention of coming back to it.

She was completely in limbo. She hadn't spoken to him for three days, but as far as their colleagues were concerned they were still engaged. *Were* they still engaged? Or as much as they had ever been, anyway? She just didn't know. And it wasn't as if she could ask.

Under normal circumstances she would have no problem asking the man in her life what he thought was going on between them, but these were about as far from 'normal circumstances' as you could get.

As the last person left the office for lunch she let out a long breath and pulled in a lungful of air. It felt like the first she had taken in days. Her shoulders dropped from where they had been up by her ears, and as she tapped away at her keyboard she felt the rest of her body follow their lead and start to relax.

Which was why she jumped when she heard the all too familiar tread of his footsteps behind her, spookily loud in the silent office. She froze where she sat, fingers still on the keyboard. Taking a deep breath, she sent it to her shoulders again, forcing them into a state of relaxation that she didn't genuinely feel but she hoped would look convincing.

She turned slowly in her chair, delaying the moment when she would have to face Joss, lift her gaze to meet his. When she eventually did, anger and sympathy warred within her.

He looked like hell.

It was clear from the black bags under his eyes and the deep lines on his forehead that he hadn't slept properly since she'd seen him last, but worse than that was the expression of pain so clear in his features.

He'd obviously been going through hell. And he'd chosen to go through it alone rather than let her into his life and trust her to support him. To be there for him.

'We need to talk,' he said, his voice cold.

Her blood ran colder as she thought he must have terrible news about Edward. But she followed him through to his office and closed the door behind them.

'How's your dad?' she asked, bracing herself for the worst.

'Better,' Joss said. 'Home now.'

The air left her in a rush of relief, and she collapsed back into one of the chairs by his desk. 'Oh, thank God for that. From your face, I thought you were coming to tell me that he'd…gone.'

Joss sat beside her his expression still grim. 'No, he's home now. That's not what I need to talk to you about. It's us.'

All of a sudden she felt that chill again. The hairs on the back of her neck prickled, and she had a sudden premonition of where this conversation was going. Or where Joss thought it was going, at least.

'What happened on Friday night—it was a mistake, Eva. I should never have let it go that far.'

'Let it?' she asked, not able to keep the note of derision out of her voice. 'I don't think you were *letting* anything happen, Joss. I think you were making it happen. We both were.'

He leaned back against his desk and looked straight at her. She felt a shiver go through her at the emptiness in his expression.

'Then that was the mistake. However it happened, Eva, it was wrong.'

Surely he couldn't feel as blank as he looked about that night. She hadn't imagined the intimacy they had shared, or the ecstasy they had found together. And she wasn't going to let him repaint it all as flat and empty just because he had got scared.

'It felt right to me,' she countered. She knew she hadn't been alone in thinking that. Not at the time at least. 'It felt pretty good for you too, if I remember. I know you, Joss. You can't fake that with me.'

'How it felt isn't the point,' Joss said, refusing to engage with her. No eye contact. No acknowledgement that what she was saying was spot on the truth, whether he wanted to admit to it or not.

Eva stood and took a step towards him, planted her hands on her hips and forced herself into his line of sight. No hiding.

'It felt right, Joss, because it *was* right. There's something between us, and I know that you know it. Whatever it was that spooked you, that has you scared and running from this connection, we can talk about that. But I will not stand here and listen to you talk about it like it meant nothing. Like I mean nothing to you.'

'I want it to be nothing, Eva. It shouldn't have happened. I wish it never had.'

The words were so unpolished, so simple, it was impossible to hide from their blow. Eva felt the blunt impact square in her chest, and had to fight not to look defeated.

'And that's why you left me—even though you knew how much that would hurt me? This is because of your divorce, isn't it?' she said, deciding that nothing short of tackling this head-on was going to get through to him. 'Your depression.'

'This is because of *you*. Because I don't want you to get hurt.'

Oh, so noble while he was breaking her heart.

'Then don't hurt me again.'

It was as simple as that. He could give up on them now, walk away as if this connection didn't mean anything to him. Or he could try again, face his past and his fears, and vow to make his future different. He could accept that this depression might return, but that if it did this time he'd find support in a relationship, rather than seeing it as a burden.

'I'm trying, here, Eva. I'm not standing here saying this because it feels good. Or because I've somehow forgotten everything that happened on Friday night. It's burnt into my memories and my retinas and my skin and I'll never be rid of it. I'm doing this for *you*. Because I want to protect you.'

'And I'm meant to stand here and take it? While you push me away when we both know that we can make each other happy? I'm sorry, Joss, but no deal. You're going to have to try harder than that.'

She didn't know where it was coming from, this fire inside her. When she had woken to that empty bed, that empty room, that empty heart, she had been sure that this was over. That nothing Joss could say to her would make up for what he had done.

But as the days had passed she'd realised she was angrier about what he was doing to their future than what he had actually done the other day. If she'd had another chance with her mother she knew she would have jumped at it. She wouldn't walk away just because she had been hurt once. She would keep trying, keep fighting to keep the ones she loved in her life.

'I didn't want to hurt my ex-wife, Eva, and look what happened,' Joss said. 'I don't want the same thing happening to you.'

'I *know* what happened.' She took a step away from him now, raising her voice and throwing her arms up—anything to try and get through to him. 'You got ill, and your behaviour while you were unwell was a symptom of the disease. When you recognised that you saw a doctor and you got better. It's sad—of course it is—that by the time you realised what was happening it was too late for your marriage. But last time I checked permanent celibacy wasn't prescribed for depression.'

'There isn't a cure.'

Joss's voice was still infuriatingly flat and she stilled for a moment, studying him, looking for any sign of the man she had spent that incredible night with.

'Perhaps not. But there's treatment. There's hard work. There's support, if you'll accept it. Most importantly, Joss, there are second chances, and they're generally not to be sniffed at. I want to be with you. I want to try loving you. Believe me, I'm going into this with my eyes wide open.'

Joss met those eyes now, staring her down. Maybe using the L word had finally got through to him.

'The last few days—'

'Have been pretty terrible. It's taken a while for me to feel ready to have this conversation. To forgive you. Believe me, if you'd asked these questions on Saturday you would have got a very different reaction.'

'The one I deserved?'

'Probably. But this is the one you're getting now. I'm not letting you off the hook, Joss. I'm not going to be complicit in you walking away. If you want to break this relationship you're going to have to try harder.'

'I'll end up hurting you again. You know it's true.'

'Would you stop talking in prophecies, Joss?'

Ugh! If she didn't feel so frustrated she'd be close to giving up on him and his fatalism right about now. There were only so many rejections her ego could take, and whatever that number was they were getting dangerously close to it. She was going to walk out of this office with dignity, whatever Joss decided. So this was it. All her cards on the table. Then Joss could take it or leave it.

'Yes, you might do things that hurt me,' she started. 'You'd be a saint if you got through any sort of relationship without occasionally doing that. I'm pretty sure I'll hurt you too. Soon, actually, if you don't start listening to me rather than talking at me. A relationship comes from moving past that. Recognising that you've done something wrong, apologising for it and trying harder next time. If you're willing to do that, Joss, then I'm still game. Because, quite frankly, I can't imagine how I could walk away from this—from you—now.'

She stood watching him as he remained leaning against his desk, still scowling, still silent. Then he looked up and met her gaze.

It was clear to see how conflicted he was. There was something about the expression around his eyes that reminded her of how passionate he'd been that night, when he'd had her beneath him in his arms, ready and wanting him. But there was a tension in his jaw that she knew meant he was still fighting it. That her words hadn't had the effect she'd wanted. He was still afraid—of himself, not of her.

'This is a lot to take in,' she said, her voice hard but not angry. 'I cleared your diary for the day. I didn't expect you to be in the office at all. Why don't you go back to the house? Rest. You look like you've not slept for days. We can talk again later.'

He ran a hand through his hair and glanced at his watch, as if it held magical answers. 'You're right. I need to sleep.'

He stood upright and took a couple of paces towards her. He was about to step past her when he stopped, laid a hand on her cheek, and she drew in a breath, wondering if everything had changed in that last fraction of a second. But when she looked up she saw from his expression that he was still holding back.

He stroked her cheek with his thumb, and Eva had to resist the urge to turn her face into the warmth of his hand. She had made her position perfectly clear; it was up to him to come closer if that was what he wanted.

'I'm sorry for hurting you,' he said.

His voice trailed off and she knew he wasn't ready yet. He didn't understand his own feelings enough to share them with her.

She pressed her lips gently to his, cutting him off before he could undo what he had just said.

'That's a start.'

CHAPTER FOURTEEN

Joss watched Eva leave his office with the touch of her lips still burning on his mouth.

She made it sound so simple. As if everything they had felt the night they'd slept together was enough to base a relationship on. As if that were enough to cancel out what he had done afterwards.

It wasn't just that he'd left. It was that he'd cut her out completely. He hadn't been able to bring himself to talk to her on the phone, knowing that just the sound of her voice would make his resolve crumble. He'd kept it up for three days, falling back into old habits and isolating himself.

When he'd walked into the office and seen her sitting there, clearly aware of his presence, his breath had frozen in his chest. Waiting for her to turn around and look at him, he had felt every emotion he had been trying to bury over the last few days flood back, hitting him with a tidal wave of longing.

And then she'd been so angry, so fierce, and so sure of what she had been saying it had been impossible to argue with her. He'd walked into the office convinced that the best thing he could do for her was get as far away as possible—emotionally, at least, even if they couldn't manage it physically. It had never occurred to him what *she* might want. That she might be prepared to give him another chance.

He thought back to the dark days of his marriage. All the times his wife had tried to offer support and he'd thrown it back at her. Retreated more and more into himself, telling himself it was for the best, that he was protecting her. And where had that led them? She'd been hurt, and he'd had to carry the guilt of that. Was he just repeating himself now?

He turned the corner to Eva's mews and looked up at the big picture window of her apartment. He'd been looking forward to getting back here, he realised. It wasn't his own home he had been wishing for when he'd been trying to sleep in that crippling hospital chair. It had been Eva's. And he wasn't so stupid to think it was the bricks and mortar he'd been missing.

Nor was it her delicious body in his bed, because a sturdy wall separated them in this house. No, it was just *her*. Being close to her. Sharing his life with her. That was what had made this feel like his home.

He traipsed up the stairs and into the bedroom, shedding his jacket and shirt as he went. By the time he reached his bed he was down to his underwear and he collapsed onto the duvet, letting his muscles relax, finally, into the bed.

As his eyes drifted closed moments from his conversation with Eva back at the office drifted through his mind until one caught at him—*I want to try loving you.*

Not the first time he'd heard that word today. He'd told his father that he loved her, but he hadn't told Eva.

And in the moment when she'd all but told him she loved him too, he'd been so intent on telling Eva what he thought she needed to know that he hadn't listened to her. Her words hadn't reached him somehow. But he was listening now. *Did* she love him? Was that what she had been trying to say?

He couldn't stop the broad smile that crossed his lips as that thought sank home. It should have been scary. It should have set off warning beacons and alarms and flashing lights. Instead it filled him with warmth, a feeling of fullness that he couldn't remember ever having before. It filled him with hope.

And as he drifted into sleep he suspected that his world had changed.

He awoke to the sun low in the window, and creases from the pillow on his face. He'd fallen quickly and easily into sleep—something that had been a trial ever since his father had given him the news of his illness. His body felt refreshed and his mind was energised, full of Eva—still going over everything she had said to him at the office. Every retort to his omens of doom. Every argument against his careful reasons why they shouldn't be together.

She actually wanted to do this. She knew the risks. She knew who he had been before. She knew that the situation with his father could only ever get worse. And she still wanted to try.

The smile that had formed on his face before he had fallen asleep was fixed in place now, because he knew what he needed to do. He couldn't let her go. Not when he felt like this. She had put everything on the line for him, told him exactly how she felt, and he owed her the same in return.

He pulled on some clothes and went through to the kitchen, pulling open the fridge and glancing in cupboards. He was certain Eva would be able to create something from what he could see, but it was definitely not his forte.

He pulled out his phone and placed a call to one of his favourite restaurants, and arranged for them to deliver something worthy of Eva's palate. With glasses and cutlery and a nice bottle of red in hand he went through to the other room and laid the table, and then dug around in drawers to find candles for every surface. If he was doing this, he was going to do it properly.

She deserved that.

She deserved everything from him.

She had shown faith in him when he had deserved it least. When he hadn't even had faith in himself. And for once he believed her more than he believed the voices of self-doubt in his head. The voices that told him he was better off alone. That no woman deserved to have to put up with him again.

He was curious too. She had seemed so strong when she was talking to him back in the office. But he knew she feared being abandoned. That it was something that had haunted her life. And then, when he had gone and done it—had left her as she had feared—she'd seemed to come out of it stronger, rather than more shaken.

A knock at the door told him the food had arrived,

and he jogged down the stairs, returning a few moments later laden with foil containers. He placed them in the oven, as instructed, and then glanced at the clock. Quarter to seven. She could be home any minute.

He had barely sat down when he heard her key in the door downstairs. He jumped up and glanced around the room to make sure he had got it right. Candles flickered, reflected and refracted in the glass of the windows. The music was low and atmospheric. And the smells coming from the kitchen rivalled anything that Maria or Eva had rustled up for him.

There was nothing more he could do to prepare. It was time for them to talk.

'Something smells good,' he heard Eva call as she reached the top of the stairs and her footsteps turned towards the kitchen. She appeared in the doorway, and he stood completely still as her eyes widened when she took in the table and the candles.

'You've been busy,' she said, and he could tell from the careful modulation of her voice that she was taking care to keep her tone even. She wasn't going to give anything away, then. Wasn't going to make this easy for him.

'I might not cook, but I can order as well as anyone,' he said, trying out a smile, wanting to break the tension between them.

This afternoon he had been so sure this was right that he had forgotten how the tension in the atmosphere ratcheted up when he and Eva were in a room together. It was never going to be the case that they could sit and have a detached, impersonal conversation about where their relationship was headed. He shook his head: what would be the point of detached and impersonal? That was the last thing he wanted. It had taken Eva to show him how stunted that had left his life. How much he was missing out on.

He wanted this to be personal, and he didn't care if it got messy. He didn't care if he got hurt. He just wanted it to be real.

'Have a seat. I'll get us a drink,' he said, heading for the kitchen and buying himself a couple of minutes to decide what he wanted to say first.

He thought back to what his dad had said to him about how he should tell her what he felt. How he had been able to see through the complications of their relationship to the fact that they cared about each other. And he was right. Whatever else was fake about their relationship, the feelings he had for her—the strength he felt from knowing he had her support—that was real.

He hoped it was for her too.

He brought two gin and tonics through and set them on the table, taking a seat opposite Eva, noticing how the shine of the waves in her hair caught and played in the candlelight.

'Did you sleep?' Eva asked. 'You look better.'

'Yeah, I did, thanks. I feel it. Everything okay in the office?'

She looked slightly disappointed at the question, and he could understand why. He was disappointed in himself for asking it. He didn't want small talk. He wanted more than that. He wanted to talk about them: what they were to each other and where they were going.

'Everything's fine. Any news from your dad?'

'He's fine too. Look, Eva, this afternoon you asked me to think. And I have. Since I left the office I've done nothing *but* think. About you.'

She gave a small nod and lifted her brows, encouraging him to go on.

'And you're right. I've been scared. Scared of history repeating itself. Scared of hurting you. When I left you alone the other night I knew what I was doing. I don't think I get a free pass on that just because Dad is sick.'

'I didn't say anything about a free pass,' Eva said, her voice steadier than his. 'Yes, you hurt me. I expect you to learn from that. And to try extremely hard not to do it again.'

'Did it make you think of your parents?' Joss asked.

It wasn't where he'd planned on this conversation going, but he was curious. Something about her had changed in the days that he'd been at the hospital with his dad, and he wanted to understand her better.

Eva nodded. 'Of course it did. But knowing what you were going through with your dad also made me think harder about them than I have before. When I was a teenager the "poor abandoned me" routine was easier to maintain. But I'm an adult now, and I don't expect the world to revolve around me. There are other things going on, and lots of interests that compete with mine. I want to be with someone who makes me a priority. But I'd rather be alone than with someone who doesn't put the needs of their sick parent above mine. My parents did what they thought was right: they lived trying to balance all of the lives they felt were their responsibility. And for them the lives of people caught up in conflict were just as important as mine. They protected me from the effects of that as much as they could, and I never gave them credit for it. I think they genuinely did the best they could, and it wouldn't be fair of me to expect more than that of them.'

Joss leaned back in his chair and took a sip of his drink. So *that* was what had changed. 'That's quite a realisation to come to after so many years.'

'Yeah, well, I had a bit of a push.' She gave him a meaningful look. 'And a weekend with nothing to do but think.'

He leaned forward and reached across the table for Eva's hand. When she turned her palm to meet his and threaded their fingers together he couldn't hold back the smile that spread across his features.

'Eva, you said earlier that you want to try loving me. Well, I want that too. I want you to try desperately hard—because I'm already so in love with you. I want to be with you, here, every day for the rest of our lives. I want to feel *this* ring...' he turned their hands over and kissed the diamonds they had chosen together '...every time I hold your hand, and remember how I felt the day we chose it. How I feel right this second.'

He paused, and looked up from her hand to meet her gaze.

'I want to hear you say I love you in every language you know. I want you to teach me to say it back, so that I'm never lost for a way to tell you exactly how I feel. I want you to be my wife, Eva.'

Her hand gripped his a little harder, and he knew he

had taken her by surprise. Well, no wonder. He'd surprised himself. He already knew he wanted to be with her, but he hadn't planned to ask that question just yet. Now that it was out there, he realised how desperate he was for her to feel the same. He looked into her eyes, tried to read her answer from the shape of her mouth, the expression in her eyes.

'Yes,' she said eventually, a smile breaking her features at last. 'Yes,' she said again as she rose from the table and took a step towards him. *'Oui.'*

At the sight of her pursed lips and the sound of those breathy vowels, he ached to pull her into his lap, but she wasn't done yet.

'Sí, sì, nai, ja,' she added as she reached him, and placed a hand on each of his cheeks.

She leaned in close, so close he could have met her lips with the tiniest movement. But this moment was all hers, and he wanted to hear her tell him yes in every language she could.

'Ano, tak, ie, na'am. I love you, Joss. Of course I'll marry you.'

At last her lips met his, and heat swept through him as he pulled her into his lap, threaded his fingers through her hair and kissed her with all the passion he'd been holding back for weeks. Part of him—no surprise which part—wanted to pick her up, carry her to the bedroom and never let her go. But there was more to this than just wanting her.

'I love you,' he told her again as he wrapped his arms tight around her waist, holding her hard against him.

'I've never wanted anything more than I want to make you happy and to deserve you.'

She smiled down at him, and he felt the connection that ran between them pull at him deep inside.

'We're going to work so hard to deserve each other,' she said with a smile. 'Every day. For the rest of our lives.'

He tipped her face down to his, and poured his whole heart into their kiss.

* * * * *

If you enjoyed this story, then don't miss
FALLING FOR THE REBEL PRINCESS
by Ellie Darkins
Available now!

If you want to indulge in another feel-good romance,
then make sure to treat yourself to
A PROPOSAL FROM THE ITALIAN COUNT
by Lucy Gordon

"You're trying out women the same way you would try on a pair of cowboy boots."

"Well, she has to fit, doesn't she?" Zach asked. "Just like a pair of boots need to fit. Otherwise I'd set the boots aside and never wear them. And I sure couldn't do that to a woman. Not after I married her and then found out the fit was all wrong."

Groaning, she looked up at the sky and shook her head. "I see. It's not about the approach, but all about the fit."

"Hey, you got it, Lydia! That's exactly right. How is it that you understand me so well?"

She looked at him, a wan smile tilting her lips. "Just lucky, I guess."

He reached over and gave her hand a squeeze. "I'm the one who's lucky, Lydia. Lucky to have found a good friend like you."

She eased her hand from his and quickly began gathering the leftovers of her lunch.

"We'd better be going, Zach. It's time for me to get back to the office."

A little stung by her abrupt attitude, he stared at her. "Lydia, did I say something wrong?"

Without looking at him, she rose to her feet. "No. You said everything right."

Then why did he feel like the sky had just clouded over?

* * *

Montana Mavericks:
The Great Family Roundup—
Real cowboys and real love in Rust Creek Falls!

THE MAVERICK'S
BRIDE-TO-ORDER

BY
STELLA BAGWELL

MILLS & BOON

First Published in Great Britain 2017
By Mills & Boon, an imprint of HarperCollins*Publishers*
1 London Bridge Street, London, SE1 9GF

© 2017 Harlequin Books S.A.

Special thanks and acknowledgement are given to Stella Bagwell for her contribution to the Montana Mavericks: The Great Family Roundup series.

ISBN: 978-0-263-92330-8

23-0917

Printed and bound in Spain
by CPI, Barcelona

After writing more than eighty books for Mills & Boon, **Stella Bagwell** still finds it exciting to create new stories and bring her characters to life. She loves all things Western and has been married to her own real cowboy for forty-four years. Living on the south Texas coast, she also enjoys being outdoors and helping her husband care for the horses, cats and dog that call their small ranch home. The couple has one son, who teaches high school mathematics and is also an athletics director. Stella loves hearing from readers. They can contact her at stellabagwell@gmail.com.

To all the editors and writers
who keep these great Montana Mavericks going.
Thank you for letting me be part of the fun!

Chapter One

"You want to do what?"

Zach Dalton pushed back the brim of his black Stetson and leaned slightly toward the woman sitting on the opposite side of the cluttered desk. Long, curly hair created a brown cloud around her head while a pair of deep blue eyes stared at him with confusion.

Tightening the rein on his patience, Zach carefully repeated his request. "I want to put a classified ad in the paper. The wanted section to be more exact. Or does *The Rust Creek Falls Gazette* have a wanted section in its classifieds?"

"Look, Mr.—what is your name?" she asked, her pencil hovering above a small scratch pad.

"Dalton, ma'am. Zach Dalton."

Her bare lips formed a perfectly pretty O, but Zach allowed himself to admire the sight for only a few seconds. He wasn't about to let this dizzy woman distract him from his objective. Zach was on a mission. He knew exactly what he wanted and had already decided the best way to go about getting it.

"Dalton? Are you related to the other Daltons who live around here?" she asked.

"That's right. There's a bunch of us, ma'am. I'm related to all of them."

The phone on the desk began to ring, and while she eyed it with an annoyed glare, a male voice in a back room yelled, "Are you asleep out there, Lydia? Pick up the damned phone!"

"Excuse me, Mr. Dalton. I'll be with you in a moment," she promised.

While she answered the phone, Zach turned and looked through a dusty plate glass window at North Main Street of downtown Rust Creek Falls, Montana. This early-September morning, the sun was shining warmly, kissing the changing leaves on the trees that grew at intervals along the concrete sidewalk. The slow, two-lane traffic was made even slower by a pair of big cattle trucks working their way to the main highway leading to Kalispell. With autumn weather soon coming, the ranchers were already sorting and selling, preparing for the long, cold months ahead.

Before Zach could let himself think about all the tragedy that had occurred back on his family ranch in Hardin, he heard the woman behind him speaking in an impatient voice.

"No. Not tonight. I have to go now, Mom. I have a customer. Bye."

When he heard the phone click into place, Zach turned back to the desk to see the young woman, who appeared somewhere near his age, shoving away the tangle of curls falling about her face. She was wearing a green, loose-fitting T-shirt with the logo of some unknown rock band plastered across a pair of rounded breasts. Apparently the newspaper staff enjoyed a very relaxed dress code, Zach decided.

"Sorry about that," she said. "Now if you'll tell me again exactly what it is you want, I'll see that your ad makes the next issue."

His gaze dropped to the nameplate resting precariously on one corner of the crowded desk. "'Lydia Grant. Assistant Manager,'" he read, then lifted a questioning glance to her. "Is that you?"

Her head made a quick bob, causing several curls to plop onto her forehead. "That's me. Assistant manager is just one of my roles at the *Gazette*. I do everything around here. Including plumbing repair. You need a faucet installed?"

"Uh, no. I need a wife."

The announcement clearly took her aback. "I thought I misheard you earlier. I guess I didn't."

Enjoying the look of dismay on her face, he gave her a lopsided grin. "Nope. You didn't hear wrong. I want to advertise for a wife."

Rolling the pencil between her palms, she eyed him with open speculation.

"What's the matter?" she asked. "You can't get a wife the traditional way?"

As soon as Zach had made the decision to advertise for a bride, he'd expected to get this sort of reaction. He'd just not expected it from a complete stranger. And a female, at that.

"Sometimes it's good to break from tradition. And I'm in a hurry."

Something like disgust flickered in her eyes before she dropped her gaze to the scratch pad in front of her. "I see. You're a man in a hurry. So give me your name, mailing address and phone number and I'll help you speed up this process."

She took down the basic information, then asked, "How do you want this worded? I suppose you do have requirements for your...bride?"

He drew up a nearby plastic chair and eased his long frame onto the seat. "Sure. I have a few. Where would you like to start?"

She looked up at him and chuckled as though she found their whole exchange ridiculous. Zach tried not to bristle. Maybe she didn't think any of this was serious. But sooner or later Lydia Grant, and every citizen in Rust Creek Falls, would learn he was very serious about his search for a wife.

He hung his hat on his knee and raked a hand through his thick black hair. "Okay. Let's start with her age. I'd like for her to be between twenty-two and twenty-five."

"That sort of narrows things down, doesn't it?" she asked as she quickly scribbled down the information.

"Well, since I'm twenty-seven, having my wife a few years younger would be best for me."

"So you're not attracted to older women?"

He frowned. "I've never dated an older woman. If that answers your question."

She shot him a clever smile. "Too adventurous for you, I suppose."

He should probably remind this woman that his personal preferences were none of her business. But she was so damned cute and quirky that he hated to come across like a jerk.

"Something like that," he said. "As for other requirements, put down that she needs to be an excellent cook and homemaker. I love homemade pies and I hate messy houses."

She began to write again. "You want that last sentence in the ad?"

"Uh, no. That was for your benefit. Just to explain," he added.

She glanced up at him and he noticed the corners of her lips were curved into an impish smile. "No need to explain to me, Mr. Dalton. You'll probably want to explain to the women who answer this ad, though. So are there any more conditions you require of your…applicants?"

She made the whole thing sound so calculated and sterile. It wasn't going to be like that, Zach promised himself. When he started dating the right woman, he figured there would be plenty of fireworks to heat things up.

"Well, yes, there are more. It's absolutely necessary that she loves kids."

"Kids," she repeated as she continued to rapidly write across the pad. "So you plan on having children with the woman who ends up meeting everything on your checklist?"

"She'll be my wife. Naturally I plan to have children with her. And plenty of them, I might add." He gestured to her notepad. "And you might as well add that she needs to get along with dogs and horses. No—change that line. She'll need to *love* dogs and horses, just as much as she loves kids. I'm a rancher. So things would never work if the woman shied away from animals."

"Dogs and horses. Got it." She lifted those sparkling

blue eyes back to his face. "Is there anything else? What about looks? Do they matter?"

Zach folded his arms against his chest. "I'm flexible. As long as she's tall and willowy with long, straight hair, I'll be satisfied."

"I'll say one thing, Mr. Dalton, you know what you want."

"I like to think so, ma'am. You see, I'm a doer. I'm not one to wait around and watch the leaves fall off the trees before I decide to get ready for cold weather to hit."

A sly smile curved her lips and Zach wondered what Lydia Grant might look like if she attempted to fix herself up. From the early morning sunlight streaming into the room, he could see there wasn't a speck of makeup on her face and she'd made no effort to confine her unruly hair. It made him wonder if she'd overslept and not had time to stand in front of a mirror applying all the gooey, colorful stuff that made women look so fetching. Could be she was just the natural sort. Or maybe she was married and her husband preferred his wife to have a casual appearance.

In any case, it didn't matter, Zach assured himself. Lydia Grant couldn't be any further from his type. He liked girlie girls who wore dresses and lace and were all soft and feminine. This woman looked like she could easily help him build fences or round up cattle.

She tore the sheet of notes from the pad and placed it by the keyboard connected to a computer tower. "If you'll give me a moment to figure this up, I'll tell you the cost. How long would you like for the ad to run? A week? Two?"

He leaned forward and was surprised when he caught a faint whiff of perfume coming from her direction.

It smelled like a particular flower. He didn't know its name, but he recalled the scent emanating from his mother's garden.

"Oh. I doubt a week will get the job done. Or even two. Better keep it up and running until I tell you to stop. I understand that will be more expensive. But in the long run it'll be worth it," he added with a wink.

She started to reply and the phone rang again. This time she let out a long breath and swiveled her chair so that she was facing an open doorway leading to the rear of the building.

"Curtis, get that, would you?" she practically yelled. "I'm with a customer!"

So much for intercom systems, Zach thought. He wanted to suggest that if money was that tight here at the newspaper, they might invest in two tin cans and a string to help with communication.

She turned the chair so that she was facing the computer. After she'd fed it a bunch of information, a printer situated on a table several feet away spit out a piece of paper. As she left her chair to retrieve it, Zach noticed she was medium height with curvy hips that filled out a pair of dark blue jeans. The brown ankle boots on her feet were the rugged hiking sort, instead of the pointy toe and high-heeled kind.

"All right, Mr. Dalton, your ad will run in each edition of the *Gazette*. I'll have the typesetter outline it in a bold box so it will be noticed. This is the cost for three weeks," she said, pushing the paper across the desk at him. "If you want it to run longer, just stop by the office and we'll start again. Is that agreeable with you?"

He reached into the back pocket of his jeans for his wallet. Pulling out a debit card, he said, "Sounds great.

I'm in town fairly often, so it won't be a problem to stop by."

He scanned his card and she handed him a receipt.

While Lydia watched him slip the item back into his wallet, it suddenly dawned on her that she'd forgotten to ask him for a photo.

Snapping her fingers, she exclaimed, "Gosh, I nearly forgot! Did you bring a photo of yourself to use in the ad?"

From the blank look on his face, she could see he'd not yet realized that he was actually advertising himself.

"A photo? Uh, no. I didn't think about that." He frowned. "Do you think a photo is necessary?"

Lydia fought hard to keep from laughing. Was this guy for real? Did he honestly not realize he was a walking dream?

"Trust me, Mr. Dalton. A woman wants to know what she's getting. And a pic of you will show her—the outside part, that is." She cast him an impish smile. "It'll be up to you to show her the inside."

Clearly deflated, he said, "I was planning on getting this project rolling today. I have my driver's license photo. Will that do?"

"Those things always look like mug shots." She opened a drawer on her desk and pulled out a digital camera. "If you're not particular about the pose, I can snap one right here."

"Right here? In this chair?"

Lydia couldn't stop her chuckles. "I'm going to focus on your face. The background won't matter much."

He tucked the tail of his plaid Western shirt even deeper into his jeans, then tightened the string bolo tie until the tiger eye slide was pushed up against the collar. After combing fingers haphazardly through his black hair, he said, "Okay. Guess I'm ready."

She studied his rugged features for a moment, then shook her head. "No. You're missing something. Put your hat on. Your potential wife needs to see she's getting a cowboy. Right?"

"Oh yeah. No chance of my profession ever changing. Not for any woman." He skewered the black hat onto his head.

Lydia lifted the camera to her eye and tried not to let out a wistful sigh as she centered the lens on his handsome face. "That's good. But a smile might help," she suggested. "You don't want to look grumpy."

His lips spread into a dazzling smile and Lydia instantly pressed the button to capture the image. Then pressed it again to make sure she'd have at least one clear pic for the paper.

"That's it for the photo. But there's still one more detail," she told him. "Do you want your name on the ad? And how do you want these potential wives to contact you? Phone? Email? Snail mail?"

"Hmm. That's a question I'd not thought about," Zach admitted. "I don't have a personal computer—unless you count my smartphone. And I'd rather keep that email for private use. I'm not sure I want to field phone calls without having some sort of background on the woman first. That might get a little awkward."

"Yes. *Awkward* might be the word," she agreed.

He thoughtfully rubbed a finger along his jawbone. "I suppose that I could do the snail mail thing, but I share a post office box with other family members, including my dad. That might get a little—uh—uncomfortable."

Lydia Grant nodded. "I don't have a father—not one that counts, that is. But I have a mother. And if I started receiving correspondence from men, I wouldn't want her to see it. That's for sure."

He looked at her as another idea struck him. "Would it be possible to have responders reply to me in care of the newspaper office? I'd be glad to pay extra for the service."

Tilting her head to one side, she studied him thoughtfully. Then after a moment, she said, "It's okay with me, but I can't speak for my boss. Give me a minute and I'll see what he thinks about the idea."

"Fine. Plead my case for me, will you?"

Grinning, she shoved a fist in the air in a typical cheerleader gesture. "Three cheers for your marriage! I'll do my best."

A few years ago when the flood had hit Rust Creek Falls, Curtis Randall had been a young reporter working at a big-city newspaper. Like countless other media people, he'd traveled to the small town to cover the tragic event. For reasons Lydia had never learned, the man had hung around during the aftermath and somehow ended up assuming the job of managing editor of the *Gazette*.

At the time, the office space assigned to his position had resembled that of a hoarder. The room had been stacked with papers and books, archaic computers, monitors and keyboards, all of which had been shelved from service years ago. After the mess had been carted from the building, Curtis had quickly turned the space into a bare, sanitized space that always made Lydia think she was stepping into a hospital room instead of her boss's office.

As for the man himself, he would definitely be a cutie if he'd ditch the cardigan and black-rimmed glasses and let his sandy-blond hair get a little mussed. But in spite of his nerdish fashion choices, Lydia found him easy to work with, and that was the most important thing to her.

Rapping on the frame of the open door, she asked, "Got a minute, Curtis?"

Scowling, he looked up from the latest edition of the *Gazette*. No doubt he'd been reading the op-ed, a piece he took great pains in writing himself.

"Sure. What's up?"

She made her way to his desk. "There's a man in the main office putting an ad for a wife in the classifieds. He wants to know if responders can contact him via the newspaper. He says he'll be glad to pay extra for the bother."

His brows pulled together. "That's rather an unusual request, isn't it? Especially for such a personal advertisement."

Lydia rolled her eyes. "If you ask me, the whole thing is more than unusual. It's downright weird. But it takes all kinds, I suppose. And we're in business to make money."

"True," he agreed. "But it might turn out to be more of a nuisance than it's worth. Is this man a local? Someone we know?"

"He's one of the Dalton gang," she told him. "I've never met him before, but I got the impression he's new in town. I'll make a prediction, though. This guy is going to get the paper plenty of attention. And we could certainly use all the free publicity we can get."

Unimpressed by her positive forecast, he waved a

dismissive hand at her. "What makes you think he'll cause extra readers to pick up the paper?"

Probably because just looking at the guy was enough to give a woman a heart attack. When the single women around here learned he was looking for a bride, all hell was going to break loose, Lydia thought.

To Curtis, she said in the most nonchalant voice she could muster, "He's a cool-looking cowboy. The women around here go gaga for his sort."

Still frowning, he tilted back his office chair. "Are you still asleep this morning, Lydia? This is Rust Creek Falls, Montana. You can find his brand on either side of the street every day of the week. But—" Seeing she was about to argue, he held up a hand to stop her words before she could get them out. "If you're willing to deal with the extra work of handling the responses to the ad, then I don't care."

A part of Lydia wanted to let out a squeal and dance a happy jig, while the more reserved part of her wondered if she was taking on a huge mess. The only thing she knew about Zach Dalton was that he had a smile that could melt a snowdrift and the type of woman he was looking for in a wife couldn't have been more opposite Lydia.

Tall and willowy? With her chin up and her shoulders back, she might be considered average height. And her build was more lush than willowy. As for the long, straight hair… Her mane could be long if she spent hours ironing out the curls that caused it to spring up several inches shorter than its natural length.

No, she decided, Zach Dalton would never look at her as a potential bride. But he might like her as a friend.

And since Lydia was a woman who knew her limitations, being friends with the man would be enough for her.

"Thanks, Curtis. I'll go tell him and get everything set up." She tossed him a clever grin as she turned to leave the office. "You're not going to regret this decision."

Snorting, he reached for his coffee cup. "That's right, I won't. But you might."

Biting her tongue, Lydia hurried back out to the main lobby, where her desk was located, and found Zach Dalton still sitting in the plastic chair where she'd left him.

Even before she gave him Curtis's verdict, he smiled at her and Lydia could only wonder why some woman hadn't snagged him before now. And what in the world had pushed him to the point of advertising for a wife? It didn't make sense to her, but then Zach Dalton's love life was none of her business.

"Good news, Mr. Dalton, Curtis is agreeable to your suggestion. So I'll have the ad direct all interested females to send their correspondence here to the paper. You'll be welcome to pick them up as they come in."

"That is good news. Thanks. And please call me Zach. We'll probably be seeing each other a few more times in the coming days."

"Sure, Zach. And you can call me Lydia."

He reached across the desk to shake her hand and Lydia complied by sliding her palm against his. The skin on his hand was tough and his grip said he didn't do anything in half measures. No milksop, drugstore cowboy here, she thought.

He released her hand and settled back in the chair. "Okay, Lydia. Nice to meet you. Are you a native of Rust Creek Falls?"

"I am. All of my twenty-eight years have been spent

right here. Except for the time I was at college in Butte, that is."

"So I suppose you were here during the big flood?"

She plucked a pencil from a can and began to turn it end over end. But it soon dawned on her that her fidgeting might give him the idea he was making her nervous. She tossed down the pencil and tried to look as casual as possible.

"I was living here during the flood," she told him. "It was a horrible time. And the damage was devastating for everyone in the area. But the town has rebuilt itself and that's helped to smooth away the scars."

"Yeah. The rebuilding has been good for everyone," he agreed. "I only moved here in July. With Dad and my four brothers. Right now all six of us are living with Uncle Charles and Aunt Rita out on their ranch, the Circle D. Until we find a place of our own, that is. These past few months I've been getting reacquainted with all my relatives that live around Rust Creek Falls. And I'm learning new faces around town. See, I've met you today," he added with a grin.

Normally at this time of the morning, the phone was ringing off its hook. Mostly from townsfolk reporting weird incidents that had happened overnight. Some even called to gripe about the prices in the grocery store ads, as if the newspaper decided what food items should cost. But since Zach Dalton had strolled into the office it had rung only twice. Wonder of wonders, she thought.

She tossed him a perky smile. "Most of us folks in Rust Creek Falls are the friendly sort. So what brought you to the area, Mr. Dalton? Your relatives told you about the Gal Rush that took place three or four years ago and you thought some of those ladies were still hanging around looking for a husband?"

A wide grin spread over his face and Lydia felt her heart do a little stutter step. His dark, rugged looks were the kind that women swooned over. And once the paper announced this man was searching for a bride, she figured there was going to be all kinds of swooning going on. Was the man clueless? Hadn't he learned by now that a little crook of his finger was enough to get the women flocking to his side? He hardly needed a newspaper ad! But selling ads was a part of her job, she reminded herself. She might as well take his money and let him suffer the consequences.

"Could be," he said, his eyes twinkling. "I've been told this place is full of beautiful women looking for husbands. And how people have come to this town from near and far searching for their one true love. From the stories I've heard, a bunch of weddings have taken place in the past few years."

Lydia chuckled. "That's true. But most folks attribute that overload of weddings and babies to Homer Gilmore spiking the punch with moonshine. Drinking that stuff made everyone in town look like a desirable catch. There were so many babies born after that incident that more doctors had to be recruited to town just to take care of the overloaded maternity ward."

He laughed. "Well, I'm not going to rely on anyone spiking the punch again. The way I see it, there's something about Rust Creek Falls that makes people open their hearts. I'm confident I'm going to find the right woman."

One that made delicious pies and kept the house spotless while raising a passel of kids. Along with making sure the straightening iron was always hot so that a stray curl in her hair never appeared. Was this guy for real?

He certainly looked real and then some, Lydia thought. In fact, he was a modern-day cowboy dream. But she'd hate to think she had to live up to his standards of a wife. Lydia's pies were purchased from a bakery, and if she left dirty dishes in the sink overnight, she didn't take a trip down guilty lane. As for her hair, her time was too precious to waste standing in front of a mirror trying to make herself look like someone she wasn't. No, if she was ever crazy enough to get herself hooked up with a man, he'd have to take her as is.

She gave him the cheeriest smile she could muster. Even though he was going about finding a wife in all the wrong ways, she still liked him and wished him well. "I'm positive you'll find her. And with a new edition of the paper coming out tomorrow morning, you might meet her sooner than you think."

Rising to his feet, he said, "Thank you, Lydia. I appreciate your help."

"You're quite welcome. And I'm sure we'll be seeing more of each other," she said, then added, "When you stop by for your mail, that is."

"Oh yeah, my mail. Let's hope I get some," he said with an outrageous wink of one blue eye. "Goodbye for now, Lydia. And thanks again."

With a parting smile, he strolled out of the office and through the glass door leading to the sidewalk.

Lydia watched him walk to the corner of the intersection, where he waited for the light to change. After he sprinted across the busy street and disappeared behind a row of vehicles, she let out a long sigh, then followed it with a muttered curse word.

How stupid could she get? Time after time her mother had warned her that marriage wasn't worth the trouble. For years, she'd watched her mother work two jobs just to keep them housed and fed. No, her mother was right, Lydia thought. A man couldn't be depended on for financial security. Most of all he couldn't be depended on for love. So she needed to quit dreaming about Zach Dalton and his quest for a bride. Instead, she needed to be thankful she wasn't his type. In the long run it would save her a broken heart.

Chapter Two

"I've never seen anything so ridiculous in my life! Advertising for a wife! Who ever heard of such a thing?"

Phillip Dalton tossed the newspaper aside and glanced down the long dinner table until his disapproving gaze landed on his second-youngest son.

Zach tried not to squirm in his chair. Not with his four brothers, two cousins, and an aunt and uncle looking on. "Dad, advertising for a wife isn't a new concept. Back in the eighteen hundreds during the gold rush days, lots of men used the mail-order-bride system."

Phillip shook his head with dismay. "That's right, son. But those men were miles from civilization. They were desperate!"

Across the table, Zach's brother Garrett let out a smug chuckle. "Zach *is* desperate, Dad!"

Phillip's stern expression grew darker. "I realize

everything is fun and games to you, Garrett. But this isn't a laughing matter."

"Oh, leave the boys alone, Phillip. Zach knows what he wants. He's just going after it in a different way than you and I did."

Phillip shot his brother Charles an annoyed look. "Damned right it's different. You and I did it the traditional way. We fell in love."

Zach purposely shoveled a forkful of roast beef into his mouth to stop himself from saying something to his father he might later regret.

Next to him, Shawn, the baby of the family, spoke up in his brother's defense. "Well, I think Zach's idea is a darned good one. It's a way for him to meet women who are interested in marriage. He can always worry about falling in love later."

"Thank you, Shawn," Zach told him.

Garrett said, "That's right, Shawn. And maybe Zach will be kind enough to give us some of his leftover telephone numbers."

At the end of the table, Phillip's expression turned to stone, while the only female at the table nervously cleared her throat and rose to her feet.

"I think it's time for dessert," Rita suggested. "Apple cobbler tonight. Maybe that will put everybody in a good mood."

Later that night, in the bedroom he shared with his older brother, Zach studied his ad in the fresh edition of the *Gazette*. His picture looked okay, he supposed. At least his eyes were open and there were no specks of food in his teeth. But he'd be the first to admit his expression was a bit goofy. Like he'd had one too many strong margaritas.

Maybe that was because Lydia Grant had left him a little dazed. Although the woman had seemed warm and friendly, he'd gotten the impression she'd believed his "wife wanted" advertisement was foolish. And that had gotten a bit under Zach's skin. He couldn't put his finger on why it had bothered him. Especially when she was clearly a person who followed a different drummer. Her opinion of him shouldn't matter one way or the other.

So why had he been wondering if the newspaper woman was married or engaged? Why couldn't he forget about all that curly brown hair or impish smile that tilted her lips and sparked her blue eyes?

"What's wrong, brother? Having buyer's remorse?"

As his brother and roommate, Booker, strolled into the room, Zach tossed the paper onto the nightstand.

"I can't have buyer's remorse. I haven't bought anything yet," Zach reminded him.

Shaking his head, Booker sat down on the opposite twin bed. "You bought an ad. One that you believe will buy you a wife. That's what I'm talking about."

Groaning, Zach stretched out on his own bed and stared up at the ceiling. The textured plaster was better than looking at his brother's know-it-all face. Not that he didn't love Booker. Zach loved all of his family deeply. But so far none of them seemed to really understand where he was coming from. And being five years older than him, Booker had a tendency to always tell him what to do and how to do it.

"I didn't hear you spouting off at the dinner table," Zach said. "Are you in Dad's court, too?"

Bending over, Booker began to tug off his cowboy boots. "Not exactly. You have to admit your plan to get a wife is a little unorthodox, but that's your choice. Not Dad's or anyone else's."

Encouraged by his brother's fair-minded attitude, Zach sat up on the side of the bed and looked at him. "I tell you, Booker, I was really surprised by Dad's reaction. He's usually open-minded about things."

Booker set his boots aside and began to unbutton his shirt. "This is different for Dad, Zach. He and Mom were crazy in love up until the day she died. They had something really special together and he wants that same thing for you. And for all of his sons."

Zach swallowed hard in an effort to dislodge the hot ball of emotion stuck in his throat. Losing his mother in the wildfire that had swept over their family ranch up in Hardin in January was still so fresh he could hardly bear the pain.

"Yeah. Well, that's exactly why I'm doing this, Booker," he said in a raw, husky voice. "For a long time now I've wanted to have a marriage like our parents had. And for just as long, I've been going the traditional route—dating and waiting and hoping to meet a woman I'd fall in love with. But that just hasn't happened. Hell, I'm even beginning to wonder if love means the same thing to me as it does to other guys."

"What is that supposed to mean?"

Zach made a palms-up gesture. "As far as I'm concerned, just having a wife who cooked and cleaned and gave me babies would be enough to satisfy me."

With a look of disgust, Booker tossed his shirt to the end of the narrow bed. "I can't see that ever working. Not for me. I'm not exactly looking for a wife, but I can tell you one thing. I'd want her to love me. And only me. Otherwise, the whole thing would be meaningless."

So Booker had the same opinion as his cousins, who'd been busily sending him text messages since his advertisement had hit the newspaper stands. All of them believed he should be thinking about falling in love first and acquiring a wife later. But that was easy for his cousins to say, Zach mentally argued. Most of them were engaged or already married. Their worries of finding a special woman were over.

Groaning, Zach raked fingers through his dark hair, then flopped onto his back. "You don't understand, Booker. Nobody seems to. But the way I see it, time is flying by. I don't want to keep waiting around hoping I'll meet some girl that puts a goofy look on my face."

"You mean like the one you're sporting in the newspaper photo?"

Zach's first instinct was to sit straight up and tell his brother to go jump in the river, but he stopped himself short. He didn't want to give Booker the idea that he was trying to hide the fact that someone had already put the look of love on his face.

"I never take a good picture." Especially when quirky Lydia had been chattering on about what a woman liked in a man. Was she a specialist on the subject? Maybe the next time he visited the newspaper office, Zach ought to ask her that very question, he thought.

Linking his hands at the back of his head, Booker stretched out on the bed. "I can understand you wanting to get married and move out on your own. As much as I love Uncle Charles and Aunt Rita, I'm getting tired of being cramped up like this. The house is about to burst at the seams. We don't have much privacy and neither do they."

Zach sighed. "You need to remember the reason we

came here in the first place. Sure, we rebuilt Dalton's Gulch after the wildfire, but we ended up selling it. The place didn't feel the same without Mom. Especially for Dad. He was grieving so much I was getting concerned about his health. I think we could all see that he needed the support of family. More than just we boys could give him. It's been good for him to be living here with Uncle Charles and Uncle Ben."

"Good point, brother. And he has been searching for property so that we can build our own ranch again. In the meantime, I guess we should just be happy he isn't sitting in a dark room staring at the wall."

"Right," Zach replied. "I only hope his anger over my newspaper ad dies down. I hate it when Dad is disappointed in me."

Booker let out a sleepy grunt. "I wouldn't worry about it, Zach. I figure by tomorrow Dad will have his mind back on cattle and hay and land. And he'll have forgotten all about your desperate quest for a wife."

Zach sat up and reached to pull off his boots. "Desperate? You got it wrong, brother. I'm determined."

"The way I see it," Booker said in a drowsy voice, "you're living in a dreamworld. But I figure there's a woman out there somewhere who's going to come along and shake you awake. And when that happens, you're going to think you've grabbed a bull by its tail."

Booker knew all about bulls. At ten years of age, he'd believed he was big enough to ride one. As a result, he was still sporting a limp from a badly broken leg. But as far as Zach knew, Booker was hardly an authority on love or women. He couldn't predict Zach's future love life any more than he could predict the Montana weather.

* * *

In a pair of yellow cotton pajamas, Lydia was sitting cross-legged on the couch as she stared in disbelief at her laptop. Only one day had passed since Zach Dalton had strolled into the *Gazette* office and placed his ad for a wife. But already the inbox on her work email was inundated with messages for the man. She'd had a feeling the response to his ad was going to be big. She'd just not estimated how big.

Scrolling to the latest message to come in, Lydia opened it and began to read.

Dear Zach,
I'm twenty-two years old and can cook a mean apple pie. I have a German shepherd named Fritz and a horse named Hula Hoop. Once I'm married, my plan is to have several children, so I truly think we'd be a perfect match. Please call.

There was a photo attached, and as Lydia stared at the beautiful young face, she felt both sick and sad. There was no doubt that Zach was going to be happy with this bridal candidate. She had the smoothest, straightest blond hair that Lydia had ever seen. Plus a pair of full pouty lips and big brown eyes. How could he not like this woman?

Her silent question was interrupted by a faint knock on the door. Since it was getting close to ten, Lydia couldn't imagine who would be stopping by.

Leaving the couch, she glanced through the peephole to see her mother standing on the small square of concrete that served as her porch. Rhoda Grant was bundled in a hooded sweatshirt and held a plastic container of food with both hands.

Lydia quickly opened the door. "Mom! What are you doing out so late?"

"Hello to you, too," she said as she stepped into the small living room. "I happened to be on my way home and thought I'd drop off some extra spaghetti we had left over from the dinner the women's club put on tonight. The funds we made will go to the flood relief. You know there are still parts of town that need to be restored."

At fifty years old, Rhoda could've been a very attractive woman. Her complexion was still smooth and her brown hair held only a few threads of gray. But instead of trying to look her best, Rhoda didn't care that her waistline had thickened and her face was as colorless as a sheet of printer paper. The few times Lydia had brought up Rhoda's appearance, she'd promptly told her daughter to take a good hard look and store the memory away. Because Lydia would look the same way if she ever allowed herself to believe a man's lies.

Rhoda handed the container to Lydia, then noticed she was already dressed in pajamas. "Were you getting ready for bed?"

"Not yet. Just making myself comfortable." On her way to the kitchen, Lydia shut the laptop so that her mother couldn't peek at the screen. "Would you like something to drink?"

"No. I can only stay a minute. My shift has changed at the nursing home. I go in at seven in the morning now, so I don't like to be up late."

For years, Rhoda had worked odd, mostly menial jobs as a cook or waitress, until finally she'd managed to study and become a practical nurse. Although the

nursing home in Kalispell where she worked required a
twenty-five-minute drive one way from Rust Creek Falls,
the pay was much better and her mother seemed to like
it. Which was saying a lot, since Rhoda was the type
of person who didn't find much happiness in anything.

"Surely you can sit down for a minute or two," Lydia
called over her shoulder as she shoved the container on
the top shelf of the refrigerator.

"How's work going?" she asked as she returned to the
living room to see her mother had made herself comfortable in the only armchair in the room.

"Same as usual," Rhoda said. "Snow Valley has gotten a new entertainment director and she's been brightening the place up with music and movies and games."

Careful to set the laptop aside, Lydia sank down on
the end cushion of the couch. "That's good. The residents need something enjoyable to do."

Rhoda let out a weary sigh. "One of these days I'll
be just like the residents of Snow Valley. Too helpless
to take care of myself and nothing left in life but a few
faded dreams."

"Mother! Would you stop it! You make it sound like
the end of your days is almost here. You're being ridiculous."

Rhoda sighed again. "You don't understand, Lydia.
You won't until you lose something that's precious to
you."

Rhoda was never guilty of being a positive person.
And most of the time she was full of self-pity, but she
usually wasn't this morbid and Lydia had little patience
for the unwarranted attitude.

"Look, Mom, you're still relatively young and you're
healthy. If you truly wanted it, you could have a very

full life. You just need to make changes. The first one being to put a smile on your face."

Rhoda scowled. "Smile? When I think of what your father—"

"Yes, Mom, I've heard a thousand times how he just up and walked out on you and me. Well, you know what? I'm not going to waste my energy or my life wondering about what he did then or what he's doing now. You've got to forget it and move on."

"Well, you'd best not forget what a man can do to a woman's life," she retorted. "Otherwise, you'll be in the same boat as your mother."

If Lydia tried her hardest she could never be like Rhoda Grant. "You mean miserable and old before your time?"

Rhoda gasped with outrage. "Lydia! That's an awful thing to say!"

Jumping from the couch, Lydia sat on the arm of her mother's chair and gave her a tight hug. "It is awful, Mom," Lydia agreed. "Because it's the truth. And I'm saying it to open your eyes. Because I love you. And I want you to be happy. Truly happy."

Shaking her head with surrender, Rhoda pushed a hand through her short, curly hair. "I know that's what you want for me, honey. But I—well, after Leonard walked out, my heart turned to stone. I don't know how to change it. Or make it different."

Lydia stared at her mother, amazed that for the first time she could ever remember, Rhoda was admitting she had a problem.

Reaching for her mother's hand, Lydia rubbed her fingers over the back of it. "I think you just made a big start in that direction, Mom."

Rhoda pressed Lydia's hand to her cheek. "You are my one bright spot, Lydia." Looking up at her daughter, she smiled wanly. "It's getting late. I need to get on home."

Lydia rose from the arm of the chair and Rhoda started to stand, then paused.

"Oh, before I go, someone at work happened to bring in a copy of *The Rust Creek Falls Gazette* and I heard a few of the women on staff talking about an ad they saw in the classifieds. Something about one of those new Dalton boys advertising for a wife. Is the ad supposed to be a joke or what?"

Lydia shook her head. "The man is completely serious, Mom. He wants a wife and thinks that's the best way to go about getting one. Frankly, I think the whole thing is ridiculous, but it's not my business to stick my nose in a customer's personal life."

Shaking her head with dismay, Rhoda stood and started toward the door. "I don't know what's come over this town. It's like some of them are still drunk on Homer's punch. Especially the Daltons. All of a sudden Travis gets himself engaged and gets on a ridiculous reality TV show. Now another one advertises for a wife. Makes you wonder what's going on with that family."

Even though Lydia agreed that Zach's search for a wife was not taking the normal route, she wasn't willing to call him either strange or wrong.

"Some folks just have different ideas, Mom. And Zach seems like a very nice guy. Not the weird sort."

With her hand on the doorknob, she looked at Lydia. "Don't tell me you're going to sigh over the guy. All day at work, the young nurses were going on and on about how dreamy he looked in the photo and all the sacrifices they'd make just to have one date with the man. It was all so silly and sickening. I hope you're smart enough not to make a fool of yourself over the man."

A strange little pang of regret touched a spot inside Lydia, but she carefully hid it with a casual laugh. "Oh, Mom, that's the last thing you need to worry about. Zach Dalton would never take a look at me. And even if he did, I wouldn't want a man who plans to choose a wife on how well she can cook."

Seemingly satisfied that she had no reason to worry about her daughter, Rhoda opened the door. "That's my girl."

Lydia walked over and kissed her mother's cheek. "Bye, Mom."

"Good night, honey."

Her mother stepped outside and Lydia quickly locked the door behind her, then turned back to the empty living room.

I hope you're smart enough not to make a fool of yourself over the man.

Her mother had spoken the words in all sincerity and that had made them all the more painful. Maybe it was true that no matter the reality, mothers viewed their children as beautiful. But even Rhoda should be able to see that her daughter wasn't the sort that men were attracted to. When a man looked at Lydia, he wasn't inspired with thoughts of babies and matrimony. No, she was the sort a man wanted on his softball team. She was the buddy he wanted to share a beer with and share his troubles about his real girlfriend.

Hating herself for having such self-pitying thoughts, Lydia walked over to an oval mirror hanging on the wall and stared at her pale image.

Was she just as guilty as her mother about giving up and giving in? What would happen if she tried to doll up her tomboyish image? Everyone in Rust Creek Falls would probably laugh and point and say she was trying to be something she could never be.

Turning away from the mirror, Lydia sat back down on the couch and opened the laptop. The screen had gone black, but once she instructed the computer to wake up, the endless emails to Zach Dalton popped into view.

As she began to read the mushy lines, pleading for a chance to become Zach's bride, she promised herself that someday she would meet a man who would love her just for being her and no other reason. And until that day happened, she wasn't going to fret about Zach Dalton and his endless female admirers.

As soon as Zach had finished his allotted share of the morning chores on the Circle D, he didn't bother changing clothes. He jumped in his truck just as he was and drove straight to Rust Creek Falls and the *Gazette* office.

When he stepped through the door, a bell above his head jangled and he looked across the wide space to where Lydia Grant's desk was situated. At the moment she was busy with a customer. A tall, older man with a bald head and an unlit cigar protruding from the corner of his mouth.

"This will take care of it, Mr. Tuttle. Your subscription is paid up for two years and will be delivered to your post office box."

"You don't plan on going up on the price between now and then, do you? I don't want to have to come back in here and give you more money," the man said bluntly. "I'm getting sick and tired of all the businesses around town going up on prices. They like to use the flood as an excuse, but if you ask me, it's just downright greed."

Zach didn't know how Lydia did it, but she gave the customer a bright, easy smile. "Don't worry, Mr. Tuttle. Once your subscription is paid in advance, that's it. You won't be charged more."

"Darned good thing," he muttered, then snatched the receipt from her hand.

As he stalked toward the door, Lydia called out cheerfully, "Thank you, Mr. Tuttle. And be sure to tell your lovely wife hello."

The customer acknowledged her with a faint grunt before he walked out the door. As Zach watched him go, it was all he could do not to grab him up by the collar and toss him onto the sidewalk. But Zach was a gentleman and had been taught to respect his elders, no matter how rude they chose to be.

When the door closed behind the man, Zach sauntered over to her desk.

"Nice guy," he said with wry sarcasm.

She laughed. "If he didn't have something bad to say, he'd be silent. How his wife deals with him is a mystery to me." She leaned back in her chair and gave him a bright smile. "So how is your day going? Ready for your mail?"

Zach felt his cheeks go warm. Even though he believed in what he was doing, there was something about Lydia that made him question his strategy. "That's why I stopped by. To see if anyone had replied to the ad."

She gestured toward the hard plastic chair in front of her desk. "Have a seat and I'll grab everything for you."

Zach eased his lanky frame into the chair and watched her walk over to a row of file cabinets lined against the back wall. Today she was dressed basically the same as yesterday, he noted as his gaze swept up and down her sexy figure. The only difference today was an army-green vest zipped over her white T-shirt.

"I've printed out all the emails that have come in so far, but since I've not looked in the past hour, there could be more. And you'll also find a few letters that were hand delivered here to the office." She placed a stack of correspondence in front of him. "That should give you a good start on your endeavor."

Zach was amazed. "All of this stuff? It's only been one day! I wasn't expecting this sort of reaction."

Her blue eyes twinkled with something like comical disbelief. "Are you for real?"

"Excuse me?"

Shaking her head, she said, "Sorry. I— Well, I'm getting the idea that you're not prepared for what you're getting into. When it comes to eligible bachelors around here, women are piranhas. I'm fairly certain you're going to be swarmed with hopeful females."

His gaze dropped to the stack of correspondence. From the looks of it, Lydia could be right. But he felt certain he could filter through them in an intelligent way until he landed on the woman of his dreams. "I think I can handle it."

She started to say something when a tall redhead somewhere in her early thirties appeared through the open doorway leading to the back of the office building.

"Sorry I'm a little late, Lydia. Tack on another ten minutes to your lunch hour. I'll handle things here."

The woman acknowledged Zach with a nod of her head, then suddenly seeming to recognize him, she walked over and offered her hand.

"You're the one! The man advertising for a wife!"

Zach shook her hand. "That's right. I'm Zach Dalton."

"I'm Jolene Sanders. I work in Proofing. I just want to tell you I think it's great to finally see a man being honest about what he wants in a woman before he ever ties the knot."

Behind Jolene's shoulder, he could see Lydia rolling her eyes.

"Are you married, Ms. Sanders?"

She smirked. "Divorced. That's why I like your style. I only wished I'd known what was on my ex's mind before I ever married him. The wedding would've never taken place."

Lydia lifted a lightweight jacket off a standing coat-rack. After tossing it over her arm, she stepped around the desk.

"I'm off. See you in an hour," she said to Jolene, then cast Zach a perky smile. "Nice to see you again, Zach. Happy hunting to you."

She started out the front door, and before Zach realized his own intentions, he grabbed up the pile of correspondence and hurried after her.

"Lydia! Wait up!"

She paused on the sidewalk and looked back at him. "Did you need something else?" she called out.

He needed his head examined. That was what he needed. But he'd worry about that later.

Trotting up to her, he tried not to stutter. "I, uh, overheard you say you're going to lunch."

"That's right. I usually go at twelve. Someone has to take over the front desk while I'm away. And Jolene would rather eat later."

The bright sunshine gave her skin a golden sort of

glow and made her blue eyes sparkle even more. The evocative scent he'd noticed the first day he'd met her drifted around him like a warm, hazy day. Zach didn't understand it, but something about her just naturally perked his spirits. And since the wildfire, his mother's death and the family's move here to Rust Creek Falls, he needed to grab what little pleasures he could find.

"I see. Well, would you like some company? I've not eaten since very early this morning. A hamburger would sure go down good right about now."

Surprise flickered across her face and then she happily looped her arm through his. "A burger sounds great to me. There's a nice little place just around the block," she said, pointing behind them to a side street that crossed Main.

"Works for me. My truck is parked right down here. I'll lock my mail in the cab and we'll be on our way."

The weather had turned cooler overnight, and as they walked, Zach helped her into the jacket she'd carried. The leaves on the trees growing out of dirt squares in the sidewalk were beginning to turn to shades of yellow and red. In the far distance the mountain peaks were still shaded in green, but it wouldn't be long before white caps of snow would remind everyone of the long winter months to come.

"It's cool today, but beautiful," she exclaimed as her jaunty walk kept up with his longer strides. "I love this time of year. When the air turns brisk and the fall is just around the corner. I start getting visions of hot chocolate and pumpkin pie. Not necessarily together, that is."

"Are you a good cook?" She was still holding on to his arm as though it was a natural thing and Zach realized he liked her easy manner. A man wouldn't have to pretend to be perfect around this woman, he decided.

"Are you interviewing me as a candidate for your wife?" she asked with a saucy laugh.

Zach felt himself blushing. He would never see Lydia as wife material. Not when she was the absolute opposite of the kind of woman he wanted. "No. Just curious."

"Okay, Mr. Curious. I can't cook. But I can open cans and pop things into the microwave."

She obviously didn't wear pretty lace or have straight hair, either. But that hardly mattered to Zach. He wasn't taking her out for a hamburger because he wanted to marry her. He simply wanted a bit of company for lunch.

"That's about all I can do, too," he said. "So we're even with the cooking."

Laughing, she said, "Yes, but we don't have much else in common. In fact, you're not like anyone I've ever been friends with."

He glanced down at her. "I don't think I've known anybody quite like you, either. But we do have one thing in common and that's *The Rust Creek Falls Gazette*. I need the newspaper to help me find a wife. And it's your job to sell ads. So we're helping each other."

"Hmm. You're right. Finding you a wife is our common ground. Let's hope we succeed."

He grinned at her. "Right now I'd be happy to get a good lunch."

She chuckled. "I might not be able to find you a wife, or even cook, but I can promise you a good meal. Follow me."

Chapter Three

A short distance down the next street, Lydia guided him to a stop in front of a redbrick building with the words Gold Rush Diner painted on the plate glass front.

"Here we are. It's small, but good," she promised.

"Where did the name Gold Rush come from? Was gold ever taken out of this area?"

"Not that I'm aware of. But I suppose anything might have happened back in the eighteen hundreds before the area was settled. Why do you ask? Are you thinking about prospecting for gold?" she asked impishly.

"The only thing I'm searching for is a wife," he told her. "And hopefully, that'll be easier than finding a vein of gold."

Zach opened the door and above their heads the rattle of a cowbell announced their arrival.

Several of the red vinyl booths were already taken

with early lunch diners, but they managed to find one in the back of the room, not far from the kitchen.

As Lydia settled herself on the bench seat and removed her coat, she could feel several sets of eyes turning in their direction. No doubt some of them had recognized Zach from the classified ad and were curious about him. Others were probably wondering what a plain Jane like her was doing with a walking dream like him.

Lydia was wondering the same thing.

When Zach had approached her on the sidewalk, the last thing she'd been expecting was for him to ask her to lunch. She wasn't sure what to make of it. She only knew it would be foolish to think it might mean more than a friendly offer.

Zach sniffed as he removed his hat and placed it next to him on the seat. "Something smells good."

Lydia chuckled. "I think that's called fried food."

He grinned and Lydia's heart fluttered in spite of herself.

"Why is it that the things we want the most are the things that are bad for us?" he asked.

He was a prime example of one of those bad things, Lydia thought. Just sitting there with him was messing with her mind and making her heart do ridiculous acrobatics.

"I don't know. But if I could figure it out, I might be able to stop my chocolate habit." Resting her forearms on the edge of the table, she leaned slightly toward him. "So tell me—what did your family think about your ad?"

He shrugged. "Well, after they ribbed me about it, my brothers mostly thought it was ingenious. Unfortunately my dad didn't see it that way. He's rather disappointed in my strategy to find a wife. I'm hoping as time goes by he'll quit lecturing and mellow about the idea."

She could see that his father's lack of support troubled him. Lydia could only wonder what it was like to have a father who even bothered to pick up the phone and say hello or drop a birthday card in the mail. At least Zach's father cared enough to voice an opinion on his son's future.

"I imagine he wants you to take the customary route," she suggested.

A frown pulled his dark brows together, and as Lydia's gaze slid over his handsome face, she figured there were already countless females who'd been sighing over his photo and plotting to become his wife. Poor guy, he was in for a bumpy ride. Unless this business of searching for a wife was just a ruse to create a dating pool for himself.

No. Lydia didn't want to think Zach was that calculating. As far as she could tell, there didn't seem to be a conniving bone in his body. But, according to her mother, every man had his own selfish agenda.

"Right," Zach said with an emphatic nod. "But I'm twenty-seven. I've been dating ever since high school and not one woman has ever felt like she was the perfect fit for me. Frankly, I'm tired of waiting."

Lydia was a year older than him and still single, but she wasn't pushing the panic button. Yet.

She was about to tell him that being in a hurry might not be wise, but before she could think how to word it in a sensitive way, a young, wiggly waitress with long black hair approached their booth.

Her entire attention on Zach, the woman placed two menus onto the table. Flashing a suggestive grin at him, she said, "Hi. How's it going?"

He smiled back at the waitress and Lydia wondered what he was thinking about all that long, straight hair. Maybe he was getting the idea that the tight apron she was wearing meant she was great in the kitchen. Or the bed. Either thought made Lydia a little sick to her stomach.

"It'll be going great as soon as we can get our lunch," Lydia spoke up.

The waitress shot her an annoyed look before settling a dreamy-eyed stare on Zach. "Aren't you the guy in the newspaper? The one taking applications for a wife?"

His face a little red, Zach shifted around on the seat. "I'm the guy," he admitted. "But the application part— I wouldn't exactly put it that way."

"He's taking résumés," Lydia said, hoping her cheery smile didn't look as phony as it felt. "And the one that has all the right answers wins the prize."

"Oh," the waitress mumbled uncertainly. "I'm not good at résumés."

Zach shot an annoyed look at Lydia, then said to the waitress, "That's not my intention. I'm just trying to find a girl that suits me."

"Then I think it's awesome," she gushed. "Like the TV show where the bachelor picks his love from a group of ladies."

Zach and Lydia exchanged amused glances.

"If you want to think of it that way," Zach said a bit awkwardly.

Thankfully, the waitress suddenly remembered why she was at their table and pulled an order pad out of a pocket on her uniform. "So what would you two like to drink?"

They both ordered iced tea, and after the young

woman hurried away, Lydia shook her head. "I'm sorry, Zach. I shouldn't have said that about the résumés. I wasn't really making light of your...effort. It's just that she was so—"

She broke off and with a sly smile Zach finished for her. "Obvious?"

Lydia expelled a long breath while wishing she could kick herself. "Yes. That's what I was trying to say. I hope you're not angry with me."

His chuckle filled her with relief.

"Forget it. I'm not offended. But I am curious. Is that really the way you see my endeavor? That I'm looking at the whole thing like a job interview?"

It was all Lydia could do to keep from squirming. "Well, to be honest, it rather looks that way. But from the little time we've spent together, I get the impression you won't marry a woman unless you're wildly in love with her. And that's all that matters."

His lips spread in a wry smile and Lydia found her gaze focusing on the dimple carving his cheek and the way his white teeth glinted against his tanned skin.

He started to make some sort of reply, when the waitress returned with their drinks. As Lydia watched her write down their orders, she wondered how the young woman could possibly know what she was scrawling across the pad. Not with her ogling gaze never leaving Zach's face.

"We'll have these orders right out, Mr. Dalton." Playfully wrinkling her nose, she let out a nervous giggle. "And if there's anything else you need, I'll be happy to get it for you."

As the waitress walked away, Lydia had to stop herself from groaning and laughing. As for Zach, he seemed unaffected by the flirtatious behavior of the waitress, which made her wonder if she'd underestimated this man. Maybe he wasn't nearly as gullible to the wiles of women as she'd first believed.

He looked across the table at Lydia and smiled. "Now, where were we?" he asked. "I believe you were saying something about me needing to be wildly in love before I picked a wife. Tell me, Lydia, have you ever been wildly in love?"

She didn't know why, but the question brought a stinging heat to her cheeks. "Uh, no. Not that I remember. When I was about twenty years old, I had a crush on a bull rider."

His jaw dropped. "A bull rider? You don't seem the sort to go for that kind of guy."

Laughing, she shrugged. "Well, he had the swagger in his walk and wore his hair a bit too long to be conventional. And guys just naturally look sexy in a pair of spurs."

"What happened?"

This time her short laugh was brittle. "Nothing. He never knew I existed."

"Hmm. What about high school? All girls at that age think they're in love, don't they?"

She shook her head. "Not me. There wasn't really any guy I could hang my starry gaze upon. You see, back then I was a little plump and my complexion was a mess. The only thing I didn't have was braces. But that was only because my mom couldn't afford them." She gave him a wide enough smile to expose her teeth. "See, my right front tooth has a tiny lap over the left one. But it doesn't bother me. None of us are perfect, right?"

"Not at all." He leaned closer, his eyes focused on

her mouth. "And I happen to think your teeth look natural and nice."

She was an idiot for letting his words thrill her. He was simply giving her a friend's opinion. But it wasn't often a man like Zach Dalton ever bothered to give her a compliment and the feeling was empowering.

"Thank you."

He took a long drink from his glass, while she peeled a straw and jammed it into her iced tea.

"Tell me if I'm being too personal, but are you hoping to get married? Have children?"

Even though they shouldn't have, the questions stung. Still, she mustered a casual voice. "Oh, back in those days of the bull rider—when I was twenty and everything about life looked fresh and wonderful—I dreamed of having a family. I expect most women do. But it just never happened. Now that I'm older, I suppose I've quit thinking so much about it. Someday I might find that perfect guy. But until then I'm content to stay busy at the *Gazette*."

His gaze scanned her face and Lydia wondered what it would be like to have him look at her with love shining in his eyes. Would any man ever look at her with such devotion? He'd be faking it if he did. That was what her mother would say.

He tossed her a teasing grin. "So you're not thinking about advertising for a husband?"

She laughed. "I think I'll wait and see how things work out for you before I go that route."

He rested his broad shoulders against the back of the booth. "I'm sure you've heard about my cousin Travis getting on reality TV."

"Oh sure. Everyone in town has been talking about

The Great Roundup! I haven't missed an episode. It's so fun watching people I know on TV."

"I've been watching the episodes at the Ace in the Hole," he said. "I have to admit it seems a bit surreal seeing Travis on TV. But so far he's hanging strong with the competition."

"I'm excited to see how the contest unfolds. Things are getting a bit nasty with some of the contestants. I hope Travis and Brenna are on the lookout for saboteurs among the group. I wouldn't be surprised if a few of them might go as far as to cut cinch straps on saddles or deliberately spook a contestant's horse."

He nodded. "My same thoughts. Last week when that big burly cowboy with the handlebar mustache got bucked off his mount, I wondered if someone might have planted a burr or something sharp beneath his saddle pad. Some folks will do anything for money. Especially the prize of a cool million dollars."

"Sad, but true," she said, then offered him a bright smile. "But Travis is a tough guy. He might just be the one bringing the million dollars home. And a new wife, too. I think everyone was a little shocked over his sudden proposal to Brenna O'Reilly."

Frowning, he picked up his tea glass. "I doubt anyone was more shocked than me," he admitted. "Proposing marriage isn't something a guy should do on impulse. But then Travis always was the reckless sort. I only hope he hasn't set himself up for a miserable fall."

"Well, from what I've seen on *The Great Roundup*, I get the sense there's a real connection between him and Brenna. That's the important thing."

"Lust or love. With my cousin, who knows? I'm still

trying to figure out if his proposal to Brenna was real or just a spur-of-the-moment thing."

Lydia tapped her fingers against the tabletop as she mentally weighed Zach's comments. "So you don't believe picking a wife from a newspaper ad is impulsive?"

Thankfully, he wasn't offended by her question. Instead, the faint grin on his face said he found it amusing. "I haven't proposed yet, Lydia. Whenever I do, it will be after a lot of careful consideration."

He sounded like a man weighing the appeal of a bologna sandwich against a rib eye steak. If he was truly in love, he shouldn't need to "consider" anything, Lydia thought. His heart would know who he wanted to spend the rest of his life with. But that wasn't her worry.

To her relief, the waitress suddenly arrived with their meals, and the interruption allowed their conversation to move away from love and marriage.

Once the flirty waitress made certain Zach had everything he needed, she left them to enjoy their burgers and fries.

"Mmm. This tastes great," Zach exclaimed after he'd swallowed a hefty bite of the thick burger. "I'll have to remember this place."

"I'm glad you approve. Being close to the *Gazette* makes it easy for me," Lydia said. "I can walk here."

"How long have you worked for the newspaper?"

"About six years. When I applied for the job, I didn't have much experience. Actually, the only experience I had was the work I'd done on the college newspaper. But at that time, the boss of the *Gazette* was nice enough to take a chance on me. Since then I've worked my way up to assistant manager. My main job is graphic design and I also do the cartooning for the paper, along with

anything else that needs to be done. Like taking classified ads, answering the phone and—"

"Fixing the plumbing," he finished for her.

Surprised that he remembered, she chuckled. "That's
right. I do know how to handle a crescent wrench."

His eyes sparkled. "I'll try to remember not to make
you angry. A woman that can handle a crescent wrench
can be dangerous."

Laughing softly, she dipped a french fry into a pool
of ketchup. "Don't worry. I can hardly bring myself to
swat a fly."

By the time Zach and Lydia finished the meal, her
lunch hour was nearing its end. After taking care of the
bill, Zach walked her back to the *Gazette*, then drove
straight to the Circle D.

As soon as he parked his truck near the barn, he
spotted his brother Cole pushing a wheelbarrow filled
with horse manure and dirty shavings toward a pile of
compost.

Expecting he was going to catch hell for being gone
part of the morning, Zach left the vehicle and walked
over to his brother.

"What's going on? Cleaning horse stalls?"

"Where have you been?" Cole demanded. "Have you
forgotten there's work to be done around here? Yeah, I'm
cleaning stalls—all by myself, I might add. Shawn and
Booker took off on horseback to go round up a bull. He
crashed through a fence at the back of the property. So
that leaves me and you to finish the dirty chores here
in the ranch yard."

"Sorry," Zach apologized. "I had to go into town."

Which was partly true, he thought. He couldn't leave personal mail lying around the newspaper office.

"To see one of your prospective brides, no doubt," Cole said with a heavy dose of sarcasm.

"Actually, I did have lunch with a woman," Zach admitted. "But she's not in the running for my wife."

Cole's expression took on a look of exaggerated shock. "You mean she wasn't that impressed with you? Wonder of wonders."

Rolling up his shirtsleeves, Zach started walking toward the barn. Cole grabbed the wheelbarrow and fell in step beside him.

"If that's the way it is, then maybe you can introduce her to me," he suggested with a wicked grin.

Zach glanced at his good-looking brother. Lydia with Cole? No. Zach didn't like that idea. Not at all.

"Forget it," he repeated in a blunt tone. "She's too old for you."

"Really? How old is she?"

"Twenty-eight."

Cole's laugh was more of a loud whoop than anything. "Guess you've forgotten I'm twenty-eight, too."

Zach frowned at him. "No. I've not forgotten. And you like younger women. Remember?"

Cole chuckled knowingly. "Wow! This ad thing worked a damned sight quicker than I expected! Zach has found the woman he's been searching for! When's the wedding, little brother?"

"Don't be stupid."

"I'm not. I can see it all over your face."

Cole couldn't see anything on his face. There was nothing to see. Lydia was a friend. Just because he wanted to shield her from Cole's clutches didn't mean he was falling for the woman.

"The only thing you need to be seeing is that wheelbarrow full of manure," Zach told him. "Let's get to work."

That evening Zach was too tired to contribute much to the conversation around the dinner table. But he was all ears when his father brought up the subject of purchasing a piece of property. Something Zach and the rest of his brothers had been praying to happen.

"It doesn't look like anyone lives there now," Phil said as everyone around the table enjoyed bowls of dewberry cobbler topped with ice cream. "The house is empty and the fences look like they're about to collapse. There's a big yellow barn on the property. From what I could see from the road, it could use some repairs, but it looked usable."

Angled to Phil's left elbow, his brother Charles nodded. "Yes, I know the property you're talking about. That's the Stockton place. It's been vacant for a few years now. Ever since Rob and Lauren Stockton were killed in a car accident. That was a real tragedy."

Rita spoke up somberly, "Especially with the couple having seven children. The way I remember it, after the accident the children split up. Some even left town. I think two of the younger girls were adopted."

"Jamie and his sister Bella are still in Rust Creek Falls," his cousin Eli spoke up. "I've not heard about the rest of the siblings."

"Who owns the Stockton place now?" Zach asked. "The siblings?"

Uncle Charles answered, "That's a good question.

You'd think if the brothers and sisters owned it, they'd be trying to keep the place from falling into ruin." He looked at Phil. "If you're interested in the property, we could ask around."

"Maybe old Grandpa Stockton owns the place," Eli suggested.

Aunt Rita grimly shook her head. "That would certainly be a travesty. The old man didn't seem to care what happened to his grandchildren. He didn't deserve the property."

"Well, the place looks like it has potential. But we'll see. Some other nice place might come up for sale," Phil said.

In the chair next to his, Cole tilted his head close to Zach's and muttered under his breath, "Let's hope it's soon. Six extra men in this house are way too many."

The house was definitely crowded, but Zach wasn't going to complain. He wanted their father to heal from the grief of losing his wife. And being with his brother Charles seemed to be working wonders for Phil's spirit. As for Zach and his brothers, they each had to deal with the loss of their mother in their own private way.

"Hush and eat your cobbler," Zach mumbled. "We'll survive."

Later that night, after Zach had retired to the bedroom he shared with Booker, he finally had a chance to look at the mail he'd collected from the *Gazette*.

Stretched out on the single bed, with his head propped on a pair of pillows, he began to sift through the emails and a few letters in envelopes that had been hand delivered to the newspaper office. Some of the women chose the short and sweet method to garner his attention, while others had gone into great detail about their cooking, cleaning and, last but not least, bedroom qualifications.

Just reading the erotic promises was enough to turn Zach's face beet red and he was glad the explicit letters had been in sealed envelopes. Just thinking of Lydia reading this sort of stuff in an email message made him cringe.

Lydia. Lydia.

He looked across the room to where the open curtains gave him a view of a bright, full moon rising over the trees. Was Lydia out strolling beneath the moonlight tonight with a favorite guy? he wondered. Or was she alone in her apartment or house, watching TV?

Hell, Zach, what is the matter with you? You have dozens and dozens of prospective brides lying right here in your lap and you're thinking about a woman who is so far from your ideal it's not even funny. Sure, Lydia is easy to talk to, but that's where it ends. And there's damn sure more to marriage than just talk. So get your mind off Lydia Grant and back on the business at hand.

Grimacing at the pestering voice in his head, he picked up another envelope and slid a letter opener beneath the flap. When he pulled out a single piece of paper, a photo fell to the side.

Picking it up, he read the brief information scrawled across the back of the glossy paper. Twenty-two years old. College graduate. Blonde with the word *natural* to the side in parenthesis. Blue eyes. Five foot nine.

He turned it over and carefully studied the image of the young woman. She was pretty enough, he thought. Slim and tall, she had an elegant air about her. She was even wearing a lacy pink top and her hair was straight as a piece of straw. He certainly wouldn't be ashamed to show up at a family affair with her on his arm. And yet the image didn't give him the slightest spark of excitement.

Telling himself he'd put her in the pile to be considered, he reached for another letter. A photo had also been attached to it, and as Zach studied the image, he decided this particular woman wasn't quite as pretty as the prior one, but she had a sweet, honest-looking face. He dropped her in the keeper pile and reached for another piece of mail.

He was slicing into the sweet-smelling envelope when his brother entered the room and tossed his hat onto the bedpost.

"What a day," he said wearily. "I think Shawn and I rode ten miles before we finally caught up to that damned bull. My back is aching."

Zach grunted with amusement as he looked up to see his brother slowly easing his shirt off his shoulders. "You ought to try mucking out horse stalls. That might get your back in shape."

"Hah. A couple of times at the dinner table tonight I thought your face was going to fall into your plate," Booker teased.

"I am tired," Zach admitted. "But hearing Dad showing some interest in a piece of property perked me up a bit. What about you?"

"Well, it's a start, at least. But that whole Stockton family thing sounds complicated. For all we know, the place could be locked up in a legal battle. Especially if there's that many siblings involved."

"Hmm. You know, when I heard Eli and Aunt Rita talking about those kids losing their parents, I couldn't help but think how lucky we are, Booker. I mean, yes, we lost our mother to a senseless fire. But at least we have Dad and other extended family. From the sound of it, those Stockton kids were scattered to the wind."

Scrubbing his face, Booker walked over and sat down on the end of Zach's bed. "Yeah. I'd hate to think of us brothers being separated like that." He eyed the pile of mail lying next to his brother. "What is that?"

Zach grinned. "Responses to my newspaper ad. Look at these photos. Pretty, huh?"

Booker picked up the photos, and as he studied the images, he shook his head in amazement. "Nice. Very nice. But what does that tell you? Not much. Those women could be shrews or spoiled princesses or—"

"They could be anything," Zach interrupted. "That's why I'll have to go through the dating process to find out."

Booker whistled under his breath. "From the looks of that mail, you're going to be a busy guy." He tossed the photos back to Zach. "You know, Dad isn't going to be too pleased if you spend your time chasing after these women instead of doing your work here on the Circle D."

Zach groaned. "I don't intend to date every female who responds to the ad. I'm going to take my time and be very selective."

Booker rolled his eyes. "And then what? What if you find The One? I'm sure your bride would be real excited about moving into a house with ten other people, nine of whom are men."

No longer in the mood to read anymore, Zach gathered up the correspondence and shoved them into a big manila envelope. "It won't always be this way. Eventually Dad will find a place where we can build a ranch as great as Dalton's Gulch was back in Hardin. Then we can all carve out a niche for ourselves."

Booker studied him closely. "You really are serious about this wife thing, aren't you?"

Zach sat up and placed the envelope in the nightstand. He wasn't going to bother locking the drawer. If his brothers wanted to poke through the mail, that was okay with him. After all, he would be the one with the dates. Not his brothers.

"I want a wife and kids more than anything," Zach told him. "I want the same thing our parents had and I don't intend to stop until I get it."

Booker gave Zach's shoulder an affectionate slap. "More power to you, brother. As for me, I'm going to take a shower and go to bed."

A half hour later, after the lights had been turned off and Zach's head was resting upon his pillow, he dreamed about having a home of his own. A big two-story with wood siding and a porch running all around. It was easy to picture the children playing on a wide green lawn. They all had the Dalton dark hair. The boys would eventually grow into tall men and the girls would become as beautiful as their late grandmother. As for his wife, Zach couldn't visualize her face. Yet he could clearly smell her sweet scent and hear her tinkling laugh.

How could that be? He'd not yet met his wife. He didn't have the foggiest clue how she smelled or how her laugh sounded.

Lydia.

That was her scent. Her laugh.

The reality caused Zach to sit straight up, and as he stared into the dark shadows, he realized his brow was damp, his heart beating hard.

Grabbing the pillow, he punched it in frustration, then tossed it back to the mattress.

"Zach? What's the matter over there?"

"Nothing," Zach said with a grunt. "Go to sleep."

Booker muttered something, then turned his back toward Zach and fell silent.

Releasing a long breath, Zach wiped a hand over his face, then forced himself to lie back down on the bed. Yet even as he stretched into a comfortable position, he knew it would be a long time before he could rid his mind of the perky newspaper woman and fall asleep.

Chapter Four

By noon the next day, Zach had made up his mind. The sooner he started his campaign for a wife, the sooner he'd forget all about Lydia. After a date with one of the lovely applicants, he was certain he'd never spend another night dreaming of Lydia's sparkling laugh or the heavenly way she smelled. No, sir, all those thoughts were going to be erased with visions of a new lady.

After randomly choosing the photo of a woman named Tracy, he called the number written on the back and was greeted by a sweet, agreeable-sounding voice that made setting up a date more than easy.

That night, as he drove into Kalispell to meet his date, he was both anxious and eager. He'd dressed in his best jeans and boots and worn a Western shirt that played up his blue eyes. Or so his aunt Rita had told him. He'd even slapped on a good measure of aftershave just to make sure the scent of cow manure hadn't followed him from the feedlot.

But now as Zach sat with his date at a nice restaurant, he wondered why the excitement he'd been feeling earlier was fading as fast as a winter sunset. It wasn't that the young woman wasn't attractive. Nearly everything about her was nigh to perfect. With long blond hair and big brown eyes, she was beautiful. She was even wearing the kind of thing he liked on a woman. A pale pink lacy dress that was as feminine as it was sexy. So why wasn't he feeling some sort of connection to her? You'd think he'd be dreaming of kissing those plump lips. Instead, he was wondering how he could cut their date short without offending her.

"Do you like living in Rust Creek Falls?" she asked as they began to eat the main course. "A friend and I drove up there one weekend and we both found it a bit hayseed."

Zach inwardly bristled. "I happen to like it very much. The people are hardworking, friendly folks. That's the main thing."

The smile she gave him was so sugary Zach very nearly lost his appetite.

"Oh, don't get me wrong, Zach. I wasn't talking about the people. Just the town itself. Compared to living here in Kalispell, there's not much to do in the way of entertainment. Don't you find it boring?"

He found her boring. That was what he really wanted to say. Instead, he promised himself to make sure the next woman he called would not be a city gal.

"No. I don't find it boring at all," he said as he sliced into the prime rib. "As a matter of fact, I'm not that interested in finding fun things to do. I'm more interested in finding a wife and settling down. Raising a bunch of kids."

Her eyes widened and she cleared her throat. "Well, yes, I noticed in your ad that those were your goals. But I thought—"

"You thought what?" Zach prompted.

A sheepish expression crossed her face and Zach suddenly realized this search for a wife wasn't going to go as quickly and smoothly as he'd hoped.

"That you were using that as a ruse—as a means to meet women."

Shaking his head, Zach reached for his wineglass. As far as he was concerned, he wished he could down the whole bottle and forget this night had ever happened.

"Listen, Tracy, I'm serious about becoming a husband and father. You're not serious about marriage?"

She coughed so hard Zach thought she was going to lose her breath. "Are you kidding? I'm only twenty-three! It'll be years before I want to saddle myself with a husband and kids. I'm sorry, Zach. Really, I am."

He swallowed another long drink of wine. "May I ask why you sent your information to me? Why you agreed to this date?"

Her face reddened. "Well, I saw your photo, Zach, and I was—uh—intrigued. I thought it would be fun to date a cowboy just once."

Yeah. Just once. If Zach's brothers heard about this, they'd never let him hear the last of it. But his brothers weren't going to hear the truth about this date, he promised himself. Nor was anyone else.

Naturally, the very next morning at the breakfast table, the first thing out of Cole's mouth was a question about Zach's date.

"So how did it go, brother?" he asked between bites

of pancakes and sausage. "Are you headed to the jewelers today to pick out an engagement ring?"

"Don't be crude, Cole," Aunt Rita reprimanded her nephew. "Give Zach a chance."

Determined to keep his cool, Zach gave his brother a sly grin. "Don't worry, Cole. I'll let you know when it's time to get out your wedding duds."

"Cole doesn't have any wedding duds," Garrett teased. "All of his clothes are stained with bull—uh, manure."

"Seriously, Zach. Did you enjoy your date?" Booker asked.

About as much as a man enjoys being bit by a rattlesnake, Zach thought grimly. Reaching for his coffee, he gave his older brother a wide smile. "Sure. It was nice. She was very beautiful. But I don't think I'll be dating her again."

Everyone at the table was suddenly staring at him. The only saving grace was that his father and uncle Charles had already eaten their breakfast and left the kitchen.

"Why?" Booker pressed him. "Not your type?"

At least that was one question he could answer honestly, Zach thought. "No. Too much of a city girl for my taste."

"Then send her my way," Cole spoke up. "My specialty is taming city girls."

Clearing her throat in a disapproving way, Aunt Rita rose from the table and carried her plate over to the sink.

Across the table from Zach, Garrett let out a loud chuckle.

"Cole, you little squirt," he said with a wicked grin.

"You've never dated a city girl in your life. Now me, I can make her forget about all those bright lights."

Zach had no ambition in changing or taming a woman into his ideal. No, he wanted her to be herself, someone who would fit just right in his arms and in his life.

A week later, Lydia was sitting at her desk trying to work on a cartoon for tomorrow's edition, but her attention wasn't cooperating. It continued to stray to the newspaper lying to one side of her desk. Zach Dalton's Search: Love or Marriage?

The provocative headline of the *Rust Creek Ramblings* column had grabbed Lydia's attention the moment she'd opened the paper yesterday. Now, a day later, she still couldn't get the opinion piece out of her mind.

Even though Lydia was the assistant manager at the *Gazette*, she had no idea who'd taken over as the anonymous Rambler since Kayla Dalton had married Trey Strickland and retired from the job. The writer could be male or female and possibly an in-house coworker. Or it could very well be an outside contributor. Either way, he or she considered Zach's advertisement for a wife clever, but lacking all romance.

Was love and romance really unimportant to Zach? Lydia didn't know why the question continued to pester her. If he was willing to settle for a loveless marriage, it wasn't anything to her. And yet the idea left her feeling totally bummed. Zach was too nice and too warm to marry a woman just for the sake of having a wife and kids.

A loud tapping on the front door of the office had Lydia suddenly looking up, and she groaned as she spotted the mailman motioning to her.

Leaving her desk, she went over and pulled open the plate glass door. "What's wrong, Barney? The door wasn't locked."

"Sorry, Lydia," the balding, middle-aged man apologized. "I thought I'd better ask you about this mail before I brought it into the front."

She frowned. "What do you mean?"

"Well, there's a lot of it," he explained. "Boxes of it."

"Then Curtis must have ordered supplies for the printing department." Unconcerned, she waved a hand down the sidewalk, toward the back of the building. "Just take the boxes around to the back entrance and knock on the door. Some of the guys there will help you with them."

Annoyed now, Barney shook his head. "This stuff isn't supplies for the newspaper. It's all going to that Dalton fellow. The one advertising for a wife. What the heck was that guy thinking, anyway? He's sure causing me a big headache."

Sighing heavily, Lydia joined the mailman on the sidewalk. "Where is the mail? I'll help you carry it in here."

Barney pointed to a mail jeep parked a few feet away. Next to it was a dolly cart stacked with two big boxes and a smaller one on top.

"You've got to be kidding!" she exclaimed. "You brought in a big box of stuff for him yesterday. All of that came into the post office this morning?"

"Yep, there's at least fifty pounds of it. I was hoping these women would slow down with the letters and packages, but instead of letting up, it's growing!"

"So I see," Lydia told him while wondering what Curtis was going to think of this fresh batch of mail. He was already grumbling about it taking up too much room in the office, along with too much of her time.

"Well, maybe the guy will get hitched soon and all of this will come to a stop. That's what I'm hoping for," Barney muttered as he headed toward the loaded dolly.

Zach soon married? Lydia didn't want to contemplate that idea.

She trotted after the mailman. "That would be sort of quick, don't you think? The advertisement has only been running for a week and a half."

"Not in my opinion. The first day I laid eyes on my wife I knew she was The One. Been wedded bliss ever since. That was ten years ago. See, I didn't need Homer Gilmore's punch to make things happen or a newspaper ad, either."

Bully for you, Lydia wanted to say. Instead, she bit her tongue and proceeded to help the mailman maneuver his load through the doorway.

"Just put them over there in the corner, Barney. By that other box of mail. I'll move them later." To where, Lydia didn't have the foggiest idea. She'd not seen Zach since the day he'd taken her to lunch and his absence had surprised her. She'd expected him to show up on a frequent basis to pick up his mail. Now, as she looked at the stacked boxes, she could only wonder if he'd changed his mind about the whole endeavor.

With several grunts and groans, Barney dumped the boxes and was on his way out when Joanna Walters, a longtime friend of Lydia's, pushed her way through the door. Both her arms were wrapped around a white box, emitting the delicious scent of just-baked pastries.

Joanna stepped out of Barney's way and carefully

made her way over to Lydia's desk. "Can I set this next to your computer? I hate to put it on the floor."

Lydia walked over to the young woman, who worked at Daisy's Donut Shop over on North Broomtail Road, a few blocks from the *Gazette* office.

"What is this? Did Curtis actually order something from Daisy's to treat his employees?" She lifted the lid to see rows of assorted doughnuts, bear claws, apple fritters and fried pies. "Mmm. Smells delicious. I hope I'm not inhaling calories."

"Sorry, Lydia. Don't let your mouth water. These aren't for you or anyone at the office. Some woman ordered them to be delivered to Zach Dalton in care of the *Gazette*." The tall blonde pulled a sealed envelope from the back pocket of her jeans and thrust it at Lydia. "This goes with it. I don't know who the woman was, but she looked like she'd just stepped out of a spa. You know the kind. Perfect nails, skin as smooth as cream and hair with more shine than a polished shoe."

"Doesn't sound like anyone from Rust Creek Falls," Lydia said while wondering what Zach would think about the woman. He might be impressed with her looks, but he wouldn't appreciate the fact that she'd purchased the desserts from a bakery rather than baking them herself.

Joanna groaned. "How can you tell anymore? There've been so many women flocking to Rust Creek Falls lately. What with the Gal Rush going on a few years back and then Travis going on *The Great Roundup*, and now Zach advertising for a wife, it's like they think this is the only place in the universe to find a husband!"

"Zach's search for a wife has caused quite a stir," Lydia agreed. "Every place I go around town people are talking about it. Females from eight to eighty seem to have an opinion about Zach and his idea to find a wife."

She carried the box of pastries over to the cartons of mail and added it to the stack.

"Mom thinks it's wonderful," Joanna said. "She wishes Dad had been that forthright about what he wanted in a wife. It took her a long time to learn what made him happy. And by the time she figured it out, she didn't care."

Like Lydia, Joanna wasn't married, but a few years ago she'd come very close to walking down the aisle. That was, until she'd discovered her fiancé had cheated on her with multiple women. Understandably, Joanna now had a major trust issue with men.

Walking back over to her desk, Lydia asked her childhood friend, "What do you think about it?"

Shrugging, Joanna said, "Well, I don't suppose he could do any worse than I did. I dated for years before I finally became engaged. And look what all that slow, careful thinking got me!" She let out a cynical snort. "If you ask me, no matter how you go about it, getting a spouse that really loves you is a crapshoot. I go home to my cat and count myself lucky."

She waggled her fingers at Lydia. "I've got to get back to work. We're shorthanded today and I've already been here too long."

Joanna hurried toward the door and Lydia called out, "Let's have lunch one day soon."

Joanna waved in agreement, then hurried on.

The bell over the door had hardly quit jingling when Curtis appeared from the back. He sniffed, then looked straight at the box of pastries.

"Did someone just deliver food?"

"Joanna brought some things from Daisy's Donut Shop. Unfortunately they aren't for us. I mean—anyone here at the paper."

Trying to ignore his scowl, she sat down at her desk and reached for the sketch pad she'd been using to image a cartoon character.

"Oh. So why are they here?"

Even though she'd had nothing to do with this overflow of mail and presents to Zach Dalton, she felt herself wearing a guilty blush anyway.

"Zach Dalton. They're from a want-to-be bride. And so is all that stuff in the boxes Barney just delivered."

Behind his black-rimmed glasses, Curtis's eyes widened. "Have you looked to see what's in those boxes? For all we know, some scorned lady might have sent him a snake!"

"No, I haven't looked. That's rather private—don't you think?"

"If Zach Dalton wanted his personal life to be private, then he sure as heck wouldn't have put his wants and wishes in the newspaper!"

Seeing Curtis was getting more than a little annoyed, Lydia jumped to her feet and began to sift through the items in the cardboard boxes.

"Just tons of letters and a bunch of baked goods. It appears these women are trying to show off their cooking skills." Lydia placed a foil-covered pie to one side and reached for a small clear plastic container. "Oh, here's something interesting. A pair of knitted baby booties. A surefire way to convince him she's sincere about motherhood, I suppose."

Curtis snorted. "Ridiculous! I've never seen so many women making fools of themselves over a man. Why, just this morning when I was eating breakfast at the Gold Rush, I had a woman approach me and ask if I could introduce her to Zach Dalton. I don't even know the man!"

Her boss wasn't a man with a short temper. But the tone in his voice said it was quickly becoming stretched to the breaking point. Turning to him, she reasoned in her most placating voice, "They associate him to the newspaper, which is a good thing. Don't you think?"

Curtis threw up his hands in surrender. "All right, I'll admit paper sales have gone up in the past few days. But that doesn't mean we have to turn this office into a dumping ground for the man's mail! Load up that stuff and get it out of here. And I mean everything."

Her mouth fell open. "But this is US Mail. We can't just throw it away."

"Lydia, don't be daft. You're not going to throw it away. You're going to deliver it to the…the wife hunter."

Curtis started out of the room and Lydia dared to call after him. "But Zach lives out on the Circle D Ranch. You want me to drive all the way out there?"

He waved a backward hand at her. "Whatever. I don't want to offend the man by demanding he come after the stuff. Just take the afternoon off if you need to and get the junk out of here."

Curtis might consider the letters and messages and gifts as junk, Lydia thought, but Zach saw it all as his future.

That morning when Lydia had dressed for work, the outside temperature had been rather cool. So she'd opted to wear a long-sleeved button-down shirt with her jeans, rather than her usual T-shirt with a slogan scrawled across the front. But now as she drove toward the Circle D, her car loaded down with Zach's mail, she couldn't help but feel a little self-conscious about wearing the pale blue Oxford. The day had warmed into summerlike weather and she could only hope Zach didn't get the idea that she was trying to gussy herself up to catch his attention. She couldn't think of anything more embarrassing.

Have you lost your mind, Lydia? Zach Dalton isn't going to notice what you're wearing. He isn't going to see anything about your appearance. Willing women from all over creation are sending him stacks of mail and gifts. He'd never consider you as bride material. He'd never even think of you as a date. Much less a wife!

As Lydia drove along the rural road toward Charles and Rita's ranch, she did her best to push the demoralizing voice from her mind. She heard enough of that kind of talk from her mother. She didn't need more of it. And anyway, she wasn't secretly pining for special attention from Zach. No, indeed. He was merely a friend and nothing more.

Eventually, Lydia passed through the entrance of the Circle D and continued to drive along a narrow road bordered on both sides with barbed wire fence. The road cut through open meadowland dotted with a mixture of hardwood and evergreens. Along the way, herds of Black Angus cattle could be seen grazing on the short grass and dozing beneath the shade trees.

She was taking in the landscape and wondering how much farther it was to the ranch house, when she spotted a truck up ahead. The vehicle appeared to be parked on the side of the road, and as she drew close enough to discern the color and make, she decided it closely resembled the Ford Zach had parked near the *Gazette* the day they'd had lunch together.

Slowing the car to a crawl, she spotted a bare-chested man near the fence. Sweat glistened on his broad shoulders as he plunged a set of posthole diggers deep into the earth.

Was that Zach? The height and dark hair resembled him, but she hardly knew what Zach looked like half-undressed. The man could very well be one of the other Dalton men.

Deciding the only way to find out was to stop, Lydia parked a few feet in front of the truck and climbed from the car.

As soon as she started in the man's direction, he looked over his shoulder toward her and Lydia immediately recognized Zach's face. All at once, her heart leaped with unexpected pleasure.

She waved at him and he waved back.

"Hi, Zach!"

While she walked over to where he was working, Zach jammed the diggers into the partially dug hole. Once he joined her at the fence, he propped an arm atop a fat cedar post.

"Lydia! What in the world are you doing all the way out here?"

Even though she was silently ordering her eyes to focus on his face, she was staring at a bare muscled chest sprinkled with dark hair and tiny rivulets of fresh male sweat.

Clearing her throat, she said, "Actually, my, uh, boss sent me out here to the Circle D to see you."

One brow arched with surprise as he lifted the straw cowboy hat from his head and raked a hand through his damp hair. "That sounds ominous. What's wrong? He wants to quit running my ad?"

Lydia felt her face growing hot and the sensation had nothing to do with his questions. It was the rugged hunk of man standing in front of her that was doing incredibly strange things to her vital signs.

"No. He would never do that." At least, Lydia didn't think Curtis would go that far. Unless the mess of mail being delivered to the newspaper office got worse. "It's your mail. You've received quite a bit of it and Curtis thought it was beginning to get in the way."

"There's actually that much of it? Gosh, I'm really sorry about that, Lydia," he quickly apologized. "I've been planning to go into town and collect it, but things have been extra busy here on the ranch."

And what about all those women who were breathlessly waiting and hoping to receive a call from him? Lydia wondered. Had he already been dating a few of them? A part of her wanted to know, while the other part revolted against the idea of knowing anything about Zach's romantic life.

"Don't worry. I've brought it all with me. But I'm sure there will be more coming. In case you haven't guessed, you're a popular guy."

Instead of looking smug or pleased at the news, Zach's expression turned rueful. "Listen, Lydia, if this whole thing is causing you problems, I'll figure out some other way. I can rent a separate post office box in town and—"

"No! That isn't necessary," she assured him. The mail was the only link she had to Zach. Without it, she'd have no reason to see him again. Lydia wasn't quite ready to say goodbye to her sexy new friend. Not yet. "Don't worry, Zach. I'll deal with it."

He smiled at her and Lydia felt like a snowflake melting on a warm tongue. Helpless and totally at his mercy.

"Thank you, Lydia. You're a real sport."

Sure, that was what she'd always attested to be, Lydia thought wryly. The good sport. The mousy girl who always helped the guy win the glamorous homecoming queen.

"You're welcome," she murmured, then deciding it was time to get to the business at hand, she glanced toward her car. "So what would you like for me to do with all the stuff? I think I should warn you, there's lots of it. My trunk and back seat are loaded."

The news clearly amazed him. "Wow, if that's the case, then maybe you'd better drive it on to the ranch house and I'll follow you." He glanced at his watch. "It's getting on toward noon, anyway. Aunt Rita usually has something prepared for lunch right about now. Would you like to join me and the rest of the family?"

Even though his invitation was offhand, it thrilled her just the same. "Oh, are you sure Rita won't mind an extra mouth to feed?"

"I'm certain she won't mind. The more folks Aunt Rita has around to care for, the better she likes it."

Lydia smiled at him. "Then I accept. Thank you, Zach."

"Great. Let me get my shirt and we'll be on our way."

Chapter Five

Less than five minutes later, they parked at the back of the big ranch house and Lydia helped Zach carry the mail into a long mudroom.

"I'll stack everything over here," Zach suggested while moving to a far corner of the room. "It won't be in the way here and I can move it to my room later tonight."

"Okay," Lydia agreed. "I'll hand everything to you and you stack it."

He shook his head. "You stand back. I can handle this."

Lydia dismissed his suggestion with a laugh and handed him one of the bigger boxes. "In case you haven't noticed, I'm not a fragile violet. In fact, in the gym I can heft a good-sized weight."

"You go to the gym?"

The surprise in his voice had her laughing again.

"Only when I get to feeling guilty about all the burgers I eat at the Gold Rush."

He suddenly lowered his head to one of the boxes and sniffed. "Hmm. Am I wrong? I think I smell food in this thing."

"You're not wrong. And you might want to tell your aunt about the baked goods. They should be eaten or frozen before they ruin."

"Good idea."

Lydia handed him the final box. "Oh, and there's another item among this stuff that you might not—uh—feel comfortable showing to your family," Lydia warned.

He shot her an anxious look. "I hope to heck you don't mean some sort of…aphrodisiac."

Zach's face began to turn bright red and Lydia couldn't stop herself from chuckling.

"No. It's nothing like that. It's more like the end result," she said. "A pair of hand-knitted baby booties. Blue ones. Apparently some woman is very serious about motherhood."

"Whew. I'm relieved it's just booties!" Chuckling along with her, he reached for her arm. "Come on. Let's go have lunch. Hopefully my brothers haven't eaten everything yet."

After washing their hands at a sink in the mudroom, they entered a big kitchen filled with conversation, laughter and the delicious aroma of home-cooked food.

Lydia's attention went straight to a long pine table situated in the middle of the room. On both sides, men were seated on benches and already in the process of filling their plates with fried chicken and hot biscuits. At the end of the table, not far from an industrial-sized gas range, an older woman was quickly rising from her seat.

"Why, Zach, we thought you were still fixing fence. Where did you find such a pretty visitor?"

A big smile on her face, the woman hurried over to them. At the same time, an older man rose from the opposite end of the table to join them.

"Oh, I found her wandering along the road like a little lost dogie," Zach answered his aunt's question. "So I thought she could use a little of your good cooking. Aunt Rita, this is Lydia Grant. She's assistant manager at the *Gazette* in Rust Creek Falls. And, Lydia, this is my aunt Rita and uncle Charles Dalton. They've been generous enough to open their home to us rowdy nephews."

Charles and Rita both gave her hand a warm shake.

"Nice to meet you, Lydia," Charles said. "Come join us at the table. There's always room for one more. I hope you'll excuse us for eating in the kitchen. We reserve the dining room for the evening meal."

"Please, there's no need to apologize," Lydia said to him while thinking the Daltons' kitchen was nearly as big as her whole house.

"Zach, you introduce her to the rest of the family while I fetch you two plates," Rita told him. "Your father isn't here, or Lydia could've met him, too."

Zach led her over to the table, where he quickly introduced her to Charles and Rita's sons, Eli and Derek. "These two are my unmarried cousins," Zach told her, then gestured to the remaining men at the table. "The rest of these guys are my brothers, Garrett, Shawn, Booker and Cole. None of them are married, either. But you can probably see why," Zach teased. "None of them are marriage material."

As Lydia's gaze encompassed the men, all of whom were dressed in rugged cowboy gear, she decided she'd never seen a more handsome group in her life. And, in her opinion, Zach was right there at the top.

"I'm so glad you were thoughtful enough to invite her to lunch," Rita said to Zach as she set a place at the end of the table. "Come on, Lydia, you can sit here at the end next to Cole. Zach, just squeeze in wherever you can find a spot."

"By all means, Lydia can sit by me," Cole said while elbowing his brother Shawn in the ribs as a signal to slide over and make room.

"I should apologize for interrupting your lunch," Lydia said to the group.

Several of the men immediately began to assure her she was a very welcome interruption, while Zach quickly stepped forward to help Lydia onto the bench seat.

"Lydia, I'd much rather have you sitting next to me than Zach," Cole said with a flirty grin. "He eats with his mouth open. Not to mention smells like a feedlot."

"That's too bad," Zach told his brother. "Because I'm going to sit between you and Lydia. She doesn't need to be next to a guy with lecherous hands."

Cole let out a loud groan of protest while the rest of the men around the table guffawed.

Lydia realized they were all teasing, yet the mere idea that Zach wanted to protect her, even from his playful brothers, left her feeling more like a woman than she could ever remember.

After the two of them were settled side by side on the bench, Rita served them iced tea, then resumed her seat.

"If I'm not mistaken," Charles said to Lydia, "our daughter Kayla used to work with you at the paper. I think I remember her mentioning your name."

"That's right," Lydia told him as she helped herself

from the bowls of food being passed to her and Zach. "Kayla worked as a reporter for the *Gazette*, so I'm well acquainted with her. Although, I've not seen her since she married Trey Strickland and they moved to Thunder Canyon. I suppose their little boy is more than a year old now."

Rita beamed. "Little Gil is seventeen months old now and quite a rowdy handful."

"Rowdy or not," Eli spoke up, "Mom loves to spoil her grandson."

"As far as I'm concerned, I don't get to see Gil nearly enough. I'm hoping they can come for a visit soon."

"The holidays will be here before you know it," Charles spoke up. "Kayla will surely want to spend Christmas here at home."

"That means two of us will have to move out to the bunkhouse to make room for her and Trey and the baby," Booker said, then looked across the table to Zach. "We can give up our room for a few days, can't we?"

"Sure," Zach agreed.

Garrett let out a snicker. "Zach won't have to worry about sleeping in the bunkhouse. At the rate he's going, by Christmas he'll be married and moved out."

Lydia refrained from glancing at Zach, but she couldn't help but notice he remained stone silent. His reaction made her wonder if his quest to get married was a sore spot with his brothers or if he was having second thoughts about the whole thing.

"Don't be pestering Zach," Rita admonished. "At least he has the fine intention of having a family."

"Yeah, Garrett," Shawn said. "All you want is a fast car and a Saturday night in the nearest honky-tonk. Nothing admirable about that."

Garrett merely chuckled. "What do you know about it, you little bantam rooster? If a woman came at you, you'd run backward!"

Shawn's face turned red, while Charles leveled a silencing glance at Garrett.

Hoping she wasn't the cause of the caustic banter between the brothers, she attempted to lighten the moment. "Mrs. Dalton, this meal is delicious. Did you do all the cooking?"

"Please call me Rita," the woman insisted, then answered, "Yes, I do all the cooking around here. Raising a big family, I've had plenty of practice through the years. What about you, Lydia? Are you good in the kitchen?"

Lydia let out a self-mocking laugh. "Not at all. I do well heating things in the microwave. I'm much better creating things with a pencil and paintbrush than I am with pots and pans."

"That's interesting," Booker said. "Are you an artist?"

Lydia nodded. "A type of artist. I do graphic design for the paper. And I also do the cartoons."

Grinning wickedly, Cole glanced around Zach's shoulder to Lydia. "You're in luck, Lydia. You don't have to worry about Zach trying to get his clutches on you. He says he's trying to find a wife, but we all know he's really looking to marry a good cook."

Lydia made herself laugh at Cole's joke, but neither he nor anyone else at the table could ever guess the hollowness she was feeling inside.

"Yes, that definitely leaves me out," she said with the cheeriest smile she could muster.

"What about your mother, Lydia?" Rita asked. "Does she do much cooking?"

Lydia very nearly choked as she swallowed a bite of

mashed potato. "No. She never had much time for cooking. You see, my dad left the family when I was really small. So Mom had to work full-time to support us. I grew up on frozen dinners and things out of a can."

Next to her, Lydia could feel Zach eyeing her in a thoughtful way. Apparently single-parent families weren't that common among the Daltons.

"Well, cooking isn't everything," Rita assured her with a gentle smile. "I'd love to be able to paint. Especially landscape art. But I'd be all thumbs. So you see, we each have our talents."

After Rita's kind words, the conversation turned to ranch topics. It was a relief to Lydia not to have to answer any more personal questions and to merely listen to the men discuss cattle and horses and the jobs that needed to be finished before the winter weather arrived.

Once the meal was over, Lydia offered to help Rita with cleaning the kitchen, but the woman insisted she could manage alone.

"Thank you, Lydia, but I've done this for years. It's nothing, really. You go on with Zach and visit with him."

"I, uh, think Zach has plenty to do without being bothered with me," Lydia told her. Then, after thanking her again for the meal, she headed toward the door leading back to the mudroom.

She was almost to her car when she heard someone calling her name and turned to see Zach jogging up to her.

"Sorry. Uncle Charles had me cornered and I didn't see you leave the kitchen. You're not going back to town yet, are you?"

Did he actually want her to stay longer? No. He was simply being polite.

"Yes. I should probably get back to work."

"Is your boss expecting you back this afternoon?"

Her eyes twinkled as she gave him an impish smile. "Actually, he said I could take the rest of the day off if I needed to. Now that you mention it, it might be nice to have an afternoon away from the *Gazette*."

He smiled at her. "Great. I was thinking we might take a little horseback ride. I could show you a bit of the ranch. Do you know how to ride a horse?"

Zach actually wanted to spend some private time with her? Lydia was doing her best not to read anything special into the idea, but her heart was already jumping with foolish joy.

"Oh sure. I've ridden horses before. As long as it isn't a bronc, I can handle it."

Curling his arm around her shoulders, he turned her in the direction of a big barn. "Great. I have the perfect mount for you. Let's go saddle up."

Short minutes later, Lydia was riding a pretty brown-and-white paint mare named Peppy Girl. Alongside her, Zach was tall in the saddle atop a black gelding he called Switch. As they walked the horses in a jaunty clip away from the barn, Lydia was still trying to figure out what had motivated Zach to invite her on this ride.

Sure, he was a mannerly guy and no doubt he was grateful to her for delivering his mail. But that didn't mean he had to take time out of his day to take her on a horseback excursion.

Quit trying to read anything special into this, Lydia. The man is a gentleman. He's simply being nice. Besides, have you forgotten all those women out there just begging for an interview to become his wife?

"Where did you learn to ride a horse, Lydia? You sit a saddle very well."

His compliment drew her out of her reverie and she tossed him a grateful smile. "Thanks. Coming from a cowboy like you, Zach, that means something. Actually, I learned how to ride when I was young. I had friends with horses. One in particular—her name was Bethann—had a great dad with enough patience to teach me how to ride." She sighed. "About the time we entered junior high, her dad's job was transferred and they moved away. After that, I missed her and her family terribly. They were— well, they were like you Daltons. A big, loving bunch."

"Do you still keep in touch with Bethann?"

Lydia shrugged. "I hear from her occasionally. She's married now with three children. She has a far different life than I do."

Was that a wistful sound she heard in her voice? If it was, she definitely hoped Zach hadn't picked up on it. The last thing she wanted was for him to think she was one of his groupies, so enthralled with the idea of becoming his wife that her eyes were blinded with stars.

Zach was as handsome as heck, and the image of him in the saddle was probably the sexiest thing she'd ever envisioned, but that didn't mean he'd make a good husband. Besides, she didn't want a husband. She didn't want to end up like her mother. Unable to hold on to her man, then spending the rest of her life in regret.

"The other day at the Gold Rush you implied you weren't all that keen on marriage and a family. But I happen to think you'd make a great mother."

Zach's comment had her staring at him in comical wonder. "I don't have a maternal bone in my body. At least, I don't think I do. Kids are noisy and rambunctious and needy and all the things that require patience. And most of my friends say I have the mind of a ten-year-old. So that disqualifies me as a mother."

He chuckled. "I don't believe that for a minute. I think you'd know the important things about raising kids. Because I—and don't take offense at this, Lydia—I think you probably missed out on some things as a child. And you'd want to make sure your children didn't miss out on those things."

Like a father? A pair of loving parents, who worked together to make a nice home for their daughter? Lydia had missed out on that and much more. Strange, she thought, how Zach had been the one to understand how that void in her childhood still affected her today.

She chuckled in an effort to lighten the moment. "Well, I don't think there's any danger of me becoming a mother anytime soon. A boyfriend usually comes before marriage and babies. And I have no prospects lined up for the job." She cast him a sly smile. "So how is your hunt for a bride really going? Your brothers were teasing you at lunch, but I'll bet they're all rooting for you to find Mrs. Right."

A wry smile spread his lips. "No luck so far. But I'm working on it."

Lydia had asked only because she thought it was the courteous thing to do. After all, she'd offered to help him in his endeavor. But at this moment she was glad he wasn't elaborating on the subject. Being alone with Zach with the beautiful outdoors surrounding them and the sun shining down on their faces was too perfect to mar with details of his dates.

Turning her attention to the trail ahead of them, she

asked, "So where are we going? Looks like we're headed toward the mountains. Where the falls are located."

"That's right. The Circle D almost reaches the mountains, but it doesn't go nearly as far as the falls."

So far Peppy Girl had been sweet and obedient and Lydia was quickly falling in love with the little mare. As the horses walked along beneath the spreading shade of a copse of elms, she stroked her hand down Peppy Girl's flowing mane and patted the side of her neck.

"When I was getting ready for work this morning, I never imagined I'd be spending the afternoon on a pleasant horseback ride."

Zach grinned. "From what I can see, you could use a little break from the newspaper office."

"It can get hectic," she admitted. "But I like my job. I do so many different things that it never gets boring. What about you? Have you ever wanted to do something other than ranching?"

"No. Never. Taking care of cattle and horses and the land—that's all I've ever known. Ranching runs through Dad's veins and I guess he passed it on to all his sons. Although, we do have other interests and hobbies. Cole is a pretty good carpenter and Garrett is a wizard at fixing anything mechanical."

"And what's your other interest?" she asked with a provocative grin. "Or maybe you'd rather not say."

He let out a low chuckle. "No. It's not women, if that's what you're thinking. My other interest doesn't actually stray that far from ranching. I like treating sick or injured animals. Back when we lived in Hardin, I had thought about working part-time as a vet assistant. But it seemed like I was always needed on the ranch, and helping my family has always been my main priority."

She nodded, thinking it had been a long while since she'd met a man who put his family before himself. "So you Daltons ranch as a group?"

"Always," he said, then lifted a brow in playful challenge. "Want to canter over to that far line of trees?"

"I'd love to."

She nudged her heels into Peppy Girl's ribs and clucked to the plucky little mare. The signal sent the mare into a fast canter, and as she and Zach raced their mounts side by side across the wide meadow, Lydia laughed with delight. With the wind slapping her face and whipping her hair into a mess of brown curls, she glanced over to see Zach was laughing, too. And suddenly the shared moment became something she'd put away in her memory, never to be forgotten.

When they reached the tree line, Zach reined in Switch to a jarring halt and Lydia quickly followed suit. While the horses danced and blew from the short run, Lydia exclaimed, "Wow! That was fun! I'd almost forgotten how exhilarating it is to ride a horse fast."

"That was definitely fast." Zach slipped from his saddle and, with Switch's reins clutched safely in one hand, moved over to her. "Let me help you down and we'll rest for a few minutes."

Lydia hardly needed help getting down from the saddle, but she wasn't about to object. Having Zach's hands firmly planted at the sides of her waist as he eased her to the ground was more than enough to leave her breathless.

"Thank you," she said, hoping he couldn't see how rapidly her heart was beating beneath her blue shirt. Or if he did, he'd put it down to the fast ride they'd just taken. "This is beautiful. Is that a little creek over there?"

"It is. I'll tie the horses and we'll walk over," he told her.

At the bank of the shallow creek, the shade grew deep and cool. Above their heads, Lydia could hear birds chattering and nearby the wind whispered gently through the boughs of a pine tree.

"Too bad there isn't a fallen tree trunk around here that we could sit on," Zach said as he glanced around the shadowy glade. "There's a big rock over there. Let's share it."

She followed him over to the boulder, which was big enough for both of them to sit on and still leave a bit of space between them.

Once she'd settled herself comfortably on the rock, she swiped back her tangled hair and let out a sigh of contentment. "This is so lovely, Zach. Thank you for bringing me here."

He pulled off his hat and placed it on the ground. Lydia found herself studying the way his dark hair flopped loosely onto his forehead. What would it be like, she wondered, to run her fingers through his hair? To touch her hands to his face, her lips to his? Just the thought of it very nearly made her shiver with longing.

"You're very welcome. It's the least I can do to pay you back for delivering all that mail to me."

All that mail. Oh yes, how could she forget the piles of letters and gifts from strangers who wanted to become his wife?

Deliberately steering the conversation away from the subject, Lydia said, "I noticed your parents weren't at lunch. I would have liked to have met them."

There was a brief pause before he replied and Lydia wondered whether Zach's relationship with his parents had become strained over his newspaper ad. He'd already mentioned his father had disapproved, but what about his mother? No doubt she'd spoken her mind about her son's unorthodox method of choosing a wife.

"Dad is out looking at land with a real estate agent. He's trying to find a piece of property with enough acreage for us to build a ranch like Dalton's Gulch—the one we had back in Hardin. One big enough for all of us brothers to build homes of our own."

"I see. So living with Charles and Rita is a temporary situation?"

"That's right. Dad isn't in any hurry about buying, though. He wants to make sure he looks at everything available before he makes a final move."

"That's understandable. You can't hurry such a big decision. Unless some perfect paradise suddenly appeared around here."

He sighed and Lydia could hear his impatience. "You're right. But I wish a perfect paradise would show up soon. Having six extra men jammed in Uncle Charles and Aunt Rita's house is a pain for everyone."

"I've only just met Charles and Rita. But while we were eating lunch, I didn't get the impression they were under a strain. In fact, both of them appeared to be enjoying all of you."

Grimacing, Zach picked up a pebble from the ground and tossed it toward a nearby tree trunk. "That's because Uncle Charles likes having his brother around. All those years we lived in Hardin they didn't have a chance to visit each other that much. Now they're making up for lost time."

Attempting to be diplomatic, Lydia said, "Well, there are times when it's good for families to be together. So what about your mother? Is she back in Hardin waiting for your father to buy a place?"

His face suddenly turned pale and stiff, and when he spoke, his voice was so strained Lydia could barely hear his words.

"I guess you could say she's still in Hardin," he said. "But not in the way you think. My mother is buried in Hardin."

Zach's admission took her by complete surprise, and as she recognized the grief on his face, she wished she could kick herself for bringing up the subject of his mother.

"Oh. I didn't know, Zach," she said gently. "Coming from a person who works at a newspaper, that sounds ridiculous. But we mostly deal in local news. If your mother's obituary was in our newspaper, I didn't remember or make the connection to you. Did you lose your mother recently?"

Without looking her way, he nodded. "Back in January. Something sparked a brush fire near Dalton's Gulch. The weather had been extremely dry and the flames were out of control before anything could be done. The fire destroyed everything in its path. Our livestock, the barns and even our home. Mom didn't make it out."

Stunned by his revelation, Lydia stared at him. How had he and his family dealt with such devastation? "I'm so sorry, Zach. I can't imagine—it's too tragic for me to comprehend. We hear about wildfires in the area, especially at this time of the year. But I've never really known anyone who's suffered through one. Was anyone else in your family injured?"

He shook his head. "All of us guys were busy hauling feed out to the herds, so when the fire broke out, we were a long distance away from the house. That put us on the outside of the fire. The house and the working ranch yard were directly in its path. We're not sure if Mom was trying to save things and stayed too long. Or if she didn't realize the place was on fire until it was on top of her. At this point, I guess it doesn't matter. Either way, we lost her."

All at once, Lydia understood so many things that hadn't been clear before. Like why Zach and his family had suddenly moved in with Charles and Rita when there was hardly enough room to accommodate everyone. Moreover, she believed she was beginning to see why Zach was in such a hurry to find a wife and make a home for himself. He'd lost his home and his mother. He wanted to replace that void in the only way he knew how.

Reaching over, Lydia placed a comforting hand on his forearm. "No one has to tell me you're a strong man, Zach. I can see that for myself. You'll never have your mother back, but you'll move forward and be happy. I'm certain of that."

His blue eyes studied her for long moments and Lydia wondered what he was thinking. That she looked a mess or that an airhead like her had no business trying to counsel anyone?

"Thank you for that, Lydia."

Lydia watched as he glanced toward the slow-moving water in the creek and absently touched fingers to the bolo tie suspended at his throat. The black braided cord was held together by an irregular-shaped slide created from a hunk of tiger eye and surrounded by engraved silver. Now that Lydia thought about it, she'd never seen him without the piece and she had to admit that the tie looked very sexy and Western on him.

"Losing Mom has been brutal, Lydia. For a long time I refused to even think about the future—I didn't want to think about it without her. But after a while, just see-ing Dad and my brothers moving on and trying to get back to a normal existence made me see I couldn't live the rest of my life in mourning."

Her heart was aching for him, and even though it was futile, she desperately wished she could take away all the hurt and loss he'd experienced these past months.

"I'm sure you were very close to your mother," she ventured to say.

A sad smile touched his face. "Yes. Very close. I like to think I was her favorite son. But in truth, Mom loved all of her sons equally." He gestured to the piece of tiger eye suspended from his neck. "Mom gave me this tie for my twenty-first birthday. Now the tie means even more to me."

The wistful tone in his voice put a lump in her throat, and before she realized what she was about to do, she reached over and rolled one end of the black cord be-tween her thumb and forefinger.

"The tie looks like a part of you, Zach. And I like it," she said softly while forcing her fingers to move back from him.

His smile deepened and she was relieved to see the gloom on his face was disappearing.

"Thanks, Lydia. I guess now you're probably think-ing I must have been a momma's boy. But it really wasn't that way. She was a good listener and I could tell her anything. And when something was bothering me, she could always make it better. She and Dad were perfect together. After thirty-plus years of marriage they were still crazy in love and devoted to each other. What they had was special and I…I want that same thing, Lydia. My brothers don't come out and say it, but I get the feeling they think I'm corny and too sentimental and I need to grow up. But I don't care what they think. I want to be happy—in my own way."

Nodding, she rose to her feet and walked to the edge of the creek bank. The still water looked cool and inviting and she wished she had time to kick off her boots and dangle her feet in the stream. How nice it would be to close her eyes for just a few moments and let herself dream, of the future she'd always wanted. A life with a loving man—like Zach. But Zach would soon belong to someone else.

"Going after your dream isn't corny, Zach. As for your mother, it's terrible that you lost her. But you're also lucky that you had her for all those years. You have memories to carry in your heart. And things—like your bolo tie. All I have from my father is a couple of grainy photographs of him holding me as a baby. He left before I was old enough to remember anything about him. And when I try to ask my mother about him, she's so resentful that everything she says is jaded. And I guess it's fairly obvious that he wasn't a responsible man, but at some point she must have loved him. It would be nice to hear something decent about my father or anything that would give me a hint at his personality. It's like I never had a father."

He walked up beside her and Lydia inwardly shivered as his hand gently curved over her shoulder and gave it a warm squeeze.

"I'm sorry, Lydia. That kind of loss is something I wouldn't know about. But I'll tell you one thing, you didn't deserve what he gave you—which was obviously nothing."

She gave him a lopsided smile. "I've learned not to

lose sleep over it, Zach. And I'm sorry I even brought it up. I guess hearing you talk about family got me to thinking about my lack of one."

His blue eyes took on a soft gleam as they roamed over her face and Lydia was suddenly and acutely aware that the two of them were entirely alone. And the urge to rest her cheek against the middle of his strong chest was so strong she had to fight like crazy to keep from giving in to it.

"You're very easy to talk to, Lydia," he said gently. "I can't explain it, but I can tell you things that I can't just say to anyone. I hope you feel the same way about me. In fact, I was just thinking we ought to do this again sometime."

Lydia was forced to cough in order to dislodge the breath of air stuck in her throat. "This? You mean go riding?"

He shrugged. "Well, sure. Or just spending time together."

As in two friends spending time together? she wondered. Or did he mean as a date?

She was frantically trying to decide how to reply in a way that wouldn't make her look like a fool, when his cell phone suddenly rang.

Pulling the phone from his shirt pocket, he said, "Excuse me, Lydia. Give me a moment to answer this."

He took a couple of steps away from her and answered the ring. As he began to speak, the flirty tone of his voice left no doubt in Lydia's mind that the caller was one of his classified-ad women. He'd never talked to her in that tone, Lydia thought. Which clearly meant he'd never viewed her as wife material. And he never would. She was as certain of that as she was that the evening sun would go down behind the western horizon.

"Yes. That sounds great," he was saying in a low, sultry voice. "Eight o'clock. No later."

He ended the call, then, without glancing in her direction, slipped the phone back into his shirt pocket.

If he was feeling a bit awkward about the phone call, Lydia could have assured him she felt far more uncomfortable.

"Uh—sorry about the interruption, Lydia. But I needed to answer that one."

The sky could have opened up with rain and it wouldn't have looked any drearier to Lydia than it did at this moment. So much for having a special horseback ride with Rust Creek Fall's newest eligible bachelor, she thought ruefully.

"No problem. That's what your newspaper ad is all about. Making dates. Finding the right girl. I understand."

The grateful smile he cast in her direction very nearly made Lydia want to scream. She didn't want him to feel grateful to her. She wanted him to look at her and want her in the most basic way a man wants a woman. She might not be a good cook or have a tall, willowy figure. And the only way her hair would ever be straight was if she fried it with a flatiron until it was stiff. Yet she wanted him to see her as a woman who could fulfill everything he was searching for in a wife. Like love, devotion and a houseful of kids.

"Thanks, Lydia. You're a real sport."

Swiping a hand through her tumbled hair, she started walking in the direction of the tied horses. "If you're ready, Zach, I really need to be getting back to town. Even though Curtis told me to take the afternoon off, I have a jillion things I need to catch up on. And I'm sure you need to return to your fence building."

He picked up his hat and tugged the brim low on his forehead. "Yeah. Sure. Work is always waiting."

He had it partially right, Lydia decided. Work was always waiting. But in his case, the women were waiting, too.

They walked the short distance back to the horses, and when Zach came around to give her a hand up in the saddle, Lydia did her best to steel herself from his touch. Letting herself fall for this guy would be worse than stupid.

Her brain seemed to have already recognized that dismal fact. Now if she could just get her heart to heed the warning, she wouldn't have a thing to worry about.

Except how to keep from breaking apart when she watched Zach walk down the aisle to marry another woman.

Chapter Six

Of all the women Zach had dated so far on his quest to find a bride, Eva-Rose Armstrong had to be the closest fit to what he was looking for in a wife. Beautiful, with long blond hair and blue eyes, she was tall and slender and incredibly feminine. Dressed in a long lacy skirt and a pair of turquoise cowgirl boots, she not only looked like a dream but smelled like one, too. On top of that, she was extremely nice.

So why wasn't Zach feeling the urge to take her into his arms? For the past three hours during dinner and a movie in Kalispell, he'd been asking himself that question over and over. Now, as they strolled hand in hand along the moonlit path to her doorstep, he still couldn't come up with an answer that made sense.

Think hard, Zach. The reason you can't get warmed up to Eva-Rose, or any other woman, is because your mind is already stuck on one particular female. All you can see is a head of brown curls, an impish little face with dimpled cheeks and blue eyes that sparkle with a zest for life.

"This has been an enjoyable evening for me, Zach," Eva-Rose told him. "Thank you for the dinner and movie. Maybe we can do it again—if you'd like."

Even though he gave her a warm smile, his mind was already wondering how much longer he could continue with the endless dating. A week and a half had passed since Lydia had delivered his mail to the Circle D, and during that time Zach had gone out with seven different women. None of them had created any kind of spark in him. As for his date with Eva-Rose this evening, he'd started out with high hopes. How could she not fit his bill for a wife? She even worked in Daisy's Donut Shop, a prime indication she'd be a good cook. He knew first-hand that she was a great baker because her pies tasted like a slice of heaven. And yet as he gazed down at her pretty face, the pace of his pulse was so slow he could have easily taken a nap. And unfortunately his libido was just as sleepy.

"It's been very nice, Eva-Rose. I'm flattered a girl like you would even agree to go out with me." Which was certainly true. In spite of the tons of messages and letters and gifts women were piling on him, most of the senders didn't have the class or elegance Eva-Rose possessed.

Her quiet laugh said she found his comment hard to believe.

"You've been causing quite a stir in Rust Creek Falls," she said. "Everyone is talking about your search for a bride."

"Being a Dalton, I can't let my cousin Travis outdo me

by getting engaged and getting on *The Great Roundup*," he joked, then deciding he'd better make sure she understood, he added, "I'm teasing, Eva-Rose. Travis and his TV gig have nothing to do with me seeking a wife."

"I never thought it did." Smiling, she gestured toward her front door. "Would you like to come in for coffee or a soda?"

This sweet, beautiful woman was offering him an opportunity to know her better, but still Zach hesitated. Something had to be terribly broken inside him, he decided. Why else would he feel like he'd been bridled and a hand kept reining him in, refusing to let him make a serious move toward any woman?

"Uh, I hope you won't mind, Eva-Rose, but I'll have to take a rain check on that. It's getting late and I have lots of work facing me in the morning. Weaning time is starting on the ranch. We're getting everything ready before the weather changes."

"No problem," she said. "I'll give you that rain check."

She rose up on her toes and kissed his cheek. Zach realized he'd look like a fool, or worse, if he didn't take advantage of the moment and give her a proper good-night kiss.

With his hands lightly holding her shoulders, he settled his lips over hers and tried to put as much enthusiasm into the kiss as he could muster. But instead of enjoying the pleasant experience and letting the sensation carry him away, he began to think. Way too much.

With his eyes squeezed tightly shut, he continued to move his mouth over hers while desperately hoping to feel some sort of jolt. He wanted excitement to ripple through him, passion to explode inside him. Instead, his mind was stuck, going round and round in working mode.

Oh hell, what was wrong with him? Had his libido gone totally dead?

The questions pounded inside his brain, forcing him to end the kiss and lift his head. When he looked down at her, he was so frustrated it was all he could do to make himself smile.

"Good night, Eva-Rose. We'll talk soon."

She'd barely had time to say good-night before Zach hurried back to his truck and started the engine.

As he drove toward the Circle D, he suddenly wished he knew where Lydia lived, or at the very least, had her cell number. Even though it was getting late, talking to her right now was the very thing he needed. Hearing her voice, seeing her smile, would make him feel better about everything.

But he couldn't run to Lydia with his problems. He was a grown man and she had her own life to lead. And from everything she'd said, she wasn't looking to include a man in her future plans anytime soon. Besides, bubbly Lydia with her T-shirts and jeans wasn't his type. Eva-Rose was exactly the kind of woman he wanted for a wife. Now, *she* would make a house into a perfect home.

So why wasn't he back at Eva-Rose's, having coffee and getting cozy with the woman? Why wasn't he trying a second or third kiss?

Zach didn't want to answer those questions. In fact, he didn't want to think about them at all. Otherwise, he might decide his entire plan to find a wife was rapidly swirling down the drain.

The next day Lydia hung up the telephone with a weary sigh and turned her attention back to the computer screen on her desk. For the past two hours, she'd been trying to create a graphic design for a large advertisement, but between an unusual number of customers walking in and the phone's incessant ringing, she hadn't made much progress on the task. And the fact that her mind kept straying to one tall, dark-haired cowboy wasn't helping matters, either.

Yesterday morning, Lydia had stopped by Daisy's Donut Shop to splurge on a glazed apple fritter, but she'd ended up getting more than a pastry and a cup of coffee. Nanette, a young waitress working behind the counter, had been practically bursting to spread the news that her coworker Eva-Rose Armstrong was going on a date with Zach Dalton. Yes! The dreamy Zach Dalton who was searching for a wife!

Feeling slightly ill, Lydia had hurried out of the doughnut shop without seeing the beautiful Eva-Rose, who must have been working in the kitchen at the time. Now, a day later, the idea of Zach and Eva-Rose on a date together was still gnawing at her. Which was stupid. Everyone in town, including Lydia, knew the man had been dating a host of women. For the past week and a half, she'd been hearing all kinds of reports of Zach squiring several lovely ladies around Rust Creek Falls. Not only that, she'd heard he'd practically been attacked by a throng of excited females in front of the gas station on Sawmill Street. Yet none of that news had affected her as much as the notion of him dating Eva-Rose.

Perhaps that was because Lydia was well acquainted with Eva-Rose. And deep down, she recognized the blonde beauty was exactly what Zach was looking for: tall, willowy, young and an excellent cook. And very nice on top of all her other perfect attributes. Lydia figured it wouldn't be long now before wedding bells would be chiming and she'd be throwing rice at Eva-Rose and Zach as they departed for their honeymoon.

"Lydia? Do you think you can beam yourself back to earth?"

Curtis's voice suddenly broke through her dismal thoughts and she turned away from the computer screen to see her boss standing at her desk. From the annoyed look on his face, he must have called out to her more than once.

"Oh, sorry, Curtis. Were you saying something to me?" she asked blankly.

His expression full of sarcasm, he gestured to the empty room. "Do you see anyone else around here?"

Lydia gave him a cheerful smile even though she wanted to throw a paper wad straight at his head. "Not at the moment. But there's been a steady stream of customers in here all morning." She made a backhanded wave to her computer. "I'm trying to put the ad design together for Abbott's Grocery. Something with an autumn theme, like falling leaves or squash. I don't want to do pumpkins because next month is October. That's pumpkin month. Anyway, I keep getting interrupted. Uh—sorry, Curtis—what did you need?"

"Only to tell you that I'm going to walk over to the library and talk to the head librarian about a book drive they're planning. Roberta was supposed to do the reporting, but she just went home with a stomach virus."

Lydia glanced toward the doorway leading to the working area behind the main lobby. Normally, she would have already been in and out of the back offices. If nothing else, just to say hello to everyone. But this morning, she'd hardly had time to take a deep breath.

"Oh. I wasn't aware that Roberta had gone home.

Gee, I hope she feels better soon. Would you like for me to do the thing at the library?" Lydia offered. "I'm not a reporter per se, but I'm sure I could get the information down."

Curtis shook his head. "Thanks, but no. You have more than enough to handle here. When are you going to lunch?"

Lydia glanced at the large-faced watch on her wrist. "I usually go at twelve. That's in thirty minutes. But I can wait until you get back. No problem."

He started toward the door. "There's no need for you to wait on me. Just make sure Jolene is here to handle the phone and be sure to tell her if my phone rings she's not to answer it. That woman can mess up a message worse than anyone I've ever known. Names, dates, times—according to her, those are unimportant facts."

Then how did Jolene ever get a job in Proofing, Lydia wanted to ask him. But she wasn't one to speak out about an employee's track record. Not when she was guilty of making plenty of blunders herself through the years. "She tries, Curtis. But I'll make sure she understands to ignore your calls."

Thankfully, he didn't hang around to say more. As soon as the door closed behind him, Lydia turned back to the ad design and stared at the monitor.

Images of falling leaves? Decorative squash? No. That didn't put a person in the mood to buy food or health and beauty items.

Beauty? That one word bounced around her brain until she unwittingly propped her elbows on the desk and stared off into space. What would happen, she wondered, if she drove over to Abbott's store and shopped for a few things in the beauty department? Something to make her eyes look smoky and her lips peachy and moist. Would that make Zach look at her in a desirable way? The same way he'd probably looked at Eva-Rose last night?

Damn it! There she went again! Letting her mind drift off in left field instead of concentrating on the job right in front of her eyes.

Determinedly, she reined in her wandering thoughts. After several minutes of doodling, drawing and arranging all sorts of banners, designs and images, she pumped her fist triumphantly in the air.

Finally! She had it! Green dollar signs mixed with orange and yellow falling leaves. All together it would represent tumbling autumn prices. Mr. Abbott would have to like it and so would Curtis, she decided.

She quickly went to work creating the design on the screen and was so engrossed in the task that she barely heard the bell over the door ring. When she eventually looked away from her work, she was beyond thrilled to see Zach strolling toward her.

"Hello, Lydia. How's it going?"

She swiveled her chair in his direction and let her eyes feast on the sight of him. He was always as sexy as heck, she thought, but today he was a wicked dream in a black Western shirt and dark blue jeans. His black hat rode low on his forehead, while the tiger eye bolo tie dangled against his broad chest. As her gaze continued to sweep over him, she decided everything about the man oozed sensuality, but today it was the playful grin on his face that was making her heart do silly somersaults.

"Hi, Zach. Everything is great with me. How about you?" Assuming he was there to pick up his mail, she rose from her chair and walked over to a closet where she'd hidden most of the boxes from Curtis's critical eye. "Your mail is still piling up. I'm beginning to think you need a secretary to help you deal with all this stuff. Ever think about picking a woman from one of these letters and hiring her to help?"

"It is beginning to be a job," he agreed. "I fall asleep every night just trying to read through most of it. Tell me, Lydia, are there really that many single women out there who want to get married?"

She tried to laugh, even though the question held little mirth for her. Maybe that was because it was becoming painfully clear she was one of those many single women without any hope of marriage or a family on the horizon.

"From the looks of this mail, it appears that way." She stacked the boxes on the corner of her desk. "Just a minute and I'll print out your email messages. Those seemed to have slowed down. I suppose the majority of women must be thinking a handwritten note will get more attention from you."

Lydia directed her computer to the mail server and the inbox filled with messages. As the printer began to work, she turned her attention back to Zach.

"You haven't been by in a few days," she said. "Is everything okay out at the Circle D?"

"Busy. Very busy. In fact, I should be there right now. We're gathering cows and calves. Getting ready for weaning. But supplies were needed from the farm and ranch store, so I was the one Uncle Charles chose to come after them."

"Lucky you. Gave you a chance to get your mail at the same time." She gathered all the messages from the printer and stuffed them into a manila envelope, which she placed atop the boxes. "There. That's it for now.

Uh—I've been wondering, Zach, do you still want to keep the ad running?"

He looked at her with surprise and for some reason Lydia felt a little embarrassed for asking the question. But taking care of the classified ads was one of her jobs here at the *Gazette*. It was necessary for her to know a customer's intentions.

"Well, sure. Why wouldn't I want to keep it running? I haven't found a wife yet."

Not even after last night's date with Eva-Rose? She wanted to shout with joy and do a pair of exuberant backflips.

"Oh. Well, I just didn't want you to have to pay for something that's unnecessary. I mean—you have stacks and stacks of applicants already. And all the women around here are aware of your search."

He shook his head. "You're right about all of that. But I'd still like to keep it running a bit longer. Someone new might come to town and see it for the first time. And that someone could just be the one I'm looking for. I'd hate to think I missed the chance because I didn't want to pay for the cost of the ad."

She gave him a cheery smile. "Then the ad will definitely stay. Maybe I should outline the whole thing with linked hearts shot with cupid arrows. That might get your ad even more attention."

He let out a good-natured groan. "Oh no! I'm already catching plenty of flak from my brothers over the ad. They'd never let me live that sort of thing down. They'd probably hang the nickname Mr. Valentine on me, or worse!"

Shoving back the cuffs of his shirt, he glanced at

his watch. "It's getting close to lunch. When do you get off?"

"At twelve."

"That's fifteen minutes away." Using one arm, he scooped up the boxes from the corner of her desk. "I have one more chore to do. If you'd like some company, I'll stop by again and pick you up."

Why was he bothering with her? All he had to do to get a lunch date would be to walk down the street or into any restaurant in town. In a matter of moments, he'd have more than one woman trying to hang on to his arm. But why question his motives, she scolded herself. All she needed to do was enjoy his company.

"That would be great, Zach. Fifteen minutes. I'll be ready."

Zach wasn't going to waste time overanalyzing his motive for having lunch with Lydia. The reason was simple, anyway. It was the middle of the day. A time when people generally stopped to eat. He was in town and so was she. There was nothing more to it than that.

Except that after he'd gotten home last night from his date with Eva-Rose, he'd spent hours tossing and turning, choking the life out of his pillow, and wondering why he couldn't get Lydia's sweet face out of his mind.

But now in the light of day, with the late summer sun shining down on the little town of Rust Creek Falls, he decided life was too good to worry about anything. Even that little matter of finding a wife.

Twenty minutes later, with Lydia safely buckled into the passenger seat of his truck and a sack of fast food balanced on the console between them, Zach drove west toward the city park.

"I hope you don't mind," he told her, "but I've already bought us lunch to-go from the Gold Rush. I thought it might be nice to eat in the park today. The weather is perfect and the fresh air is good for you."

Lydia chuckled. "I especially need the fresh air today. I've had a very hectic morning."

"Lots of news to write about? Or just crabby customers like Mr., uh, what was his name? Tuttle?"

She laughed again and Zach was amazed by how much better the sound made him feel. Her laughter always made him smile, always reminded him of the special joys of life.

"Thankfully, Mr. Tuttle didn't come in this morning. Actually, all the customers were nice, but there were so many and the phone has been ringing and ringing. As for the news, I actually don't write news pieces. Roberta collects the news and Artemis—we call him Artie— does most of the writing. Along with Colette. She's very young and has only been out of college a short time, but she's doing a super job so far. She's been writing about Travis and Brenna's progress on *The Great Roundup*. So if I miss seeing an episode, she can always catch me up on what's happened."

She leaned over and sniffed at the sack of food. "Do I smell chili in there?"

He nodded. "Chili dogs and fries. If you don't like them, I'm going to be in big trouble."

"Oh, Zach, I love chili dogs! How did you guess?"

Her reaction made him feel like he'd just stumbled onto the end of a rainbow. "Oh, you just look like a chili-dog girl to me."

"Sure," she said with a wide grin. "It's easy to imagine

me with chili smeared all over my mouth. I'm a messy girl."

She might picture herself in that way, but Zach was beginning to think of her as a girl who was full of life, who wasn't so self-absorbed she worried about having every fingernail perfect and every hair in its proper place. God help him, but he was beginning to think of her as perky and pretty and adorable.

Zach, as soon as you finish lunch, you need to see a doctor. Because something has caused your thinking to tilt way off base. From the time you were old enough to get your driver's license and take a girl on a real date, you haven't picked one that looked or behaved like Lydia Grant. You've always wanted your lady companions to be delicate, refined and ultra-feminine. You've never been interested in a gal who could step up and play first base on the baseball team!

Thankfully, by the time Zach turned onto Buckskin Road, the admonishing voice in his head had faded to little more than a distant echo and he was determined to keep it there.

Rust Creek Falls Park was a large grassy area surrounded by a split rail fence and dotted with clusters of tall spruce trees. Zach stopped the truck in the dirt parking lot, and after helping Lydia to the ground, he grabbed their lunch.

"So take your pick, sweet lady. Where would you like to dine? I see a picnic table and a few park benches. Or we could sit on the grass. I'm game for anything."

Smiling, she looped her arm through his. "Hmm, that's quite a choice. Let's go over to the park bench in the shade of that tall spruce," she suggested.

"Great choice. We can see Rust Creek Falls High

School from there. The image might bring back some old memories you'd like to share with me. Like your prom date? I'd enjoy hearing about him."

She let out a good-natured groan. "I don't have to see the school building in order to remember some of those embarrassing memories."

The two of them strolled through an opening in the fence, then along a hard dirt path until they reached the wooden bench. Once they'd taken a seat, he placed the bag of food between them and began to divvy up the carefully packaged items.

"Since school has started, the park is rather quiet," Lydia observed.

As he handed her one of the chili dogs, a child's cry carried across the grassy lawn. Both Zach and Lydia turned their attention to a young mother trying to pacify a boy somewhere between three and four years of age. At the moment he was kicking and stomping and desperately trying to pull his hand from the woman's grasp.

"He's cute, but he sure is an angry little guy," Lydia commented. "I'd say he doesn't want to go home."

"Yeah. My guess, too. Makes you realize parenting isn't all fun and games."

She slanted a wry look at him. "Does seeing a temper tantrum like that one make you want to forget about having kids?"

He passed her a foam cup filled with crushed ice and cola, along with a paper-covered straw. "No. I still want lots of kids. And hopefully I'll have lots of patience to go with them."

"I guess having several brothers would make you feel that way." She unwrapped the chili dog and bit into the end. After she'd swallowed a mouthful, she exclaimed, "Delicious! This is hitting the spot, Zach."

"Don't forget your fries. Would you like ketchup?" he asked.

"Absolutely. What's french fries without ketchup? That's like a biscuit without gravy. It's just not the real deal."

She was eating with the same gusto he remembered and the sight made him happy. Apparently she was one of those lucky persons who could eat what she wanted and never gain a pound. Because it was clearly evident beneath her blue jeans and T-shirt that her figure was nicely formed. Not too skinny or overly pudgy. Everything was exactly right. And Zach figured all those curves would look even better if he saw her without the simple pieces of clothing.

Zach didn't know why such an erotic thought had suddenly popped into his head. But the image it created was enough to make him feel more than uncomfortable.

Giving himself a mental shake, he forced his thoughts back to her last comment.

"Biscuits and gravy," Zach repeated. "Now you're talking my kind of food. Aunt Rita makes both of them really well. Just like my mother did."

Lydia said, "You know, when I was having lunch the other day with you and your family at the Circle D, I was trying to picture myself with a bunch of siblings and cousins like you have. Being an only child, it's hard for me to understand how you connect to each one of them. I mean, they're all different, yet you're close to them all."

He swallowed a piece of his chili dog before he answered. "I never really thought about it in that way, Lydia. I grew up with older brothers watching over me and a little brother trying to tag along after me. Each one of us is different, but in some ways we're all alike. There are times we argue, but for the most part, we all get along. I'm lucky, I guess."

"Not lucky, Zach. Blessed. Because you and your brothers were raised by a pair of loving parents. They obviously taught you siblings to love and respect each other."

Zach usually thought of Lydia as a fun girl who didn't take life too seriously. But sometimes, like now, she came out with remarks that told him she had deep thoughts, too. About people and families and…love. The notion had him regarding her even more closely and wondering if somewhere beneath her sparkling eyes and wide smile, she wanted the same things that he was searching for. Someone to love and children of her own.

"I can't imagine not having siblings," he said. "I'd be pretty lost and lonely without my brothers around."

"It's hard to miss something that you've never had, Zach." Sighing, she shook her head. "When I was small, I used to beg Mom to find me a daddy and to give me brothers and sisters. I was too young to understand what all that entailed. I only knew that I wanted the things my friends had. But Mom closed off her heart. I guess it just wasn't meant for me to be in a big family."

The idea of Lydia as a child, longing for a father, tore at Zach's heart. Regardless of what had gone on between her parents, she'd not deserved to be abandoned, as though she was unimportant. It wasn't right that her mother had allowed her own bitterness to cause Lydia to miss out on some of the most precious things in life. But life was rarely ever fair and Lydia seemed to realize that fact more than anyone he'd ever met. She didn't go around feeling sorry for herself, or moping about with a huge chip on her shoulder.

He smiled at her. "Maybe someday you'll marry into a big family. Then you'll be dealing with a bunch of in-laws."

Her short laugh was brittle. "I can't see that happening anytime soon. Besides, being on my own has made me very independent. A husband might start trying to run my life. Telling me what to do and how to do it. That would never work with me and then I'd be saddled with the word *divorcée* attached to my name. Everybody in Rust Creek Falls would be saying 'Look at Lydia. She couldn't hold on to a man any more than her mother could.' No. I'm okay just like I am."

Perhaps she was right, Zach thought as he continued to eat his lunch. If she wanted to live her life as a single woman, it was none of his business.

After a stretch of silence, he asked, "Did you attend the event the PTO put on for the kids here in the park last month? Aunt Rita and Uncle Charles and Dad all came to town to watch some of the events. From what they said, everyone had loads of fun."

"You must be talking about The Great Roundup Kids Competition," she said. "Actually, I did stop by and watch for a while. The park was overflowing with people that day. I have a few friends with kids that competed. None of them won an event, but they didn't care. They were having fun. And that was the main objective."

"I imagine the kids around here are following *The Great Roundup* about as much as the adults," Zach said. "It's a big deal for the town to have two of its own featured on a TV series. And speaking of *The Great*

Roundup, the next episode is on tonight. Are you going to drop by the Ace in the Hole to watch it?"

Chuckling, she dipped a fry into a blob of ketchup. "Mom thinks the Ace in the Hole is a den of iniquity, but I go just the same. If I'm caught up on work, I'll probably show up."

"Great. I might see you there."

She shot him an odd look that Zach didn't quite understand and then she said, "I heard you had a date with Eva-Rose Armstrong last night. How did that go?"

Her question shouldn't have surprised him. After all, she'd been helping him in his quest to find a wife. It was only natural that she wanted to hear about his progress.

"Okay, I guess. She's a very nice girl. Do you know her?"

"I've known her a long time and I see her almost every day in Daisy's Donut Shop. When I heard you were going out with her, I thought she's just what you're looking for."

On paper she was perfect, Zach thought. In person she'd hardly excited him. But maybe if he tried a second date with Eva-Rose, things might be different. He'd not yet ruled out the possibility.

"She is—sort of. I mean, she meets all the criteria. But one date isn't enough to tell if you're going to click with a person or not. And I feel like I need to keep broadening my choices first. I don't want to limit myself."

She leveled a pointed look at him. "In other words you're enjoying yourself too much to stop now."

He felt his face turning a bit red and he wondered, not for the first time, why Lydia should make him feel self-conscious. He was twenty-seven years old. He shouldn't be embarrassed to admit he liked dating women.

"This isn't a game, Lydia. It's a mission."

She shook her head. "I'm sorry, Zach. Game. Mission. It shouldn't be either one of those things."

With his chili dog eaten, he wadded up the wrapper and tossed it at a nearby trash barrel.

"And what should it be, Lydia?"

"Sorry. I shouldn't have said anything."

"No. I'm serious. I'd like to know your thoughts on the subject."

He looked around to see her head tilted to one side, her gaze studying him thoughtfully.

"Okay. It shouldn't be anything," she said. "It should just be a natural progression. Nothing contrived or planned. You meet a girl. Maybe you do that through a friend or relative. Or maybe you just walk in somewhere and see her for the first time. Anyway, if your interest is sparked, then you should date her and let nature take its course. But you're trying out women the same way you would try on a pair of cowboy boots."

"Well, she has to fit, doesn't she? Just like a pair of boots need to fit. Otherwise I'd set the boots aside and never wear them. And I sure couldn't do that to a woman. Not after I married her and then found out the fit was all wrong."

Groaning, she looked up at the sky and shook her head. "I see. It's not about the approach, but all about the fit."

"You got it. That's exactly right. How is it that you understand me so well?"

She looked at him, a wan smile tilting her lips. "Just lucky, I guess."

He reached over and gave her hand a squeeze. "I'm

the one who's lucky, Lydia. Lucky to have found a good friend like you."

All of a sudden, she eased her hand from his and quickly began gathering the leftovers of her lunch.

"We'd better be going, Zach. It's time for me to get back to the office."

A little stung by her abrupt attitude, he stared at her. "Lydia, did I say something wrong?"

Without even looking at him, she stood up. "No. You said everything right. Just what I expected."

Then why did he feel like the sky had just clouded over? Why in heck did it matter what Lydia thought about him or his marriage plans? He was going to find a wife. A perfect wife. With or without this woman's approval.

Rising to his feet, he tossed the last of his cola into the trash. "Come on," he muttered. "It's time we both got back to work."

Chapter Seven

"This is delicious, honey. It was thoughtful of you to bring this by. Especially after the shift I just finished."

Lydia watched her mother dip into a pint-size container of cherry chip ice cream. The flavor was Rhoda's favorite and it never failed to put a smile on her face. Something that Lydia wished she could see more often.

"It's been a few days since we talked and I didn't have a load of work to take home tonight. I thought I'd stop by and see how you've been doing," Lydia explained to her mother as the two of them sat at Rhoda's small kitchen table. "So how have things been going at Snow Valley? Any new residents?"

Her mother nodded as she swallowed a spoonful of the ice cream. "Actually, we did get a new patient a few days ago. A gentleman about five years older than me. He had some sort of accident and broke his leg. Poor guy's going to need weeks of care and lots of therapy to get his leg back in working order."

"No kids around to help take care of him?"

"No. He has a son, but he lives way off in Georgia, or somewhere down south. Saul doesn't want to be a burden to him or anyone, so he checked himself into Snow Valley. I admire him for that. You know how most men are whiners, but this one doesn't seem to be."

Lydia stared at her mother in stunned fascination. She'd never heard her say anything complimentary about a man in a long, long time. Not only that, she'd called this man by his first name, as though she'd already gotten to know him socially. That just wasn't like Rhoda Grant. Wonder of wonders. Was there a glimmer of a chance that her mother might possibly be changing? Lydia could only hope and pray.

"So this man is expected to recuperate and be able to go home eventually?" Lydia asked.

"Oh yes. I expect he'll be back home in three or four months." Rhoda put the lid on the ice cream. "It's always good for the nurses' morale when we have patients that are going to get well and be able to go back to a normal life."

"I'm sure. It's good to have hope for ourselves and everyone around us." Frowning, she watched her mother carry the leftover ice cream to the freezer. "Mom, aren't you feeling well? You usually eat every bite of cherry chip."

"I feel fine, honey. I've just been thinking it would be good for me if I cut down and lost a few pounds."

For the past five years Lydia had been preaching to her mother about the benefits of losing weight to remove the stress on her knees. But Rhoda had always dismissed her advice with negative remarks, or simply ignored her daughter altogether. Lydia was beginning to wonder if during the past week some sort of magic fairy had twinkled happy dust over Rhoda's head. Or had magic come in the form of a man with a broken leg?

"That's great, Mom." She gave her mother a bright, encouraging smile. "With a little weight off, you might even get the urge to buy a few new clothes."

Instead of deriding her daughter, Rhoda surprised Lydia yet again by letting out a girlish laugh and running a hand down the side of her hip. "Imagine me looking slim and svelte. I might get some new scrubs and maybe even a dress. The holidays aren't that far away. I could use some sprucing up before Snow Valley has its Christmas party."

Lydia could no longer hide her excitement over Rhoda's new attitude. Leaving the table, she crossed the room and gave her mother a tight hug and a kiss on the cheek. "Mom, I'm so happy to hear you talking like this."

Rhoda patted her arm. "You're a good daughter, Lydia. And I know I'm not always the best of mothers, but you've always loved me in spite of that. I'm going to do better. I promise."

With an affectionate groan, Lydia pressed her cheek against her mother's. "Oh, Mom, we'll both do better. Together."

Lydia stayed at her mother's long enough to watch the weekly airing of *The Great Roundup*. The episode turned out to be interesting and fun.

Since haying time had begun on the dude ranch where the contest was taking place, the major challenge was hauling hay from the field to the barn. The team that ended up getting the most bales properly stacked in the hayloft within the allotted time would be the winner. With each bale weighing a hefty sixty pounds, most of the female contestants were given the job of driving the flatbed trucks, while the men loaded the vehicle with the hay. Then later that evening, as a minor challenge, the groups were given the task of cooking some sort of dessert in Dutch ovens over a campfire.

Brenna and Travis's team were strong and steady in the haying challenge and ultimately declared the winners of that event. But their peach cobbler didn't stand up to Wally Wilson's bread pudding.

As the show ended for the evening, Rhoda said, "I'm not surprised that grizzled old cowboy Wally and his team won the dessert contest. He's had experience as a cook on a ranch. And he won the chili cook-off in one of the earlier episodes. So he gets a prize of another restful night at the cushy ranch lodge."

"Well, Brenna and Travis did win the big event," Lydia replied, "so there's no danger of them being eliminated from the contest for the next challenge."

"Too bad that blonde tart Summer Knight hasn't been voted off," Rhoda remarked. "But I have to admit she was darn good at the hay challenge. She handled her team's truck like she'd been driving one all her life."

Lydia chuckled. "Yeah, the same way she handles the men—with plenty of experience. I just keep hoping Travis can see through her flirting ways."

Rhoda nodded. "She's cunning, that's for sure. But I think Travis is smart enough not to let her get her claws in him."

Lydia nodded thoughtfully as the ending credits rolled and a car commercial flashed on the TV screen.

"You know, I kept watching the way Travis and Brenna were interacting with each other and it looks to me like they're really in love."

"Hmm. Well, why wouldn't they be?" Rhoda asked. "They got engaged, didn't they?"

"Yes. But I think a lot of folks around town are wondering if it was just a sudden whim sort of thing. At least, that's what Zach believes. He thinks Travis's proposal was just an impulse thing."

Rhoda scowled at Lydia. "Zach? Are you talking about Zach Dalton? The guy with the ad in the paper for a bride?" She rolled her eyes with disgust. "He's a good one to be talking about a marriage proposal. If you ask me, he's nothing but a lothario. And the sooner these women around here learn what he is, the safer they'll all be."

"Mom! Earlier in the kitchen I thought you—"

"I know, honey. I'm sorry. I am trying to change for the better. But in this case, I'm not being jaded just because Zach is a man. I can admit that deep down there are some good men in this world."

"Hallelujah," Lydia practically shouted. "I think that's the first time I've ever heard you say anything like that."

Rhoda gave her a cheeky smile. "See, I'm trying. But as for this Zach guy, I just can't believe he's genuine."

Oh Lord, what would she think if she knew Zach considered his search for a wife as a mission? That he needed to make sure a woman fit him like a pair of boots? She'd be labeling him as something far worse than a lothario.

This afternoon, when Lydia and Zach had left the park, she'd been more than a little disappointed with him. His talk about finding a woman who fit him and then calling Lydia a friend had left her feeling as though she was one of those plain-faced nannies. The kind a man trusted to take care of his children, but would never dream of marrying.

"He's just confused, Mom. He lost his mother recently and I think he believes getting married will fill some of the void."

"That's not the right reason to take a wife."

"No. But that's his business. Not ours." Lydia left the couch and began to pull on her jacket.

"Are you leaving already?" Rhoda asked.

"Already? I've been here for hours. I need to get home." She walked over to her mother and kissed her cheek. "See you soon."

"I'll call you," Rhoda promised. "Maybe you can come over to Snow Valley and have lunch one day soon."

"I'd like that," Lydia told her, then with a little wave, she let herself out of the house.

Minutes later, she was driving down North Broomtail Road, still pondering the change in her mother, when she passed by Daisy's Donut Shop. Although the eatery was closed for the night, Lydia's thoughts suddenly turned to Eva-Rose. Had the woman been as instantly infatuated with Zach as all the rest around Rust Creek Falls appeared to be? After one date, was Eva-Rose desperately wishing she would be chosen as Zach's bride?

For Eva-Rose's sake, Lydia hoped not. The woman was too gentle and nice to set her heart on a man who wanted little more than a cook and baby machine. Eva-Rose deserved to be loved.

And from Zach's comments about his date with Eva-Rose, love hadn't been anywhere on the radar. His half-hearted attitude about the beautiful blonde had taken Lydia by complete surprise. No one fit his list of requirements more perfectly than Eva-Rose. So when Lydia had asked him about the date, why hadn't he been grinning from ear to ear and singing her praises? Instead, he talked about broadening his horizons and dating even more women.

The whole idea made Lydia wonder if her mother had been right in describing him as a lothario. Maybe all this advertising and fanfare over finding a wife was just a glorified dating game with him.

This isn't a game, Lydia. It's a mission.

His words caused her back teeth to grind together. She'd never heard such a calculated bunch of hogwash and she'd desperately wanted to tell him so. She'd wanted to cut loose and let him know how she really felt about his wife want ad. That he was never going to have the kind of love and marriage his parents had enjoyed. Not until he actually understood what loving someone really meant. But expressing her true feelings on the matter would've crushed their friendship. And, heaven help her, having Zach as a friend was better than nothing at all.

At the intersection of North Broomtail Road and Sawmill Street, Lydia made a left, which would take her to the west outskirts of town where her house was located. The street passed directly by the Ace in the Hole, and as Lydia slowly approached the nightspot, she saw the parking lot was jammed with vehicles. Cowboy hats were everywhere as animated folks spilled from the front entrance. A few couples were walking hand in hand toward their cars, while others had their arms wrapped tightly around their partner's waist.

As usual, *The Great Roundup* viewing at the bar had drawn a crowd of people and Lydia could only wonder if Zach was among the sea of cowboys in attendance.

The thought had scarcely entered Lydia's mind when she caught a glimpse of him on the far edge of the parking lot, and before she realized what she was doing, she abruptly turned the car into the lot and stopped at the first empty place she could find.

By then she could see that Zach was not alone and her heart sank all the way to her feet as she gazed at the woman standing at his side. Tall and slender with long dark hair that brushed the back of her waist, she was definitely a beauty, Lydia thought sickly. Designer jeans tightly outlined shapely legs that appeared to go on forever. As for the woman's perky behind, Lydia wondered how long she had to work out on the elliptical machine each day to look that good.

As Lydia watched him help his date into the cab of his truck, she felt herself going cold inside and the feeling made her angry. What was the matter with her, anyway? From the first moment she'd laid eyes on Zach Dalton, she'd known he was out of her league. So why was she letting herself pine over something she could never have? It was stupid. And she had better things to do. Like go home and stare at the walls.

The next afternoon, Zach and his brother Garrett were inside the Circle D barn, saddling a pair of horses with plans to ride fence line.

"So did you manage to see any of *The Great Roundup* last night?" Garrett asked as he tightened the cinch on his saddle.

Frowning slightly, Zach continued to brush the bay he'd picked to ride. "Why are you asking that? You went to the Ace in the Hole last night to see the latest episode just like I did."

Garrett shot him a shrewd glance. "Yes. But I didn't have a hot date with me like you did. Boy, oh boy, she was something, Zach. I hope you wrote her number down in permanent marker."

"I think I still have her number. Why? Would you like it?"

Garrett jerked the stirrup into place before he turned an incredulous look on Zach. "Are you kidding? You mean you'd actually give me her number? Man, she must have struck out with you."

Zach reached for the saddle he'd balanced on the hitching post. As he swung it onto the bay's back, he said, "She was a beauty, but she knew it. If you're looking for Miss Diva, then give her a call. I won't be guilty of dating her again."

"Miss Diva, huh? Well, it might be fun to date a girl like that once or twice. My dates are usually so homespun I have to pick the hay out of their teeth," Garrett joked.

Normally Zach would have laughed at his brother's corny attempt at humor, but this afternoon he didn't feel like laughing. He was getting nowhere fast with his search for a wife. And all because of Lydia Grant. He should've never taken her to lunch at the Gold Rush. He was out of his mind for inviting her on that trail ride. And then yesterday he'd succumbed to another weak moment and taken her to lunch in the park. Those outings with the curly-haired newspaper woman should have never taken place. Especially the picnic lunch yesterday. Damn it, he didn't know what had happened during the little outing, but something had put her off with him.

When he'd dropped her off at the newspaper office, she'd barely taken the time to mutter her thanks before she'd jumped out of the truck and raced into the building. For one second, Zach had considered going after her, but just as quickly he'd stopped himself. What would have been the point? Lydia wasn't the woman he was after. He wasn't trying to win her heart and persuade her to be his bride. He needed to stick to his checklist and forget about Lydia.

But all last night, when he should've been enjoying his date with April Rogers, he'd been thinking about Lydia, and wondering what he'd done to raise her hackles.

"April was too high maintenance for me, but if you're willing to spend lots of money and attention on her, then you two would get along fine," Zach told his brother.

"Hmm. I'm not sure I'm willing to go that far," Garrett told him. "After all, we're working cowboys, not millionaires. The closest we might ever get to that kind of money is Travis. He and Brenna are still hanging in there. I'm beginning to think if they're careful and don't make any silly mistakes, one of them might actually win *The Great Roundup*. Wouldn't that be a hoot?"

"It would be a hoot, all right," Zach agreed. "But they still have a long ways to go before the competition ends. And those other cowboys are just as determined to get the million. Like Lydia and I were talking, some of those contestants are downright cutthroat. Just like that sneaky, wannabe cowboy with the red mustache. If Fred hadn't turned around just in time to catch him, he was going to dump a box of salt in his dessert dish."

"Yeah. He's a sneaky lowlife. No one deserves to win anything by cheating. I'm glad he was voted off." As Garrett untied the buckskin's reins, he glanced over at Zach. "Uh, by the way, who's Lydia? I thought your date's name was April."

Leaning a shoulder against the bay's hip, Zach shot

him a tired look. "Garrett, does anything stay in your mind except a fast car? Lydia had lunch here on the ranch with all of us. Remember? The newspaper woman."

"Oh. Oh yeah, the cute little gal with the curly hair. I'd forgotten her name." Garrett frowned with confusion. "I didn't know you'd been dating her."

Even though Zach had already made certain everything was straight and tight on his saddle, he turned and pretended to adjust the latigo.

"I haven't been dating Lydia. We're just friends. And we talk."

A clever grin cocked one corner of Garrett's mouth. "Hmm. If that's the case, then maybe you could give me Lydia's number. She'd be a gal a guy could have fun with."

Garrett's comment struck a sore spot in Zach and he turned to glare at his brother. "Don't talk that way about Lydia!" he warned. "She isn't that kind of woman!"

Garrett's brows shot straight up. "Whoa now, brother! You took that all wrong. When I said fun, I meant fun, not hanky-panky. I thought Lydia was nice. I liked her. She's the kind of woman a man can be himself with. And that's the best kind."

Zach's eyes narrowed as he carefully studied his brother. For some reason he didn't like the idea of Garrett and Lydia together. No. That was something he couldn't abide, Zach thought.

"How would you know that's the best kind? You've never had a serious thought in your head about a woman."

Annoyed now, Garrett backed the buckskin away from the hitching post and slung himself into the saddle. As he settled the toes of his boots in the stirrups, he looked down at Zach.

"Don't try to act all righteous with me, little brother.

This thing you're calling a wife hunt is nothing more than a dating game. Getting serious starts here." He tapped a forefinger against the middle of his chest. "Not from a stack of mushy letters."

Trying to hold on to his temper, but failing, Zach untied the bay and stepped into the saddle. As he reined the horse alongside Garrett's, he flung more questions at him, "What the hell do you know about it? You don't care if you ever get married."

"I can tell you one thing," Garrett muttered. "I'm not about to get married just for the sake of having a wife. If I ever get married, it's going to be for love. Not for homemade pies, or kids, or a housekeeper!"

Before Zach could make a heated retort, Garrett urged his horse forward and out the open door of the barn. As Zach watched his brother kick the buckskin into a long trot, he felt his shoulders slump with defeat. Garrett was right. A man should marry for love. But so far Zach couldn't find the elusive emotion. And what if he never found it? Was he supposed to spend the rest of his life alone, with no children or wife? No home to call his own?

She's the kind of woman a man can be himself with. And that's the best kind.

As Zach urged the bay into the bright sunlight, Garrett's comment about Lydia rolled through his head. Zach had thought the same thing about her—until yesterday at the park when all of a sudden she'd turned cold on him. And that bothered him far more than he wanted to admit.

Determined to put the woman out of his mind, Zach urged the bay into a canter until he caught up to Garrett, then slowed his mount to match the buckskin's trot.

"Uh, sorry about that back there," Zach said to his brother. "I got out of line."

Garrett looked over at him and grinned. "I got out of line, too. So let's forget it and go check some fence. Ready?"

"Heck, yeah. Let's race to the old windmill," Zach challenged.

"Yeehaw! You're on!"

Zach spurred his horse into a fast gallop with Garrett following right behind him.

"This is getting ridiculous," Jolene commented as she watched Lydia dump an armload of letters and email messages into a cardboard box. "What makes Zach Dalton so special? Sure, he's cute. Well—okay, more than cute, he's dreamy. But there are plenty of other hot cowboys in and around Rust Creek Falls. Like his brothers, for instance. They're all handsome guys. So why have so many women gone gaga over Zach?"

Sighing, Lydia shoved the box in the kneehole of a spare desk, another space she'd purposely created for the overflow of Zach's ad responses.

"Women are after him because he's made it clear he has marriage on his mind. That's the difference between him and the rest of the hunky cowboys around here. And let's face it, most young women have one objective in life. Snag a man and live happily ever after." Lydia didn't bother to hold back a snort. "I'm beginning to think that's a fool's dream. Besides, a woman hardly needs a man at her side to keep her standing upright. If you ask me, we can do that just fine on our own."

"Why, Lydia, what in the world has come over you? It's not like you to be so cynical. You must be spending extra time with your mother. And I don't mean that in a nasty way. But we both know she can make a woman feel pretty negative toward men."

Since Lydia had worked with Jolene for several years, the two had become friends and, as such, Jolene had witnessed firsthand how jaded Rhoda could be. Now Jolene was putting Lydia in the same sour category. It was horrible.

Straightening to her full height, Lydia shook her head at Jolene. "I did have a long visit with Mom last Friday night and you're going to find this hard to believe, but I enjoyed it. Mom was actually bright and upbeat. She's making an effort to lose weight and talking about buying new clothes for the coming holidays. I'm telling you, Jolene, for a while there I thought I was dreaming."

Lydia walked back to her desk and Jolene followed. "Wow! What's going on with her? Something must have pushed your mother around the corner and into the light of day!"

Lydia glanced in the direction of Curtis's office, then remembered he'd left twenty minutes ago to attend a chamber of commerce meeting and wouldn't be back before the office closed at five.

Easing into her desk chair, Lydia looked at her friend. "This sounds incredible. And I'm not sure I believe it— yet. But I think it's a man. She told me about a new patient and talked about how nice he was. Mom never talks about a man. Unless it's in an unflattering way."

Totally bemused, Jolene eased a hip onto the corner of Lydia's desk. "No! I don't believe it! Besides, old people are the only kind that live at Snow Valley. Right?"

"No. Not necessarily. Sometimes patients arrive that are young or middle-aged. Some of them have been in accidents or have health issues that require them to have a few more weeks or months of medical care. After they've been released from a hospital. As for this mystery man, Mom said he was five years older than her. Which would put him around fifty-five."

"Oh. So this man isn't old and decrepit. Have you met him?"

"No. But I'm hoping to. As far as I'm concerned, anybody who can put a spark in my mother's life deserves a medal."

"Well, this is good news," Jolene agreed, then narrowed her gaze on Lydia. "So why have you been so crabby lately? Are you not feeling well?"

Had her dismal mood really been showing that much? The idea made her angry at herself. Thinking about Zach Dalton was a waste of time and energy. She had to stop it or risk becoming the biggest fool in Rust Creek Falls.

Forcing a cheery smile on her face, she shook her head. "Sorry if I've been crabby, Jolene. I'm just overworked. I'm convinced Curtis believes I'm an octopus and can work all eight arms at one time."

The redhead gave her a sympathetic smile. "That's what you get, Lydia, for being Super Woman."

Lydia let out a rueful laugh. "Sure. I really look like a superwoman, don't I?"

Jolene grimaced. "I wasn't referring to your appearance. I was talking about your ability to do a thousand things and do them all well. But now that you've brought it up, I think you'd be a ravishing beauty if you'd just give yourself a little boost. Maybe a dash of makeup. A few pieces of clothing—something soft and feminine."

Feeling worse than self-conscious, Lydia picked up a pencil and began to absently doodle on a small notepad.

She'd heard this sort of thing from Jolene before. But this time it struck her deeply. Seeing Zach with the dark-haired beauty in the Ace in the Hole parking lot had made Lydia even more aware of her own lackluster appearance.

"That's not me, Jolene. Everyone knows the fairy tale of turning an ugly swan into a beautiful princess is just that—an impossible dream."

Jolene stood up, her arms folded against her chest and a disgusted look on her face. "Stop it! You have all the requirements to be a very lovely woman. Instead, you choose to hide all your pretty assets. And we both know why, don't we?"

The pencil slipped from Lydia's fingers as she stared at Jolene. "We do? What are you talking about? I've always been like this. I'm not a delicate flower, Jolene. I'm more of a dandelion weed."

"Dandelion weeds are beautiful, too. You've just listened to your mother so long, you're afraid to try to attract a man. Afraid if you do catch him, you'll never be able to hold on to him."

If anyone else had said such a thing to her, Lydia probably would've gotten angry. But she couldn't get angry at Jolene. She had a huge heart and was a genuine friend who was always ready to lend a helping hand if Lydia needed it.

"You mean, like my father?"

Placing a hand on Lydia's shoulder, Jolene nodded. "Listen, sweetie, none of that stuff with your father was your fault."

"To this day he's never shown his face here in Rust Creek Falls," Lydia grimly reminded her.

"Sorry. Self-absorbed jerks don't have the guts to show their faces to the ones they've wronged. Think about it. You and your mother didn't need that sort of worthless man in your life. Furthermore, you don't need to let the loser affect your happiness now. Got it?"

With a smile of concession, Lydia said, "Okay. I got it. But can I ask you something personal, Jolene?"

"Sure. What is it?"

Lydia said, "I know you divorced Neal because he cheated on you. So how did you keep all that from crushing your self-confidence?"

Jolene shook her head. "Oh, Lydia, for a long time my self-esteem was nonexistent. It took a long time for me to remember I was worthy of more than what Neal dealt me."

Lydia was surprised. "After your divorce I remember you being very angry, but I never thought you seemed down on yourself or that you were lost."

Jolene chuckled. "Give me an acting award, then, because I fooled you and a lot of people. True, I was angry, but deep down I wondered why I hadn't been enough woman to keep Neal faithful. I wondered what I was lacking. It took me a while to figure out that he was the one with the problem. Not me."

"I'm glad to know you're not acting now," Lydia said. "And you've gotten yourself together."

Jolene gave her a saucy wink. "I've gotten my mojo back, all right. And when the right man comes along, I'm going to use it on him."

The right man. Maybe Lydia would find the right man, she thought wistfully. Someday. After she exorcised Zach Dalton from her heart.

"Oh, yikes! Lydia, why didn't you remind me about the time?" Jolene gasped as she glanced at her watch. "I have work to finish before we close up shop."

The redhead rushed out of the front office, leaving

Lydia to return to the project she'd started earlier this Monday afternoon. As usual, she'd worked her way through dozens of interruptions. But her real lack of concentration could be blamed on a tall, dark cowboy with an easy smile. A cowboy who was clueless of the havoc he was causing to her heart.

Instead of focusing on the graphic design on the screen, she was looking down at her black T-shirt and boyfriend jeans.

Since Curtis wasn't a stickler about any kind of dress code for the staff, she'd always taken the easiest and cheapest route. But if her boss ever changed his mind, she'd be frantic. Could she walk into this office wearing a dress without being laughed out of the building? And what would Zach think if he saw her in something soft and feminine, like Jolene had suggested?

Lydia, forget about what Zach would think! Sexy clothes, makeup, come-hither looks—none of that is going to turn his head. He's stuck to that damned list of his and you're not on it!

Fighting back at the nasty voice in her head, she forced her attention to the graphic design and began to move the bold lines and borders displayed on the monitor. She wasn't going to let Zach interfere with her work or her life, she promised herself. Her mother had seemingly turned a new leaf. She was putting the man she'd lost in the past and was finally beginning to think toward the future. Lydia had to do the same.

Chapter Eight

At five minutes past five that evening, Zach pulled his truck into a parking spot a few yards from the *Gazette* and jumped out, barely taking the time to shut the door behind him.

"Lydia! Wait! Are you locking the door?"

As he trotted down the sidewalk toward her, she glanced in his direction. From the look on her face, she was surprised to see him. But then he'd never shown up this late in the day before.

"Yes, we're closing," she told him. "Did you want to pick up your mail?"

Halting a few steps away from her, Zach noticed she was dressed in her usual jeans and T-shirt, but today she'd pushed back her hair away from her face with a braided headband of tiny flowers. The pale yellow petals formed a halo around her hair and gave her complexion a golden glow.

The difference, even though small, had him staring at her in wonder. Garrett had called her pretty. Strange how Zach had never really noticed just how pretty she was, until now.

Clearing his throat, he answered, "Uh, yes. But I wouldn't want you to go to a lot of trouble."

Drawing her shoulders back, she gave him a smile, but the expression looked more forced than sincere. Apparently she was still miffed at him. Zach had spent most of the weekend wondering what he'd done and why it was so important that she forgive him.

"It's no trouble," she told him.

He smiled back at her. "Well, it would save me a trip into town tomorrow."

"There's no reason for that." She stuck the key back in the lock and gave it a twist. "Come with me and I'll fetch it for you."

Inside the office, the overhead lighting had been turned off and the blinds closed on the windows, making the room dim and shadowy. Zach stood just inside the door and waited as she walked through the low, fence-like partition that separated the customer space from the work area.

Zach said, "I was trying to get here before closing time. But Garrett and I were out repairing fence and didn't make it back to the ranch before late."

"Don't worry about it. I have it all gathered and ready to go."

When she returned to him, she was carrying two cardboard boxes. Zach quickly took them from her and balanced the lot against his chest.

"Wow, I'm surprised there's still so much of this

coming in." He sniffed at the top one. "Any baked goods in here?"

A faint grimace pulled her brows together. "No food this time. But plenty of letters. I didn't think there were that many women in the state of Montana."

Zach felt his face turning a hot shade of red. Which was ridiculous. The whole town was aware that hordes of women were chasing after him. Why should another box of letters put an awkward look on his face? Maybe because Lydia seemed so disgusted by it, he thought.

Lowering his head, he thumbed through the top box. "Well, some of the senders are repeats," he said in an attempt to justify the indecent amount of mail.

"Hmm. They must have serious intentions or they're very persistent."

She stepped around him and opened the door. "That's all your mail," she informed him. "So if you don't mind, I'd like to lock up."

He'd never heard her sound so blunt, and her cool attitude bothered Zach far more than he wanted to admit. What had happened to that sunny, bubbly woman who'd made spending time with her feel very special?

Without making any sort of reply, he followed her out of the building and paused while she locked the door.

"Thanks, Lydia. It was nice of you to do this for me. Uh, what do you say we go have a bite to eat at the Gold Rush?"

He wasn't sure why he'd made the impulsive invitation. Except that ever since they'd picnicked in the park, he'd been thinking about her. That day she'd clearly gotten angry with him, and though he hadn't yet figured out what had prompted her ire, he knew he wanted to get on her good side again. That was far more important to

Zach than going through a stack of letters from women he'd never met.

"Thanks, but I'm not hungry."

Not willing to give up, he said, "Oh, well, if it's too early for you to eat dinner, then we could have a snack and cup of coffee at Daisy's."

"The doughnut shop will be closing soon."

Frowning, he glanced at his watch. "Not for two more hours. What's wrong? Are you still angry with me?"

Her gaze lifted to his, and as he looked into her blue eyes, Zach felt a strange flutter in the middle of his chest.

"I was never angry with you."

"Come on, Lydia, be honest. When we left the park the other day, you were anything but happy with me."

"I was annoyed with you, that's all. Because I didn't agree with some of your tactics of finding a wife," she admitted. "But I still like you, Zach, and consider you my friend."

That wasn't exactly what Zach wanted to hear, but at least she was talking. "Good. Then there's no reason we can't have a cup of coffee together. Let me put this away and we'll walk to Daisy's Donut Shop."

She studied him for another long moment, then shrugged, as though the idea of spending time with him bored her, but she'd do her best to suffer through it. Her attitude was quite a change from all the women who'd been fawning over him for the past month.

"Okay," she agreed. "I could use a jolt of caffeine. It's been a long day."

"Great. Wait here and I'll put this stuff away."

Once he'd dumped the boxes in the truck, he hurried back to her side and they started down the sidewalk. After a few steps, he impulsively reached over and looped his arm around hers. When she didn't protest or pull away from him, Zach considered it a major triumph and the silly grin he was feeling inside remained with him all the way to the bakery. Early evening was a slow time of the day for business at Daisy's. Other than the server behind the counter, the place was empty. After purchasing a pastry and coffee for each of them, they sat down at one of the small tables near the front window.

"Looks like we're the only ones in the mood for sugar and caffeine," Zach commented as he unwrapped a bear claw drizzled with icing.

"Unfortunately I have trouble resisting either one." She glanced at him as she stirred cream into her coffee. "So how did your weekend go? I saw you leaving the Ace in the Hole Friday night. You must have been watching *The Great Roundup*."

Surprised that she'd been anywhere in town that night, he asked, "Were you at the bar? I looked for you but didn't see you."

Her expression was suddenly a mixture of sarcasm and disbelief. "Really, Zach, you don't have to say anything like that to me. It's cheesy. In fact, I don't appreciate it."

"What do you mean by that? All I said was that I looked around for you."

She peeled back the wax paper on her cinnamon roll and took a bite. After she swallowed, she said, "You had a gorgeous woman at your side. You hardly would've been thinking about me, much less looking around the bar trying to spot me."

He shook his head. "Sorry, but you're wrong. I knew you'd been keeping up with *The Great Roundup* and that day in the park you mentioned you might go to the Ace in the Hole to watch. That's all."

A sheepish expression stole over her face. "I'm sorry. I don't know what's wrong with me, Zach. I'm sounding like a shrew."

"Forget it. As long as we're still friends, the rest doesn't matter."

She reached over and touched her fingers to the back of his hand. The gesture warmed him, and before he could stop himself, he turned his hand over and wrapped his fingers around hers.

Her gaze met his, then darted to a spot across the room, and Zach used the moment to study the profile of her straight little nose and the full curve of her lips. Did she ever want to kiss a man with those lips? he wondered. Moreover, did she ever want to make love? If Garrett was sitting across from her now, he wouldn't be wondering about those things. He would've already gotten the answers directly from her.

She said, "I didn't go to the Ace in the Hole that night. I was visiting my mom. We watched *The Great Roundup* together."

"So how did you see me and my date?" He wanted to know.

"I drove by the bar on my way home."

"Oh."

Lydia looked at him. "She was gorgeous, by the way. You think she's The One?"

The One. Sometimes he thought he should just throw up his hands and surrender. He'd dated at least a dozen women here lately and boredom was about to set in with the whole effort. Clearly it wasn't meant for him to find the love of his life. Not one single woman he'd gone out with had made him feel good or special. Not one had felt as though she was meant to be by his side through the rest of their lives.

"No. She isn't The One. In fact, I won't be seeing her again. She wasn't my type at all."

"What part didn't she fit? The cooking? Or did becoming a mother put her off?"

He chuckled ruefully. "Besides being a diva—a boring one at that—she obviously lied about herself and the kind of life she's looking for."

"You mean she actually admitted she wasn't truthful with you?"

Zach shook his head. "No. But it was easy to see the truth for myself. She didn't know one thing about cooking. I doubt she'd ever sunk one false fingernail into a sink of dishwater. And she knew even less about kids."

"That's too bad. But it's not like you don't have more to pick from. Judging from the mail you've received, you could probably date a different woman for the next three hundred and sixty-five days. I'm sure you'll eventually find what you're looking for."

"Do you really mean that, Lydia?" he asked earnestly. "Or are you just trying to be nice?"

"I happen to think that everyone has a special someone out there. You just have to wait until fate bumps you together and then everything will fall into place."

He gave her a pointed look. "Is that what you're thinking about your future? That you're going to bump into a man who will turn into your Mr. Right?"

She let out a short, humorless laugh and the sound had him smoothing his fingers over the back of her hand. Her skin was soft and warm and the sensation of touching her was so pleasant he realized he didn't want to stop.

"He'd probably have to do more than bump into me. He'd most likely need to crash into me to make me notice. I have a bad habit of living in the clouds. My head is always buzzing with work."

"There's more things to life than work."

She pulled her hand from his and picked up her coffee cup. Zach wanted to reach for her other hand, just so he'd be connected with her, but he had to remember that she was just a friend. She might get the wrong idea if he started getting all touchy-feely. And he might get the wrong idea, too.

She sighed, then cast him a gentle smile. "One of these days I'll have my special someone. And so will you."

"Yeah," he murmured. "One of these days I'll have what my parents had. I can't give up on that."

"So how is your dad's search for land going? Has he found anything that interests him?"

With a faint grunt, Zach reached for his coffee cup. "He's having as much trouble finding land as I am finding a wife. Although, he did come across one property that caught his attention. But Uncle Charles and Aunt Rita tell us it's most likely bound up in legal issues."

Curiosity peaked her brows. "Oh, where is it? Close to Rust Creek Falls?"

Zach nodded while thinking how pleasant it had been to have Lydia riding horseback with him that day on the Circle D. Not only had he been impressed by how well she'd sat a horse, but he'd also been struck by how perfect it felt to have her by his side. It had set him to wondering how she might fit with ranching life. Not that he was thinking about her as a prospective bride. No. She wasn't his type. But she would probably make some other rancher a great wife and partner.

He answered her question, "I think so. The place supposedly belonged to the Stockton family. Do you know them?"

A sad shadow crossed her face, but then she quickly shook it away and gave him a wan smile. "Yes, I do. I imagine Charles and Rita told you their parents were killed in a car accident?"

He nodded. "That's why buying that particular piece of land might be next to impossible. The children own it jointly and they might not all be in agreement to get rid of the place. And the way Uncle Charles and Aunt Rita talk, some of them might not be easy to locate."

"Hmm. That's true. Jamie and Bella are still around, but shortly after the accident the older boys left town and I haven't heard anything about them in years. I expect your aunt and uncle are right. That property is probably locked up in legal issues. It could be a pretty place, though, if someone bought it and fixed it up. Have you driven by there for a look?"

He shook his head. "No. I know the general location, but I've purposely avoided the place."

Confusion pulled her brows together. "But why? I thought you were anxious for your father to come up with another ranch for your family."

He shrugged. "I am. But I think Dad has already decided pursuing that piece of land wouldn't be worth going through the legal headache. If I saw the place and fell in love with it—" Pausing, he shook his head. "That would be a big disappointment and I don't want to go through any more of those."

Peering over the rim of her cup, she leveled a pointed

look at him. "I'm sorry, Zach, but life will always have disappointments. We can't always have the things we want—or *think* we want."

That was a lesson he was learning more and more every day, Zach thought.

"You're right," he said. "But it's heartbreaking when you see your dreams hanging right in front of you and your arms are always just inches short of grabbing them. You know what I mean?"

He figured the faint twist of her lips was supposed to be a smile, but it looked rather sad to Zach.

"I understand exactly. Once upon a time I grabbed so hard and so many times that my shoulders started coming out of their sockets. I finally quit trying to reach for them. Nowadays if I spot a penny on the ground, I'll reach for it. But the dreams—they'd have to fall right into my lap."

"You make it sound as though we should forget about our dreams, period."

She tore off a piece of the pastry and popped it into her mouth. After chewing the bite, she said, "I'm sorry, Zach. I don't mean to sound negative. That disappointment you were talking about—well, I guess I've had too many of them. But that's not to say I'm unhappy. I like my life. It's going along just the way it should. Why should I mess things up by chasing after dreams?"

Zach was trying to decide how to answer her question when the only waitress on duty appeared at their table carrying a glass carafe of steaming coffee.

"Would you two like a refill?" she asked.

"Thanks, Nanette," Lydia said. "I'll take a little warm-up if you don't mind."

The young woman with short dark hair filled Lydia's

cup, then looked at Zach. "What about you, Mr. Dalton? There's plenty here and I need to get rid of it before closing time."

"Sure. Fill it up," he told her.

A clever little smile wrinkled the waitress's nose and Zach decided she probably hadn't been out of high school for more than a year.

"I'd tell Eva-Rose to come out from the kitchen and say hello," Nanette said to him, "but she's already left for the day. Bet that disappoints you, huh?"

Lydia laughed. "Don't say any more, Nanette, or you'll have Zach weeping in his coffee."

Even though it was obvious that Lydia was teasing, Nanette didn't appear to catch on. As she stared at Zach, her eyes grew wide and so did her mouth.

"Oh, you mean Eva-Rose has gone to the top of your list? Wow, she hasn't let out a peep about it!"

Zach and Lydia exchanged droll glances.

Zach said, "Sorry to disappoint you, Nanette, but I don't have a list. Not yet. But you can certainly tell Eva-Rose I said hello."

Nanette's confused gaze traveled from Zach to Lydia and back again. Apparently she was just now putting the two of them together and trying to figure out the connection between him and Lydia. Good luck on that, Zach thought. He was still trying to figure out how to label their relationship. He wanted to think of her as his friend. Yet what he felt for her was far more. She was Lydia. A woman he wanted to be with.

"Okay. I'll do that," Nanette finally replied. "You two enjoy your coffee."

Behind them, the bell over the door jangled and two older women walked in and headed straight toward the glass display case filled with cakes, pies and pastries. Nanette hurried away to wait on the customers and Zach grinned at Lydia.

"She's obviously one of your groupies," Lydia said. "Why don't you thrill her and ask her out?"

He frowned at her. "Are you joking? She's a baby. She might be perfect for my little brother, Shawn. But not me. I like my women a little more mature."

Lydia laughed. "Twenty-three? Twenty-four? You must put me in the geriatric category."

Her laughter always got to him and his chuckles instantly joined hers.

"I don't think you're quite ready for a walking cane," he assured her.

"Thank you. When I get home, I'll take a bunch of vitamins—to make sure I maintain my vitality."

The playful sarcasm in her voice had him laughing again. "Lydia, you always make me feel good. Did you know that?"

Her smile faded, while her gaze fell to the cup in front of her. "That's me. Good for a few laughs."

Zach didn't understand the abrupt switch in her attitude. The last couple of times he'd been with her, she'd had these sudden attacks of seriousness. They seemed totally out of character, but then he needed to remember he'd met her only a few short weeks ago. There were probably many sides to Lydia that he'd never seen before. And strange as it seemed, he wanted to see all of them. Even the moody ones.

"That's a nice ability to have, Lydia, to make a person feel good and happy. You're blessed."

Her gaze met his and then a smile slowly spread

across her face. "Thanks, Zach, for reminding me of that fact."

He ate the last of his bear claw, then eased his shoulders against the back of the wooden chair. "I've been wondering what's going on at the *Gazette*," he told her. "The Rust Creek Rambler keeps writing pieces about me. What's the deal? Aren't there more important things going on around town than my search for a wife?"

Her brows lifted. "Does that bother you?"

He shrugged. "I've been trying to let it all roll off my back. But I have to admit some of those comments make me feel like an idiot. Still, I can't complain. I put myself in the position to be ridiculed and mocked. I wouldn't be much of a man if I couldn't take the good with the bad. I just wondered why the Rust Creek Rambler has to make me the constant subject. Who is this person, anyway? Not you, I hope!"

She chuckled. "Hardly. I have enough responsibilities at the *Gazette* without taking that one on, too. Actually, I don't have a clue who writes the column. Nor does anyone else. He or she writes anonymously."

He studied her with disbelief. "Are you kidding? How could you not know? You work right there in the office."

She shook her head. "For a long while your cousin Kayla was the Rambler. But it wasn't until she quit the paper and married Trey that the cat came out of the bag and we all learned it was her. After that, someone mysteriously began to pick up where Kayla left off. I've tried to snoop and find out. So has Jolene. But neither one of us can get to the real identity. She says the columns appear on her desk for proofreading without any clue as to who put them there. It's always neatly typed and stuffed inside a plain white envelope. Jolene says the spelling and grammar never needs correcting."

"Hmm. How very strange. Clearly whoever writes it is educated and knows how to write for a newspaper. The narrative has that sort of feel about it."

Lydia nodded in agreement. "I've often wondered if it might be Curtis. But some of that mushy stuff the Rambler has been coming up with lately doesn't fit his style at all. Unless he's trying to make people think a woman is writing the column. Whatever the case, the readers seem to enjoy it. We get lots of feedback on the column. And many readers are sending in their opinions on your ad for a bride."

Somehow that shouldn't surprise him, but it did. He expected his relatives and friends to voice their opinions on the matter, but not total strangers. "I'm sure most of them are saying I'm too calculated, unromantic, a fool in the first degree. Any of those fit?"

Smiling, she crumpled the empty wax paper. "Yes, yes and yes. But to be fair, there have been plenty of positive comments about you, too. Mostly that you know exactly what you want and you're not afraid to go after it."

But did he really know exactly what he wanted? Zach was beginning to doubt his initial plan and that couldn't be good. Not if he expected to succeed. Still, he intended for his marriage to last. He wanted to make sure the woman he picked was someone he could love and cherish until the end of their days.

"Hmm. Sometimes I'm asking myself if my wants are a bit askew."

"What do you mean by that? Are you talking about the requirements you stipulated in the ad? Well, don't worry about that. It's no problem to revise the wording."

If only it could be that easy, Zach thought as his gaze slipped over her soft features. "It's not the wording, Lydia. It's… Oh hell, I don't know what it is. But I'm beginning to wonder if I'm limiting myself."

"You're thinking you need to include other types of women? Is that it?"

Her blue eyes widened and Zach could only wonder what she was thinking. That he was wishy-washy or, even worse, a phony? Well, at least he'd not impulsively proposed to a woman the way his cousin Travis had before the start of *The Great Roundup*.

"Something like that. It would be a shame to miss out on finding my one true love just because I had tunnel vision."

To his surprise, a broad smile crossed her face. "Zach, that's the smartest thing I've heard you say."

"You think so?"

She nodded emphatically. "There are dozens of women out there who might not meet all your requirements, but they'd make wonderful wives. And that's your objective."

A wonderful wife. Sure, Zach wanted that. But why hadn't Lydia mentioned anything about love? Did she not realize that was the one thing he wanted most of all?

What Lydia thinks about that issue doesn't matter, Zach. All that matters is that you love the woman you marry. It will all be very simple. Especially if you'll leave Lydia out of the equation.

The nagging voice in his head reminded him he'd sat there long enough, gazing at a woman who would never be the mother of his children.

Giving himself a hard mental shake, he pushed back his cuff to glance at his watch. "Oh hell, I'd better get going. By the time I get back to the Circle D, it'll be time to do the evening chores and my brothers will be mighty angry with me if I'm not there to help."

Rising to her feet, she said, "Yes, I need to be getting home, too."

They gathered the empty wrappers and, on their way out the door, dropped them into the trash.

On the walk back, Zach held on to Lydia's arm and matched his longer stride to hers. The evening sun was quickly disappearing behind the distant mountain, sending long shadows over the sidewalk. A touch of coolness had moved in with the glow of twilight and for one wild second Zach wished he was taking Lydia home with him. He wished he could spend the rest of the night with her at his side, hearing her voice, touching her skin, smelling that sweet fragrance in her hair.

"Here we are. Thanks for the coffee, Zach."

Lydia's voice pulled him out of his strange reverie and he looked around to see they were standing beside his truck.

Drawing in a deep breath, he glanced down at her. "It was my pleasure, Lydia. And from now on I'll try to be timelier about picking up my mail."

"No problem. I got a yummy pastry out of the deal. And some nice company."

He stood there, not wanting to let go of her arm, his gaze fixed on the shadows flickering across her face, and suddenly nothing else mattered except that he kiss her.

"Yes. Very nice company," he murmured, then bent his head and touched his lips to hers.

She tasted like sugar and her lips were incredibly soft. The urge to draw her into his arms and deepen the kiss was so strong it left a buzzing in his ears. But they were standing on the street out in the open and he wasn't supposed to be doing this sort of thing. Not with Lydia!

Pulling himself away, he did his best to give her a casual grin, just to prove to her that all was cool and the earth wasn't shaking beneath his feet. But in reality he felt as though there wasn't a cell in his body that wasn't trembling.

Her eyes were dark and wide as she stared up at him. "What was that?"

Her voice was little more than a hoarse whisper, but Zach managed to hear her question. Now if he could just answer it in a way that made sense.

"Just a little kiss, Lydia. That's all. Friends do kiss, don't they?"

She licked her lips and Zach realized he wanted to kiss her again. Only this time he wanted to do it in a deep, meaningful way.

His thoughts must have shown on his face, because she suddenly stepped back as though she feared he was going to lock his arms around her.

When she finally spoke, her gaze was directed down the sidewalk rather than at him. "Well—uh—yes. Sorta. Just not exactly like that."

"Sorry if I offended you, Lydia. I was trying to tell you that I like you. That's all."

"I like you, too, Zach."

He cleared his throat and continued to pretend that nothing major had just occurred. "Well, I'd better hit the road. Will I see you at the Ace in the Hole this coming Friday? Things are really heating up on *The Great Roundup*. It'll be fun to see what happens."

She smiled at him, but Zach could see the expression

was far more strained than happy. Apparently that kiss hadn't been nearly as sweet to her as it had been to him.

"I'll try to make it," she promised half-heartedly.

"You have my cell number. Send me a text and let me know if you're going. Okay?"

"Sure. Maybe I'll see you there. Goodbye, Zach."

Before he could say anything else, she turned and hurried down the sidewalk.

Zach stared after her until she disappeared around the corner of the building, then giving himself a hard, mental shake, he climbed into the truck and headed toward the Circle D.

With Rust Creek Falls disappearing in his rearview mirror, he glanced at the boxes of mail in the passenger seat. Any other time he'd be excited to get home and dig into the letters and messages and photos. But this evening the idea held little appeal.

At the moment he couldn't see himself finding a wife in those boxes. The only thing he could see was Lydia walking down the sidewalk and everything inside him yearning to run after her.

Chapter Nine

There days later, before most of the household had climbed out of bed, Zach made his way to the kitchen with plans to have a quiet cup of coffee with his aunt Rita. But as soon as he stepped into the big, warm room with its smell of rich comfort food, he spotted his father sitting at the table. The latest edition of *The Rust Creek Falls Gazette* was propped in front of him, and considering the scowl on Phil's face, Zach could only surmise his father wasn't pleased with the news.

"Good morning, Dad, Aunt Rita." He walked over and plucked a cup from the cabinet, then filled it from a big graniteware coffeepot sitting on the stove.

"Good morning, Zach," Rita replied. "You're up very early this morning."

"I woke up thinking about your biscuits, Aunt Rita. No man can sleep with the taste of them on his mind."

She laughed. "Why, thank you, Zach. It's nice to be charmed so early in the morning."

He pecked a soft kiss on her cheek, then carried his cup over to the table. As he took a seat, Phil put down the paper and slanted a pointed look at him.

"Good morning, son. Seen the paper yet?"

"No. I've barely had time to open my eyes."

Phil aimed a finger at the middle of the page. "You're getting to be the biggest news around Rust Creek Falls. Almost as big as Travis and his TV adventures."

Zach groaned. "Don't tell me. The Rust Creek Rambler is at it again."

"How did you guess," Phil said with plenty of sarcasm. Then he began to read.

"'Playboy or Family Man?

Seems like Zach Dalton is trying to have his cake and eat it, too, as he's been spotted around town squiring a new lady every night of the week. Now tell me, dear readers, does that sound like a man with matrimony on his mind? More like a wolf on the prowl to me.'"

His expression grim, Phil cast the paper aside. "I could keep reading, but it only gets worse."

"I'm sorry, Dad. But I can't control what an anonymous gossip columnist writes about me. Besides, I doubt anyone pays that much attention to such nonsense."

"Nonsense! You certainly got that right, young man! This whole scheme of yours is just that—a bunch of bull manure! And I want to know when you're going to put an end to it."

Zach clutched his coffee cup as he tried to keep his

patience in check. He loved his dad dearly, and up until Zach's decision to advertise for a wife, the two had always gotten along well. Now it cut him deep to know that he didn't have his father's support. Especially over something that was so important to Zach's future.

"I can't answer that, Dad. I haven't found a wife yet. Until I do, I'm going to keep looking."

His jaw tight, Phil once again pounded his finger on the newspaper. "I just read this to you. Is that how you want people to think of you—and your family? That you're some playboy with only self-gratification on your mind? I sure as hell don't want folks around here thinking I raised a son with that sort of character."

So now he'd become an embarrassment to his father, Zach thought dismally, and most likely to his brothers, too. Although, they'd been kind enough not to express their feelings to his face.

Zach was wondering how he could defend himself to his father when he felt his aunt Rita's hands settling on his shoulders.

"Phil, don't you think you're being a little hard on the boy? He only wants what you had with Diana," she gently suggested. "And he's going about finding it the best way he knows how. Things have changed, Phil."

The older man glowered at his sister-in-law. "You're damned right they've changed! Zach's mother is dead— that's how things have changed. If she was alive today, he wouldn't be behaving in this outrageous manner!"

Biting down on his tongue, Zach rose from the table and gave his aunt a grateful hug. "I'll have something to eat later," he said close to her ear, then quickly left the kitchen before he said something to his father that he might later regret.

* * *

A short while later, beneath the dim glow of a single light bulb, Zach stood in the quiet barn, stroking a brush over the bay gelding. The red-brown hair sliding beneath his hand was beginning to grow long and thick, predicting a cold winter would soon be arriving.

Zach tried to imagine what the mountains and valley floors would look like decorated in snow, but his mind was having trouble moving that far into the future. Not when it was still dwelling on his father's hurtful words.

It wasn't like Phil Dalton to be short or disapproving with any of his sons. In fact, Zach couldn't remember the last time he'd gotten on his high horse with them. Until now. Zach tried to tell himself that his father was still grieving and that losing his wife had changed him. But that reasoning only made things harder to deal with. He didn't want his father to be changed. He wanted that same strong, steadfast man who'd always encouraged him to succeed. Not the father he'd left fuming at the kitchen table.

The gelding's ears pricked to attention a moment before Zach heard the light footsteps approaching from behind.

Glancing over his shoulder, he was totally surprised to see his father walking toward him.

"It's a little early to be saddling up, don't you think? Your brothers are just now stumbling into the kitchen for breakfast."

"I wanted to give Rascal a good brushing."

"The cool nights have started the horses growing their winter coats." Phil patted the bay gelding's hip. "I'm glad we shipped our horses from Dalton's Gulch down here to the Circle D. It's comforting to ride a horse who's already your buddy."

Zach's throat tightened with emotion as he turned back to Rascal and continued to brush down the horse's shoulder and beneath his belly. "Yeah. At least we'll have a few horses of our own to take with us whenever you do find a piece of land. We'll need them when we start building a herd of cattle."

Phil sighed. "I realize you boys are cramped and wanting your own place, but some things just don't happen overnight."

"Like finding a wife," Zach couldn't help adding.

There was a long pause before his father finally spoke. "I'm sorry about that back there in the kitchen, Zach. I didn't mean to get so harsh. It's just that I'm trying to deal with so many changes right now. And then to have you— Well, I can see you're not happy. If you ask me, this whole thing about finding a wife has made you miserable. And I want you to be happy, Zach. Truly, I do."

There was no mistaking the genuine affection in his father's voice and that was all it took to erase Zach's resentment.

"I know, Dad. I guess all of us have been dealing with a lot of changes. Every night before we go to sleep Booker talks about having our own house, our own barn and cows. But missing Mom is what hurts us all the most. It has to be even worse for you."

Stepping forward, Phil rested a hand on Zach's shoulder. "It's not easy, but I'll be okay. Diana gave me five dedicated sons—that's a lot to live for. We'll build our own Dalton spread again. As for you wanting a wife—"

Zach interrupted before Phil could get started again.

"Dad, I honestly never meant to make a spectacle out of this thing. I never expected so many women to make themselves available to me. It's almost a put off. Do you understand what I mean?"

Phil nodded. "I do understand. Most guys don't feel good about being chased. So why don't you end this thing and remove the ad from the paper?"

Zach let out a long sigh. "I've considered the idea. But then the whole town would call me a quitter. I can deal with being labeled a playboy better than I could a quitter."

His father studied him for long moments and Zach figured he was using the time to summon up a sermon. Instead, he laid a hand of support on his arm.

"All right, Zach, you started this thing, so you'll have to be the one to finish it. I only wish that you'd find one girl and stick with her. That's the last I'll say on the matter. Except good luck," he added with a wry grin.

Zach didn't often hug his father. Phil and his five sons were rough and rugged ranchers. Expressing their love for each other in a physical way didn't occur on a daily basis. But this morning Zach found it very easy to wrap his arms around his father's shoulders and hug him tight. "Thanks, Dad. And I promise I'm going to find that one girl. Just as quick as I can."

Friday afternoon, Jolene sat on the corner of Lydia's desk, waiting for her friend to finish reading the latest *Rust Creek Ramblings* column.

"Oh, I've read this thing at least twenty times since it came out in yesterday's paper and it's still just as terrible! Awful!" Lydia tore her gaze from the paper long enough to glance in the direction of Curtis's office. "What is our boss going to think if he figures out the Rambler is talking about me? This is so embarrassing and so wrong! Damn it, I wish I knew who was writing this stuff. I'd give him or her a piece of my mind."

Jolene was incredulous. "You mean someone did actually see Zach kissing you? Out on the sidewalk in broad daylight?"

"Well, yes. But it's not like the Rambler makes it sound. It was just a little friendly kiss. Nothing more. Really, Jolene, think about it. Do I look like a woman Zach Dalton would be going after?"

Bending her head close to Lydia's, Jolene said in a hushed voice, "Like I told you before, there's nothing wrong with your looks. And men don't restrict their appetites to just one type of woman."

"Well, I can assure you that Zach is just a friend." He'd certainly made that clear enough last Monday evening when he'd placed that little kiss on her lips. He'd kept insisting over and over that there'd been nothing to the intimate contact, and after the nonchalant way he'd behaved about the kiss, she could certainly believe him. "He's still going through piles of mail, trying to pick out the lucky winner who will ultimately be his bride. Yuck! Is that the way you'd want to be chosen for some man's wife? Not me."

Jolene wrinkled her nose. "To be honest, the idea of being 'picked' like a lottery number is not appealing to me at all. I want to be romanced and cherished. Mostly, I want to be loved."

"Well, I don't think that is going to happen here in this office—on Lydia's desk!"

The sound of Curtis's voice had Jolene jumping to

her feet and Lydia pushing the newspaper away from her keyboard.

"Oh, I...I was just—uh—discussing the Rambler's column with Lydia," Jolene stuttered. "If you'll excuse me, I'll get back to work."

Jolene started to scurry back to her office, but Curtis quickly stopped her.

"Wait a minute, Jolene. Come back here. I want to talk with you and Lydia."

"What have we done wrong?" Jolene asked as she skirted around Curtis and stood next to Lydia's chair.

He shook his head impatiently. "You haven't done anything wrong. I wanted to see if either of you is going to the Ace in the Hole tonight? I want to do a piece about the impact *The Great Roundup* is having on the bar. I hear they've been having rip-roaring viewing parties. But Artie is busy tonight and so is Colette. Roberta is tied up with another project. And I have a prior out-of-town engagement. I need someone from the *Gazette* to be there and give me a firsthand account."

"I'd love to go," Jolene said. "But I've already made plans with relatives tonight. I suppose I could break them. That is, if Lydia can't go."

Curtis leveled a look on Lydia. "What about it?"

"I hadn't thought about it. But I could go."

Who was she kidding? All week long she'd been thinking about going to the Ace in the Hole just to see if Zach really would be watching for her. On the other hand, she'd been telling herself that the less she saw of Zach, the better off she'd be.

Curtis looked immensely pleased. "Great, Lydia. No need to bother with a notebook or anything. Just take some mental notes and we'll put something together Monday."

"I haven't done any reporting since my college days," Lydia warned him. "But I'll try to take extra notice of everything."

"I'm sure you'll do fine," he told her, then purposely glanced at the clock on the wall. "We still have time to get something done today, don't you think, ladies?"

He left the room and Jolene glanced ruefully at Lydia. "Back to the grind. Have fun tonight. And for Pete's sake, if a man asks you to dance—go for it!"

"I'm not going to dance," Lydia argued. "I'm going to report."

Shaking her head, Jolene left the room and Lydia reluctantly picked up the newspaper scattered over her desk.

Has Zack Dalton finally found his Mrs. Right? Or was the kiss in front of the *Gazette* just more of his fun and games?

Snorting at the Rambler's ridiculous questions, she folded the paper and shoved it in a drawer. Out of sight and out of her mind. At least, until tonight.

Zack had been helping his brothers finish up the evening chores around the barn when Lydia's text message came in to let him know she'd be at the Ace in the Hole. After waiting all week and not hearing a word from her, the little note had left him ecstatic, and he'd showered and changed for the evening ahead in record time.

When he arrived at the popular nightspot in Rust Creek Falls, the parking lot was already overflowing with vehicles, an indicator the bar would be equally packed. His assumption was right. A line had already formed at the entrance, so he joined the end and waited his turn to pay the cover charge.

Several minutes later, he finally entered the honky-tonk, only to see it was crammed with people standing, sitting at tables and lined up at the long bar. Music spilled from a jukebox and, over on the small dance floor, couples were dancing elbow to elbow.

His brothers Cole, Garrett and Shawn were probably somewhere among the crowd, but finding them wasn't Zach's priority. His main thought was to find Lydia.

"Hey, Zach, you managed to make it in before they shut the doors?"

Zach turned toward the voice to see his cousin Eli sidle up to him. "I've been here about two minutes," he told him. "Have they really shut the doors?"

"That's what I heard someone say," Eli replied. "The fire marshal wants to make sure the place doesn't exceed capacity. If you ask me, it's already gone beyond that."

Zach could only hope that Lydia had already arrived.

"So where's your date for tonight?" Eli asked. "Gone to the powder room?"

Zach shook his head. "I didn't bring a date tonight."

Eli looked shocked. "Are you kidding? This is the kind of night that brings out the best in a woman," he said, then grinned as a loud female laugh sounded over the din. "Or maybe I had that backward. Maybe it brings out the worst."

From the corner of his eye, Zach caught a glimpse of a head of curly brown hair. Although the woman sitting at a table had her back to him, he felt certain it had to be Lydia. No woman had hair like hers.

"I, uh, just needed a break," Zach told him. "Sometimes a man needs some time alone."

Eli chuckled. "Yeah, that's why he comes to a bar packed with people."

Zach laughed along with his cousin. "Well, you know what they say. A person can be in a crowd and still be alone."

Eli glanced curiously at him. "Hmm. How is your hunt for the perfect wife going?"

Perfect? Zach was beginning to believe the list he'd made for the perfect wife was coming back to haunt him.

"I'm working on it. So how is your love life going now? You have a special lady hidden away somewhere?"

Eli grimaced. "No one hidden. I haven't met anyone that interests me."

"Eli, there are plenty of gorgeous women around here. All you need to do is go after the one that suits your fancy."

"I don't have your self-confidence, Zach," he said with a wry grunt, then motioned with his head toward the bar. "Let's go see if we can wedge our way in and get a beer."

"No, thanks. You go ahead," Zach told him. "I see someone I want to say hello to."

The cousins parted and Zach began to work his way through the crowd, toward the billow of brown curls. But before he could reach her, two young women he'd met at *The Great Roundup* viewing the week before waylaid him.

"Zach! We've been looking all over for you," the blonde exclaimed as she crooked an arm tightly around his.

"That's right," her friend chimed in as she latched on to Zach's opposite arm. "We were afraid you weren't going to show. And the night just wouldn't be the same without you here."

"It's good to see you, ladies. But actually I was, uh, on my way to see a friend." He started to extract his arms, but both women held on tight.

"You can't run off now," the blonde exclaimed. "We just found you!"

"That's right," the second woman said with a happy giggle. "You can at least have a drink with us first."

Deciding the easiest way to get himself out of this fix was to have a quick beer and then make his exit, he said, "Okay, ladies, let's see if we can make our way to the bar."

Lydia wished she'd never promised Curtis she'd come here tonight. The place was so jammed with people she wondered if there was any oxygen left in the room. Along with that, the noise had reached an unbearable level. If Zach was here, she'd probably never see him.

The thought of Zach had her glancing down at her outfit. She didn't know what had possessed her to put on a pale blue blouse with a low neckline and a pair of tight black jeans. She hadn't worn this kind of clothing since she'd gone to a rock concert in Billings and that had been a few years ago. Now she felt like everyone was staring and wondering who, or what, she was trying to be.

"Hi, Lydia. Is it okay if Janie and I join you? Or is someone else sitting at your table?"

Lydia looked up to find Anne Lattimore, the blonde divorcée who worked as a receptionist at Dr. Brooks's veterinary office. Her young daughter was gathered close to her side.

Relieved to see a pair of familiar faces among the

rowdy crowd, she gestured to the empty chairs. "Hi, Anne. Please join me before any more strangers come along and carry the chairs off to another table."

"Thanks. I was beginning to think Janie and I were going to have to stand up during the show."

Mother and daughter settled themselves in the seats across the table from Lydia. Both of them had bottles of soda with straws. As good as the drinks looked, Lydia would have paid dearly for a beer. Anything to dull the thoughts of Zach going through her head.

"I told Janie we'd probably be able to see the show better at home on our own TV, but I'd promised we'd come to the Ace in the Hole for the viewing tonight." Anne glanced affectionately at her daughter. "Janie's in a blue mood. She's missing her best friend."

Lydia looked at the young girl who appeared to be around nine or ten years old. She was the spitting image of her lovely mother, but there was a sad look on her face. "Who is your best friend, Janie? Maybe I know her."

"Abby Fuller. She has two little sisters. Kiera and Kaylee."

"Oh sure. Those are Marissa Fuller's girls. I heard they all went to Paris with that billionaire guy she's going to marry."

"Yeah," Janie mumbled miserably, "and they're still gone."

Anne exchanged a helpless look with Lydia. "Yes, she and Autry Jones and the girls are still in France. But I keep explaining to Janie that her best friend won't be there forever."

Lydia gave the child an encouraging smile. "That's right. And when your friend comes home, she'll have all kinds of exciting stories to tell you. And you'll be able to catch her up on everything that's happened in *The Great Roundup*."

Janie tilted her head to one side and the other as she digested Lydia's suggestion and then she shrugged both shoulders. "Yeah. I guess you're right. I'd better make sure I remember everything that happens on the show."

Anne looked at Lydia and smiled her thanks and for the next several minutes the three of them talked about the show and other things that had been going on with mutual acquaintances around Rust Creek Falls.

Then just before the music went quiet and the big-screen TV flickered to life, Anne and Janie left the table to find a spot in the room where Janie could see over the heads in the crowd.

Lydia decided to make her way to the bar and was relieved to find an empty stool with a decent view of the TV.

A young waitress with short red hair leaned across the bar toward Lydia. "Want anything to drink, honey?"

"A beer, please," Lydia told her. "And don't bother with a glass."

The waitress started to turn away, then paused and looked back at Lydia. "Say, aren't you the newspaper woman?"

"That's right. I'm the assistant manager at the *Gazette*."

A curious look on her face, the waitress leaned over the bar again. "Then maybe you can settle an argument between me and my girlfriends. We're all wondering who Zach Dalton was kissing in front of the *Gazette*. I say it had to be Collette. She's the youngest and cutest gal that works for the paper. One of my friends thinks it might be Jolene. She's older, but she's sexy. And another has the idea his kissing partner was someone that wasn't connected to the paper at all. Do you know?"

Of course they wouldn't be guessing Lydia would be the woman whom Zach had kissed. She should be relieved, but in a way, it made her feel like a squashed bug.

"Sorry. Only the Rambler knows and he or she isn't telling."

"Aww. That's a bummer. He's here tonight. Zach Dalton, I mean. If I have a chance, I just might ask him myself," she said with a playful grin, then turned to go. "I'll be right back with your beer."

Zach was here. Just hearing the man was somewhere in the bar set her heart to pounding. And though she told herself not to bother, she swiveled the bar stool first to the right and then the left as her gaze roamed over the crowd for a glimpse of his face.

When she finally spotted him, he was completely encircled by a group of women, and from the looks on their faces, they were hanging on his every word. Not to mention his arms.

Eenie, Meenie, Miney, Mo. Which one would he choose for a bride? She didn't know who was more stupid. The women clustered around him or herself for wishing she was one of them.

The sound of a beer bottle being placed onto the bar in front of her pulled Lydia's attention away from the flirty scene and she quickly handed the waitress cash to pay for the drink.

"Keep the change," Lydia told her.

"Thanks. Enjoy the show."

It was a show, all right, Lydia thought grimly as her gaze slid back to Zach and his flock of groupies. From what Lydia could see, even more women had joined the little party.

Why had he even bothered asking Lydia if she was coming here tonight? He'd implied he wanted to meet up with her. He'd even asked her to text him and she'd been stupid enough to comply. But so far, he hadn't bothered to acknowledge her presence.

The thought had Lydia taking a long swig from the beer bottle. If it wasn't for promising Curtis to take mental notes of this rowdy event, she'd be gone in a heartbeat. She'd be far away from the sight of Zach and his potential brides.

Suddenly, the jukebox went quiet, announcing it was time for *The Great Roundup* to begin. Relieved for the distraction, Lydia turned her attention to the big screen.

For this episode, the contestants were required to saddle and ride their horses over a long, demanding obstacle course. The route included going under a waterfall, across a wide creek, climbing a steep gully and maneuvering over a network of fallen logs, before ultimately racing down a long flat stretch to the finish line.

The crowd in the bar was quick to react as each group took their turn at riding the arduous trail. Whoops and hollers erupted as riders struggled to keep their horses going as fast as possible without veering off the track or having their mounts balk completely. When one man lost his seat in the saddle and was nearly trampled by the following horse and rider, a collective gasp sounded around the room, and then the crowd went silent as medical personnel rushed in to make certain the cowboy wasn't seriously injured. Thankfully, he was only shaken by the mishap, but his mount ran away during the mayhem, instantly disqualifying him from finishing the obstacle course.

When it came time for Travis and Brenna's team to go, Lydia was holding her breath. There was no doubt that Travis could ride the rugged terrain without a problem, but could Brenna?

As the contest unfolded, Lydia realized her fears were unwarranted. Although Travis could have raced ahead of the group, he remained close to Brenna and even stopped and dismounted in order to help her lead her skittish horse through the waterfall.

Zach could say what he wanted about Travis's marriage proposal being impulsive, but it appeared to be the real deal to Lydia. The tender way Travis looked at Brenna couldn't be faked. No more than the affection that was in Brenna's eyes whenever she was near Travis. True love. Yes, Lydia could see it. Why couldn't Zach recognize it?

Because he didn't understand anything about true love. He wanted long legs, a willowy body and silky hair. And don't forget the pies. Oh no, Lydia couldn't let herself forget the cooking requirements.

Tilting the bottle to her lips, she realized it was empty and quickly decided she needed at least one more beer to finish this assignment.

She motioned to the barmaid and after a moment she arrived with another drink.

"Great episode tonight, don't you think?" the young woman asked. "Travis and Brenna are doing great. One thing's for sure, no matter who ends up winning the million dollars at the end of the show, Brenna is going to be the real winner. She'll have Travis."

"Yeah. She's got him all wrapped up," Lydia agreed.

"Too bad the men around here can't be more like the Daltons."

"You mean take-your-breath-away handsome?" Lydia asked.

"That part doesn't hurt. But I was thinking more along the lines of wanting marriage and a family. Like Travis and Zach."

Lydia's gaze cut furtively to the group of women crowding around Zach. At the moment they were giggling and pawing at him as though he was the only man in the room.

Playboy or family man? Ha! Lydia could give the Rust Creek Rambler the answer to *that* question. Zach Dalton was all about fun and games. And even if she'd been invited to join in, Lydia didn't want to play.

This evening was turning into a disaster, Zach thought as he attempted to watch the last leg of competition on the night's episode of *The Great Roundup*. So far he'd managed to watch only snippets of the show. As for Lydia, he hadn't had a chance to even say hello. Damn it! She was the real reason Zach had come to the Ace in the Hole tonight. Not to see his cousin on the big-screen TV or to have strange women throwing themselves at him.

I only wish that you'd find one girl and stick with her.

His father's words suddenly drifted through his thoughts, prompting him to look at the women ringed around him. He had to admit that some of them were beautiful. Some probably met all the requirements for becoming his wife. But none was giving him that deep-down happy feeling that Lydia gave him.

"Sorry, ladies, but you'll have to excuse me for now."

Without a backward glance, he walked away from the group and began to work his way to the bar, where Lydia was perched on a bar stool at the very end.

He hadn't noticed exactly when Lydia had left her table and moved over to the bar. But he had noticed that since she'd changed her seating, she'd been steadily tilting a beer bottle to her lips. The sight worried him greatly. Not for anything did he want her climbing into a car and driving home.

"Hello, Lydia," he said as he slid onto the stool next to her. "Having a good time?"

Her head slowly turned in his direction and she looked at him with exaggerated surprise. "Well, Zach Dalton, imagine you being here tonight! I would've never guessed. How are you? Still looking around for that special cook?" She giggled, then shook her head. "Oh, I'm sorry, I meant to say 'wife.' A cook. A wife. They're hardly the same, now, are they?"

She was rattling, and though Zach suspected she hadn't really drunk that much, it was obviously too much for her.

"The show is nearly over," he said soberly. "I think I should drive you home."

Her mouth fell open as she stared at him. "You? Drive me?" The idea left her cackling. "Zach, you're getting funnier every day."

"I'm not joking. I'm going to drive you home. Do you have a jacket?"

He put his hand on her arm, but she jerked it away.

"I'm not going anywhere with you. Go back to all your pretty women. They need you. I can take care of myself. I always have and I always will!"

Frowning, he wrapped a hand firmly around her

upper arm. "Lydia, do you have a jacket?" he repeated the question.

She scowled at him. "Why would I have a jacket? It's hot as blue blazes in here!" She used one hand to fan her face. "I'm sweating. Are you?"

He wasn't sweating at the moment, but he would be, Zach thought, if he didn't get her out of there.

"No. I'm fine." He slid an arm around her back and urged her off the bar stool. "Come on. The show is ending. Let's get out of here before the parking lot gets crazy."

To his relief, Lydia didn't argue with him this time, and with a bit of careful maneuvering, he managed to get her out of the bar and inside the cab of his truck.

After he'd carefully clicked the seat belt over her and started the engine, he asked, "Where do you live?"

"In a house. All by myself. That's where."

He let out an impatient breath. "Lydia, what is the address? Do you live here in town?"

Her brows puckered in a thoughtful frown as she looked at him and then around the confines of the truck cab. "What am I doing here with you? There are women back in there." She jabbed a finger in the direction of the bar. "You need to be with them. Not me."

Hoping to catch her attention, he said, "Maybe I should call Curtis—your boss. He can probably tell me where you live."

"Curtis? Oh Lord, now that man really needs a woman to loosen him up. He keeps his shirts buttoned right here." She drilled a finger into the hollow of her throat. "Tight as a piggin string. Makes me wonder how he breathes."

Seeing he was making no headway, he was wondering what to do next when she suddenly leaned across the console and touched her fingers to a bare spot of skin at the base of his throat.

"See, you don't button your shirts like that. I bet you can breathe just fine."

Even though this was a slightly altered Lydia who was touching him, she still had the power to affect him and he quickly grabbed her hand and placed it back in her lap before he forgot he was a gentleman.

"My breathing is just fine, Lydia. You sit back and let me…"

The rest of his words trailed away as he spotted her handbag lying on the floorboard near her feet.

Quickly he grabbed it and rifled through the contents until he found her wallet.

"Hey, what are you doing?" She reached over and attempted to pluck the driver's license from his fingers. "You don't need my credit card!"

Zach quickly read the address on the plastic card, then handed it to her. "Put it back in your wallet. It's your driver's license."

"What's the matter? You think I can't drive?"

As he pulled out of the parking spot, he glanced over to see her dropping the license into her open handbag, instead of returning it to the safe spot in her wallet.

"I think you need some coffee. That's what I think."

Ten minutes later, Zach had found Lydia's house. The little bungalow was one of a few that sat on a graveled road on the far west edge of town. A bulb had been left on over a tiny porch to shed a pool of yellow light over the front door.

He parked the truck and they walked to the porch. Though she managed to walk on her own, her movements were still a little slow as she dug around in her handbag for the house key.

"I can't find it." Her voice was full of irritation as she peered into the leather bag. "Guess you'll have to climb in a window. No. You're too tall. I'll climb through the window."

Not bothering to argue with her, he began to search around the porch for a hidden key. He finally found it slipped between a crack beneath the wooden threshold and the concrete porch.

"No need to climb anywhere," he told her. "I found the key."

Once he opened the door, he stepped aside and allowed her to precede him inside.

"Um…the light is right here…somewhere…on the wall."

She must have located the switch, because an overhead fixture came on to light a small living room. While she flung her handbag in the direction of a short red couch, Zach glanced around at the simple furnishings and the walls lined with shelves jammed with books. Apparently Lydia's preferred form of entertainment was reading. Or it could be that a book was her escape from the everyday grind. Either way, the discovery didn't surprise him. Clearly she wasn't a party girl. He figured after a long day of work at the newspaper office she'd much rather relax with a book than to go out with friends.

"This is nice," he said.

"Not nearly as nice as the Ace in the Hole—surrounded by a bunch of oversexed, pea-brained women." She waved a hand toward the door that was still partially open. "You'd better get over there before they close the place."

Zach's only intention had been to drive her safely home, but he decided he couldn't leave now. Not when she seemed so angry and mixed-up.

"I'm not going anywhere." He shut the door behind him and locked it. "So, where's the kitchen? Aren't you going to invite me for coffee?"

A comical frown twisted her features. "Coffee? What for? Your women are waiting."

For some reason she seemed to be fixated on the idea of *his* women. A fact that annoyed him far more than her consuming too much alcohol. He hadn't even taken a date to the Ace in the Hole tonight because he'd wanted to spend some exclusive time with Lydia.

Damn it, so far nothing about this night had turned out the way Zach had planned.

"No one is waiting for me," he said patiently. "I'm waiting on you to show me the kitchen."

His words must have registered, because she latched on to his hand and led him out of the room. "The kitchen. Right this way, Mr. Dalton."

The kitchen was a tiny rectangle but was fully equipped with small but modern appliances and a little round wooden table with two matching chairs.

"You sit down," he ordered. "And I'll make the coffee."

Spotting a drip machine on the counter, he crossed to it and dumped an inch of leftover brew from the glass carafe and washed it out.

Lydia didn't obey his suggestion to sit, but she did step out of his way as he began a search through the cupboards for ground coffee and filters.

"I don't keep very many groceries in the house," she said, then let out a mocking laugh. "Remember, I can't cook anything. I have to concentrate real hard just to boil water. What do you think about that?"

Other than the coffee and a box of saltine crackers, the cabinets were bare and he wondered if the refrigerator was equally empty. The idea bothered him greatly. Not that he thought she was going hungry. But because she was living so completely alone, her home spared of things that made a house warm and inviting.

"I think you can read and follow directions on a recipe. I think you just don't want to try. Because you don't have anyone but yourself to cook for."

He spooned coffee grounds into the machine, then quickly added the water. Over his shoulder he saw that Lydia had finally taken a seat at the table. If he was lucky, she'd remain there until he got some sobering coffee into her.

The amused look on her face disappeared. "So now Zach Dalton is a psychiatrist. Woo-hoo. That should come in handy with picking a wife. You can psychoanalyze her first—make sure she's mentally capable of being married to you."

He didn't bother to make any sort of reply to that. In the first place, he didn't understand why she was being so sarcastic. And second, he didn't want to talk about his search for a wife. Not tonight.

The coffee seemed to take forever to brew, but finally there was enough in the carafe to pour a cup for each of them. He found a small carton of half-and-half in the refrigerator, and after stirring a bit into hers, he carried the cups over to the table.

"Here. Drink this. It will make you feel better."

"Better? If I felt any better, I couldn't stand myself," she retorted.

Cradling his cup with both hands, he leaned back in the chair and let his gaze take a slow survey of her appearance. Not only was she acting out of character tonight, she looked different, he decided. Her pale blue blouse was soft and feminine and showed just a hint of cleavage, while her black jeans were tight enough to reveal the curvy shape of her hips and legs. She'd pinned one side of her hair back with a glittery barrette and he was stunned to see a pair of silver earrings dangling against her neck.

So Lydia Grant could be one sexy woman. Why hadn't he seen this side of her before? Or had it always been there and he just hadn't been able to see it?

"Try your coffee," he told her. "Before it gets cold."

She took a few sips and studied him through lowered lashes. "Why are you still here?"

"What is going on with you, Lydia? Why are you angry with me?"

Her lips formed a perfect O. "Angry? I never get angry."

He rolled his eyes. "Okay, you're vexed with me. Why?"

"Really? You have to ask?"

He'd heard his father say more than once that women were hard to understand. Well, tonight Zach had to agree. He was certainly having trouble following Lydia's riddles.

"I'm asking, aren't I?"

She squinted at him. "Sort of. Uh, what was the question?"

Zach stifled a groan. "Why are you miffed at me? What have I done?"

"Nothing. That's what. You can't even lift one hand and waggle a finger at me. Oh no, that would be asking too much."

His mind was beginning to spin as he tried to follow

the gist of her conversation. "I take it you were expecting me to wave at you or something?"

Her eyes widened as pink color splashed across her cheeks. "Or something! You're hilarious, Zach."

"Then why aren't you laughing instead of glowering at me?"

She gulped down more coffee. "I don't feel like laughing." She wiped a hand across her brow. "I feel hot. Do you? I think I'll open the window."

She started to rise from her chair, but Zach put a hand on her shoulder and gently eased her back down. "I'll open the window. You swallow some more of that coffee."

Leaving the table, Zach went over to the sink and pushed the window slightly up to let in a small stream of fresh air.

"You have your phone with you?" she asked.

He glanced over to see Lydia was rubbing the tips of her fingers back and forth against her forehead.

"Yes. Why?"

"Do you ever look at your messages?" As soon as she'd spoken the question, she began to shake her head vehemently, sending her brown hair flying about her head. "Oh, I'm so sorry. I'm not thinking straight. You only read the ones from prospective brides."

He rejoined her at the table. "I read your message and I replied."

The nod she gave him was greatly exaggerated. "Yep. 'See you there.' That's what you said. 'See you there.' Well, you saw me, all right. Guzzling beer and sitting there all alone—like somebody with the flu or the measles. I'm not contagious. And I don't think there's anything wrong with your feet." She pointed down at his boots. "No. They're both there—just like they always are."

In spite of everything, a smile began to spread across Zach's face, and before he knew it, the smile had turned into laughter.

"What's so funny?" she asked.

Still smiling, he leaned across the table toward her. "You're so cute even though you are a bit tipsy."

Shadows suddenly filled her blue eyes. "Cute? Don't patronize me, Zach."

From the serious tone of her voice, he could tell she was sobering up very quickly.

"Believe me, Lydia. You're more than cute to me." He reached across the table and cradled her face with his hand. "You're adorable and special."

"So what do you want?" she asked with a dose of heavy sarcasm. "For me to say I'll keep boxing and handling all your love letters?"

"No. That isn't what I want at all."

Something was suddenly pushing him to his feet and straight at her. The next thing Zack knew, he was drawing her from the chair and into the circle of his arms.

Her head fell back and she stared up at him in stunned fascination. "Zach, what are you doing? This is—"

Deciding she'd said enough, he bent his head and silenced her with a kiss. He hadn't expected the contact to cause an explosion. He'd only kissed her to stop her angry rant. But something caused an instant eruption to take place between them. All at once, their mouths were fused together, searching, pushing the kiss to an even deeper connection.

At some point, Zach felt her tongue probing at his teeth and he opened his mouth to allow her search to go even deeper. The all-consuming taste of her was enough to take his breath away, but still it wasn't enough. With his arms tightening against her back, he pulled her body tightly to his and reveled in the wondrous excitement pouring through him.

Lydia wasn't supposed to be making him feel this way. Making his head spin. Blood was rushing through his head, singing in his ears. What did it mean? What could it mean?

By the time Zach found the strength to lift his head, both of them were breathing hard and he was fairly certain the ground had literally shifted beneath his feet.

"Lydia." As he whispered her name, he stroked her soft cheek. "I don't know what just happened. Do you?"

Her eyes blinked as they struggled to focus on his face. "No. But it was good. Don't you think?"

He released a long, shaky breath and realized he was far drunker right now than she'd been back at the Ace in the Hole.

"Too damned good," he whispered. "We shouldn't be doing this."

"Why not?" she gently challenged.

Why? Try as he might, Zach couldn't come up with one good reason to resist the very thing he wanted most. And that was Lydia.

"You're right," he murmured. "We both want this and that's all that matters."

Her arms slipped around his neck and then her lips were moving provocatively against his. "Kiss me, Zach. Let's not think about tomorrow."

No. He wasn't going to think about tomorrow. He wasn't going to think about anything, except making love to Lydia.

Chapter Ten

How could this be happening? One minute Lydia had wanted to kick Zach in the shins for being so utterly clueless, and the next thing she knew, his arms were pulling her close, his lips kissing her like she was the tastiest dish he'd ever sampled.

Why her? Why now? A part of her wanted to tear her mouth from his long enough to ask him those questions. But the more he kissed her, the less she cared about getting answers. The fiery desire that was crashing through her was all that mattered. Having him touching her, loving her, was too thrilling to resist.

When he finally eased his mouth from hers, she was already lost in a dreamy fog and her only compass was his strong body next to hers, his hands anchored at the sides of her waist.

"The bedroom—where is it?"

Even as he asked the question, he was guiding her backward and out of the kitchen. As they slowly moved from the room and into the hallway, Lydia hardly recognized the familiar walls and floors of her house. Instead, she felt certain that Zach must have already lifted her to some other place. One she'd never visited before.

"Behind you," she said, her voice rushed and breathless. "On your right."

When they stepped through the open door of her bedroom, he fumbled along the wall until he found the light switch. The glare of the overhead light illuminated a standard-sized iron bed with tumbled covers, a nightstand and lamp, and a chest and dresser made of dark wood.

Moving away from him, she began to hurriedly snatch up the clothing she'd left strewn over the footboard of the bed. "Sorry about the mess. I—"

She didn't have a chance to say more or finish her tidying. He flipped off the light, then made his way to the lamp on the nightstand. Once the small glow lit the side of the bed, he returned to her. She gazed up at him in bemused fascination as he plucked the clothing from her hand and tossed it aside.

"I don't see any mess. All I see is you," he murmured. His hands slid from her shoulders and down her arms before wrapping around her wrists. "And what I see is making me very happy."

"Zach, you're not right in the head. I think—"

"Don't think." His lips came down on hers, hot and demanding, provoking her into a hungry response. "Just let me look at you. Touch you."

Her breaths coming in rapid gulps, her heart hammering out of control, Lydia watched as his fingers moved to the tiny buttons at the front of her blouse. His hands were strong, the skin tough from doing a man's work. The feel of them against her skin caused a friction that sent goose bumps up and down her arms and across the back of her neck.

When he finally pushed the fabric off her shoulders, his gaze fell to the white lacy bra cupping her breasts.

"Mmm. I knew underneath those clothes you'd be all woman."

He touched the soft flesh spilling over the garment, then quickly decided to rid her of it. The instant her rounded breasts were exposed, his hands cupped their weight while his thumbs raked back and forth across her tight nipples.

"Beautiful, Lydia," he whispered. "So perfect."

The way he said the words sounded so genuine, even loving. But that was probably because she wanted to think in those terms. She wanted to believe that to Zach she was a beautiful woman. One that he desired the most.

Her throat aching with emotion, she shook her head. "You don't have to shower me with sweet words, Zach. You don't have to pretend. There's a mirror right over there on the dresser. I can see. At best, I'm average-looking."

A scowl furrowed his forehead. "Pretend? Average? Stop selling yourself short," he gently scolded, then dipped his head to the curve of her neck. "I can see for myself. And I can appreciate beauty when it's right in my hands."

The sensation of his lips moving against her skin, his warm breath brushing her ear, was enough to turn her knees to mush. Latching her hands on to his shoulders, she tilted her head, giving him access to her neck. He pushed aside her hair as he nuzzled his way to her earlobe. After treating it to a gentle bite, his lips spattered light, taunting kisses across her cheek, down the bridge of her nose and finally onto her trembling lips.

This time as he kissed her, his hands went to work with the rest of her clothing. When her jeans slid to her feet but stuck at her boots, he lifted her onto the bed and knelt to remove them.

Lydia wanted to tell him she felt like Cinderella and he was the prince, preparing to slide a glass slipper onto her foot. But this wasn't a fairy tale and she hardly wanted Zach to think she was having such childish dreams about him. It had to be enough that he wanted her.

He tossed her boots aside and then her jeans quickly joined the discarded footwear. His gaze slid up her bare legs, till it was riveted on the minuscule scrap of lace that served as her panties.

As he continued to gaze at her, a wicked grin curved one side of his lips and Lydia felt sure her whole body was blushing bright pink.

"So there is a very feminine side of you." He leaned over her and slid a thumb beneath the waistband of her panties. "Why do you keep it hidden all to yourself?"

If her heart beat any faster, she was quite certain she was going to pass out before she ever had a chance to make love to him.

"I, uh, can't very well walk around naked. I have to keep it hidden."

The low chuckle in his throat vibrated right through her, and the sound warmed her as much as the touch of his hands.

"You don't want anyone to know you're a sexy little minx, do you? But I've discovered your secret. And the surprise is all mine." His voice lowered, along with his head. When his lips touched one puckered nipple, he whispered against it, "Tonight, you're all mine."

Lydia couldn't hold back her groan any more than she could stop her arms from wrapping tightly around him.

His tongue made lazy circles around each nipple before he finally fastened his lips around the sensitive flesh and drew it deep within his mouth. The sensation caused helpless little groans to sound in her throat, her body to ache with sweet agony.

Need had her squirming, shifting and searching for a position that would bring her even closer to his rock-hard body. Zach recognized her frustration, and easing away from her, he stood and began to remove his clothing with awkward jerks.

Lydia lay back and watched as each garment fell away until he was wearing only a pair of dark gray boxers. Even though she'd seen him without his shirt before, she still wasn't prepared for the depth and strength of his chest, the sinewy arms or the long, powerful legs. The sight of his rugged masculinity in the raw flesh was enough to cause her breath to catch in her throat.

When he returned to the bed, he stretched out beside her and, with a hand at the side of her waist, rolled her until the front of her body was pressed tightly against his.

"Now, this is better," he murmured against her neck. "Much better. You feel like a piece of warm velvet and taste like a marshmallow. All soft and sweet and good."

As he nuzzled her throat, his hands began to race over her, touching her in places she'd never been touched before. His fingers left rivulets of fire behind them and in a matter of moments she felt sweat dampening her face and belly while the rest of her skin sizzled like drops of water on a roaring flame.

Just when she thought she was going to be consumed by the heat, his hands cradled her face and his thumbs were tilting her mouth up to his. This time the movement of his lips on hers was hungry and ravaging, driving her desire to heights she'd never dreamed she could reach.

While he kissed her over and over, she clung to him, her whole body trembling, aching to be joined to his. When she couldn't bear another second, she reached for the hard shaft of manhood pressing against the thin fabric of his boxers.

When her fingers closed around him, he groaned deep in his throat and quickly rolled away from her.

"Do you use any birth control?" he asked, his voice raw and raspy.

A cynical laugh hung in her throat, practically choking her. "Me? Why would I need birth control?"

The look he shot her said he was questioning her sobriety. But Lydia could've assured him she was stone-cold sober and her mind was crystal clear. He was the one who'd gone a little off the beam. Otherwise, he would have already recognized she wasn't sexually active. One guy in the last five years hardly warranted the need for birth control.

He tried to answer. "I— Well, I just thought…you're single and attractive and you might want to be prepared for anything."

"No. I've not had any reason to be prepared," she said, then wondered if her admission would open his eyes and make her see she wasn't the type of woman a man desperately yearned to take to bed. Moreover, she wasn't *his* type of woman.

But apparently he wasn't put off by her revelation. Instead, he gave her a reassuring smile. "No need to worry. I'll take care of it."

He plucked his jeans from the floor and fished something from the pocket. When he slipped off the boxers and turned his back to her to ready himself, she felt a sting of tears prick her eyes.

Maybe Zach did want her for real, she thought. At this moment, she had to trust her heart and believe she was more to him than just a willing female body.

Returning to the bed, he gathered her close. With his nose nuzzling hers, his hand wiped the tangle of brown curls from her face.

"Lydia, if this is something— Well, if you're not sure, we can wait."

Even though her breasts were squashed flat against his chest, she tried to press herself even tighter against him. "Wait? Are you— Have you changed your mind? You don't want me?"

With a needy groan, his hands flattened against the base of her spine and urged her hips closer to his. "Oh, Lydia, I want you. More than you can know. But I don't want you to regret this. Not tonight, or ever."

Regret making love to this man? It was like a fairy tale come true. Tonight would be a memory she would carry in her heart forever.

She pressed her lips to his. "No regrets, Zach. Just make me all yours. Now. Right now."

Her whispered plea was all it took to convince him. Before she had time to draw a deep breath, his hands were planted on either side of her head, his body hovered over hers.

She dared to look up and her heart swelled with emotion at the soft tenderness she saw in his eyes.

"Zach."

His name came out as a husky plea, and then with his gaze still locked with hers, he spread her legs and drove himself into her.

Lydia thought she was prepared for the moment their bodies connected, but she'd not been expecting the instant euphoria that exploded inside her. Each cell that made up her being was wrapped in incredible warmth, and for a few delicious seconds her body went limp with exquisite pleasure.

And then he began to move in a taunting rhythm and everything changed. Hot desire took over and pushed her body into an excited rush to give and take. Mindlessly, she wrapped her legs around his and met his thrusts with a strength she hadn't known she possessed.

Time stretched on, but for Lydia it seemed that only seconds had passed before the need in her began to twist tighter and tighter into a flaming vortex, and the need for relief was the only thing driving her movements.

Pants for air intermingled with her moans, and then he was swallowing up those sounds as his lips covered hers and his tongue thrust deep into her mouth. The frantic connection was all it took to push her up and over the brink.

She needed to breathe. She needed to call his name. But she could do neither. He refused to relinquish his hungry hold of her mouth, and then suddenly it didn't matter whether she ever drew another breath of oxygen into her starved lungs. She was flying among the stars, her whole being headed straight for the moon.

Somewhere along the brilliant journey, she felt his

arms lifting her upper body off the bed, crushing her in an embrace that was so consuming she was certain her body had merged with his.

She was drifting helplessly when she felt his mouth finally tear away from hers. He cried her name, the sound raw and guttural, as he thrust deeply inside her one more time. Then suddenly she felt the mattress against her back and he was above her, shuddering with a final spasm of aftermath.

When he eventually rolled his weight away from her, Lydia fully expected him to rise from the bed and start dressing. Instead, she was completely stunned when he placed a hand on her hip and rolled her into the curve of his damp, warm body.

"Mmm." He nuzzled his cheek against hers as his fingers tangled themselves in her wild curls. "Do you have any idea what you've done to me?"

She eased her head back and tried to study his face in the dim lighting. It was damp with sweat and his black hair had fallen in a devilish wave over his forehead. A wry grin was curving one corner of his lips, and try as she might, she couldn't find one ounce of regret on his face. Or was she simply blinded by the pleasure that was still humming through her body?

"You mean you're not disappointed?"

The choked sound he made was full of disbelief. "You really are clueless about yourself, aren't you?"

"I'm not an experienced lover, Zach."

He brushed his lips against hers. "That's good. I'll spend the rest of the night giving you lessons."

Her eyes widened. "The rest of the night?" she asked incredulously.

His low, sexy chuckle sent shivers of anticipation over her bare skin.

"That's right. We're only getting started."

To prove his point, he began to kiss her again, and at that moment Lydia realized she was totally lost to him.

Where was she? And was that coffee she smelled coming from the direction of the kitchen? No. It couldn't be. She lived alone. And her coffeemaker was too antiquated to have a timer on it.

Rising groggily up on one elbow, she stared around her bedroom in stunned fascination, then down at the indented pillow next to hers. Had Zach really been in her bed, making love to her for most of the night? The memory of it seemed so real, yet the light of day told her she had to be dreaming. Zach Dalton wouldn't have been in her bed!

Her head flopped back against the pillow and the crash vibrated like a thousand tiny hammers pounding at her skull. "Oooh!"

She was clutching her head and moaning when Zach appeared at the side of the bed, a steaming cup of coffee in his hand.

Shocked by the sight of him, she grabbed for the sheet at the same time she realized she wasn't wearing a stitch of clothing.

"Good morning, sleeping beauty," he said with a cheerful smile. "Ready for coffee?"

Groaning, she rose to a sitting position while attempting to hold the sheet to her breasts. "Zach, what are you doing here?"

His expression bemused, he handed her the coffee.

"Are you telling me you've already forgotten last night? You really know how to crush a man's ego, Lydia."

Frowning, she squeezed her eyes shut as images of the two of them in bed began to flash through her mind. "No, um, I remember everything. It's just that I expected you to be gone this morning."

"Oh. You think I'm that sort of guy."

The disapproving tone in his voice had her opening her eyes to look at him. Disappointment was clearly written across his face and that confused Lydia even more. Surely Zach didn't care what she thought about him. He had loads of women standing in line to date him and persuade him that they were perfect wife material.

"I don't know what to think. This thing that happened between us was rather unexpected. Don't you think?"

"Well, yes. Sort of," he reluctantly agreed. "But that doesn't make it any less real."

Sipping her coffee, she studied him through a veil of lashes. The sex had been real, all right. But the feelings behind it? She couldn't imagine him having any genuine affection for her. Sex and love were entirely two different things. If she ever expected to hold on to her pride, she had to remember that. Not for anything did she want Zach to discover she'd been slowly and steadily falling in love with him.

He reached over and touched a hand to her forearm. The gesture brought a tight lump to her throat. Zach was everything she'd ever wanted in her life. And yet she was smart enough to know that even if they did try for a lasting relationship, it wouldn't work. She could never hold on to a man like him. She'd land in the same situation her mother had found herself in. Alone and looking back with anger and sadness. No, she thought.

Better to stop things now before they ever reached the point where her heart would split right down the middle. Or was she already there?

"Lydia, last night you promised you'd have no regrets. Do you still feel that way?"

Unable to meet his gaze, she stared down at the bed-covers. "No. I don't regret anything." Which was true enough, Lydia thought. Someday, after years had passed, she'd be glad for her memories. Glad that she was able to experience the heights of passion with this man. "But listen, Zach, just because we were together last night doesn't mean I expect any sort of commitment from you."

"You don't?"

The confusion in his voice had her glancing back up to his face.

"Why, no. I've always been an independent woman. And that's the way I intend to stay."

"Independent," he repeated. "Like without a man."

She did her best to plaster a smile on her face while hoping he'd never guess just how plastic the expression actually was.

"That's right. I like being free—with no one to answer to but myself. And you have your hunt on for a wife. We really need to just keep things casual, don't you think?"

Stung by her cavalier attitude, Zach walked over to a pair of double windows and stared out at the small back-yard enclosed by a chain-link fence. There were no trees or lawn furniture. No doghouse or even a stray cat. The grassy square appeared to be as empty as he felt.

Last night had been the most perfect night of his life.

Lydia had been the most perfect woman he'd ever held in his arms. And this morning as he'd dressed and made coffee, he'd been bowled over by happiness. He'd finally found the woman he wanted to live with for the rest of his life.

Now she was telling him she didn't want any part of his future plans. What was wrong with her? Had last night only been an evening of pleasurable sex? And what was wrong with him? Why hadn't he realized long before now that Lydia was the woman he should have been pursuing?

"So you think I should keep up my hunt for a wife?"

"Well, sure. That is what you've wanted for a long time. And I'm not about to stand in your way of finding your dream."

You are my dream, Lydia. Can't you see that? Didn't you feel it last night when we made mad, passionate love?

Aloud he said, "I guess I should be thankful you're being so considerate about my future plans."

"I want you to be happy, Zach. That means a lot to me."

He thought he heard a slight quaver in her voice. Or maybe he'd imagined the emotional sound. Maybe he simply wanted to believe there was a part of her that genuinely cared for him.

Turning, he walked back to the bed. "And I want you to be happy, too, Lydia. If that means giving you space, then I'll go along with your wishes."

For right now, Zach thought. But later? No. He wouldn't be much of a man if he let the woman he wanted most slip right through his fingers.

She smiled at him. "Great. We can still be friends after this. Maybe better friends than even before."

"Sure," he said, trying his best not to sound flippant. "Best friends. So if you'd like to get dressed I'll take a friend to breakfast."

She laughed softly. "See, there are some good sides to not knowing how to cook."

The following Tuesday, Lydia had used her lunch hour to visit her mother at Snow Valley. Now, as she prepared to return to the *Gazette* office, Rhoda followed Lydia onto the long front porch of the nursing facility to say goodbye.

"Lydia, honey, are you sure you're not ill? You look like you've lost ten pounds since I last saw you."

"I could stand to lose a few pounds, Mom. I'm fine, really. It's just that I've been very busy at the newspaper office, that's all."

Busy trying to forget she'd had one too many beers at the Ace in the Hole and had ended up making love to Zach as though there would be no tomorrow, she thought ruefully. But try as she might, she couldn't forget that night any more than she could ignore the fact that he was a man on a mission. With an endless supply of willing women at his beck and call.

Her mother's hand suddenly wrapped warmly over her shoulder. The comforting touch brought an unexpected lump of emotion to Lydia's throat.

"I hope you're not disappointed in Saul," Rhoda said. "I was really hoping you'd like him."

A few minutes ago, Rhoda had taken her by Saul's room and introduced her to the man. Lydia had been pleasantly surprised at his positive spirit and genuine kindness. He was exactly the sort of man her mother needed in her life.

"Oh, Mom, Saul is very nice. I'm not disappointed at all. In fact, I'm thinking you'd better lasso him before he gets that cast off his leg. You don't want to let him get away."

Rhoda giggled like a schoolgirl and Lydia was amazed by the playful reaction. A month ago she would've never guessed a man would come along and make such a change in Rhoda Grant's lonely life. Too bad the man who'd walked into the newspaper office and turned Lydia's heart upside down hadn't changed her life for the better. Ironically it was Lydia who'd turned into a miserable fool over a man she could never have.

"You're right, sweetheart. Saul is a keeper. And I think he likes me. Don't you think?"

Lydia smiled at her mother. "He looks at you like you're an angel, Mom. I'm certain he likes you."

Lydia kissed her mother's cheek. "It's time I got back to the office. I'll call you soon," she promised.

On the drive back to the *Gazette*, Lydia tried to shake away thoughts of Zach, but they seemed to follow her no matter where she was or what she was doing. Over the past four days, she'd been struggling to convince herself she'd done the right thing by telling him they needed to keep things casual between them.

When Lydia had told him she wanted him to be happy, she'd sincerely meant it. Losing his mother had affected him deeply and filled him with an urgency to have a family of his own. He wouldn't be happy if he let go of his dream to find the perfect wife. The one who could bake like a pastry chef and look like a model while doing it. No, Lydia wasn't Zach's type. And for both their sakes, she had to remember that.

Later that afternoon, she was at her desk, taking an ad over the phone, when the bell on the door rang. Glancing up, she spotted Zach's long, tall frame entering the newspaper office and her heart began to pound so rapidly that the customer's voice in her ear faded to a dim muffle.

Today was the first she'd seen of him since last Saturday morning, when he'd served her coffee in bed. Yet the memory was still so vivid it sent a warm flush over her face.

Jerking her attention off him and back to the customer on the phone, she said, "That's right, Mrs. Weaver, the ad will appear in the next issue of the *Gazette*. If you want to make any changes after that, all you need to do is give me a call."

Although her gaze was focused on the notepad on her desk, she could still see his boots coming closer and closer until they parked themselves in front of her desk. His presence jolted her so much she was practically stuttering into the phone.

"Uh, yes, thank you…No—it'll be fine—I'll take care of it…Yes—that's right—goodbye."

She hung up the phone, and as she attempted to gather her scattered senses, she called upon every dramatic skill she possessed to give him a cheerful smile.

"Hello, Zach. Here for your mail?"

He sank his lanky body into the plastic chair positioned in front of her desk, and immediately Lydia's gaze traveled over his rugged face and down to his broad shoulders. Today he was wearing a Western shirt of brown plaids, the ubiquitous tiger eye bolo tie loose and resting against his upper chest. And without even trying she was suddenly picturing him with the shirt peeled away. All those hard muscles would flex with each little movement he made.

The erotic image was enough to make her breath catch in her throat and she coughed in an effort to break the spell.

Smiling at her, he said, "Actually, I thought we might go to lunch at the Gold Rush. That is, if you've not eaten yet."

Regret swamped her, but she quickly told herself it was for the best that she'd already taken her lunch break. The less time she spent with Zach, the better it would be for both of them. She needed to move on and let him get on with the business of finding a wife.

"Oh, I'm sorry, Zach. I had lunch with my mother at her workplace."

He shrugged and for a moment Lydia actually thought she saw a bit of disappointment on his face. But that was foolish thinking. The man could hardly walk down the sidewalk without women following after him. He hardly needed Lydia's company.

"I should've called first," he said.

"Well, I'm sure there are plenty of women here in town who'd love to go to lunch with you. Why don't you call one? Right now." She gestured to the phone. "Or better yet, go by Daisy's Donut Shop and see Eva-Rose. She's perfect for you."

Her suggestion appeared to completely confuse him. "You think that's what I ought to do?"

The smile she forced on her lips made her entire face feel as though it was going to crack. "Sure I do. What man wouldn't want a woman like her?"

He cleared his throat and shifted in the seat, and Lydia

had to fight to stop herself from racing around the desk and flinging herself into his arms. Having his lips on hers and his arms wrapped around her would make the world feel right again. But ultimately that would take her down a dead-end street. And she didn't want to spend the next several years pining for what might have been with Zach.

"I don't know," he answered. "Men like all types of women."

"Yes, but you're focused on one type and Eva-Rose certainly fits the bill." In spite of the sick clench in the pit of her stomach, she gave him another broad smile. "I'll get your mail. I'm sure you're eager to dig through it."

Rising from her chair, she hurried over to the space between the file cabinets where she'd been stashing Zach's stacks of correspondence. As she pulled out the boxes, she squeezed her eyes shut and willed away a sting of tears.

He said, "Actually, Lydia, I wanted to talk with you about the ad. I think it's time I put a stop on it."

Certain she'd heard him wrong, she gathered the cardboard boxes in her arms and walked back over to her desk. "You're going to stop the ad? But why? You haven't found a bride yet. Or have you?"

A shade of magenta came over his face and the nauseated feeling in Lydia's stomach grew worse.

"I, um, I'm fairly certain I've found her. I'm just not sure she's ready to accept my proposal."

Was this what it felt like to be dead and still be breathing? she wondered.

She asked, "What's the matter with the woman? Is she crazy?"

He cut a pointed glance in her direction. "I'm beginning to think she is a little mixed-up. But I'm hoping her head will clear in time and we can have a wonderful life together."

Lydia plopped the boxes down on the desk in front of him. "I see. Well, until that happens, you need to keep going through this stuff. A woman admires a man who sticks to his plans and sees them through. If you stop the ad now, it will make you look like you've quit paddling in the middle of the stream. That wouldn't leave a good impression."

Damn the impression, Zach thought. Damn the whole mess! He'd been crazy to believe he could find a wife through a newspaper ad. His dad had been right. Picking a wife from a list of applicants was a bunch of bull manure. A man needed to be in love.

Zach only wished he'd recognized he was in love with Lydia before he'd slept with her. With more time, he might've convinced her that the two of them were right for each other. But like a clueless idiot he'd not realized what was happening to him until he'd taken her home and then to bed. Making love to Lydia had opened his eyes and his heart. Unfortunately the whole night had seemed to have the opposite effect on Lydia. Not only did she seem dead set on staying single, she appeared to be distancing herself from him.

Oh Lord, what was he going to do? Keep going through the motions of this farcical search while all along he wanted to drag Lydia to the nearest preacher and have her say "I do" before she could change her mind?

Totally frustrated and confused, he leaned toward her and lowered his voice. "Lydia, about the other night… Are you sure you're not miffed at me?"

For one second something flashed in her eyes that made him think she was about to make an angry lunge for his throat. But he must have been mistaken, because a provocative smile suddenly curved her lips.

"Miffed? Of course not. It's not like we're in love with each other or anything close to it. We had a pleasant night together. I'm not making any big deal out of it. And neither should you."

A big deal? It was the biggest, most earth-shattering experience he'd ever encountered with a woman and he was supposed to forget it? Damn it all!

Shaking his head, he snatched up the boxes of mail and rose to his feet. "Okay. I'm convinced. Keep the ad running. In fact, make it even larger and put a bold banner around the whole thing! I want some real attention!"

Too annoyed with her to even say goodbye, he stalked to the door, only to have her call after him.

"Where are you going? To see Eva-Rose at the doughnut shop?"

"Hell yes! At least she appreciates my company."

Outside on the sidewalk, he swore again as he strode toward his parked truck. He might as well inform his family he was going to enter a monastery. Because he was never going to make love to another woman for as long as he lived!

Chapter Eleven

"Lydia, could you come back here, please?"

The next afternoon, the sound of Curtis's voice rattled Lydia's concentration, and with a heavy sigh, she saved her work on the computer and hurried back to her boss's office.

"You needed me?" she asked as she approached his pristine desk.

He gestured toward the empty wooden chair angled toward one end of his desk. "Sit down, Lydia. I have something to talk over with you."

Uneasy now, she took a seat. She hated change and that was exactly what she'd heard in Curtis's voice.

"Is anything wrong?" she asked before he had a chance to begin.

Frowning, he pushed his black-framed glasses higher on his nose. "Not at all. In fact, I couldn't be happier with the way things are going with the paper. You know, you were right all along, Lydia. I should listen to you more."

Stunned, she stared at him. "Really? What was I right about?"

"Zach Dalton, of course. And his ad for a wife. At first I hated all that clutter the mailman was dropping off here at the office. But it didn't take long for me to recognize the publicity was selling papers. We've sold more copies in the past month than we did in all of last year! The man has turned out to be a gold mine for the *Gazette*!"

Lydia shifted uncomfortably on the chair. "Zach was in the office yesterday picking up his mail. I think I should warn you that he was considering stopping the ad. But I managed to talk him out of it. For now, at least."

He shot her a look of relief. "Good work, Lydia. This plan I have won't work unless it's obvious to the public that Mr. Dalton is still searching for a wife."

She leaned forward as her uneasiness turned into pure dread. "What plan?"

"That's the reason I wanted to talk with you. I want to have the townsfolk of Rust Creek Falls decide who would make the best bride for Zach. We're going to invite everyone to write in with their vote, along with an explanation as to why this certain woman should become Zach's wife. Then after a certain length of time—say a week or something like that—we'll throw a big announcement party at the Ace in the Hole and reveal the winner of the contest. I think we should call it Zach's Perfect Bride Contest. Who knows, it might turn out to be an even bigger event than the viewing of *The Great Roundup*."

Lydia was completely appalled by the whole concept. "A contest? Oh, Curtis, I can't believe you came up with this crazy idea. It's not like you at all."

"Well, maybe the idea isn't like me. And I'll admit it originated from someone else. But that's insignificant. I think the whole concept will be great. The readers will love getting involved with Zach's quest. And in my opinion, the man could use some advice. His hopping from one woman to the next makes him look confused and indecisive."

I'm fairly certain I've found her. I'm just not sure she's ready to accept my proposal.

Zach's words from yesterday were suddenly marching through Lydia's head all over again. If he'd already found the woman of his dreams, he hardly needed any interference from the newspaper. But she couldn't be the one to burst Curtis's bubble. Besides, Zach was a grown man. He didn't have to follow the townspeople's advice. Not unless he wanted to.

"I think you'd better run this contest by Zach first," she cautiously suggested. "You certainly wouldn't want a lawsuit against the *Gazette*."

Thoughtful now, Curtis leaned back in his chair. "Hmm. You have a point there, Lydia. Perhaps you should be the one to run the plan by Zach. After all, you're friends with the man."

Unable to remain still any longer, she jumped from the chair and began to move restlessly about the room. "We're not exactly chummy anymore."

"Oh. Does that mean you don't want your name thrown into the pot of potential brides?"

And have all the townspeople writing in about her shortcomings? And why she was the last woman on earth who should be Zach's wife? Not in a million years!

Horrified by the whole notion, she stopped and stared at him. "That's exactly what I mean! If I ever catch a husband, it's going to be the old-fashioned way. Not because I've won some idiotic contest."

Curtis studied her suspiciously and Lydia suddenly realized she'd been protesting far too loudly and vehemently.

"I…I'm sorry, Curtis. I got carried away there for a minute. Your plan is ingenious. And I'm sure it will be great publicity for the *Gazette*. It's just that I…I'm not the marrying kind."

His expression relaxed and Lydia let out a silent breath of relief.

"I see. Well, I'll call Mr. Dalton myself. In the meantime, I'd like for you and Jolene to put your heads together on this and come up with a list of at least three women for the readers to vote on. Once that's done, the rest will easily fall into place."

Pain was suddenly pounding in the middle of Lydia's forehead. How in the world was she going to hide from this fiasco? Not for anything did she want to be around when this perfect bride for Zach was going to be announced. She wanted to be somewhere far away. Where she could forget she'd ever met the man. And thoughtlessly fallen in love with him.

Two days later, Zach and Booker had been riding a far west pasture on the Circle D for most of the day, searching for any weanlings that might have been left behind during a roundup they'd made of the herd yesterday. So far the men hadn't found any calves. A good sign that none of the babies had been left behind.

"It's hot as heck for the end of October," Booker said. He pulled a kerchief from around his neck and used it to mop his face. "I'll be ready for a tall glass of iced tea when we get back to the ranch house. And later a beer at the Ace in the Hole. You going to *The Great Roundup* viewing tonight?"

Zach had no desire to go to the bar and have a bunch of women pawing over him. And he sure as heck didn't want to see Lydia there again. He didn't want to be reminded of last Friday night when he'd wound up taking her home and making love to her for hours on end. That night had changed everything inside him. Thanks to her sweet lips and giving body, everything he'd ever thought he wanted was no longer on the list.

Last night, he'd tried another date with Eva-Rose. He'd even splurged big-time and taken her to a ritzy restaurant in Kalispell. During the fancy meal, the candlelight had made her even more beautiful and her company had been pleasant. At the end of the evening, he'd been eager to kiss her again, hoping against hope that something would spark and burn the memory of Lydia's lovemaking from his mind. But kissing Eva-Rose had been like kissing an old friend. Nothing had clicked. Not with him, or with her, as far as he could tell, and he'd driven home feeling even more frustrated.

"I don't think so," he finally answered Booker's question. "I'm not in the mood to face that crowd tonight."

"You're going to be facing more than a crowd whenever that newspaper contest comes to a close," Booker commented. "By the way, Dad isn't too happy about that development. What in the world were you thinking? You're gonna let the folks of Rust Creek Falls pick your wife? You're nuts, brother!"

"Gee, thanks, Booker. That makes me feel even better about the whole damned mess!"

Booker stared at him. "You mean you're not happy about the Zach's Perfect Bride Contest?"

Happy? He was angry and sick and everything in between. "Hell, no! I didn't want any part of it. But when the newspaper editor called me about the whole idea, I couldn't very well tell him no."

"Why not? You don't owe the man anything."

Zach shrugged. How could he explain to his brother that the only woman he'd ever loved worked at the *Gazette*? Damn it, he couldn't explain anything. Because Lydia had made it clear that she didn't give a hoot about him.

"He's Lydia's boss," Zach eventually replied. "I didn't want to make problems for her."

"Lydia? Why should she matter? I didn't see her name on the list of contestants." Booker laughed, then rolled his eyes toward the wide blue sky. "Sorry, I shouldn't have used the word *contestants*. One of these women is supposed to become your wife."

As the horses slowly plodded along the trail leading back to the ranch yard, Zach shook his head and tried to push away the heavy nausea roiling in his stomach.

"None of those women is going to be my wife, Booker. I've already decided who I want to marry."

Surprised, Booker glanced at him. "You have? Who?"

"I'm not going to say," Zach said with grim determination. "Not until I've had a chance to work things out with her."

Booker snorted. "The way I see it, you'd better work fast. By next Saturday night, Rust Creek Falls is going to pick your bride."

Booker was right, Zach decided. He had to come up with a plan and he had very little time to waste. But how was he going to convince Lydia that she was the marrying kind and the only woman he wanted for a wife?

"Lydia, you look as sexy as all get-out in that skirt."

The exclamation came from Jolene as the two women stood in a dressing room in the back of a little boutique located a few blocks away from the *Gazette*. Normally, the staff never worked on Saturday, but Curtis had decided to print a special edition to capitalize on Zach's Perfect Bride Contest, so all the staff had been called in for the day. Somehow, during their lunch break, her friend had talked her into buying something new to wear to the big party tonight at the Ace in the Hole. But so far everything she'd tried on had looked frumpy.

"I couldn't," Lydia argued as she stared at the image of herself in the full-length mirror. The black leather did cling to her hips in the best of ways, but the short hemline showed off her legs. Something Lydia wasn't accustomed to doing. "I look like a—"

"Rock star!" Jolene finished for her. "Because you're certainly rocking that look."

To further make her point, Jolene grabbed up a black satin tank top and held it up to Lydia. "This will make the outfit complete. You have great arms and shoulders. Let everyone see them."

Everyone didn't matter, Lydia thought. What would Zach think if he happened to see her at the party tonight? That she was making some sort of last-ditch effort to catch his attention?

Lydia, you have to be the silliest woman in Rust Creek Falls. Probably the whole county. Zach isn't going to have one single thought about you tonight or any night to come. You pushed him away. You told him you weren't the marrying kind. Now the townsfolk have chosen a bride for him. In a few hours, the big announcement will be made. And you can kiss any chance at snagging Zach a final goodbye.

Irritated at the mocking voice in her head, Lydia stepped out of the black leather skirt and tossed it toward her friend.

"You're right, Jolene! I am ready to rock this night and to heck with what anyone thinks." She tugged on her jeans. "Now if you'll help me find some heels to go with this getup, we should make it back to the *Gazette* before our lunch hour is up."

Jolene shot her a wicked grin. "Now you're talking, girl!"

For the remainder of the day, Lydia tried to focus on her work and not think about the party or Zach, but as the minutes began to tick down to quitting time, she desperately wanted to make one last plea to Curtis to allow her to skip the *Gazette* party. But she'd already tried once and the response she'd gotten from her boss had made it very clear she had to be at the Ace in the Hole tonight, or she wouldn't be sitting at her desk Monday morning.

Several hours had passed since then and now she found herself standing at the edge of an enormous crowd, trying to pretend she was any other place than the Ace in the Hole. But she was failing miserably. Especially when Zach suddenly walked up to her.

Apparently he was already having thoughts of a wedding, she decided as her gaze swept over his crisp white Western shirt and familiar bolo tie. She'd never seen him look more handsome, and to make matters worse, the smile on his face was the sweetest she'd ever seen.

"I'm glad you made it to the party, Lydia," he drawled. "Tonight is a very special night for me. And without you here, none of it would feel right."

Confused by his odd statement, Lydia studied his handsome face before she glanced down at the small cup of punch in his hand. Had Homer Gilmore been doctoring the punch bowl again? she wondered.

She said, "I can't imagine why my presence would make any difference."

"You can't? Well, you will." His gaze swept over her face, then all the way down to her toes. "Wow! You look fabulous, Lydia. This must be a very special night for you, too. The idea of me finally getting married must be making you very happy."

She wanted to kick him in the shins, or kiss him senseless. But since the crowd around them made either choice unacceptable, she kept her response to a wan smile.

"In case you've been wondering, this contest was not my idea, Zach. But I'm glad to see you're sticking with it. A woman admires a man who keeps his commitments."

His head bent close to hers. "Yes, I recall another time you told me those very same words. I remember a few more things you said, too. When you were in bed. Naked. With a just-loved look on your face."

Her jaw clenched as pain rocketed straight through her. "A gentleman would never bring something like that up on an occasion like this. That night has nothing to do with this one."

"If you hadn't been so stubborn, the both of us would be somewhere else instead of here. And this whole party wouldn't be happening!"

He was talking in riddles that she couldn't decipher. But none of it mattered anyway, she thought grimly.

After Curtis announced the winner of the Perfect Bride Contest, she could put him and this whole mistake behind her.

"Hey, Zach," Jolene greeted as she sidled up to Lydia. "Ready for the big announcement?"

He nodded a greeting at Jolene, then settled a stare on Lydia's face.

"I've never been more ready for anything."

His words were like cactus needles driving deep into her flesh. By tomorrow, she expected her whole body to be festered and sore from the wounds he was inflicting on her.

"In case you didn't know, Curtis assigned Lydia and me the task of making the list of perfect brides for the townsfolk to vote on. It was actually harder than I thought. There are so many lovely women around here who fit your requirements. I hope you were pleased with the women we chose for you."

Zach continued to look at Lydia in a strange way.

"Don't worry about it," he said bluntly. "The woman Curtis announces will be the absolute perfect wife for me. Now if you ladies will excuse me, I need to speak to one of my brothers."

He walked off and Lydia blew out a pent-up breath.

"Gee, he didn't look a bit happy," Jolene commented, then glancing at Lydia, she added, "As far as that goes, neither do you. What's going on, anyway?"

Lydia started walking in the direction of the bar. She needed something far stronger than a glass of fruit punch to get her through this ordeal. Which was rapidly turning out to be worse than a root canal.

Glancing over her shoulder, she saw Jolene following close on her heels.

Lydia asked, "Do you have any idea who came up with the idea for this contest? Curtis told me it wasn't him. And I'm inclined to believe him. This isn't his style."

"Trust me, Lydia, I've tried to snoop around the office and find out who came up with this, but everybody seems to be clueless. Why? What does it matter, anyway?"

Grimacing, Lydia continued to maneuver her way through the crowd. "Zach doesn't deserve this. And neither do I."

"Lydia, you're not making sense."

"Nothing about this night is making sense," she barked at Jolene. "Come on, let's see if we can get a drink or two, or three, before Curtis starts the show."

Unfortunately the bar was so crowded neither Lydia nor Jolene could wedge their way through. And then it was too late for a chance to numb the ache inside her with alcohol. Curtis was stepping up to the microphone and the excited crowd was turning their attention to the man with the answer everyone was waiting to hear. Who was the perfect bride for Zach Dalton?

After greeting the crowd, Curtis slipped into a long speech about all the hardworking cowboys around Rust Creek Falls, how many of them had already found the loves of their lives, and how fitting it was that the townsfolk had a hand in helping find the ideal bride for Zach.

Curtis droned on, "I want to thank all the *Gazette* readers for writing in with your votes and expressing the reasons you think your choice is the right one for our marriage-minded cowboy—Mr. Zach Dalton."

Curtis gestured to Zach, who was standing a few steps away from the slightly elevated stage, and as Lydia looked over at him, she wondered if she could feel any worse than she did at this moment. Did he really intend to marry the woman who won this debacle of a contest? Surely love and commitment meant more to him than that!

"But I think everyone here at the Ace in the Hole is going to be surprised at the results. As I scanned through the letters, I certainly was amazed," Curtis continued. "Ladies and gentlemen, I now must reveal that the winner of the bride contest is not any of the three women on the list."

Surprise rippled over the crowd. Some folks even let out loud gasps. Lydia and Jolene exchanged confused glances.

"What's going on?" Jolene hissed in Lydia's ear. "Has Curtis flipped his lid or something?"

"The punch must have been spiked again," Lydia muttered, then glanced again to Zach.

Oddly enough, he didn't appear to be fazed by Curtis's unexpected announcement. In fact, there was even a faint smile of approval on his face.

"Who's the winner, Curtis?" some man in the crowd yelled.

"Yeah! Spill the beans, will ya?" another called out. "We're tired of waitin'!"

Holding up a hand to call for patience, Curtis reached behind him and plucked several sheets of paper from a plastic container. After clearing his throat, he began to read, "All right, I'll get to it. The first letter states that Zach's perfect woman is caring and genuine. Another says she's lovely and real. The next, that she's compassionate and hardworking. And this one says she's the most beautiful woman to walk the streets of Rust Creek Falls. These are just a few of the reasons why Lydia Grant will make the perfect wife for Zach."

Lydia Grant! Instinctively, one hand crept to her throat as she stared around her in stunned horror. Was this some sort of cruel joke? Surely she'd misunderstood what Curtis had read into the microphone!

"Me?"

She must have squeaked the question out loud, because every eye in the bar seemed to turn to her.

"That's right, Lydia," Curtis answered, his expression equally shocked. "You are the winner of the Zach's Perfect Bride Contest."

Next to her, Jolene's jaw dropped. "What the hell is going on?" she whispered to Lydia, who by now was too dazed to answer anything.

Her mind racing wildly, Lydia's gaze found Zach's in the crowd and her heart gave a drunken lurch. Was he a part of this farce? To embarrass her? Get back at her? But for what? She'd not done anything to him, except give him her heart and soul.

For one second she wanted to take off running through the crowd and hide somewhere so deep and dark that no one could ever find her.

"Lydia, please come forward to collect your prize," Curtis called out.

Numb with embarrassment, Lydia forced one foot in front of the other until she reached the stage where Curtis stood behind the microphone stand.

"Her prize is Zach!" a woman in the crowd yelled. "Give her Zach! Give her Zach!"

The whole crowd began to loudly chant the phrase until Curtis was forced to signal for quiet. Once the noise had dropped to a low, restless rumble, he handed Lydia a long envelope.

"As winner of the prize, the *Gazette* is giving away

dinner for two at a four-star restaurant in Kalispell. Along with weekend accommodations at one of the city's finest hotels."

Confused, she took the envelope while shaking her head. "Curtis, you have something wrong. I—"

Before she could finish the protest, Zach was suddenly at her side, reaching for her hand and clasping it tightly.

"Nothing is wrong, Lydia," Zach said gently. "In fact, everything is right. More than right. You see, I wrote every letter in that box. And every word is the truth. Right from my heart."

Curtis awkwardly began to cough. "Folks, this is highly irregular, and from Zach's confession it's clear that the rules of the contest have been violated."

"Hang the rules! My brother has the right to fix anything that concerns his bride-to-be!"

Lydia recognized Garrett Dalton's voice, the adventurous brother of the family. But she didn't have a chance to hear more of the exchange between Curtis and the rest of the crowd. Zach was drawing her to one side of the stage, where a few feet of space separated them from prying ears.

By now her eyes were blurred with tears, yet amazingly she could see a tender smile curving his lips. "Zach, why have you done this?"

"Here. Read some of these and you'll understand." He handed her the box with all the letters he'd written. "Like I said, I meant every word."

Doing her best to ignore the restless crowd behind them, Lydia quickly scanned through the sheets of paper. On each one a specific note had been written depicting the times and places they'd been together. Some even had quotation marks around the exact words she'd spoken to him about love, marriage and children. All the things a man and a woman considered important to their happiness together.

Unable to stop the tears from spilling onto her cheeks, she lifted her head and stared at him in amazement. He really had seen her as a woman all this time! He honestly did want her! Lydia Grant!

"Oh, Zach, I never thought—"

"Forgive me, Lydia. Ever since I've come to Rust Creek Falls I've had this idea of finding the one woman to help me put down roots and make a family." His expression pleading, his hands made a warm steeple over hers. "But all this time I was blindly looking for love in all the wrong places. Advertising for a wife was a stupid idea. But ultimately, the ad and this crazy contest of Curtis's helped me find her—you!"

Her head swung side to side as she tried to search for words, but she couldn't think of anything that made sense. "But, Zach, I'm none of the things you were looking for."

"Wrong. You're everything I'm looking for. Furthermore, that night after we made love, you should have had more faith in yourself. And you should've had a lot more faith in me. I was trying to tell you that I was committed to you and only you. But you wouldn't listen."

She let out a rueful groan. "I was afraid, Zach. That's why I tried to push you away. I was scared that I'd never be able to hold on to you. Just like my mom couldn't hold on to my dad."

"I finally figured that out, Lydia. But you don't need to fear anything. Not anymore. I'm never letting you go and I have the ring to prove it."

Still stunned, she watched him pull a small box from his jean pocket. When he flipped open the lid, a gorgeous diamond ring winked brightly at her.

She gasped at the sight of it and so did the crowd. A short distance away, Curtis frantically motioned for the *Gazette* photographer to start snapping. Apparently her boss saw a big story unveiling right before his eyes and he meant to take advantage of the opportunity.

"Lydia, I'm waiting for your answer," Zach urged.

Shaking her head, she tore her gaze from the diamond to look blankly up at him. "Did you ask me something?"

Everyone in the bar began to roar with laughter.

"If you're going to propose marriage, you'd better do it proper, Zach," some man shouted from the back of the crowd.

Taking her hand, Zach asked, "My sweet Lydia, will you do me the honor of becoming my wife?"

Happiness was suddenly pouring through her, choking her to the point she could hardly speak.

"I will," she whispered, then repeated it in a voice loud enough for everyone to hear. "Yes, Zach Dalton, I will be your wife."

Zach slipped the diamond on her finger and then, with a loud whoop of joy, he scooped her up in his arms and carried her straight through the cheering crowd. Once they were outside the building and in the quiet darkness, he pulled her into his arms and kissed her with a tenderness that only came from a love that was deep and real.

"We'd better go back inside," she said with a happy laugh. "There's an engagement party going on."

"In a minute," he promised. "But first I have to kiss my perfect bride-to-be just a few more times."

Epilogue

The bed in the Kalispell hotel was so enormous a person could get lost in it, but there wasn't a chance of that happening to Lydia. Her head was resting on Zach's shoulder, while his arm kept her body firmly wrapped close to the curve of his warm body.

"Mmm. Curtis is a nice guy," Zach murmured against the crown of her brown curls. "Since I broke the rules of the contest, he could have demanded that you return the prize. But I'm glad he decided to let you keep it. This is like a mini-honeymoon before the wedding."

A week had passed since Zach had proposed to her at the Ace in the Hole and subsequently her life had turned into a joyous whirlwind. At first she'd been fearful Rhoda would frown upon her sudden engagement, but it turned out that her mother was ecstatic. Especially with Zach showing her he was a real gentleman by asking for her daughter's hand in marriage.

Twisting onto her side so that she was facing him, Lydia said, "You know, you still haven't told me how you managed to change all the readers' letters without Curtis or someone else from the *Gazette* seeing you."

He chuckled and the happy sound was like a song she would never tire of hearing.

"Easy. Before the crowd ever arrived at the Ace in the Hole, I saw Curtis put the container of letters on a shelf beneath the bar. So while he and the soundman were checking the microphone, I made the switch. And he never suspected a thing. Until he started sifting through them."

Lydia laughed. "No wonder Curtis had a stunned look on his face when he started reading. He probably thought his eyes were failing him."

"Well, he and everyone else in Rust Creek Falls can now see how I feel about Lydia Grant. I cherish every beautiful inch of you, my darling."

She nuzzled her cheek against his. "I was so relieved your father approved of our engagement. I was afraid he might think you'd proposed to me on impulse."

"You mean like Travis did with Brenna?"

"Something like that." Easing her head back, she pushed her fingers through the black hair hanging over his forehead. "I understand you didn't necessarily approve of your cousin's sudden proposal to Brenna. But now I think you'll have to agree that it looks as though there's something very real between the two of them. During last week's episode of *The Great Roundup* you could practically see the chemistry sizzling between them."

"Yeah," he said gently. "Even if they miss getting the million dollars, Travis and Brenna have already won. Love is much more precious than a stack of green bills."

Catching her hand, he placed a kiss in the middle of her palm. "So tell me, Lydia, what do you think of having a springtime wedding? Like April or May? The grass will be green and the flowers blooming."

"Sounds wonderful to me. Only, I'd better warn you right now that I'm not the kind of gal that's up on all that fancy wedding stuff. Like color schemes and tasting menus."

With a groan of contentment, he pulled her naked body into the tight circle of his arms. "Who cares about any of those things? We'll hire someone to take care of the details. Right now I think we should start practicing for our honeymoon. We want to get it right, don't we?"

Laughing deep in her throat, she brought her lips next to his. "If we ever expect to have a half-dozen babies, we'd better get it right."

"My thoughts exactly," he told her, then proceeded to kiss her with a love so perfect it was destined to last a lifetime.

* * * * *

*Look for the next installment of the new
Mills & Boon Cherish continuity*

MONTANA MAVERICKS:
THE GREAT FAMILY ROUNDUP

*Daniel Stockton left Rust Creek Falls a decade ago,
blaming himself for his parents' deaths. But he never
got over his high school ex, Anne Lattimore.
And when he finally comes back to town, will love
give them a second chance?*

Don't miss

THE MAVERICK'S RETURN
by USA TODAY *bestselling author
Marie Ferrarella*

*On sale October 2017, wherever Mills & Boon
books and ebooks are sold.*

MILLS & BOON®

Cherish™

EXPERIENCE THE ULTIMATE RUSH OF FALLING IN LOVE

MILLS & BOON®

EXCLUSIVE EXTRACT

Crown Prince Frederick of Lycander needs a wife and an heir, and discovering he has a secret son with beautiful supermodel Sunita makes him determined to claim both!

Read on for a sneak preview of
CLAIMING HIS SECRET HEIR

'You have a baby?'

Frederick's hazel eyes widened in puzzlement, a small frown creasing his brow as he took another step into her sanctum. His gaze rested on each and every item of Amil's.

'Yes.' The word was a whisper, all Sunita could manage as her tummy hollowed and she grasped the door jamb with lifeless fingers.

'How old?' Each syllable was ice cold, edged with glass and she nearly flinched. No, she would not be intimidated. Not here. Not now. What was done was done, and, rightly or wrongly, she knew if she could turn back time she would make the same decision.

'Girl or boy?'

'Boy.' Each question, each answer brought them closer and closer to the inevitable and her brain wouldn't function. Instead, all she could focus on was his face, the dawn of emotion – wonder, anger, fear and surely hope too? That last was so unexpected that it jolted her into further words. 'His name is Amil.'

'Amil,' he repeated. He took another step forward and instinctively she moved as well, as if to protect the life she had built, putting herself between him and her home. 'Is he mine?'

For an instant it was if the world went out of focus. She could almost see a line being drawn in the sands of time – this was the instant that separated before and after. For one brief instant she nearly took the coward's route, wondered if he would swallow the lie that Amil was Sam's. Then realised she could not, would not do that. 'Yes. He is yours. Amil is your son.'

Now she understood the origins of a deafening silence. This one trolled the room, echoed in her ears until she wanted to shout. Instead she waited, saw his body freeze, saw the gamut of emotion cross his face, watched as it settled into an anger so ice cold a shiver rippled her skin. Panic twisted her insides – the die had been cast and she knew now that whatever happened, life would never be the same.

Don't miss
CLAIMING HIS SECRET HEIR
by Nina Milne

Available October 2017
www.millsandboon.co.uk